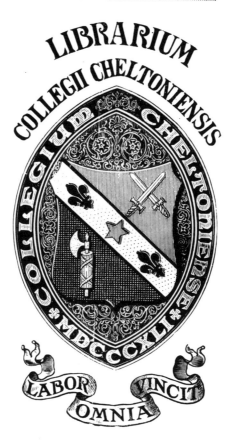

MACABRE

MACABRE

Stephen Laws

Hodder & Stoughton

First published in Great Britain in 1994 by
Hodder and Stoughton
A division of Hodder Headline PLC

10 9 8 7 6 5 4 3 2

British Library Cataloguing in Publication Data

Laws, Stephen
Macabre
I. Title
823.914 [F]

ISBN 0450 60690 2

Typeset by Avon Dataset Ltd, Bidford-on-Avon

Printed and bound in Great Britain by
Mackays of Chatham, Chatham, Kent

Hodder and Stoughton
A division of Hodder Headline PLC
338 Euston Road
London NW1 3BH

This Novel is Dedicated With Love
To Joan and Rob Laws

Acknowledgments

I'd like to thank the following good friends for their advice,
assistance and support:

Antony Harwood, Keith Durham, Humphrey Price,
Sheena Walshaw, Dawn Bates.

Laurie Brown (Captain of 'The Owl')

And with Love to Melanie and Eve – for being there.

PART ONE

THE FORLORN

ONE

The thought came to him unbidden: more people die at four in the morning than at any other time. Who the hell had told him that in the first place? It always slipped into his mind when he was working the graveyard shift and it always depressed the hell out of him. He shrugged off the chill he'd been feeling all night and concentrated on the road ahead.

He didn't like working this shift, usually preferring late morning to evening. But there were more taxi licences being given out these days, more black cabs on the streets than ever before – and he was behind in the repayments. Good income weeks usually compensated for the bad weeks, but lately there seemed to have been more of the latter.

Sleep had become increasingly difficult for him of late. The dreams were always bad, but seemed to have been getting worse. Same stuff, run over and over like a video replay. He wondered why the simple repetition of those dreams hadn't dulled the horror. But it never did, and he always awoke from whatever fitful sleep he'd been allowed, soaking in sweat and with that name clenched in his teeth. Surprise, surprise – he hadn't been able to sleep at all tonight, had finally thrown back the bedclothes and lit another cigarette. He sat for a long time looking out into the night as blue smoke curled around his face. And then he'd pulled on his working clothes again, cursing all the way. If he couldn't sleep, then he might as well be out there working.

He was still cursing. It was three thirty in the morning, and he hadn't been flagged down once since he'd started. And now, just when it seemed that things couldn't get worse – it was starting to rain.

"Great!" he hissed through clenched teeth as the first ribbons of water began to streak the windscreen.

A figure moved in a shop doorway up ahead. Tony quickly flipped the windscreen wipers on, hoping that it might be a punter taking shelter from the rain, and now in need of a taxi. But as his black cab drew level with the doorway, Tony could see that he was wrong. The shadowed figure was a vagrant, or a drunk – whether male or female he could not tell. As the car swept by, he just had time to see the figure pulling together a makeshift mattress out of a soiled potato sack and newspaper. Tony gritted his teeth and kept going.

And now – another figure was standing on the other side of the road, opposite the park gates and directly under a streetlamp. Now here was someone definitely looking for a ride – why else would he or she step out into the road like that, as if to flag him down? But no . . . the figure was looking on past him, and Tony cursed under his breath again when he saw that it was *another* tramp, wearing a heavy, ragged overcoat and a skintight woollen balaclava.

"Where the bloody hell are they all coming from these days?"

Was it just his twisted perception in the past few months, or did there seem to be more vagrants on the streets at night? Were there more kids in shop doorways under cardboard, more shambling derelicts than ever before? Sometimes, it seemed to him as if they were *gathering* on street corners, gathering to watch. And to wait for something. As if they knew that something bad was coming, and they were just standing or sitting or squatting there, waiting silently for it to happen . . .

He tried to shrug off these familiar feelings. His sense of melancholy and depression always seemed to deepen on the late shift as he cruised the streets and saw more of them bedding down for the night on the pavements, in shop doorways or in park shrubbery.

The walking wounded.

The phrase made him shudder, made him think back. Why the hell didn't he seem to see as many of them during the day? There were faces that he recognised during daylight hours, but he never seemed to see any of them on the streets at night. And the shambling, derelict figures who tottered and shambled and weaved on the sidewalk, or stood under the streetlamps, or stood silently in doorways, seemed only to come out at night – like ghosts. He wondered sometimes if any of those spectral figures who silently watched his taxi slide by in the night had once been in the army. But it was another one of those renegade thoughts, which only served to make him more depressed. He wondered just what the hell he would do, just how the hell he would *feel* if he recognised one of those figures as one of his ex-army companions.

The figure under the streetlight was far away behind him, still standing with one foot in the road and the other on the kerb; looking back in the opposite direction as if waiting for someone or something. The figure made him uncomfortable, and Tony switched on the taxi radio in an attempt to defeat the creeping blues. He laughed bitterly.

Just his luck to pick a blues song. He twisted the radio tuner again until he'd found a good heavy rock number . . . and the taxi glided on through the black watches of the night like some darkened, mobile disco: the music stabbing the night as it passed, making those behind the darkened windows of these terraced streets grunt and turn in their sleep.

The identification photograph containing Tony's taxi-driver registration number hung on the dash before him. The photograph depicted someone who was trying to look blank, as if he was trying to conceal something. He'd torn up the first photograph that had come out of the public booth. He had been trying to smile on that one, and that smile looked dreadful. As if he'd smelt something bad, or just remembered an unpaid bill. The second one showed an impassive face with troubled eyes. Anyone looking at the photograph would guess that the driver was about forty years old, but they'd be wrong. Tony Dandridge was thirty-three. But what he had experienced, what he had seen in the Falklands campaign as an enlisted soldier (5th Battalion Parachute Regiment, or "Five Para"), had given him those seven extra years. They wouldn't wear off, and would probably stay with him for life. The ribboned medal which he kept in the bedroom cabinet drawer of his boarding house testified to the fact that he had performed "above and beyond the call of duty" during that action. But on that one horrific day, his best friend had also been killed in that action – and the feelings of bitterness, horror and betrayal had refused to be placated by the stated but elusive gratitude of his country.

There had been no place for heroes on his return to civvy street. He had enlisted at twenty years old, not being able to find a proper job in the midst of a recession. He had served hard time in Northern Ireland, seen some pretty bad things over there, had even got used to being a permanent target on the Shankill Road. But that one night in a slit trench on a filth-encrusted mound near Mount Longdon had stripped away a great deal from him. That one night was responsible for his insomnia and, when he did sleep, the nightmares that always jerked him awake. He had been invalided out of the service, with a fragmented bullet in the thigh that had left pieces of itself in there, and which still gave him a bad time on cold nights. On his return to civilian life, he had found that his pension just wouldn't pay the bills. The irony was not lost on him, but brought no humour. There had been no job opportunities for him before, which had led to him enlisting. Now, it seemed that his experience with the regulars had done him no good whatsoever. There were no job opportunities for a former professional soldier. Nightclub bouncer, security guard, or crime. He had tried all of this, but it had only served to erode him

5

further. Taxi-driving had presented the only way to supplement his army pension and to keep his head above water.

Cruising through the city, Tony watched as the night-time people seemed to be taking over the city, watched as the kids on the street smashed up the shops and threw paving slabs at passing cars, saw the figures lying in the gutters. His own taxi had been stolen twice by kids whose only thrill was the thrill of a joyride, the thrill of a quick buck, a quick fight, a quick fuck. Watching them on the streets, he could feel that they were all just one big bomb, waiting to detonate. You couldn't switch on the television or the radio these days without feeling that the tension was real, the threat overwhelming. People were staying indoors, watching ever-increasing crime statistics on bleak news programmes. The fuse was lit, but how long would it take for that bomb to explode? Tony saw all these things on the streets where he plied his trade and felt that, just as surely as the fabric of society was disintegrating, the good and the decency and dignity was disintegrating within himself.

He checked the clock on the dash as he drove. It was just after four, and the rain was now pouring down. The pavements were awash and the drains were gobbling water as his taxi slid through the sheets of dirty water. Neon from empty shops, businesses and apparently deserted nightclubs glittering on the pavement and the roads. Now it seemed that he would never get a punter. This rain would keep everyone off the streets, or cowering under cover.

"The hell with it."

Now he knew that he was just burning up petrol on these empty streets. Far from catching up on those late payments, he was now going to have to work even longer shifts to make up for tonight's wasted escapade. His ploy to beat insomnia now meant that he was more out of pocket than before. Maybe it was time to give up.

He turned the cab at the bottom of an unfamiliar street where a crooked streetlamp threw angular shadows through the rain and over the slick, black pavements. The headlights swept over the frontage of a derelict and dilapidated shop. He seemed to recall that this had once been a Government Job Shop, and laughed ruefully as the headlights swept back up the street down which he'd just come.

There was a figure caught in the headlights just ahead of him, waving frantically from the pavement.

As he swerved the cab across the street in a spray of water, Tony could see that it was a young woman. Even from this distance, in the glare of the headlights through this slashing rain, it was clear that she was about twenty-five years old and wearing clothes not meant for this kind of weather. She was wearing what seemed to be a party dress,

6

for crying out loud. Nineteen fifties style. Her blonde hair was soaked, clinging to her head and with wild strands across her face. Her clothes were absolutely sodden as she stood there in the downpour, frantically waving . . . and as the cab pulled up sharply beside her, Tony could see with surprise that she had a child.

The baby was wrapped up tightly in an all-enfolding blanket against the rain, and the girl had the child clutched to her breast with one arm, so that Tony could see no details of its face. She was still frantically waving at him with the other, even as the cab stopped. Obviously anxious to be out of the rain as quickly as possible, she lunged for the back door of the cab. Tony's foot came off the brake pedal, to allow the safety catch on the door to unsnick.

"Hell of a night to be out," began Tony. "Better climb in before . . ."

And Tony shrank back as the girl pulled out an automatic pistol from the baby's shawl, yanked open the cab door and climbed quickly inside. Her face was white and grim, the eyes sparkling with deadly intent; not moving from his face as she dragged the door fiercely closed and held that gun at arm's length from her – and with the barrel no more than three inches from Tony's own face. The gun looked much too big for her slender white hand. Unable to move, hands rising from the wheel in an involuntary act of surrender, Tony could see that this soaking girl had a beautiful, classic face, but that beauty had assumed a glacial mask of purpose. The gun may have been too heavy and large for her hand, but it did not waver as the baby began to cry. The woman glanced quickly out into the night again. And Tony could tell now by looking at her face that the girl was obviously being followed by someone, and that she was also terrified.

"Drive," she said.

"Okay, okay. Take it easy. But where do you want to . . . ?"

"Just *drive!*"

Tony turned quickly away, still *feeling* that gun barrel at the back of his neck. He shoved into first gear, and the cab roared away from the pavement in a spray of rainwater. The girl slid back away from him on to the seat, but quickly compensated. Tony saw her in the rearview mirror as she pushed forward again until she was sitting on the edge of the seat, shushing the child with one arm, crooning a low, wordless song as she cradled it against her breast – and with that gun still held pointing at him. It made a bizarre sight.

"Faster!" snapped the girl, glancing back out of the rear window the way they'd come. And yes, there was a very real fear on that girl's face at something back there, as well as the determination. Tony quickly changed gears. They had reached the end of the street.

"Right or left?"

"Just fucking *drive!*" Now Tony became aware of the girl's accent. She was American.

There was only waste ground and a building site to the left. If he pulled in there, God knows what she would do. He swerved to the right, and now the windscreen was only a blur of water and darkness as they drove straight into the rain. This was a long stretch of road, guaranteed to get her away from what she feared – unless her pursuers also had wheels. Apparently not, for now the girl had slid back into the seat and was breathing a sigh of relief. Still cradling the child and crooning her low lullaby, she raised her gun hand so that she could wipe the rainwater from her face with her forearm. She caught sight of him looking at her in the rearview mirror and her eyes flashed.

"Okay, okay!" said Tony. "I'm driving, I'm driving."

The child's tears began to subside, and Tony watched her bend to kiss its face, her long hair straggling over the shawl.

"If you're in trouble," volunteered Tony, "maybe the police . . . ?"

Again, that flash of anger in her eyes. The grip tightening on that bloody huge handgun. Further conversation was obviously not required.

They drove for a further five miles, pretty much in a straight line. The traffic lights were with them all the way, and Tony thanked God for it, wondering just how she would react if they suddenly had to stop.

"All right," she said at last. "Stop here."

They were miles from anywhere. This was the edge of an industrial estate. No housing developments, no council estates. Just the wind rattling a rusted iron fence at the side of the road, a faint silhouette of deserted factories against the blacker backdrop of the night sky and torrents of dirty water running in the gutters at either side of the road.

"Are you sure . . . ?"

"Stop the *car!*"

Now, the barrel of the handgun was pushed up hard against the back of Tony's neck. The distance that they'd put between themselves and the girl's pursuers had not really relieved the tension or put distance to her fear after all. The cab slid to a halt.

Tony gripped the wheel tight.

Drugs.

It had to be. Why else the manic desperation? And if that was the case, just what the hell could he expect now that he'd stopped the car? There wasn't much cash in his bag, just loose change. But she didn't know that. And if she was desperate for a fix, or to pay a pusher off . . . why then, wouldn't she just finish him now and take it?

The cab door swung open and the girl climbed out, hugging the child tight to herself against the rain and still with the gun levelled at

8

him. The door stayed open as she moved around the front of the car, full into the headlights. That gun barrel remained unwavering and pointed straight at him through the windscreen. She was coming round to his side of the cab. For an instant, he weighed up his chances. If he slid quickly into gear and ducked low, could he drive straight on ahead and ram her down?

But the kid, for Christ's sake!

Never mind the kid, you idiot. What about you? She's going to take that loose change and then she's going to blow your head off.

Too late, the moment had gone.

But he realised as she stepped gingerly around to his side of the cab that he would never have made it anyway. She was waiting for a movement – *any* kind of a movement from him – and she would have shot him in the face without any hesitation,

He gripped the steering wheel even tighter. Was this the way it was going to end after all? Not in the mud on some mound in the Falklands, but in a battered cab on the outskirts of a dilapidated industrial estate – for seventy-five fucking pence.

She reached his window.

"Wind it down!"

Tony just looked at her. Why the hell should he assist in his own death?

"I said *open it*!"

Tony shook his head.

He watched her as, breathing heavily, she reached carefully for the door handle – and with that gun only inches away from his face on the other side of the glass. She flung open the door, taking two quick steps back as if she was expecting him to throw himself at her from the cab. Although still holding the child tight to her chest, the girl's hand fumbled down past the neckline of her dress, hunting for something in there. She was having difficulty finding whatever it was, and the gun wavered. Tony's hand moved on the wheel.

"*Don't* . . . think about it."

She had found it now, and stepped guardedly forward in the rain. Awkwardly, she flipped that something from her hand on to Tony's lap, quickly readjusting her grip on the child again and standing back.

It was a ten pound note.

Tony looked at it in bewilderment.

"It says eight pounds fifty on your clock in there," said the girl. "Keep the change, it's a tip."

Tony looked at her in astonishment as she continued to back off into the darkness, always with that gun levelled at him.

"What . . . ?" he began.

9

"I always pay my way," said the girl.
In the next moment, she had vanished into the darkness.

TWO

When Tony had carefully parked his black cab on the concrete driveway outside his lodging house, he climbed out and slammed the driver's door hard. Rain shimmered on the roof and sleek bodywork. His anger was such that he couldn't at first get the key into the car lock. Pausing to draw a deep breath to calm himself down, he carefully locked the car door and then hurried to the battered front door of his lodgings.

Of all the bloody luck. One punter all night – and she turns out to be Ma Barker and Kid.

Cursing at his wasted night and rotten luck, Tony hurried up the litter-strewn steps to the front door. The apartment block was pre-war (*Pre-Crimean* War, one of Tony's fellow lodgers had muttered one day when his water pipes had burst in the bathroom), and had once been a fashionable hotel called the Rex. The old Rex sign was still discernible high up on the fascia of the building, partially obliterated by pigeons' droppings. The original owners had gone bust, and the place had stood derelict for a full seven years before being bought by a property developer. Attempts had been made to renovate the property for sale as individual private apartments, but then the property developer had also gone bust and the half-completed renovations had halted – while the mice and the rats and the pigeons returned to their former abode. Finally, the place had been acquired by a housing conglomerate and now the old, turreted building, standing in one of the less salubrious parts of the city, was rented out to "transients": lorry-drivers, salesmen . . . and one taxi-driver. The conglomerate had refused to pour any more money into modernising the place. Maybe they were aware of the jinxed history of the old building. But that lack of modernisation meant that the rent charged was just about affordable for Tony. He had been living there ever since leaving the army twelve years ago.

He had lived in worse conditions.

The entrance hall always smelled of mould, irrespective of the weather. He hardly noticed it now as he pushed in. A blast of wind and rain enveloped him as he slammed the door shut. Now he was in total darkness as he fumbled at the wall for the timer switch. He found it, flicked . . . and the old iron-balustraded staircase stretched up and away before him, four storeys high. His apartment was at the top. As he began quickly to ascend, gripping the iron balustrade tight, he thought back to his bizarre encounter with the girl and her baby.

Should I have told the police? Maybe somebody else out there might fall foul of Mother Bonnie and Baby Clyde.

The timer switch was a constant challenge that Tony always took up, and tried to beat. He usually managed to reach the third landing before the light switched off. Maybe one day he would beat it and reach his own apartment door before the stairwell was plunged into blackness. It was a good form of exercise. He stabbed at the switch and sprinted up the stairs, thinking about what he should do about tonight's little escapade. The police?

Nah, what's the point? It means a day and a half sitting in the police station, trying lo describe her. Wasted time and wasted earnings. I'm already behind with the bloody rent for this place – I've got to get out there early again in the morning and earn some cash to keep my bloody cab.

He had reached the second landing now, swung around the banister and headed for the third, rummaging in his jerkin pocket for the key to his front door.

Drugs. Has to be drugs. He thought of the child again, of the poor little bastard's plight, saddled with a manic, drug-crazed mother. And then he blanked it out. He couldn't afford to start thinking like that, because when he did the depression always set in. And that depression always catapulted him back to the Falklands, to what had happened there – and how it had changed the whole tenor of his life, and his attitude towards living.

On the last staircase leading to the top floor, the light flicked off. Tony instantly slowed, breath tight. The exercise had been good for him. It had burned out a great deal of the anger that had been building up at what had happened to him that night. He paused then for a brief moment in the utter darkness until he could get his bearings a little clearer. One of the handrails up here was a little loose. He'd complained about it on several occasions but was still waiting for that lazy bastard of a landlord to do something about it. Okay, the lack of maintenance and decor was one good reason that the rent always remained manageable. But all it needed was one drink too many, that bloody light-timer flicking off, one stumbled step – and a grab for that handrail. It was a good sixty-foot drop down into that stairwell.

Gradually, the outlines of the handrail and the walls became clearer and Tony started up again.

Then he stopped.

He turned and looked down into the stairwell, expecting to see that someone else had come into the lodging house, expecting to see that the door which he had just heard opening was now being closed. But there was nothing down there, no movement. The door was still shut; there was no tell-tale spill of light on the hallway carpet from the streetlight outside. But he could have sworn that he'd heard a door opening down there . . . and more than that . . . the sound of something like a long and echoing *sigh*. He shrugged it off and continued to ascend in the darkness. Perhaps one of the other lodgers had heard him, and opened their own door to take a look-see.

The noise came again. Sibilant, long-drawn-out. And somehow terribly, terribly *hungry*. It made Tony shudder. There was something about the tone of the sound which made him feel very uncomfortable.

Getting scared of the dark now, Dandridge? On top of everything else? You pathetic specimen.

It was obviously the sound of traffic out there in the rain. Perhaps a car passing through a rainwater pool outside. A backward glance still revealed no movement in the depths of the stairwell. Finally, he had reached his own floor. A chill wind blew into that corridor from a window that had been jammed half open for over a year now. He flicked the light back on, looking down to confirm that there was no one down there, following him up – and of course, the stairwell and staircase were empty. The girl and the gun had obviously spooked him.

Why the hell did she pay the fare after all that?

Tony strode down the top floor corridor to his own door, and let himself in.

In seconds, his jacket was thrown over a battered chair, and Ry Cooder was playing a quiet moody piece on the stereo to wind him down. Tony stood in the small kitchen looking at the rain streaking the window, listening to the wind moaning and soughing around the eaves of the flat. Coffee, or whisky? Neither. It would only wind him up — not down. Now, more than anything, he needed sleep to get him ready for a long hard day ahead. He ran his hand through unruly brown hair and wandered into the living room-bedroom. Throwing himself onto the bed, he groped at the bedside cabinet until he'd found the cigarettes. Maybe he should get pissed after all? No, maybe not. Those extra shifts, remember. He finished his cigarette and lay there listening to Ry Cooder, hoping that the songs would help drift him off to sleep.

But sleep was still not coming easily tonight.

Something about the girl and her baby – and the look of fear and determination on that girl's face – would not leave him alone.

He kept telling himself that she was drugged.

No she wasn't. I could tell by her face. She was just desperate to get away from something that was following her, and I was the first car on the road she could flag down.

He kept telling himself that she was mad.

No, there was no insanity on that face. Just a desperation and a determination to protect her kid and get away from there as quickly as possible. I've seen that sort of gutsy determination before. When we knew that we were stranded and outnumbered, and all we could do was stand fast and take whatever was coming over the hill at us.

He kept telling himself that she was obviously on the run from the police.

No, not the police. I don't know what in hell she was running from, but I'm glad that – whatever it is – it wasn't after me.

Tony stared at the ceiling, watching his cigarette smoke curl in the air – and tried to sleep.

THREE

"Are you hungry?" asked the shadow, leaning down.

Jamesy slapped out at the proffered hand. In his stupor, he thought that a scene from twelve years ago was being re-enacted. He had been on the streets even then. And on that particular day, he'd been given a gift from heaven. God knows how he'd come across it, or been able to pay for it, or who the hell had given it to him – but he had suddenly become aware of a half-bottle of good whisky in his grubby overcoat pocket. One minute he had just been walking on a High Street somewhere, the next he had fumbled in his pocket – and there it was! A full half-bottle. Energised as if he had just won the City lottery, he screwed off the cap and lifted it to his lips. Wait a minute, wasn't this just a little too good to be true? This *couldn't* be whisky in here. It was a joke, wasn't it? Just like the jokes some of those young office kids liked to pull on him when he was sleeping it off in the park. They'd put it in his pocket – they must have. They'd probably found an empty bottle and then . . . well, then they'd probably pissed in it or something. He held the bottle to his lips. But the odour was unmistakably liquor. One quick sip had confirmed this miracle of the holy spirit. He had retired to a shop doorway to finish it before any of the other thieving beggars spotted him with it and came ambling over, hoping for a snort. He had fallen asleep then, the bottle shoved back into the same pocket – just in case the same angel or good booze fairy decided to bless him again, and fill it up while he was asleep. Next thing he knew, he had been woken up by this bloke standing over him, shaking him awake and offering him some money. And who the hell had it been? Well, it had been a bloody bum-bandit, hadn't it? A bloody homo. Wanting to know what he'd do for a fiver. Jamesy had blundered to his feet, shoved the stranger back out of the way and had staggered off down to the embankment. His good mood had been ruined – and the good booze fairy had not returned to refill his bottle. He had smashed it against a shop wall.

Now, it seemed that this event was being replayed as the figure said again, "Are you hungry?"

"Fuck off and leave me alone!"

Jamesy blundered to his feet, shoving out at the stranger. But the young man (was it a young man?) quickly stepped back into the darkness, out of the way. Reeling, Jamesy steadied himself, and then realised that this was not the same man, the same place, the same time. He was on a building site. The place where the council had been demolishing a block of flats and clearing the land. He had fallen asleep behind a jumble of shattered concrete and pilings. Now he was aware of the cold in his legs. He began to massage them as the figure just stood back and was silent.

After a while the figure again said, "Are you hungry?"

Jamesy looked up.

It was a young man. Maybe twenty-five years old. Well dressed, with a long dark raincoat. His hair seemed to be brilliantined in the darkness. He was wearing spectacles. Jamesy could see the moon reflecting in them. He remained unmoving, watching Jamesy as he rubbed his legs.

"You a poof?" asked Jamesy at last.

"No," said the figure, "I only want to help. You looked uncomfortable."

"Even more bloody uncomfortable since you woke me up, aren't I?"

"Sorry. But if you're hungry . . ."

"I'm always hungry. Me metabolism, see?"

"I understand. Well, maybe I can give you something to warm you through. Soup and a bun, perhaps. And then – only if you want – a place to sleep." The figure stood to one side, waving a hand back. And now Jamesy could see that there was a van parked on the other side of the demolition site. It had a fold-down flap on it, like a hot dog van. Now at last, Jamesy knew who the young fellow represented.

"Salvation Army?"

"Salvation," said the young man. "Yes." He took a step backwards, waiting to see if Jamesy would follow. Jamesy waved impatiently at him.

"All right then, all right. I'm coming. Me legs, see. Seizing up, aren't they?"

Jamesy's clotted hair concealed a scar in need of stitching. His teeth were charred stumps and there was an ominous rattle in his chest. He suffered from patches of fungal infection on his buttocks, had a scar from a perforated ulcer in his stomach and the tracks of scabies parasites between his fingers. His knees were arthritic, ankles swollen, and he had trench foot and poor circulation. *(Not to mention the*

16

dandruff, he liked to joke to anyone willing to listen to his catalogue of woes.)

The young man turned and began to walk back towards the van. Muttering, Jamesy began to follow. He was hungry, but if anyone started to wave a Bible at him or started lecturing him on the error of his ways, then somebody might get a split head for their trouble.

It was late, Jamesy had no idea how late. But he was surprised that there was no one else here on the building site to take advantage of the free handout. Although this wasn't one of the sites that the handout people usually visited, some of the people he knew from the street made a habit of following these vans around, of knowing just where they would be. The Salvation Army and other welfare organisations knew the usual haunts for many of the street people and occasionally had their vans there well in advance when the weather was bad. But occasionally, vans would cruise looking for impromptu gatherings. This was obviously one of the latter. Maybe there *had* been other street people here, but he'd been sleeping and missed them all. Maybe he was the last, and this young guy had spotted him snoring behind the concrete pilings just before they were ready to pack up and take off. Well, all right. He would take some soup and bread and anything else digestible off their hands. But he wasn't taking up the offer of somewhere to sleep. He'd spent too much time in Men's Palaces, and there were too many people there with grudges against him. You couldn't relax there, couldn't sleep for fear of some bastard creeping up on you with a razor blade. Far better suffer the winters on the street and keep your wits about you. It occurred to him that if there *had* been others here tonight and he'd let down his defences enough to sleep – then he had already placed himself in potential danger. Muttering about getting old, he followed the young man right up to the van. Now he could see that it wasn't quite the same design as the other Sally Army vans he had seen around. There wasn't a fold-down flap on the side as he'd first presumed in the darkness. This one served up the grub from the rear, and its double doors were open to the night, spilling a welcoming, warm orange light on to the rough rubble-strewn ground.

The young man reached the rear doors. Smiling, he looked in at someone there and said, "Another customer." He turned back to Jamesy as he finally drew level.

"Tea, coffee or soup?" he asked.

"You said soup," rejoined Jamesy as if the man had gone back on his first offer, shuffling up to the doors. The young man stepped aside to give him access to the light and the warmth.

Suddenly, the light was switched off

And then hands clawed out of the interior of the van.

Jamesy cried out in alarm as those hands fastened on his shoulders, his arms and in his hair. He reeled, trying to pull away . . . but the young man had seized him from behind and propelled him forward into the van. The force of that shove sent him tumbling against the steps of the van – and then the clawing, grabbing hands were hauling him roughly into the van's dark interior. Jamesy tried to scream for help, but something was jammed into his mouth. He lashed out with his feet, felt his boot connect and heard a curse. Those hands had pinned him to the floor now. He heard the door slam shut as the young man climbed inside after him.

"Hold him," said a voice in the darkness. It was a young woman's voice.

"Let me up, you stinkin' . . ."

And then someone seized him by the hair and punched him full in the face. The impact slammed his head back hard to the van floor.

In his dream, the good booze fairy had refilled his bottle and he was lying back in that same shop doorway twelve years ago.

FOUR

Jamesy jerked awake in darkness. This time, there was no befuddlement, no wondering where the hell he could be. With that awakening, he was instantly seized by the damned *outrage* of what had happened to him in that van. He sat up quickly and the pain in his head and face made him retch. He fumbled at his face in the darkness and felt the stickiness of congealed blood. His nose had been broken before. He reckoned that it had been broken again.

"Some bastard's going to *pay* . . ."

The words echoed back to him. He was obviously no longer in the van. When he felt at the ground, it was not metal or carpet . . . but rough soil. Had they simply tipped him back out of the van on to the building site? No, he had spent too long on the streets to know instinctively whether he was inside or outside. He was inside. Somewhere. And he could hear a very faint trickling of water.

He sat for what seemed a long time, listening for voices or any sound of movement. But apart from the slow and constant trickling of water, there was nothing. At last, he began to make out outlines in the darkness.

He was in an ancient basement of some kind. As he'd felt and guessed, the ground beneath him was rough soil. The walls surrounding him were of bare stone, and now he could see water running down those walls. Yes, he was definitely underground. He shifted again, peering into the murk – and this time he put his hand into something sticky. He recoiled, looking down at his fingers. There was a viscous substance on his hand – like candle wax.

"Shit!"

From somewhere in the darkness, Jamesy heard what seemed to be a bolt being shifted in a door. That sound reminded him of the time he had spent in prison; just like a bolt on a cell door. Had he been *locked* away down here? He struggled to rise as a dim light spilled down one of the far walls, revealing an arched stone alcove. That light had issued

19

from the alcove, and shadows were moving in there now – spilling downwards to reveal stone stairs. Someone was coming down.

Jamesy may have been on the streets for twelve years, may not have been as fast or as strong as he'd been in his youth. But he'd learned a lot during that time and he was no easy touch. He'd been kidnapped and beaten up. Someone was going to pay for that very dearly. He bunched up his fists, hawked and spat. He was ready.

The first of the figures entered the basement.

It was a young woman, mid-thirties. Well dressed. Her presence seemed incongruous here, not at all menacing. And she was *smiling* as she stepped down calmly off the last rough-hewn step and walked towards him.

There was a man behind her, maybe Jamesy's own age. Again, clean-cut and very ordinary. He was wearing a bland, dark suit and tie. For all the world like a bank manager – and sharing the same smile as the woman.

There were eight of them in all. Another middle-aged man in a cardigan and wearing jeans, looking like a lorry-driver. As each figure entered, Jamesy expected to see the young bastard who had first approached him on the building site. But he was not one of the eight. When they had all entered the basement, they stood quietly looking at him. No sign of menace on their faces, no threat. Just the same good-natured smile. Jamesy shuffled uneasily. There wasn't one of them looked hard enough to take him, or stop him if he just wanted to get out of here.

"Right!" he said. "Right . . . there's a law against kidnapping in this country, in case you didn't know."

The eight figures remained motionless, still smiling, still unconcerned.

"All right, all right. Who's first, then?" Jamesy bunched his fists and waved one at them in a *Come on!* gesture.

The eight figures just stood and watched.

The water trickled on the walls.

Jamesy took a tentative step forward. None of them moved aside or towards him.

He took another step.

"What the hell do you want then, eh?"

No response. He began to walk slowly towards them, step after careful step.

"Somebody's going to have to pay for this, you know. Can't just rough people up and kidnap 'em. You're going to have to cough up a little cash if you want me to keep quiet about this, know what I mean?"

And now it came to Jamesy that no one was going to stop him if he wanted out of this place. These weren't drug-crazed hippies, or serial killers, or religious maniacs. They were . . . well, bloody hell . . . they were just *ordinary* people. Ordinary, *soft* people. And he could take anybody who tried anything on.

"Well, what about it, then? Twenty quid to keep quiet?"

The same smiles, the same lack of concern.

"All right, a tenner. That's my last word. A tenner, or the boys in blue . . ."

He was only a few feet from this strangely quiet bunch of people. He looked them over – a clerk, a housewife, a lorry driver, a bank manager. A couple of nondescript teenagers, boy and girl. An older woman, a pensioner maybe. And some spotty Herbert in an anorak who could be a train spotter. Whatever or whoever the hell they were, they wouldn't stop him leaving.

Uttering a growl of disdain, Jamesy shoved through them towards the rough stone stairs.

They fell on him like a pack of wild animals.

Again, hands clawed in his hair, seized his arms and shoulders.

Enraged, he lashed out at them. But the full weight of eight people was on him before he could get his bearings and really land a blow that would count. Yelling in rage, Jamesy crumpled under them. The weight bore him down as he flailed, and then two feet from the ground he collapsed completely as if he was at the bottom of a rugby scrum, the flats of his hands pounding on the rough dirt, his feet kicking and thrashing. He was suffocating. He screamed for air, the exertion making him even more breathless. The darkness spangled before his eyes and then . . .

. . . they were turning him over on to his front. Sobbing, he gasped in the air, unable at the moment to fight back as those rough hands straightened him out. He moved his head, and tears of pain filled his eyes at the agony in his nose and forehead. Now, they seemed to be waiting again. Holding him down and waiting for something.

Or someone.

Jamesy heard the sounds of movement from the stairs and turned, sobbing, to look. A shadow spilled down over the stone stairs from the opened doorway somewhere above. He looked back up at his captors, expecting to see the same bland smiles. But now those faces had changed dreadfully. They were grinning from ear to ear. Those faces seemed distorted from his perspective. The eyes glittered in the darkness. As he watched, he saw a thin string of spittle fall like gossamer from the mouth of the elderly woman whose hand was gripped in his unkempt hair. Those faces seemed . . . hungry. Jamesy twisted back to look at the staircase and saw that the shadow was coming down the stairs. But something must be wrong with this person. He didn't know just what in hell was wrong – but something about this shadow on the bare, dripping stone walls was filling him with even greater fear. At last, the shadow stepped down into the faint light.

It was a young girl – perhaps nineteen years old. She was wearing a simple, plain grey dress that looked more like a smock. Her legs were bare, she wore scuffed suede shoes. Her hair was long and red and tied in braids.

And even from where he lay, Jamesy could see that the girl was blind. Her eye sockets were black and hollow.

At the bottom of the stairs she stopped and cocked her head to one side, as if listening. Jamesy looked back at his captors. Their expressions seemed now even more dreadfully expectant than before. Somewhere, someone gave vent to a small, nervous giggle in the excitement of what was coming. The blind girl moved to the left and Jamesy tried to follow her movements, but the hand in his hair held fast. Now he could hear something, like the grating of stone on stone. A second later, the blind girl had moved back into his line of sight.

"*Let me UP!*" shouted Jamesy, his breath found at last. He thrashed to rise, but the weight of the bodies above held him down. Again, the old woman slammed his head down hard on the ground.

The blind girl smiled, as if this sudden noise had confirmed where everyone could now be found. She moved silently towards them, hands held out in front of her. There was a dreadful confidence in her movement, as if she was not blind at all – just pretending.

Jamesy could smell something as he thrashed and screamed to be up. It was the smell of his own naked terror. The smell of his own urine.

Something glittered in one of the blind girl's hands as she fumbled her way downwards, hunting for his face. Light sparked somehow in the darkness, and within that fragment of light, Jamesy was sure that he could see the face of a haloed saint.

At the last, before the hideous nightmare of agony and torture began, Jamesy could see what the girl was holding.

It was a sliver of glass from a church's stained-glass window.

FIVE

Ranjana knew that something was wrong as soon as she put her key in the front door lock. She tried to shrug the feeling off as she pushed into the hallway passage, but it just seemed to get worse as she stepped inside and closed the door.

There was an unfamiliar coat hanging on one of the pegs in the hallway. A lightweight, grey raincoat. It didn't belong to either of her two brothers.

She nervously put the shopping bags down on the floor just as someone laughed in the living room. It was Patel, her elder brother. She strained to listen and was now aware of mumbled conversation. Then Rajinder, her younger brother, put his head around the living room door and saw her.

"Ranjana!" he exclaimed, as if her arrival was somehow unexpected. "Thought I heard the front door. We've got company."

"Who?"

"Come and see," replied Rajinder, vanishing back into the living room. Invisible, he said, "She's here." And then she heard the sound of an unfamiliar male voice grunting acknowledgment.

Ranjana took off her coat and walked slowly to the living room door.

"Come on," said Patel from inside. "We're waiting."

Both of her brothers seemed to be standing . . . well, *awkwardly* in the room. Rajinder stood against the far wall, his hands behind his back, almost bowed at the waist and straining forward to take in the conversation. Patel was sitting on the window ledge, looking much too eager to please. Beside him was the owner of the third voice. This stranger was sitting in the most comfortable armchair in front of the television. It had been Father's chair before he'd died. But this man was in his mid- to late forties. Bald, with strands of hair combed carefully but with limited success across his head. He was wearing a business suit, and the frames of his spectacles were thick and dark.

"Ah, Ranjana," he said. He made as if to rise and greet her, but Patel

23

had moved quickly from the window ledge and guided him back into his seat.

"This is Mr Gupta," said Patel, easing himself back to the ledge. His eyes didn't leave their visitor, didn't acknowledge Ranjana's presence.

"Hello, Ranjana," said the man called Gupta. "You look so much more mature than fifteen years old. Compared to the photographs, I mean."

At first, Ranjana could not speak.

"How are you?" asked the visitor. "Been working hard at the shop?"

Ranjana turned to look at Rajinder. But he was looking down at the floor now, at his feet. She could see from his expression that he knew what she was thinking, and that he was uncomfortable. She turned back, and this time Patel was looking at her with anger in his eyes.

"*Answer* Mr Gupta, Ranjana. He's come a long way to see you."

But this surely could not be Mr Gupta. He looked nothing like the photographs that her brother had shown her. The Gupta from those photographs was in his early twenties. There was no middle-aged paunch, no horn-rim spectacles. And he had hair: rich, dark, curling hair.

"I'm sorry . . ." she began. "How are you?"

"Delighted. I can't tell you how nice it is to meet you at last."

"Mr Gupta has come up from Bradford," continued Patel. "His business is expanding and he hopes to open up one or two branches here in our town. Not only that, but he may be buying property here, Ranjana."

"Yes," said Gupta. "That's entirely a possibility. Which will have a big effect on our personal plans."

"There's a chance that we can bring the wedding forward," said Patel.

The smile on Patel's face as he spoke was too much for her.

"Excuse me," said Ranjana. "I have to get a drink of water." Quickly, she hurried from the room and into the kitchen next door. As she left she heard Gupta say, "Is she *all right*?"

In the kitchen, Ranjana gripped the rim of the sink and took a deep, shuddering breath. Then, she grabbed a glass beaker from the draining board and filled it with water. As she drank, she thought: *They lied to me. Both of them. They LIED!*

She whirled at the sudden noise behind her.

Rajinder had followed after her.

"How?" she hissed at him. "How could you do it?"

"But we've talked this all through. You've known for years, Ranjana." His face carried no conviction in what he was saying.

24

"Yes, I agreed. Because that's what Dad wanted just before he died. But he wouldn't agree to this – not the way you want it to be. You've both lied to me, Rajinder. Those photographs you've shown me must be twenty years old at least. How old did you say he was?"

"Well, we said he was . . . well, a young man . . ."

"Young? *Young?*" Ranjana turned back to the sink for a moment, gripping the rim, trying to control herself. Her voice was deliberately calm when she turned back to her younger brother: "But that's hardly the point, is it? I know this is all to consolidate the business and to keep Patel happy . . ."

"That's not fair, Ranjana. And you know it!"

"Don't talk to me about being bloody fair."

"Dad was right, you're too westernised."

Ranjana took a step forward, suddenly aware that she had raised the glass beaker as if to throw it at her brother. He flinched back, and Ranjana fought to control herself again.

"Don't you dare say that to me," she said. Her voice was hard and tight. "I'm proud of who I am and I'm proud of my family – with two notable exceptions, right now. Before Dad died it was all agreed in principle. And I was happy with the idea of an arranged marriage. But . . . and there are two big *buts*, Rajinder. Number one: you've lied to me about Gupta. Whether he's eighteen or eighty doesn't matter. The point is you *lied* to me. And that just serves to show me that I was right all along. This whole thing is all about the fact that Mr Gupta's a 'pillar' of the business community and can move Patel into that business by our families becoming related. That's obviously more important than my happiness . . ."

"Ranjana, it's not . . ."

"And number two: we agreed that we would only marry well after I'd finished my degree at university and decided on a career. Now you're telling me that he's coming up here *soon*."

"He's a nice man, Ranjana."

"That's not the *point!*"

Patel appeared in the doorway. "What the hell is happening? Get yourself back in here now."

"You lied to me, Patel."

"Now!"

Ranjana glared at him for a long while. Then she said, "Where's Mother?"

"Upstairs. In her room."

"You mean *you* sent her there while the men discussed business."

"Ranjana, I want you to come next door and talk to Mr Gupta."

Steeling herself, Ranjana walked stiffly past her brothers and down the hallway. She paused briefly at the doorway, felt Patel's rough guiding hand at her back and shrugged it off.

"Is everything all right?" smiled Gupta.

"Perfect," Patel smiled back, flashing his teeth as they entered. He resumed his seat on the window ledge.

"The photographs don't do you justice," said Gupta.

"Neither do yours," replied Ranjana. From the window ledge, Patel flashed a dangerous and angry look. "Did you know my father well?"

"Not your father, no. But your uncle and I were quite close."

"Perhaps we could have a few words alone?" asked Ranjana – and this time it looked as if Patel might fly from the window ledge and smack her across the face.

"But of course," said Gupta, finishing any comment from Patel before it was made. Forcing that same smile back on to his face, Patel clapped his hands together instead and shoved away from the ledge.

"Absolutely." He waved at Rajinder to follow him as he headed for the door. "Maybe you're hungry, Mr Patel. I'll get Mother to make us something."

"That would be nice."

Ranjana resented the fact that Patel had given Gupta her father's seat. There were other comfortable chairs in this room. Why should he have chosen that one?

"Why don't you sit down?" asked Gupta. And this somehow made things even worse. Now, he was acting as if she was the guest, and he the host.

"No, I'll stand. Mr Gupta . . . I appreciate that these arrangements only came about because my father . . . well, it was what he wanted just before he died."

"I've known your family for a long time, Ranjana. Through your uncle, of course."

"But I was hoping that there would be a little more time. My cousins married by arrangement and they're both very happy. But they had a period of time for . . . for the . . ."

"Courtship?"

"Yes, I suppose you could call it that. I was hoping that we'd have more time to get to know each other before . . ."

"Yes, I know that things seem a little faster, a little more *organised* than may usually be the case. But as your brother said, I'll be coming here to live. And I'm anxious that we should move things along as quickly as we can."

"I see. Have my brothers told you about my university plans?"

"Out of the question, I'm afraid."

"I beg your pardon?"

26

"I'm not a young man any more, Ranjana. And one of the things that I've missed – one of the things that I want to rectify as quickly as possible – is having a family of my own. A man in my position needs to have sons, to pass on the family business. I would need my wife to be a full-time wife and mother."

"What?"

Gupta smiled indulgently. "I know everything seems a little fast, but . . ."

"Fast isn't the word for it. You're saying that my plans for university aren't important. That all you really want me for is to have your children?"

Gupta shifted uncomfortably. This conversation wasn't going the way he wanted at all.

"Maybe we should just start now, then?" continued Ranjana. "With the sex, I mean. Here on the carpet. May as well just get me pregnant straight away. Why wait for a marriage ceremony? Hell, why wait for a *courtship*?"

"Well, really. I don't think that . . ."

But Gupta was talking to Ranjana's back now as she stormed out of the room, swinging the door wide.

Rajinder was standing in the passage. He had obviously been listening.

"Ranjana!"

She shoved him back hard at the wall.

I'm not going to cry, I'm NOT going to cry!

"You liar, Rajinder. You bloody liar."

Patel was in the kitchen. He saw what was happening and lunged at her, dark eyes flashing. Ranjana cried out, yanked her arm away from his grasp and ran up the stairs, fighting back the tears. At the top of the landing, she hit the toilet door with both hands and clattered inside. She could hear her brothers' feet on the carpeted stairway as she slammed and locked the door.

The door handle twisted as she backed off to the sink.

"Ranjana!" hissed Patel. "Come out at once!"

The tears were coming. There was nothing she could do that would stop them. She grabbed two fistfuls of toilet paper from the holder and crammed them to her face, trying to squeeze the tears back. But they came anyway. She made no noise as she wept.

"You're shaming us!" continued Patel. "Don't you know that? If Father was here, he'd hate you for what you're doing. It's what he *wanted*, Ranjana! You're ruining our family dignity and respect."

Her sense of betrayal overwhelmed her. She sank to her knees beside the toilet bowl.

Outside, she seemed to hear Rajinder protesting.

Then, with sharp, shocking violence – the toilet door flew open. Patel had put his shoulder to it. She crammed the paper against her face and tried to curl up into a ball. Patel seized her by the wrists and dragged her to her feet.

"No," said Rajinder behind them on the landing. "This can't be right, Patel. We haven't handled it right."

"Shut up!" Patel dragged Ranjana to the landing again. "Ranjana!" he hissed the words directly into her face, glancing back downstairs to make sure that Gupta hadn't heard anything. "You'll do this, forget all about that bloody university and just do as you're told. Do you understand? This is important. Important to me."

Ranjana's anguish gushed out of her in a wailing sob. She could not control herself now.

"Ranjana!" Patel dragged one hand from her face and slapped her hard.

"No!" Rajinder dragged Patel's hand back. "You're wrong, you bastard! Leave her alone!"

Patel rounded on Rajinder. They were going to fight again. And now the bedroom door at the far end of the corridor had opened and her mother emerged. Ranjana had fallen to her knees. She held out her arms to her mother like a child needing comfort.

Her mother moved back into her room, and closed the door.

From somewhere downstairs, Gupta said, "What on earth is going on up there?"

And then the feeling of wrongness that Ranjana had felt on opening the front door descended to overwhelm her. The anguish and the sorrow crowded into her head. She felt it happening again. The Bad Thing.

"Shit!" said Patel as she slumped back against the landing wall.

Her eyes had turned up into her head. Her face looked waxen. Now, her legs began to thrash and squirm on the floor as her body tilted unconscious towards the carpet. Spittle sprayed from her mouth as she rolled over.

"Shit, shit, shit, shit!"

Rajinder lunged downwards to grab her. "Oh no, Ranjana! Oh no . . ."

"Shit!" Patel punched the wall, heedless now of whether Gupta could hear anything. He could see that Gupta was standing in the living room doorway, looking up in bewilderment. "Shit . . ."

"Get the stuff, Patel," hissed Rajinder. "For God's sake, hurry. She's having another fit."

"*Fit?*" said Gupta from the living room doorway.

Shit, thought Patel, and tried to smile.

28

* * *

And in her dream, Ranjana saw the Running Man again.

The Running Man, surrounded by light. Arms outstretched, reaching for her in slow motion.

She could not tell whether this man was black or white. There seemed to be something wrong with his face. Like a white man with a smeared black face. His clothes seemed ragged, his arms and legs also somehow smeared. The light suffused him as he ran. His mouth worked soundlessly in a silent, screaming plea. Those eyes were filled with agony – and he needed her desperately.

"What do you want?" screamed Ranjana in her dream as those arms reached out to enfold her and the brilliant light engulfed her. "WHAT DO YOU WANT FROM ME?"

SIX

"Up, thief!" said the kindly woman in Randall's dream, and he could not understand why she was being so angry with him after she'd been so nice. He had entered a room full of roses, and this kindly old lady had asked him how old he would be on his next birthday. When he answered, "Nineteen, coming up twenty next month," she had smiled as if he had just answered a very important question correctly. She turned to the table behind her and gave him a blank photograph. Then she had suddenly turned nasty . . .

Nasty . . .

As Randall realised that the voice was the voice of a man, not a woman. The dream had blinked away, and a rough hand was shaking his shoulder.

"Up, thief!" The voice was definitely masculine; the accent Glaswegian. "Come on, get up out of it and tell me where you've hidden it!"

Randall groaned, pushing out at that calloused hand. But his sleep-blurred resistance seemed to drive the voice into a rage.

"I said *get up!*"

That same rough hand cuffed Randall hard across the top of the head. The jarring pain smacked him out of sleep instantly. He struggled into a sitting position, hair awry, as the figure which had materialised in his bedroom took a step back, sihouetted in the opened bedroom doorway by the dingy orange light from the landing outside. The voice, the unsteady wavering of the figure, and the tell-tale smell of whisky on his breath brought with it instant identification.

His father.

"What the hell's the matter with you?" groaned Randall.

"The matter? I'll give you 'What's the matter', son!"

The silhouette lunged forward and this time seized his hair with both hands, yanking him from the bed. Randall cried out in pain and rage, grabbing at his father's wrists as he was wrestled to the floor.

30

He thrashed to get balance, but although Randall was a strong young man, his father had seen plenty of street action in his time and knew just exactly what he was doing. Randall could not get that balance, could not get his feet properly beneath him as his father dragged him bodily across the room. Randall hurled obscenities at him. But all his father would say as he struggled was, "I'll show you the matter, I'll *show* you the matter . . ."

There was someone else in the doorway, holding on to the door frame and weaving drunkenly. As he twisted, he recognised that figure as well. Etta – his father's latest drinking partner and so-called girlfriend. Fifty-five years old, going on nineteen. Hair like candy floss. Black leather mini-skirt and varicose veins. In her free hand, she was holding a fish and chip supper, wrapped in newspaper.

"Show 'im, Andy. You show him."

Randall was dragged to the fireplace, and now he could see that his father was groping there for something. The old terraced house had a decrepit fireplace in each room, even the bedrooms. Sometimes, in the really bad winters, Randall would start a fire there to try and warm the bloody place up before going to bed. As a result, he had an iron "blazer" in the corner, and a coal scuttle and . . .

A poker.

Randall heard it rattle against the cracked tiles at the side of the fireplace as his father grabbed for it.

" . . . show you . . ."

"He took it, Andy!" shrilled the wavering figure on the threshold. "He definitely did. Definitely."

" . . . show . . ."

The poker was in his father's hand.

But he only had one hand ravelled in Randall's hair now . . . and Randall twisted, seizing the hand that gripped his hair with both hands. As he flipped over to his knees, he twisted that hand hard. His father uttered a hoarse, guttural cry. The poker spun from his other hand in an uncompleted arc – an arc that would have been completed when it connected with Randall's head – and clattered to the bare floorboards of the bedroom.

"Show him!" shrieked Etta from the doorway. "Don't let your own son get the better of you! Show him, you soft twat!"

Randall hauled his father over until he had sprawled on the floor. Then he leapt back agilely to his feet. He was naked – and felt naked.

"Dad! Calm down – and tell me what the hell's going on!" He held his hands wide in supplication. His father writhed in agony, gripping his wrist, then began to rise again.

"Show him, then!" warbled Etta.

31

"It's you, isn't it?" accused Randall, stabbing a finger at the woman in the doorway. "Both out of your heads with the drink. And you've been filling his head with fucking fantasies again."

"Don't talk . . ." and Etta belched. " . . . pardon me . . . don't talk to me like that, you bastard! Show him, Andy!"

" . . . show you . . ." said Randall's father, rising and bunching up his fists.

There was a photograph on the mantelpiece over the fireplace. An old photograph on the hearth taken in so-called happier days. Randall could see it now, reflected in the landing light. A day on the beach, with his father and mother smiling – and he was smiling too, even though he had two broken ribs from his dad, and couldn't play football on the beach with the other kids because of it.

His father stepped forward, fists raised. The eyes weren't somehow focused on him. They were fixed on a point that seemed to be a good six feet beyond Randall. The rage, the bitterness, the things that had been eating his dad's guts for over twenty years were all *there* – right on the other side of Randall. And the old man (Old? His father was forty, and bloody fit. Twice as old as his son, but fit and bloody dangerous). Once again, Andy Garrett was going to square up to the things that he hated. And, once again, Randall seemed to be there in front of it all, focusing it all.

The old man skipped. Even drunk, he had a natural rhythm which belied the fact that he'd spent some time in the ring in his youth. The fists juggled professionally for the first blow.

The photograph on the hearth reflected the landing light again, drawing Randall's eye once more. In that instant he saw his own face again, still so open and fresh and full of innocent happiness for the camera, despite everything that was happening.

And now, there was only one overriding emotion after so much abuse, both physical and emotional. The sudden sense of it was bitterly overwhelming.

Betrayal.

And with that bitter surge came a sense of sorrow that flooded his soul.

Not for him. Not for Randall Garrett, twenty years old; unemployed since leaving school apart from brief casual labour and hopeless government training schemes, training kids for industry that did not exist. Not for him, the streetwise man who had learned to come up the hard way. Not for him, who'd been in as many street fights as his "fatha" by the time he was twenty.

But for the boy in the photograph – the nine-year-old who had cried when he was beaten. The sickly kid who had stopped crying *while* his father was beating him, because the old man was telling him with each blow that only girls and nancy boys cried. So that while his father was beating the shit out of him, he was still trying to please the old man by not crying and pretending to be brave while he took his punishment.

Randall stepped quickly forward, took his father by the collar and gave him an uppercut. It was what his father would describe as a classic.

Randall heard the old man's jaw snap shut with a hard *clack*! In the next moment, he had fallen to the floorboards like a bull with the humane killer touched to its forehead.

For a moment, Etta was frozen speechless. She hung in the doorway, momentarily frozen rigid and unwavering. Andy was out for the count. Randall just stood and looked. Then he turned and moved to the battered wardrobe where he'd hung his clothes.

"You've *killed* him . . ." said Etta. She tottered into the bedroom, high heels clacking on the boards. With practical difficulty because of her leather mini-skirt, and with more theatrics than a silent screen heroine, Etta knelt down beside her paramour. She placed the newspaper bundle reverently down beside his head as if it was some kind of offering.

Randall did not look back as he roughly pulled on his clothes.

"Baby, baby, baby . . ." Etta began to shake Andy by the collar. Then, turning back to Randall: "You little bastard!"

"Not so little," said Randall, pulling out a holdall from one of the shelves. He began to stuff his meagre possessions into it. "But definitely a bastard. He never married my mother."

"I'll get the police."

"So get them." Randall shoved his only other pair of jeans and another shirt into the holdall, zipping it up savagely. His father had begun to groan as he strode past them both on the floor.

Etta tried to take a swipe at his legs as he passed. "I will! I'll get the *police . . .*"

"Get the telephone number for the Alcohol Advice Centre. It'll do you both more good."

"Fuck off!"

Randall headed down the staircase.

He knew that it was the last time he'd ever walk down these stairs.

Near the bottom, he heard a fumbling commotion at the top of the staircase, but did not turn as he reached for the door.

"Fuck *off*!" screamed Etta, and this time Randall whirled when something soft and wet hit him between the shoulder blades. It was the fish supper in its newspaper wrapping. Chips and batter littered the staircase. Randall brushed his back as he pulled the door open.

33

"Happy New Year," he said and stepped out into the darkness.

He slammed the door hard and walked away. It occurred to him that he would never find out what he had done to incur so much wrath.

The nine-year-old boy inside was crying, but this time Randall wasn't listening.

SEVEN

He walks in the rain.

His name is Mac, but no one knows whether this nickname is derived from his first name or his surname. He isn't Scottish, so it can't be that.

He is a tall man, perhaps six feet four inches, and he carries himself well for someone who lives on the streets. His hair is unkempt, dark curls pleat around his ears and hang on his shoulders. He wears a long grey coat, and the stitching has begun to burst along the left seam. Although a big man, he looks bigger. This is because he has prepared for the bad weather on the way. He wears two shirts and three pullovers, all cast-offs found during the course of his wanderings, retrieved from waste bins, skips, or torn black plastic bags filled with rubbish and awaiting collection from back alleys. There are long johns under his jeans, and the jeans themselves would be a perfect advert for the company who made them if not for the wearer himself. He has worn them for six years, and they have shown little signs of wear and tear. The shoes are heavy Doc Martens, passed on to him by a girl in a Salvation Army dress who took them from a vagrant found dead in a car park. Literally a case of dead man's shoes. Beneath the shoes, three pairs of socks.

His face, at first seeming to be dirt engrimed, is actually tanned to the colour of leather. He is fastidious about washing. But closer examination of that face brings with it a feeling of unease. A beard masks most of it, but if not for that covering, one would be tempted to think that the face itself seems somehow unreal; like the face of a tailor's dummy. The features are somehow too regular, too clearly defined. No one has really got close enough to see that this face has in fact once been badly ravaged – burned, perhaps. If not for the beard, the tell-tale thin white tracing of a surgeon's scalpel can be seen around the man's hairline, around his neck and beneath his eyes.

The eyes are a startling blue. And they never seem to blink, another result of surgery. When he sleeps, those eyes remain open. And it is this

35

apparent icy stare that makes life so difficult when it comes to handouts from passers-by on the street. The eyes seem intimidating. But his face never seems to betray any sign of emotion. He is, for the most part, a silent man. But when he does speak, his voice is soft but resonant with no hint of an accent. The voice does not hinder a feeling of strength ... of danger. His age seems indefinable, and could be anything from mid-twenties to mid-forties. And he has been on these streets longer than most of the others.

He has been walking for a long time today, unconsciously following the same route he has been taking for over ten years now. It is an astonishingly complex circuit of the city, radiating in and out of the centre like the spokes of a wheel. He follows the same streets, the same alleys, the same part of the waterfront. But no one can predict when and where he will appear. Timetabling is not a factor of his route, but he never deviates from it.

When he stops by the waste bin next to a bakery, it is his first stop for five hours. It has been raining now for over two hours, and the contents of the bin are soggy as he rummages through it. No luck. No one has dumped any food today. He turns and looks into the bakery doorway where office workers are queuing for lunchtime sandwiches, ignoring the looks of hostility and disgust. He jangles the loose change in his pocket ... then continues on his way.

Overhead, the darkening sky fizzes blue-white. Seconds later, the thunderclap seems to shake the windowpanes in the office blocks as he walks past. As if in answer, the rain intensifies. He grips the overcoat collar tight to his throat. Again, another thunderclap – and the rain is becoming torrential; a white spray of it splashes back from the pavement. When the third explosion in the sky comes, much nearer now, he stops and looks up.

"Three, seven, four, oh-two," he says – and continues walking.

A premature darkness has descended with the storm, and the man called Mac continues on his way, head down. His lips are moving; he is repeating the same numbers over and over again. Time loses its sense and meaning again. There is only the rain, and the darkness and the sounds of thunder in the sky. Mac's tread is paced and measured, as if on a long, hard march.

As he passes a furniture store, someone calls his name.

He stops and looks into the shadowed alcove. It is not a good place for anyone to take shelter during this rain. The doorway is on a slight inner cant, and a dirty pool of rainwater has gathered. When he steps forward, he can see that someone is lying in that doorway, in the middle of the pool. The figure raises a weak hand in his direction.

"Mac ... ?" The voice breaks into a spasm of coughing.

The big man moves forward.

36

"Christ, Mac. I think I'm . . ." The words choke off again. " . . . think I'm dying."

Mac sees something else now as he looks at the figure in the doorway. He doesn't see the sodden man in the doorway; he sees another figure, in the same position, also with hand outraised in a plea towards him. But the fine spray-mist of rain which surrounds the figure is no longer rain. It is the opposite. It is fire. Blue-white petrol fire. And the figure in that doorway is not drenched, but hideously burned. Mac lunges forward, and takes the upraised arm. Quickly, he stoops in the doorway and lifts the burned (wet) man shakily to his feet. He stoops again when the figure is standing, and scoops him up onto his shoulder.

"Jesus . . . Christ . . . Mac . . . please . . ."

"Okay," says Mac. "Okay."

He steps back out onto the pavement. A young man and woman make a wide detour around them as they pass. For a second, Mac stands there with this man on his shoulder, adjusting the weight. The man's arms and legs swing limply. Now, he has made his mind up on the direction to take. He strides away down the street through the pouring rain, back in the direction from which he's just come.

The sky explodes again.

Mac ducks slightly, looking up at the clouds. The movement makes the man he's carrying begin to cough again.

"Easy," says Mac. "Easy. We'll make it back."

EIGHT

It had been quieter than usual in the Casualty Department, which made Linda wonder whether the Fates were planning something bigger than usual for later on. Was this literally the lull before the storm? As if in answer to her thought, the windowpanes rattled as thunder rolled again in the sky.

She had been on shift for an hour and a half. Her raincoat was still drying out on its peg behind the reception desk. So far, there had been one workman who'd fallen off a ladder on a nearby building site and possibly broken his arm. He was still sitting on one of the seats in front of the reception desk, glaring at her. He'd been seen by a doctor, then told to wait. Clearly, he held her responsible. She might just as well have given that building site ladder a push. An eight-year-old kid with a gash on his hand. An old guy who had at first seemed to be concussed, but then had turned out simply to be drunk – and was quickly thrown out. And a DIY enthusiast who'd dropped a hod of bricks on his foot.

Maybe that petrol tanker was even now bearing down on a busload of kids? Perhaps that accidentally turned-on gas tap was just waiting for the first cigarette match to be struck?

When the Casualty doors banged open with terrific force, slamming against the interior walls, she spun in her seat – expecting to see an ambulance crew bustling through.

It was a big man in a long coat, soaked to the skin. At first, she thought he must be a wrestler and that he had his opponent on his shoulders, ready to give him a body slam to the floor. But no, the man was spinning as if looking for help. The man on his shoulders was clearly unconscious, and by the look on his white face clearly in need of help. They sprayed water as the big man looked for assistance.

"*Medic!*" shouted the big man, striding into the middle of the reception area.

The DIY man had jumped up from his seat despite his injured foot,

MACABRE

and was standing behind it now as the big man reached the centre of
the room and spun again, still looking for help. Linda grabbed for the
telephone, but it was only halfway to her ear when the plastic screen
curtains at the rear of the reception were dragged back. Dr Indrahan
and a nurse were hurrying over even now. The big man saw them
coming, stooped and headed for the rows of seats. The boy with the
gashed hand was dragged open-mouthed out of his seat by his mother
and over to stand protected by the coffee machine, as the big man
carefully placed his companion down on one of the seats. The doctor
and nurse quickly moved to him. As the big man stood back, Linda
could see that both he and his companion were completely soaked to
the skin.

She moved to come around from behind the reception desk, but
stopped when the big man turned and headed towards her. Something
about him, something about the man's eyes, about his size and the
strength of him, made her stop in her tracks. She fought to find her
voice.

"Are you all right? Can I . . .?"

"Three, seven, four, oh-two," said the big man.

He walked past her, out through the reception doors, and back into
the torrential rain.

NINE

No one knew it, but Gerry's bedroom was a shrine.

There were things in there which must never be touched. Ordinary things . . . and not so ordinary things. Of the ordinary: the bedside lamp must always be on the windowsill, not on the bedside table. His wife had moved it once, and he had nearly slapped the stupid tart – hard. The same shirts had to hang on the same hangers in the wardrobe, the same shoe boxes had to be in the same position under the bed. He'd wanted to change the posters on the wall, but couldn't. They had to stay up there, even if they were beginning to get tattered and were peeling away from the wall. Hell, he hated some of the bands that were up there now; couldn't understand why he'd liked their fucking music in the first place – but the posters had to stay. Sharon had mumbled something about redecorating the place recently, but one look from him had told her that nothing – but *nothing* – in that room was going to be changed. That room had once been their marital bedroom, but he had thrown her out to sleep in the spare room weeks ago, when the first "visit" had taken place.

On the first night it happened, Gerry had been lying there thumbing through a tattered old book about war atrocities. War in the Philippines stuff. He'd left it open at page twenty-three. Then it had happened.

That book was still on the bureau, still open at page twenty-three. And it was going to stay that way.

There were other things about the room that were more than ordinary.

There was a semen stain down by the side of the bed. Gerry renewed that stain regularly. It musn't ever be washed off

And under the bed, next to the shoe boxes, another cardboard box about the same size. But there were no shoes in that box. Whatever was in there had been there on the first night, so it had to stay just the same. The only trouble was that it had started to smell. And Gerry knew that he couldn't do anything about it. Even spraying it with air

40

freshener or turps or something would be no good, because that would bring a new odour to the room. Everything, even the smells, had to be exactly the way it had been on the night of the first visitation.

Gerry stood in the centre of his room, looking around. He checked everything. The shirts, the book, the stain. There were bound to be some things that he hadn't noticed on that first night, but as long as he *tried* to keep everything as it was, that was the most important thing. He moved to the bedroom window and looked out across the council estate. It was night, and the ranks of streetlamps stretched all the way from this house in a perspective line, through the maze of streets and alleys, to the main highway. He could see traffic glittering past on that highway, moving fast. None of it was taking the sliproad down to the estate. All those well-off bastards and fat cats, just heading straight on by. Very soon, no one would be passing him by again.

Somewhere out there in the night, he could hear a police siren. Maybe a police car chasing one of his own gang in a joyride car.

"Go for it!" Gerry shouted at the window. "Go on, leave those pigs standing!"

" . . . you all right . . ." came Sharon's faint voice from downstairs.

"Stop fucking prying!" shouted Gerry, turning quickly from the window. "*Right?*" There was no answer. Gerry hawked and cleared his nose, then looked around the room again. It was good. He moved back to the bed, lay on it and put his hands behind his head. After a while, he lit a cigarette. That was okay, because he had been smoking on the night that it had first happened.

He was excited now. He felt sure that he would be coming again. Gerry had a name for him, even though he had not been given a name by the Man. It summed him up. Not only the way he looked, but the way he felt. That look and that feeling connected very profoundly with him.

The Man Who Shines Black, thought Gerry.

And with that thought came the same tingly feeling in his arms and legs that always presaged an appearance.

Gerry sat up to attention, stubbing out the cigarette. He straightened himself, earnestly leaning forward. This was where his eyes usually went blurry, like he had a headache coming on or something. The doctors had shown a big interest in the early days about those headaches, when he was a kid. He had been ten years old then, was twenty-two now. He remembered the questions they'd asked about whether or not he heard voices when he got one. About whether he'd seen anything. Well, he had heard a voice once. But that was it – only once. But he'd never let on to his parents, or to the doctors. He'd been sniffing glue that week, so it must be that. But if he'd told them

41

anything about it, they would have locked him up and thrown away the key. It had been a woman's voice then, some stupid bint just going on about housework or something. Like he was tuned into a radio. Crazy. Anyway, he'd never heard anything like it since. But these headaches were the same, just the same as . . .

And the flecks of light began to appear in the middle of the room.

As he watched them again, filled not with fear but with a deep excitement, Gerry realised that those specks looked just like the slow-motion film of a light bulb exploding. Lots of glittering, fine shards.

That cascading, tumbling jumble of light was getting bigger than a light bulb now. It was blossoming outwards, spinning faster. And starting to take shape. Now it seemed to Gerry that it was as if something was approaching him down some long, reflecting tunnel. Getting bigger and nearer all the time. Gerry shaded his eyes. Shadows from the light were leaping and rearing all around the room. *There should be noise*, thought Gerry. *There's so much light*. But everything was silent in the room. Gerry could still hear the police siren dying away outside in the night. The headache pulsed bad behind his eyes and Gerry groaned, holding his temples.

The light flared and then died. Like someone coming in and shutting a door.

When Gerry opened his eyes again, the Man stepped from nowhere into the middle of the room.

The jumble of fractured light was gone.

But the Man was there. A silhouette, with no discernible features, no discernible face. Just a shape of a man, glistening black as if his blackness was somehow wet – the way that rain will shine on a black waterproof. The Man stood and looked at him, and even though Gerry could not see his face, he knew that he was smiling.

The Man Who Shines Black. And it was the Man speaking now. *That's a good name, Gerry. I like it. You're an imaginative man.*

And Gerry loved the sound of the Man's voice.

It's been . . .

" . . . a week," finished Gerry.

A week, said the man. *Since I last came. Make me happy. Tell me things to make me happy.*

"It's getting bigger," said Gerry eagerly. "The way things are organised, I mean. Remember that gang from Albion Street, the lot who had control of Penner estate? Yeah, well they don't no more. I just did what you wanted, showed them that trick you taught me." Gerry laughed in glee, hugging his knees on the bed. "It was so fucking easy. There was only the two to worry about. You know? Dobsy and Tanner. They were in charge. Once we got rid of them, it was easy to have the others come in with us. Dobsy and Tanner are in Intensive Care. I had the guys fuck them over. Some of their own mob even joined in. Couldn't believe it!"

That's good, Gerry. Very good news. It's important that you be in control. Just follow my advice.

Gerry heard a noise on the landing outside his room. Then Sharon said, "Do you want something to eat?"

"I'll tell you *when!*" he shouted, looking nervously at the silhouette standing in the middle of the room. He listened as his wife headed downstairs again, knowing that no one could hear the Man. Even if the door was to open now, and the stupid tart came in, she wouldn't be able to see him. And it wasn't the booze, or the drugs. This was *real.* The first real thing that had happened to him in a long, long time.

Real, said the Man Who Shines Black. *Yes, I'm real. And what I can give you is very real, too. Look inside . . .*

The Man waved his hand in a languid gesture, as if lazily trying to dispel invisible cigar smoke. In that one moment, Gerry was suffused with a profound sense of who and what he was, and what he could become. Gerry Tomelty: twenty-two years old, in trouble with the law since he was twelve. Joyrider supreme at the age of fourteen. A long list of "form". Arson, burglary, assault and battery, intimidation – a rapist at the age of fifteen. And the leader of one of the biggest and most organised gangs on the council estate. In a series of breathtakingly stimulating images, Gerry saw his gang doing what they loved doing best – intimidating the local Asian community on the estate. He saw an old man and his wife going down under heavy boots, saw blood flow and a pair of spectacles being trodden underfoot. He saw Paki cars being stolen and burned out. He saw a young mother being fucked by two of his mates in a back alley, and knew that she would be too afraid to tell anyone about it. Not her husband, not the police. Nobody. It had been good sport, but now it was –

Essential, Gerry. Absolutely essential. And Gerry was back in real time again when the Man spoke. *This is the most important thing. You must continue to intimidate them. It's important to make sure that your own people are made to hate them.*

" . . . yes . . ."

They're reacting to you now. You know that, don't you? They're reacting to what you do. And this is good. Because the more the black bastards react to their shops being smashed or looted, the more you must make your own people ready to respond.

"Serious retaliation."

Perfect, Gerry. A perfect term. Your own must be made to feel that they're only retaliating when the blacks fight back. You are currently drawing together the biggest, most organised street gang. This latest development on the Penner estate is very pleasing to me. You are a most excellent pupil. I am well pleased at my choice.

"When, though?" asked Gerry. "When are we going to split this fucking estate wide open?"

Don't be impatient. Just listen to what I tell you, and follow my directions. It's coming soon. In only seven weeks, since I first came to you, you have come a long way. I promise you that very soon you will be able to reap the rewards.

The Man Who Shines Black talked just like that English teacher at school that Gerry had hated so much. So stuck-up and full of poncey words, and with the accent that just seemed to say: *I'm something, you're shit.* But the Man was different. He talked the same way, but the things that those words did to Gerry – inside his head – filled him with . . . something like love. But that couldn't be right, because only homos thought stuff like that. Whatever, it was different. And this Man was much more of a man than his weakling of a father had ever been before the old tosser had drunk himself to death.

"Okay," said Gerry. "You're the boss. Just tell me the next part of the plan and I'll do it."

Again, Gerry knew that the Man was smiling, even though Gerry could not see his face.

No, Gerry. I'm the tutor. You're the boss. Very soon now, you'll be bigger than you ever dreamed.

Gerry hugged his knees, smiled like a little boy, and listened.

TEN

After what had happened to him – the mad girl passenger and her baby – Tony believed that there was no way he would ever sleep at all that night.

Nothing would work: not the shot of whisky, not Ry Cooder's music. Apparently to confound his expectations, sleep crept up on him unawares as he lay on the bed, thinking and letting the music play over him.

But there was to be no peace in that sleep for him again.

The dream began.

"We're cut off, and he fucking knows it," said Moxy as he slumped down next to Tony.

"How is he?"

"He's not going to make it."

The subject of their talk – Lieutenant Dennis Crawleigh – lay twenty feet away. Willis was their nearest thing to a medic, although they'd all had the training, and he was busy trying to staunch the blood flow. It was no use, Crawleigh had been shot in the guts. Despite his wound, Crawleigh had been trying to tell them that everything was okay. But to a man – eight of them – they knew that they were separated from the main division by an almighty cock-up.

Orders had been given for the capture of Mount Longdon, Two Sisters, Mount Harriet and Goat Ridge. They'd realised from manoeuvres at home how much of this landscape resembled the Dartmoor Tors – long exposed hillsides linked by saddles of high ground and surmounted by outcrops of rock.

In clear weather, the Argentinian defenders had excellent visibility, less so at night. There had been no unusual artillery preparation and the attack had proceeded as silently as possible in the early stages. Five Para had joined with Three Para in the assault on Mount Longdon, with Two Para in support. After the initial assault, heavy gunfire

45

support had been laid down for the next stages.

The Argentinian 7th Infantry Regiment had dug themselves well in among the crags of Mount Longdon – and were using their night snipers to deadly effect.

And, thanks to Crawleigh, they had blundered straight on to a machine-gun nest without protective cover. The nest had been wiped out with phosphorus grenades, but Crawleigh had bought one in the guts in the process.

Now, crouched behind a rough mound and in utter confusion, Moxy had seen the figures breaking cover in the night and heading their way.

"They're ours," hissed Moxy. "They must be ours."

Cameron shoved himself up too far over the lip of the mound for safety.

"No, they're fucking not," he said calmly.

And the next thing Tony knew, Cameron had lifted his 7.62 mm SLR and let rip.

"Christ!" yelled Willis from the other side of the mound.

And a pair of boots suddenly appeared in Tony's line of vision. He ducked back instinctively – and the first of the Argentinian soldiers leaped directly over him and landed, whirling. Cameron fell back, finger still tight on the self-loading rifle as he fell next to Tony – and the lethal blast of fire caught the soldier as he landed and before he could let off the round which would have taken Tony's head off. Tony saw the soldier explode like a sack of blood and offal.

The mound had suddenly become hell.

More grey-green, uniformed figures were leaping over the mound. The sounds of gunfire and men screaming were deafening, the mound itself lit in a mad tracing blaze of insane sparking light as weapons discharged. Tony saw an Argie land on Moxy, feet first, smashing him to the ground. He struggled to raise his semi-automatic Browning, but was too late to stop the bayonet coming down full-force and two-handed under his chin. Moxy made no noise as the Argie pulled the bayonet free, but Tony was screaming now, unable to let the bastard have it as another Argie came over the top directly towards him. Moxy's killer was gone in the mêlée, but Tony was screaming and bringing his weapon up as his own attacker landed in the dirt. Screaming, he pulled the trigger – and the Argentinian's head vanished chaotically into the night.

Somewhere, Willis was cursing fit to bust. Cameron was gone and Tony scrabbled in the dirt for better purchase.

And then someone or something punched him on the right thigh. His leg went from under him and he rolled in the dirt, seeing another silhouette appear on the lip of the mound. Its own automatic weapon blazed, but strangely Tony could hear nothing. He fired at it, just as the

46

*silhouette leapt at him. The figure slammed into him. And now the pain
in his leg and the suffocating body blow had taken Tony away from this
hell. He was sliding, going to sleep. The sounds of the hand-to-hand
fighting all round him were distant. Someone seemed to be shaking him
by the shoulder, but he just wanted to turn over and go to sleep.*

*Now, somehow, he was lying across the lip of the mound. Someone
had hauled him there. There were bodies lying back down in the mound,
but Tony got the feeling that somehow the battle had moved on, beyond
him into the night. Now, he was aware that two people were helping him
over the mound and a voice hissed right into his face: "Come on,
Dandridge! Fucking move it if you want to get out of this alive. Come
on, you bastard. All the others are dead!"*

*"Dead?" he heard himself say, and almost laughed at the stupidity of
the statement. His leg was hurting now. Had it gone to sleep?*

*"Come on!" This time he recognised the voice, saw the faces as his two
rescuers finally hauled him over the mound. It was Cameron, the man
who had already saved him from death, and Willis. And what Tony
thought at first was mud on Willis's face he now realised was a mask of
blood from the parallel bayonet gash across his forehead.*

*Someone else was coming. Striding purposefully through the night
towards them. Another silhouette, carrying something like a vacuum
cleaner. And Tony knew that this must be a dream, because people didn't
suddenly walk into hell carrying vacuum cleaners. He smiled at this
ridiculous shape that the two others had not seen yet, and said, "Who's
that?" as if expecting them to let him in on the joke. "He been sent to
clean up, then?"*

*"JESUS CHRIST!" yelled Willis, suddenly letting go of Tony's arm and
running back to the mound. Tony fell, with Cameron's grip still tight on
his other arm. He saw the ridiculous silhouette with the vacuum cleaner
turn calmly as Willis raced from them, heard Cameron say, "Shit!" as
he suddenly let go and dodged, weaving through the night. Tony laughed
aloud. This was all too silly for words.*

And then the night roared into bright orange flame.

*A blossoming cloud of black-orange fire had leapt from the nozzle of
the "vacuum cleaner". Tony saw it lance in a blazing arc towards Willis,
saw it envelop him and pass on, saw the burning, thrashing shape that
had once been Willis leap and tumble over the rim of the mound in a
shrieking, blazing mass.*

*And could laugh no more as the silhouette came on towards him. The
cloud had blossomed and died, but traces of liquid fire were still dripping
from the flame-thrower nozzle as the Argentinian came on.*

*The safe fantasy of the dream had gone. His leg was in agony and he
couldn't rise to his feet. Uttering hoarse cries of fear, Tony tried to scramble*

away from the advancing figure. The night-black figure and its dripping hose of fire came on relentlessly. He didn't want to die this way – oh Christ, not THIS way! He held out a hand in a silent plea.

The figure adjusted the controls on the thrower. A flower of orange-black spurted from the nozzle.

And that flower whipped upwards and away into the sky. Someone yelled and the advancing Argentinian went down.

Tony could see that someone or something had leapt out of the night on to the Argentinian. They had both gone down in a thrashing tumble of limbs. They thrashed on the muddy ground in the darkness, both figures cursing and uttering hoarse cries. Tony recognised the voice of his rescuer – Cameron.

"Use your gun!" yelled Tony, and began to crawl towards the figures as they rolled on the ground. A cloud of sparks gushed in the air. The figures were rolling around in those sparks now. "Use your fucking gun!" Tony clawed at the sparse withered grass, hand over hand, screaming at Cameron. It was too dark to make out what the hell was happening, but it seemed that Cameron was on top of the bastard, with his hands round his throat. The Argentinian thrashed beneath him. Tony heard the clunk and jiggle of the canisters on the Argie's back.

And then Cameron cried out in pain as the Argentinian managed to get one leg between them. He kicked out savagely, one foot planted on Cameron's chest – and Cameron was thrown clear.

"No!"

Cameron hit the ground hard and struggled to rise.

"No!"

The Argentinian was on his knees, and the nozzle swung around.

"NO!"

Tony saw the orange-black cloud leap hissing from the nozzle at Cameron, could smell the petrol.

And Cameron had struggled to his feet, ready to launch himself back at the Argie – just as the orange fire-cloud enveloped him.

"NOOOO!"

Cameron had become a human fireball. Tony looked in horror at the blazing marionette which had once been his best friend. Somewhere within that roaring mass of orange flame, he could still see the human outline as it turned – almost calmly – from the Argentinian and blundered away, lighting up the night.

And Tony was on the Argentinian. The pain in his leg was as nothing, it didn't prevent him from leaping at the kneeling figure as its attention remained focused on the blazing man-thing that had been Cameron. The fire snuffed out from the nozzle as the Argentinian went down under him. One hand was around his throat as he screamed obscenities of hate and grief into the Argentinian's face. Something snapped under them and the Argentinian shrieked. Tony screamed like an animal, hoping that the sound was a leg breaking.

The bayonet was in his hand.

And then it was jammed under the Argentinian's chin, to the hilt.

Hot red liquid was spilling and slopping over Tony's hand like soup as he kept it there, screaming. The Argentinian began to twitch and jerk under him.

When it was over, Tony looked up sobbing.

Out there, in the blackness of a Falklands night, he was sure that he could see a distant burning figure, running into the dark, its outline shining like a beacon as it ran, and ran, and ran . . .

Tony could not stop screaming in rage and pain and grief.

The fire blinked out.

And so, at last, did Tony.

ELEVEN

Tony was awake again, bathed in sweat.

How many showers do I have to take in one day? he asked himself, groaning, as he rubbed a hand across his moist face in the darkness. He struggled to sit up, leaning for the bedside lamp. His hand froze in mid-air. The music was still playing on his stereo, so he couldn't have been asleep for long. Just long enough to relive the same events in dream form, the same unrelenting horror. He paused to listen. It was still Ry Cooder's guitar, but something had happened to the speed on his tape deck. The music was playing too slow, it was running down: Cooder's guitar notes hanging too long in the air: thick, heavy long-drawn-out bass chords. Like all of the bedsprings in his mattress slowly breaking under his weight. Then Tony remembered that he had fallen asleep with the bedside lamp switched on. Now, it was off.

Power cut, he thought, but reached for the switch anyway.

And the bedside light came on.

Someone was standing in the room.

Tony rubbed his face, convinced that he was still dreaming.

When he looked back, the figure was still there. Indistinct, standing in deep shadow between the wardrobe and the door. But the figure of a man nevertheless.

"Where is she?" asked the shadow.

"What the hell are you doing in my . . . ?"

"Where is the girl, and the child?"

And now Tony was no longer sleep-blurred. The dream, the persistence of the past horror which deprived him of sleep, the experience with the girl and her child – and now the fact that someone had just walked into his room – all of this coalesced into a pure rage. Tony swung out of the bed, fists bunched. He wouldn't ask for explanations – he'd just take this bastard by the scruff of the neck and throw him down the stairs.

A hand emerged from the shadows.

50

The figure was holding a gun on him.

The sight of it halted Tony in his tracks. He stood, arms apart, swaying as he instantly corrected the lunge which would have slammed this intruder hard up against the bedroom wall. He turned in rage, facing the other wall, holding his hands up in the air.

"I do not bloody *believe* this! Twice! Twice in one bloody night!"

Tony spun back again, away from the man.

"Where is the girl and the baby?" asked the figure again. The voice was calm, well modulated – and the gun did not waver in the shadows.

"What the hell are you talking about?"

And now the figure stepped out of the shadows. Other than the gun – a standard .38 automatic by the look of it – the man himself presented no threatening presence. He was middle-aged, dressed in what looked like a "respectable" business suit. To Tony, he could have been an accountant, an estate agent or a bank manager. The man wore spectacles, and strands of dark hair had been carefully combed from left to right over a balding pate.

"Don't play games with me, Mr Dandridge," said the man. Again, the voice was calm, but now there was a trace of impatience. "We don't have the time. You will tell me where they both are."

"Look," Tony moved carefully back to his bed, sitting on the edge. "If you mean that nutcase and her kid who I picked up in the taxi, I've no idea."

Was that the sound of the man grinding his teeth?

"Honestly," continued Tony. "She just told me to drive. Someone – I guess it was you – was following her. She just wanted to get away."

"And you just took her, without question?"

"Listen. She had a gun at the back of my neck. Of course I just went where she wanted. I dropped her off in the middle of nowhere, somewhere. She vanished and I came back here."

"You're sheltering her."

"Look around then! You won't find her here! And let me tell you, I am a bit fucking sick of having guns waved in my face tonight."

The man sidled to the right, still keeping his eyes on Tony. He moved to the wardrobe door, pulled it open and glanced quickly inside.

"Are you joking, or what?" Tony was laughing now. A harsh barking laugh of derision. "You think they're hiding in the wardrobe?"

"Get up from the bed and walk ahead of me. I'm going to search the rest of your flat."

"How did you get in?" asked Tony as he rose. He couldn't believe that someone could just pick the lock and creep in without him noticing. Sleep had become such a fitful affair for him.

"Walk ahead," said the man.

51

Tony raised his hands and moved ahead.

"What's through there?"

"Kitchen and bathroom," said Tony. "That's all there is."

"Are there any more rooms?"

"Like I said, that's all there is."

"Keep your hands raised."

"Watch a lot of westerns on television, do you?"

The man jabbed the gun hard into the small of his back as Tony stepped through the kitchen door.

"Shut up!" he hissed.

It was what Tony had been waiting for. He spun quickly, catching the man's wrist and dragging it down. Off balance, the man grunted and went down on one knee. With his free hand, Tony seized the kitchen door and yanked it back hard so that it slammed into the man's head. The door was light wood, but the shock effect was what he'd planned on. The man sprawled, crying out in pain as Tony snatched the gun out of his hand. The man was on his knees now, balance gone and dazed. Tony braced himself, planted a foot on the man's chest and shoved hard. The man tumbled back into the living room, sprawling in a heap.

"Little bit of army training goes a long way," said Tony grimly, weighing the gun in his hands. "Now just who the hell are *you* and what the hell is going on?"

The man was whimpering now, scrabbling across the living room carpet towards the door.

"Stay where you are, you little sod!"

The man scrabbled to his feet, looking back at Tony in anger and fear. He dived for the door handle. Tony held out the gun towards him.

"Stop right there!"

But in the next instant, the man had flung the door wide. It slammed against the interior wall, and the man lunged out into the darkness. Tony heard his feet blundering down the corridor in the darkness, heard the man's frantic breathing echoing back. He rushed to the door after him, gun still held at arm's length.

"I'm telling you, you bastard!" he shouted down the corridor, just as the man rounded the corner and headed down the stairs. Tony ran after him. When he reached that corner and the balustrade beyond, he could see the silhouette of the intruder blundering away down the winding staircase beneath him.

"You better stop now, or I'll let you have it!" yelled Tony.

But the man kept on down, bouncing from balustrade to wall in the frenzied impetus of his flight.

At the bottom, in the hallway, the man stopped and looked back. A shaft of moonlight illuminated his face from the part-window in the front door.

"You're lying!" he shouted back at Tony. "We *know* you're lying!"

Tony leaned over the topmost banister, pointing the gun, at arm's length, straight down at him.

"I said *stop!*"

"You're sheltering her. You know where they are." Even from this distance, Tony could see that the man was trembling. With anger, or exertion, or simply with fear he could not say. "And you'll be sorry for this, Dandridge. Very, very *sorry!*"

"How the hell do you know my name?"

The man hurled himself at the front door and yanked it open. Moonlight flooded into the hallway, silhouetting him again.

"Something will come for you, Dandridge." The figure skipped out into the night, turned fleetingly and shouted again, "Something will come . . ."

And then the man vanished into the darkness. Tony listened to his running footsteps as he disappeared into the night.

Somewhere below, on the second landing, another door was yanked open. Tony moved quickly back from the banister into the darkness when he heard the landlord's voice say, "What the *hell* is going on here?"

Seconds later, he was back in his flat, quietly closing the door.

He stood in the middle of the room, looking at the automatic pistol in his hand for a long time. Finally, he tossed it on to his bed and gave vent to a long, weary sigh.

"It's been a hard day's night," he said, and went to make coffee and watch the sun come up.

TWELVE

Ranjana looked at her reflection in the train window, oblivious to the scenery which flashed by outside. She had been looking at her face for a long time, to the point where it now seemed to be the face of a stranger. She held the dark brown eyes in her gaze, hoping that she could find some answers; hoping that the strange face which seemed to know her so well could give the answers she was so desperate for.

When she had recovered from her "attack", Mr Gupta had gone. Her mother was wiping her face with a damp towel, and the first thing she saw when she opened her eyes were the tears in her mother's own.

She was in the living room again, on the sofa. Rajinder was sitting on the sofa, a look of concern on his face. Patel still sat on the window ledge, staring out angrily at the street – probably in the direction which Mr Gupta had taken. Her mother had wanted to bring a doctor, but Patel had snapped "No!" without turning to look at her. Ranjana had struggled to a sitting position then and asked for a drink of water. Rajinder had gone to get it, and then Patel had asked their mother to leave the room.

"Don't think it's over," said Patel when she had left. He was still looking out of the window. "Don't think that your little act has spoiled anything. We can still arrange it . . ." Patel began to nod as he looked out into the street, as if trying to convince himself. "We can still do it. Might take some talking around, but I know that I can swing it with Gupta . . ."

Later, while she was still resting on the sofa, Ranjana had heard her brothers arguing upstairs. She knew that Rajinder had changed his mind about it all, knew that although he was now on her side, Patel would have his way, whether his younger brother liked it or not. It wasn't just because Patel was the older brother, but because Rajinder was too weak to help her. The death of their father had destroyed any

54

will or confidence that her mother had left – something upon which Patel was quick to capitalise.

Her mother had gone shopping.

Rajinder had stormed out of the house, unable to meet Ranjana's eyes.

After a long, hearty-sounding telephone conversation – presumably with Mr Gupta – Patel had also left the house, slamming the door behind him. Obviously on his way to the bridegroom-to-be; no doubt fully able to explain away the "fits" that troubled his bride-to-be.

And when the house was empty and quiet, Ranjana had gone upstairs and packed her travelling bag. All the while she was doing it, all the while she was placing her clothes and most important personal possessions in it, she was unable to think about what exactly she was going to do. Someone else seemed to be wearing her skin when she jammed the bag shut. Someone else was guiding her actions as she let herself out through the front door and into the street. Half an hour later, that same strange person inside had drawn out her secret savings from the building society. And one half-hour after that she had been standing on a station platform, waiting for a train.

She had no plans.

She only knew that she had to get away.

She was heading south.

She had travelled only four stops, but had covered one hundred and fifty miles. She was barely aware that she had alighted in a town which she had never visited before. And after twenty minutes walking on a cold and badly lit street, she had stopped at the first boarding house sign she had seen. It was an old terraced house; the felt-tip pen sign in the downstairs window had almost faded in the sunlight. She couldn't recall now whether she had had a conversation with the old woman at the so-called reception desk. But she had paid for three nights bed and breakfast. And during those three days she had stayed mainly in her room.

She had slept a great deal. Wept a lot. And still felt the after-effects of her latest "fit". Usually, she had recovered after twenty-four hours, but this latest attack had been bad, and her mind was still confused. Finally, after the three days, she had drifted back to the same station, had bought another ticket and boarded the first train to arrive there. She was unsure now whether she had been away for three days or three weeks.

A voice over the internal train Tannoy woke her from the trance. She looked nervously down the length of the train. The voice was explaining that refreshments were available in the the buffet car, but although she had eaten nothing all day, she was not hungry. There was an emptiness inside which could not be filled, and she still felt nauseous after her blackout.

The image from her "dream" was still strong.

The glowing, shining Running Man. Crying out to her in an agonised, silent plea for help. For reasons she could not explain, that dream image distressed her deeply. That man was in indescribable torment and wanted her to put an end to it, but the distress somehow went much deeper than that.

Neither dead nor alive, the thought came to her. Now what on earth did *that* mean?

The second-class, four-seat alcove in which she was sitting was occupied only by herself facing the engine, and a young man sitting directly opposite her, next to the window. She couldn't remember seeing the young man's face. Everything about boarding the train seemed blurred. She seemed vaguely to recall that the man had helped her to lift the travelling bag on to the rack above, but she could not be sure. She looked up to check that it was still there – and a small voice inside asked her just what she was planning, and just where she was going. She refused to listen to that voice, felt a bitter sorrow welling up inside.

Then she looked across at the young man, and the newspaper that he was reading. And recoiled back in her seat when she saw the front-page photograph and its caption.

The caption read: *"Missing: Have you seen this girl?"*

And Ranjana's own face was looking back at her. It was a photograph from the family album, taken perhaps three years ago in happier times.

Ranjana shrank down in her seat, now trying to hide her face, now trying to lean forward and read what was written there – but fearful that the young man might lower his newspaper and see her face properly for the first time.

Panic threatened to overwhelm her. She forced herself to climb out of the seat, gaze still fixed on the newspaper and the man hidden behind it, willed him not to put the newspaper down. Then she slid out from the seat and headed for the toilet. It wasn't far behind her. Quickly, Ranjana stepped inside and slid the door shut. She sat on the toilet seat and looked at her hands. The toilet cubicle was filled with the rushing sounds of the train's passage.

And then something strange began to happen to her.

That feeling of desperation and loneliness was becoming something else. That feeling began to gather momentum like the sounds of the train hurtling on to her unknown destination.

How *dare* Patel organise her life like this? How *dare* anyone stand by and see her life made subservient to someone else's will, for someone else's financial gain? Her mother and Rajinder had stood on the sidelines and let it happen. And she had simply allowed things to take their course.

I was being faithful to my culture, faithful to what Father wanted, said a voice inside.

Yeah, but it's not supposed to work like this, is it? My own brother has organised this for his own advantage, and what, Ranjana, would your father be saying now – if he was still alive – about this? What would HE say to the way you feel and what you're being forced into?

. . . he wouldn't allow this to happen to you . . .

Right! Exactly right! And another thing – how dare, how DARE they put a photograph in the newspaper? How dare they make it look as if I'm a bloody fugitive!

. . . they're worried about you . . .

Worried my arse! He wants me back so that he can "sell" me to Gupta.

Ranjana stood up sharply and flung open the toilet door. A woman and child shrank back in alarm as they passed on their way to the buffet car.

"Sorry," said Ranjana, but her voice contained steel.

She strode back to her seat. The young man opposite to her was still holding the newspaper up, still reading. She sat calmly. When she looked up at the suitcase in the rack, she remembered something that was in there, something that perhaps had really been at the back of her mind all along, even when her mind seemed to have blanked out when it came to definite plans.

There was an address book in there. And on the first page, under "A", was the address of an older school friend. Andrea Gordon had been her best friend at school and the only person she felt comfortable with when it came to discussing future plans. Andrea understood her family pressures, the expectations about leaving school to work in the family supermarket business. Above all, she had given her strong moral support about further education, urging Ranjana to follow in her footsteps by going on to college after school. Now, she remembered her words: *If you ever change your mind, if you ever need a friend . . .*

Ranjana spent a long time thinking about it. Her thoughts only returned when the young man opposite finally put the newspaper down. But now she was no longer worried. She studied his face, to see whether or not he was going to recognise her own. But when their eyes met, he looked quickly away as if in embarrassment. He took a Sony Walkman, plugged himself in and folded his arms. When he closed his eyes, Ranjana could not help a small laugh.

When the train finally arrived at her destination, Ranjana lifted down the travelling bag. She watched the platform sliding by and then, carefully, leaned over the table and tapped the young man on the arm. He had been dozing, and awoke with a start. He pulled out the earplugs as she smiled at him.

"Excuse me . . . ?" said the young man.

"You really should be more observant," said Ranjana, tapping the newspaper on the table. Still smiling at him, she hoisted her bag and turned away.

Still puzzling, the young man watched her vanish past the window and away along the platform.

THIRTEEN

Randall swung his holdall around to the other shoulder and kept walking.

His left shoulder had been injured six years ago in a street fight, and the muscles occasionally gave him gyp if he overexerted. He thought back to that fight now as he trudged on down the isolated and barren stretch of road on which he'd found himself. He had been standing with friends in a Chinese takeaway, waiting in line. The pubs had just closed, and there was a great deal of drunken banter taking place. Then a couple of hard lads had shouldered through the queue, shoving a weedy-looking guy and his girlfriend out of the way. They had stopped shoving when they'd come to Randall and his mates, rightly sussing that they might be in trouble if they decided to get past this lot. But Randall didn't like the look on the young guy's face as he was shoved aside, knowing that he couldn't do anything about it; didn't like the crushed look on the girl's face. This was something that he couldn't let pass. He had shoved one of the offenders in the chest, shoved him hard – and told the young lad and his girfriend to take *his* place in line. The trouble had started then. Randall had told the others to keep out of it, had flattened one of them easily enough. But then the other had pulled out a flick knife, and stabbed it into Randall's shoulder. It had remained sticking in there when Randall had flung him out of the takeaway doorway and on to the pavement. They had run away then . . . and Randall had been forced to do without supper, and substitute it for an evening in the Casualty Department instead. The young lad and his girlfriend hadn't been able to look at him when the ambulance arrived. They had vanished into the night with their suppers. The two pushers-in hadn't been seen in local boozers since.

Randall rubbed at the aching shoulder muscle and stopped momentarily, looking down the road. It seemed to stretch on for ever, right to the horizon. Scrawny trees dotted the roadside and he couldn't see a signpost anywhere. The first lorry-driver he'd been able to flag down had dropped him off over two hours ago, and he hadn't had any luck since. Cars had flashed by, oblivious to his raised thumb. Maybe he shouldn't complain. Who the hell wanted to pick any solitary male hitch-hikers up these days, anyway? Who the hell wanted a homicidal maniac or a rapist in the back seat? He wondered what had happened to the simple "trust" that his father used to espouse in the early days.

"Dead as a doornail," he said, and kept on walking. At least it wasn't raining.

As if bidden by the thought, Randall felt the first light touch of a raindrop on his face,

"Someone up there having a good laugh," he said to the sky.

He looked at his feet as he walked, trying to remember good times. It was hard to do. Most of the good time memories were spoiled by wretched prologues and postscripts. He remembered a birthday party when he was twelve, but couldn't glean any comfort from the happiness of it because of the memory of the beating he received afterwards for dropping something on the carpet. He couldn't take any joy from the caravan holiday they'd had at the coast when he was thirteen, because of the memory of the beating his mother had taken when she had been packing the holiday bags. He decided to think of nothing from childhood, just to look at his feet and to count the steps.

He would find work down south. Everyone knew that the opportunities for casual manual labour were a bloody sight better down south than they were in the north. It didn't matter what the hell he did, just so long as he could get some cash into his pocket. Just enough to feed himself, keep some kind of a roof over his head and keep dry.

Dry. The word was conjuring more water from the sky. He looked up again and could see a brooding mass of cloud heading his way from the east.

"Shit!"

But now he could see a huddle of buildings up ahead where the road met the skyline. A small, silhouetted jumble – and something that must surely be a neon sign. A motorway café? Yeah, it must be. And as he quickened his step, he could see that there were at least three lorries parked in the rear of the place. Hot coffee and the possibility of a lift. Maybe his luck was picking up. Randall hurried on ahead, hoping that he could beat those stormclouds before they reached the café.

FOURTEEN

No one there knew who had started the fire. But it had been burning all night, and they were grateful for it. Someone had dragged several shattered spars of timber across the rubble-strewn site and dumped them in the middle of that waste ground. Old sacking and other combustible rubbish had been thrown in there, and maybe petrol had been poured over the lot to give it a good start. Now, that great mound of guttering orange flame lit up the waste ground and the twenty or so figures who sat around it. Some leaned against the one remaining rough brick wall, others sat in the rubble and engaged in confused, heated and barely connected conversations with each other; reliving old arguments, redressing grievances with people now hundreds or thousands of miles away in place and memory. One or two had wrapped themselves in blankets and had fallen asleep in the cardboard boxes they'd retrieved from the council dump at the end of the street. One silhouette staggered to its feet, bottle in hand, and began to sing "Moon River" in a tuneless vibrato. A couple of teenagers snorted solvent from a plastic bag.

Tonight was going to be a cold one. If they could keep that fire going all night, and not have some interfering copper coming around – or some interfering sod telephoning the fire station, then everything would be fine.

The man called Mac had been sitting in the same position for a long time. Legs crossed, back braced against a slab of concrete. He was close to the flames, perhaps too close for safety, and he was staring into the glowing orange innards of that fire. When the others walked by him, they kept a reverential distance. No one spoke to him, but everyone looked at him as they passed.

Dalby was not a tramp, was not a down-and-out, was not without cash. But he was a man with problems. The business had gone bust, and because of that his wife had left him. He'd known all along that she'd never have the guts to stick by him if things turned bad. And he hadn't been surprised to find that note waiting for him when he got back from the casino. He'd used the last five grand to try and win back what the stocks and shares had lost him. Now, he had two hundred and fifty left. That was it – all his worldly goods.

They said it all had to do with the drink problem. He knew he had been hitting it hard, of course. But in this day and age, in the garment business particularly, you had to cope with those pressures. Booze was the one thing that had seen him through, and the warnings of his doctor, friends and bitch of a wife were all attempts to deprive him of the one and only fuel which his engine needed. He'd been out on the streets before; minor lapses when that fuel had temporarily burnt out his engine, but nothing to worry about. Once, when he had discharged himself from the drying-out clinic. The bloody money he'd wasted there! He'd spent the next three days on the streets, had met some interesting people, had learned from their own stories that he wasn't anything like them at all. He was in control. They were not.

He had been walking for a long time, nursing the half-bottle of whisky. (Good stuff, too. Not the rotgut he'd seen those other has-beens drinking.) It was late, and he'd lost all sense of direction. The street in which he'd found himself was obviously derelict, with empty houses awaiting demolition. Then he'd seen the clouds of sparks rising above one of those roofs, drifting and blossoming upwards like the promise of a warm welcome. He had staggered through the darkness towards those sparks and the smoke, had found a "cut" between the houses and up ahead had seen the brightly lit waste ground area

Now, sitting on a wooden spar, Dalby had set about finishing off the half-bottle. He had shoved away any attempt by any of the no-hopers to sidle up and use their bonhomie to get a swig from that bottle. When one of them had turned aggressive, he had jumped up with a housebrick in his hand. He had stood there, swaying, until the would-be companion had sidled away.

Dalby was fascinated by the big guy who just sat and stared into the fire. He had finished off his whisky and watched him. He didn't move, and surely he must be too close to that fire for comfort. Once, when someone threw another piece of wood into the fire, the wind had taken that sudden upward whirling of sparks and enveloped him in it. But the big man didn't stir, didn't leap to his feet trying to swat them off his body. Hell, he didn't even seem to blink. Later, Dalby had watched in fascination as one of the down-and-outs had approached the big man. This man was about sixty years old, in a real shabby state. But he was approaching the big man, with . . . well, with something like reverence. He had a bottle in his hand – vodka or gin, maybe methylated spirits. Still a good few feet from where the big man sat, he stooped down (Christ, like he's bowing to the king or the queen, or something) and offered his bottle. For a while, the big man still didn't move, didn't blink. Then, very *slowly he reached out and took the bottle . . . and, bloody hell, the older guy was backing off now like he really was in the presence of royalty, and he'd just made an offering. The big man nodded, still staring into the fire, and then took a deep drink. The older guy backed off into the deeper shadows on the periphery of the derelict space. And now, Dalby was feeling really sleepy. The fire was warm and comforting. The strange sight he'd just witnessed was also somehow strangely comforting. The whisky had numbed him to the extent where the rough rubble beneath him wasn't uncomfortable. There was another half-bottle in his coat pocket. He pulled it out, screwed off the cap and swallowed. Then he thought about throwing the empty bottle into the fire. But the presence of that big man so close to the flames somehow deterred him.*

Dalby slid down against a concrete block and drank again.

The flames leapt and danced. Someone was singing.

And the big man just kept looking into the fire.

Maybe life wasn't so bad after all.

He was asleep and dreaming, but he wasn't comfortable any more.

In this dream, he was being pulled about and jostled. He was in a dark place, and the place itself seemed to be bumping and moving around. His ears were filled with a rushing, roaring, rattling sound, and when he tried to steady himself in this mad place, hands fastened on his arms. His body was suddenly jarred as the black place gave an even greater lurch, and he felt his jaw snap shut under the impact. Somewhere, someone – perhaps a woman or a child – said, "Be careful!"

Dalby didn't like this dream and willed himself to wake up.

The dark place tilted to the left and he groped for purchase again. The hands held him firm. Who else was in this dream? Now he was jerking backwards as the dark place suddenly ceased to move. Was that the sound of screeching tyres?

With a rattling clatter, two doors swung open in the darkness and Dalby could see that this had been done by two silhouetted men. The hands were now pulling him to his feet, but he couldn't control his balance and slid to the floor of what he could now see seemed to be a van. He giggled, and was hauled aloft again. Twisting his head, he saw a young girl smiling at him. On the other side, a man about his age – again with that smile. Maybe this was a good dream, after all? There were others in the van. Perhaps eight or ten people, all helping to guide him down from the van into the arms of the two men who had been pulling open the doors.

" . . . have a party?" laughed Dalby, waving one limp arm as the two men took him and began carrying him over rough ground. He liked the look of the young woman from the van, could hear them all following behind. He hoped that this was going to be a wet dream.

There was a building up ahead. Stark and black against the dark night blue of the sky. Dalby could see a Gothic arch just ahead. Was this a church? He laughed again and said, "I'm not a believer . . ." He twisted to look at the two men who were carrying him. One had a moustache, the other was clean shaven. And they were both smiling.

The Gothic arch swam up to Dalby and he was engulfed in darkness.

The footsteps of the two men, and then of those who followed, were echoing now in the blackness. It was cold in here, cutting through Dalby's alcoholic fog. Was this a dream, or not? They emerged from the utter darkness into semi-light. He looked up. Yes, they were in a church – but this place was derelict. The roof had partially caved in and he could see stars through the timber-splintered gaps. Rubble had fallen into the church and Dalby could see shattered pews beneath old blocks of dark stone. There was mould on that shattered stone. They were carrying him down the aisle towards where there should be an altar, but was now only a huge pile of rubble and broken beams. He tried to turn and look at those following behind, but his carriers would not allow him to turn.

Maybe it was time to wake up?

At the bottom of the aisle the two men swung to the left and headed for another arch. Vaguely, Dalby could see a heavy door with massive iron studs. He wasn't sure about this at all now.

"Okay, enough. I'm . . . I'm waking . . ."

And as the door swung towards him, something seemed to hit him hard on the back of the head.

Blackness again.

Yes, this must be a dream after all. So there was nothing to worry about.

And yes, this was going to be a good dream after all. Because now he was lying on his back somewhere in the semi-darkness. And the same young woman he had seen in the van was leaning over him. She was unbuttoning his shirt, and the way she was smiling and licking her lips was already arousing him. Other hands seemed to be helping her in the darkness, taking off his shoes and socks, now his trousers. But that didn't matter. All that mattered was the beautiful face above him with her long, golden hair and her sparkling eyes – and the way she lovingly and slowly unbuttoned his shirt. Her other hand had moved to his groin, was expertly pulling down his underwear. *Oh God, please don't let me wake up yet!* The same invisible hands that had undressed him were now holding his arms and legs. The girl had finally finished unbuttoning his shirt and moved downwards towards his groin and out of view into the darkness. *You can hold me down for this if you want to – but believe me, sweetheart, you don't have to!*

Another face suddenly moved into view.

A different girl, with fiery red hair. And Dalby could see with a sudden churning of horror in his stomach that her eye sockets were dark and empty. Just dark, empty holes where the eyes should have been. She smiled at him, but that smile was more like a hideous grimace.

When the girl held the long shard of glass up in front of his face, Dalby screamed. Even in the darkness, he could see that it was a broken shard from one of the stained-glass windows in the church.

His screams reached a new pitch when the blind girl gripped him below and swept the shard viciously down.

They sweat and strain in the darkness when it is all over.

The spades and shovels have been retrieved from the stone sarcophagus at the other side of the basement. But it is a joyful exertion, for they know that they will soon be reaping their rewards. They take turns to dig, men and women. The soil down here is heavily compacted and it is hard work. But their enthusiasm and vigour seem boundless, and in a very short time the grave has been completed. It is only four feet square, but will serve the purpose.

The body is unceremoniously dumped into the hole. It crumbles and folds at the bottom of its grave. No one speaks as the soil is returned; indeed, no one has spoken since their arrival. When the grave has been filled, they compact the soil again with their feet.

One of the men who had carried him from the van takes something out of his inside pocket. He stoops and sticks it firmly into the soil over the grave. The girl with the blond hair strikes a match and kneels, applying the flame.

It is a solitary black candle, and its guttering light reveals that there are dozens of pools of black wax elsewhere in this underground place.

They stand silently around the candle. The One Who Was Chosen speaks in unknown tongues.

And then they file out of that underground place, up the stone stairs and away into the night.

The solitary black candle gutters in the darkness.

And the black van goes out again into the night.

PART TWO

STREET PEOPLE

15

The derelict industrial estate where Tony had dropped off his strange customer had been scheduled for demolition two years ago. Once a thriving engineering complex, it was now the industrial equivalent of a ghost town. Rusting cranes stood like dinosaur skeletons, chains swaying and rattling in the breeze. Corrugated tin roofs flapped and banged when the wind was high. The only sounds in the sheds and warehouses were the scuttling of night animals and the flutter of nesting pigeons' wings.

The local council had scheduled demolition, but cutbacks in finance had deferred this major task, and it was "re-prioritised". But now two children had been hurt playing there. One had fallen through a roof and the other had been injured trying to rescue him. Now, the priorities had shifted again at the outcry of public opinion and the necessary finance had been found. In two months, the bulldozers would move in.

And Gerry would have to give some more thought to where his combination acid house/rave parties were going to take place. Up until now, the industrial estate and its warren of alleys between the warehouses had provided a perfect venue. Even if the noise was heard and reported, it took the pigs ages to get in there, and escape for the punters was always easy if they were carrying.

As usual, word of mouth was all that was required to publicise the event. Tonight, there were at least three hundred punters. Johnny Spence had reported the numbers to him dutifully after a head count.

"You sure?" said Gerry from the back of the Volvo that Johnny had stolen that night.

"At least three hundred."

"Good. Don't want Andreas getting more than his share. That's your job tonight, Harry."

Harry Bennet was sitting in the passenger seat up front. His nose had been broken so many times that it hardly seemed to exist any more. Only the nostrils gave an indication that it was there. "Andreas got more heavies than normal, tonight."

"So? You telling me you can't handle it with the other guys?"

"No, Gerry," said Harry quickly. "We're on top of it. Just thought you'd want to know."

"So now I know."

Andreas represented the off-estate pushers – a part of what the newspapers liked to call organised crime. They were organised, hard and dangerous. But Gerry and his own gang "owned" the housing estate, and to avoid any potential aggravation between the two, a meeting had been set up three years ago. Gerry would provide the punters and the venues, Andreas would provide the stuff. For the co-operation, Gerry and his own "representatives" would receive a cut in the profits. So far, it had worked out all right – but there were unofficial rules to the game which were observed by both sides. When the Volvo screeched around the corner of one of the industrial alleys and they saw the rusted sign for Robson's Electronics above the warehouse entrance where the rave was taking place, Gerry prepared himself for the "game".

They hadn't been able to hear the music when they entered the industrial estate, but now it was full blast. Once again, Gerry cursed the council for bringing its plans for demolition forward. This was the perfect venue. All of this rusting crap deadened the sound. Blue and red lights flashed through the vent in the huge double doors that fronted the warehouse.

"Okay, let's do it!" snapped Gerry – and the first part of the ritual began.

There were at least six of Andreas's men at the warehouse door. Another four strolling around the periphery just watching. The rave had been on the go now for about an hour and a half, but there were still kids waiting to get in. Johnny floored the accelerator and the Volvo screeched into the forecourt. Gerry grinned as Andreas's men looked up in alarm, and then Johnny dragged the handbrake on. The car skidded and swerved, facing back in the direction they'd just come from. Even inside the car they could smell the burning rubber, could see wisps of blue smoke curling past the window.

Then the other cars screeched in after them, all performing the same deadman's swerves. There were five cars, all of them taken from the streets that night. Gerry sat for a moment, watching as two of the big men at the warehouse door ducked inside to report. Andreas was in there all right, and they'd be telling him that they'd arrived.

"Okay," said Gerry – and the ritual continued.

Harry climbed out of the car, all macho swagger, stood back and opened the rear door. Gerry climbed slowly out and stood for a long time looking at the warehouse as Harry stood back. Point made on who was in charge here, he began to walk slowly towards the warehouse – and at that moment, the occupants of the other five cars also climbed out, slamming their doors. Gerry smiled, aware that they were gathering around him protectively as he walked on. Most of them had showed tonight. Only Andy Grantham wasn't able to make it – he was still in hospital with a gash in the gut after they'd taken over the East End gang on the estate.

The four men who had been patrolling the warehouse moved to join their colleagues at the front doors as Gerry and his own crowd of twenty-three approached.

Gerry recognised three of the men. They were all wearing sober business suits. Most of them were a decade older than anyone in Gerry's gang.

"Been to a funeral, Jimmy?" asked Gerry, stopping at the doors.

"Evening, Mr Tomelty."

"Private party, or can anyone join in?"

Jimmy Taggart was as hard as they come. Tight curly black hair, eyes like slits, shoulders that you could stand two pints of beer on. Gerry knew that he had once been a semi-professional boxer.

"You're the co-organiser, Mr Tomelty. You and your—" Jimmy paused, looking at the crowd behind Gerry – "*collective* always have special reservations." Gerry looked back at his own and on cue they gave an extravagant moan of delight at this description, as if they were the audience of a quiz show, being shown the star prize of the evening. Jimmy's face remained unchanged as he and three of the others pulled the doors aside. Gerry entered, and the others followed.

Into a suddenly overwhelming barrage of electronic scattershots exploding over digitised drumbeats and the strobing of red and green lights. The thrashing mass inside worshipped at the altar of the Orb and the Shamen.

Gerry was pleased to see that Johnny was right. There were at least three hundred – and the takings would be good. The warehouse floor had been cleared of debris and rusting junk and the DJ had set up his equipment at the far end. A sea of heaving kids thrashed and jostled to the music.

And now, on the left, Gerry could see his counterpart; also surrounded by protectors, now giving a barely perceptible nod of the head to acknowledge his presence. It was Andreas. Trendy suit, hair swept viciously back over his head and then hanging down to his shoulders in a ponytail. Maybe thirty years old. Perfect teeth, like he was advertising toothpaste. Gerry returned the slight nod.

71

"Smooth bastard," said Gerry, but his voice was swallowed by the music. Gerry turned to Johnny and Harry, nodding again. They gave out the permissions, and now most of Gerry's gang were moving into the crowd, ready to party. Ten previously selected members of Gerry's own gang would remain with him, just as Andreas had his own men. And neither of the co-organisers would communicate throughout the night. *Mexican Standoff*, thought Gerry and began to move into the crowd, his own gang creating a wake through the crowd for him. There was a bar at the right-hand side of the warehouse; their raves were never dry. He would position himself there for the night.

"Good buzz," yelled Johnny to someone, laughing, as they moved through the thrashing crowd.

Gerry grimaced. He couldn't remember the last time he'd had a *buzz*. Ecstasy didn't give him what he wanted, no drug did. He wanted something more than that, something more tangible. He wanted to be in control. *Really* in control. He didn't want to be a co-fucking-organiser with anybody.

The Man Who Shines Black had promised to show him how.

At the bar, Gerry stood with a beer and watched the thrashing crowd, listened to the pounding music. And as he watched the punters, watched Andreas and his own men, listened to the inanities of the new DJ, Gerry thought: *The music and the booze and the drugs and the lights – all of it makes you think you're acting in a video, Andreas. Look at the way you're posing. You stupid jerk. You think you're a movie star, don't you? Well, I'm not fooled by it all, you ponce. And I'm going to give you all a buzz, all right. A buzz like you never fucking believed. So enjoy yourselves while you can, 'cause there's changes coming. Big fucking changes . . .*

The rave was still going on when they left in their stolen cars.

It was four a.m., and one of them had been forced to peel off when a copper car had recognised the number plates and given chase. They had whooped in glee when the car had executed a handbrake turn and zoomed off into the night, the pigs' car following with its siren wailing. They would never catch them. Now if only everyone else's car was reported in, that would mean the pigs would be chasing Gerry's gang all over the estate. Once they got into the warrens of the estate roads, there wasn't a cop car could follow for fear of hitting a civilian – even at this time in the morning. But there was no such luck.

The buzz had remained elusive for Gerry all night – as it usually did. Everyone else was sky-high, but Gerry was morose. Now it was time to change all that.

"Stop here!"

Johnny slammed the brakes on and the car screeched to a halt in the middle of the street. Johnny and Harry looked at him in puzzlement. Two of the other cars that were still with them screeched past, did handbrake turns and stopped.

"Time for some fun." Gerry leaned forward and snatched the bottle of vodka from Harry's hand. There were only two or three mouthfuls left in it. Gerry drained it.

"Gimme your tie, Johnny!"

"What for?"

"Just gimme it!"

"Awww, come on, Gerry," said Johnny, taking it off and handing it over the back seat to him. "You're not going to rip it up, are you? That thing cost a fucking fortune . . . Aww, fuck!"

Gerry climbed out of the car and walked to the boot. Flinging it open, he looked back to the stores that lined the street. Their car was directly opposite a newsagent with a formica sign reading: *Singh and Son.* Gerry leaned in and took out the petrol can, standing back while he unscrewed the cap and began to pour it into the vodka bottle,

"Wakey,wakey!" yelled Gerry, and now Johnny and Harry were leaning out of the car, and began laughing when they realised what Gerry was going to do. Johnny wasn't so bothered about his tie now when Gerry ripped it lengthwise to expose the soft inner lining and stuffed it into the neck of the bottle. "Come on, then! Wake up, you Paki bastards!"

"Yeah!" shouted Harry when Gerry moved to him with the bottle. Harry flicked his cigarette lighter and applied the flame.

"Dreaming of all the money you're making out of us, then?" shouted Gerry.

The tie caught immediately, blue-green fire flaring around the neck of the bottle.

"Stealing our fucking jobs!"

Gerry ran at the store window.

"Go back to your own fucking country!"

He flung the bottle hard at the window. It exploded inwards in great shards, the petrol bomb shattered on the shelves inside and a roaring cloud of greasy orange-black flame unfurled instantly in the shop. Gerry swung the petrol can in his other hand. It whirled into the shop, in a twisting ribbon of petrol. The fire cloud *whumped* and roared anew. And then Gerry dashed back to the car, flinging himself into the back seat again. He could hear the others laughing in their cars further down the road.

"Look at that!" yelled Johnny laughing, and pointing to the flat above the store. A bedroom light had come on.

"Rise and shine, you fuckers!" said Gerry, and then Johnny floored the accelerator and the Volvo screeched off into the night again.

This still wasn't the buzz that Gerry was looking for – but it was the closest that he'd come to it that night. As he settled back in his seat and listened to Harry and Johnny laughing in the front seat, he felt sure that the Man Who Shines Black would be coming again tonight. And if he did, he just knew that it was going to be for a special reason.

16

It was two days after Tony had picked up the woman and her baby, and then had woken to find the intruder in his flat.

And in that time Tony had worked long and hard, putting in the extra hours that he would need to pay the bills. Nicotine and caffeine had been his greatest allies. Business was still slow, but gradually he had been able to make up the shortfall. And for most of that forty-eight hours he had been trying to piece together what had happened. Now it seemed clear. The woman and her child had been on the run from the guy who had turned up at his flat. Obviously, he was the husband – and this was the unknown someone from whom she'd been fleeing. Tony found it difficult to imagine that the very ordinary-looking bank manager/estate agent could be someone who could engender so much fear. But then again, he did have a gun. What was it with that little family unit and guns? He wouldn't be surprised if the kid had also got a derringer under its shawl. And there was an obvious reason for the guy knowing Tony's name. It was, after all, on the doorbell list just outside the front door. Perhaps the guy had taken Tony's licence plate number. Whatever – there was bound to be a reasonable explanation. Once again, he had decided against going to the police. He just didn't have the time – and he had a lot of taxi-money to make up. The hire-fee on the car was due soon.

Tony let himself into the flat again. As always, he hadn't been able to beat the landing light. The window at the top of the landing was half open and cold night air was cutting through it. He'd tried to shut it, but the bloody thing remained stuck.

How the hell was the little guy able to let himself in here like that? Without my seeing or hearing him. And what's to stop him just doing the same thing again?

"If you're in here," said Tony as he closed the door behind him, "I'll have to kick your arse again."

He smiled as he threw his jacket over the chair and made for the kitchen. The automatic pistol was safely under a loose floorboard in here. He meant to throw it out, when he remembered. Tony plugged in the kettle for coffee, switched on the stained and battered radio on the kitchen bench. It was cold in his apartment – central heating for each of the apartments was not a feature of the Rex. Tony moved back to his bed and turned on the small paraffin heater which stood beside it.

Later, lying on his bed and watching the flickering images on the small, portable television set, Tony found his mind drifting back to Five Para again – and to the instant replay dream.

He'd come around in a makeshift military hospital to discover that Mount Longdon had been taken by the Brits. He'd been lucky. Another division of Three Para had come across the site of their conflict in a forward sweep. None of Tony's mates had survived, and it was only the sputtering sparks from the Argentinian's flame-thrower that had drawn their attention to him. The Argentinian was dead, of course. Tony had seen to that. Back at HQ he had reported on what had happened. The fact that his detachment had found themselves so hopelessly adrift and away from their target was all Crawleigh's fault – but he had no doubt that no blame would attach to their commander. Crawleigh's daddy was, of course, Somebody Big.

They had never found Cameron.

Even after Tony had been flown home and eventually invalided out of the service because of the bullet wound to his leg and the subsequent nerve damage, he had tried to find out just what had happened. He knew that Cameron had run screaming into the night, a human fireball. But surely his body was there somewhere. Despite his investigations, Cameron had remained "Missing in Action – Presumed Dead". Even if the poor bastard had been burned to a crisp, surely there must be something left on the body that could give his identity? Tony felt an obligation born out of comradeship to try and follow through. He owed that much to Cameron's family. After all, the man had saved his life twice. Afterwards, when he was well enough recovered, Tony had sought out Cameron's only remaining family member – his father. He was a man whom Cameron had talked about with great affection; someone he had tried to mould himself on. The old man lived in Salford and Tony had travelled up there for a meeting.

But standing on the pavement outside Cameron's father's home, on a bleak and wintry November morning, he had been unable to go through with it for reasons that he found difficult to explain. Instead, he had about-faced and returned home apologising to him later by letter. And in that letter he had tried as non-graphically as possible to explain what had happened, and how much he owed to Cameron. He still felt badly about the way he had handled the whole business, wished that he could turn back the clock and try again. Later, he found out that Cameron's father had died and that had compounded his feeling of guilt massively.

Tony reached for his cigarettes again, lit one and watched the smoke climb up to the ceiling. It had begun to rain outside again, tear-like splashes running in rivulets across the window.

Something will come for you.

Wasn't that what the man had said? It had certainly sounded like that, although Tony couldn't be exactly sure. After all, the man had been downstairs standing in the passage, and he had been on the top landing.

Tony swung away from the bed and walked to the window. The street below was empty, the road and sidewalks gleaming like ebony. Somewhere a dog was barking.

Something will come for you.

Tony returned to the kitchen. He was getting low on coffee, and settled on tea instead. The kettle began to hiss like the rain outside as he yawned, stretched and moved back into the living room.

Still yawning, he saw the strange reflection in the window.

Tony paused, stifling the yawn, and turned to look back in the kitchen. Was there something in there, something that he had switched on, which could make such a peculiar reflection? There was nothing in there. The kitchen light was on of course, but when he turned back to the window he could see the orange reflection of that light at the top right-hand corner of the window.

But this strange, flickering white reflection was growing bigger now. It was a fluttering of light, and the first thing that Tony thought of was how his late mother had described the lights she got in her eye when she was suffering from a migraine attack. This strange, blurry flutter of light and darkness looked just the way she described. Now, Tony realised that the light wasn't reflecting from behind. It was out there somewhere, in the night. Perhaps something from the street; maybe the spinning light from a police car.

Tony moved towards the window,

Something will come for you.

And suddenly froze in his tracks as that light began to grow larger and brighter. It was approaching the window at one hell of a speed – and the intruder's threat now seemed to be somehow very real and very near. The fluttering light was like some lamp hung on the front of a locomotive and that soundless locomotive was even now hurtling through the night, directly towards Tony. Its hideously fast approach instantly conjured up a feeling in Tony's gut. Something that he hadn't felt for a long time, not since his days on active duty in the Paras. Something that had been born in him again when the girl had pulled the gun on him in the taxi. It was a deep-rooted feeling of fear in his guts.

And travelling at such a speed, this thing – whatever it was – must surely *impact.*

Tony flung himself bodily to the floor as the hideously fluttering light filled the window frame. The room was lit with a brilliant white light.

And then the window exploded with a roaring detonation.

Grenade! thought Tony instinctively, hands covering his head as he hit the carpet. The room was filled with whirling glass and shredded curtains. And after that initial detonating impact, the room was suddenly filled with the roaring of a great wind.

Night had come into Tony's room, just as surely as if it was a living thing.

The lights in the flat had instantly fused, all the light bulbs exploding simultaneously. But there was still a blinding white light in the room, and as Tony clambered to his feet, a raging whirlwind was destroying the flat; tearing open drawers and scattering his clothes. The wardrobe in the corner juddered, its doors flew open and his shirts began to whip out into the room. The clothes on the bed suddenly jumbled and leapt from the bed, one by one, as if they were being plucked and snatched away by invisible hands.

Tony steadied himself against the wall, staring in stunned amazement.

The whirlwind calmed, but only slightly. Clothes and debris still danced in the air. But the shrieking sounds which had accompanied the wind were quieted, and as Tony watched in utter astonishment and shock, he saw that something was beginning to form in the middle of the room.

It was a shape.

And he could see that this indistinct "something" was also surrounded by the same bubbling black and white light that had exploded through the window. It was a vague and insubstantial blur, but something about the darker contours of this thing suggested the shape of a man; the same size, the same height. But it was also a constant jumble of movement, as if the thing – whatever it was – was constantly changing its form.

The fear that Tony had felt two days ago was as nothing to the fear he could feel now. It was greater by far than the fear he had felt in the army – in Ireland or the Falklands. Because something about the *thing* which had erupted into his flat exuded an utter and sheer menace like nothing he had ever experienced before. Whatever in hell this thing was, it was vile and deeply frightening. Instinctively, Tony knew that it was not only the most evil thing he had ever experienced – but that it was also immensely capable of carrying out, of executing *evil* in a very physical and very deadly way.

The wind swirled around it.

Tony knew, despite its constant shape-shifting, that the thing was facing him, that it was aware of him and was simply waiting. Like some hideous spider waiting in its web as the fly struggled, just waiting to move – nightmarishly fast and deadly, in Tony's direction. Tony remained frozen, steadying himself against the wall. Now, it looked as if the thing was like . . . a monk? . . . was like . . . and Tony recoiled back to the wall when this forgotten childhood phobia emerged again. It was like some human-shaped praying mantis. Head bowed but insubstantial; shadow-face still looking at him, hands (claws?) clasped in front of it as if in prayer. And weaving slightly, the way that those insects did before they uncurled and lunged forwards to take their prey in those hideously oversized claws. Light shifted and melded on the shape as if it was somehow now composed of ragged cloth – and steel. Tony could not take his eyes from it, realising now that he could also see right *through* the thing. It was somehow transparent, and the wall behind it was clearly visible. That transparency did not diminish the hideous and deadly aura surrounding it.

"Where are the girl and the child?"

There was no movement on that insubstantial face to suggest that this was its voice, but Tony knew that it was the thing talking to him. And something about that voice made him dry-heave. He fought to control himself. The voice was the parody of a human voice; like a tape playing at the wrong speed, up and down. Dragging and then speeded. And behind that simple query, the voice carried with it the most horrific and malevolent threat.

Something will come for you, the man had said.

And here it was.

Tony tried to speak, but his first attempt was strangled.

"I told you . . . told him . . . I don't know."

The thing was silent, still with hands/claws clasped before it. Still weaving, as if toying with its prey.

"Tell me."

"I've told you, I just don't *know!*"

Another horrifying pause.

"Tell me . . . or I will let loose upon you."

The words were strange, but Tony knew without doubt what the thing wanted most; knew that this nightmare *preferred* him not to have the answer that was required; knew that it actually *wanted* more than anything else to have the excuse to "let loose upon him".

And at that moment, the apartment door burst open.

Tony flinched in shock, expecting the thing to launch itself at him. But now he could see *through* the hideous apparition that there was a figure standing in the doorway. It was Sangster – the landlord.

"What the bloody hell have you *done,* Dandridge?" The wind picked at Sangster's clothes, at his opened waistcoat, ruffled his thinning hair.

The Nightmare Thing turned slowly from Tony to look at the intruder. Still looking directly through the transparent monstrosity, Tony could see the look of horror on Sangster's face; knew that he too was instantly suffering the same instinctive gut-fear when he saw what was standing in the middle of the room. Sangster took a step back, uttering a grunt of horror, disgust and fear. He paused for only a moment – and then lunged sideways, blundering back to the door.

But somehow, that door slammed shut as if on command, trapping Sangster in the room.

Tony knew that the thing had done it.

Sangster tugged at the door handle, still keeping his eyes on the thing. When it would not budge, he turned and tugged at the handle with both hands.

"*Who?*" said the thing.

"Sangster," said Tony, not realising that he was going to answer the thing. "My landlord."

"*Where are the girl and the child?*" it asked Tony again.

"For God's sake, I don't know. That's the truth."

"*Then watch,*" said the thing, and began to glide across the apartment floor towards Sangster.

"No . . ."

Sangster looked back over his shoulder in stark fear, his eyes widening when he saw that the thing was heading towards him. Uttering a hoarse cry of terror, he blundered through the whirling wind towards the shattered window aperture. Glass crunched underfoot.

"For Christ's sake, Dandridge. Keep it *away* from me!"

Now, Tony realised that the great wind was emanating *from* the thing itself as it bore down on Sangster. He clung to the wall beside the shattered window aperture, and Tony could see that he was desperately darting glances out into the night air, deliberating whether or not he could make his escape there. And Tony could not move, remained frozen against the bedroom wall as . . .

The shape reared and enfolded Sangster.

A shrieking began, louder even than the storm which had erupted into Tony's apartment. At the same instant, Tony could hear something that sounded like ripping cloth; each rip accompanied by Sangster's shrieks of pain and despair. The twisting commotion by the window frame suddenly blurred across the room, and Tony could vaguely see Sangster's shape within it, thrashing and kicking with horrifying desperation.

Something flew out of that mad dance, whirling at Tony. He cried out, instinctively slapping at it, knocking it away from his face. It fell to the carpet with a wet flopping sound, and Tony could see that it looked like . . . looked like . . .

Sangster's arm, torn off at the shoulder.

The landlord continued to scream as the mad dance careened across the room. The ripping-cloth sound was the most hideous thing that Tony had ever heard.

The twisting, slashing grey blur collided with Tony's bed. Tony saw flame guttering as his paraffin heater was overturned. Damp-blue flame surged at the foot of the bedspread, and the thing whirled away from the bed again as Sangster screamed, "Oh *Chrissssssttt!*" His scream turned to a frightful, liquid gargling at the sound of another long and tearing rip . . . and then Tony saw something round and tattered fly out of the twisting maelstrom in the middle of the room. It hit the far wall with a wet smack, mercifully falling out of sight behind Tony's overturned music centre.

There was no conscious thought now, no decision-making, as Tony lunged away from the apartment wall. The horror had finally galvanised him on a completely subconscious level. He was going to die if he stayed frozen in terror at that wall. The bed was burning fiercely as Tony lunged towards it, aware of movement behind him. Sangster was quiet, the ripping had stopped. Tony could feel the hideous death-wind focusing on his back as the thing turned towards him.

His whisky bottle was lying at the foot of that bed, where it had been thrown from the bureau by the hell-wind. Without pausing in his headlong dash, Tony stooped and seized it by the neck, smashing it against the bureau as he passed. He flung it on to the burning bedspread, and a great gout of flame flared up to the ceiling. In one brief but gut-wrenching moment of horror, Tony could see from the corner of his eye that the thing in the wind had discarded Sangster's horrifically mutilated body and was gliding across the apartment towards him – in an act of horrifying embrace. Yelling in fear and revulsion, Tony gripped the quilt cover on the bed and heaved it with both hands from the bed itself. The blazing quilt flapped into the air in a blazing canopy of smoke, sparks and fire. It enfolded the advancing

81

shape – and then Tony turned and hurled himself at the apartment door.

Some crazily rational part of his mind registered how he had complained to Sangster once upon a time about the paper-thin walls and doors of the apartments, and the resultant lack of privacy. Now, he was grateful for it.

Tony's shoulder-charge took him straight through the door, the middle section punching out in one complete piece. He slammed into the corridor wall on the other side, but felt no pain. Rolling and scrabbling to his feet, and with the hell-wind from his apartment now gusting into the corridor, Tony hurtled down the passageway towards the staircase. Behind him, something raged and howled like some angry, primeval beast. Tony staggered, righting himself at the end of the corridor. The staircase lay before him; four storeys down to the main entrance where the man who looked like a bank manager had told him that something was going to come for him. He grabbed the handrail and looked back.

And something erupted from his apartment, straight through the wall and into the corridor in a great explosion of plasterboard, brick and gushing dust.

He would never make it down those stairs.

As something within that shattering dust cloud twisted and writhed in his direction at hideous speed, Tony turned and flung himself at the window at the top of the stairs. It was still jammed half open, and somehow Tony had slithered through it quicker than a snake. It was a four-storey drop, but the prospect gave him no greater fear than the terror which had already enveloped him. He had stood at the window before, looking out into the night – knew that there was a drainpipe on the right. Heedless of the drop, aware only of the horrifying thing that was right behind him, Tony twisted, grabbed the drainpipe and let gravity pull him down. Dropping hand over hand, fingernails tearing on the pipe, Tony dropped and clambered frantically away from the window.

"No!"

His twisting legs found no purchase, and the weight of his body dragged his hands away from the drainpipe.

Tony fell.

Something yanked at his body viciously, snapping his jaw shut. His neck felt whiplashed and something had torn his shirt, scraping his side against the rough stone wall. When he refocused, he realised that his right hand had caught hold of a windowsill. Quickly, his scrabbling left hand had found the drainpipe again. He hugged the drainpipe tight, gasping in exertion and fear. Looking up, he could see that he had dropped one storey. Miraculously, he was still alive. Panting, begging the Fates, Tony started down again.

Above him, the window frame through which he had made his escape exploded like a bomb out into the night.

Tony hugged the drainpipe again as a rain of broken glass, brickwork and other debris fell past him. When it had dropped past, Tony kept on clambering down. He did not have to look up to know that something defying even the logic of nightmare was looking down at him with bestial hunger from the shattered window aperture.

Still twenty feet from the ground, Tony dropped the rest of the way.

There was a rough, grassed area down here at the side of the apartment block. Tony bounced and rolled, colliding with several rubbish bins awaiting collection.

Gasping, sobbing for breath, he looked up to see that the thing was no longer there. But black smoke was gushing from the window. The fire from the paraffin heater and the thrown quilt cover had set light to the rest of the building. Somewhere inside, someone was screaming.

He knew that the thing was coming down after him.

Tony pulled himself upright, and ran into the night.

17

Alighting at the station, Ranjana had gone straight to the nearest public telephone and tried Directory Enquiries. She had given her friend's name and address, but the operator had been unable to give her the telephone number, saying that it was unlisted. Perhaps she meant that it was ex-directory?

There was a policeman standing at the station entrance, and for a moment Ranjana considered whether she should go and talk to him, explain the position, and vent her anger at the fact that her brother had reported her missing. Surely if she explained what was going on, everything would be all right? On the other hand, she was still fifteen, under the legal age of consent. Patel had betrayed her; what other tricks might he have up his sleeve if she just decided to come clean? More than anything else, Ranjana needed time to think. Her mind was still too fogged by everything that had happened. Once she had found Andrea, had been able to stay with her for a while – maybe talked like they used to talk at school – she could sort out the mess inside her head. She would have to decide soon. The money she'd drawn from the building society was not going to last for ever.

Ranjana turned away from the policeman and hurried to the coffee shop. Once inside, she ordered black coffee and then took the street map out of her bag, the one she'd purchased on her arrival at the station. Andrea lived in the Marylebone area. Anchorage Street was just a short walk from Anchorage Underground station.

"How much?" asked a voice.

Ranjana looked up. There were two men standing beside her. Both about her father's age; one wearing a donkey jacket and woollen cap, the other a long dark raincoat. It was the second man who'd spoken. They were both shuffling their feet as if the cold in the station was too much to bear.

"Pardon?"

"I said how much?"

"How much what?"

The man in the donkey jacket snorted in laughter, but seemed unable to look at her face.

"Don't give me that, love. You know what I mean."

"Go away."

"Come on, we saw you hanging around. Stop beating about the bush. Give us a price for two."

"I'll give you a smack in the fucking mouth for nothing."

"She charge extra for talking dirty?" snorted the donkey jacket again.

"See this," said Ranjana, holding up her coffee cup. "You'll get this in the face if you don't get lost. Both of you."

"Fucking dyke," muttered the man in the long coat. Both men shuffled away.

Ranjana felt knotted inside. She watched them idle around the station, occasionally looking back her way when it was obvious that they weren't going to find anyone else hanging around the station. The policeman had gone. Finally, she finished her coffee and tucked the street map back into her bag. When she headed for the Underground station, she saw with apprehension that both men were slowly following in her direction. She hurried ahead, pushing through the crowds and down the staircase.

Nervously glancing behind her as she made her way down, she decided that she would jump on the first tube train that came, just to ensure that these two perverts weren't following her. Then she could change and head back to Marylebone.

But her luck was in. The first train to arrive at the Central platform was the one that she wanted.

It was raining again by the time that Ranjana emerged on the street outside Anchorage station. Ranjana took the street map out again and kept walking, clutching that book tight to her chest as if afraid that her ex-school friend's address might suddenly vanish from the pages.

The streets seemed lonely and desolate, but Ranjana marched on ahead. The bag seemed very heavy now, she would be glad when she had a chance to rest. There were two tower blocks ahead. Could Andrea be living in one of these? She passed both, but the addresses were different. She checked again, knowing full well that Anchorage Street was beyond the tower blocks; third street on the right. A car zoomed past in the rain, a dirty wave of water soaked her legs.

And then something hit her from behind – hard. Ranjana spun, falling to her knees. Someone shouted: "Come on, then!" And something dragged savagely at her arm.

Two men.

85

No – *the* two men from the station.

They had followed her after all, and one of them had grabbed the handle of her bag, trying to yank it away from her. That handle had been over Ranjana's shoulder, had slipped to the crook of her arm as the donkey-jacketed man had grabbed it, and pulled her down as he tried to run on past her. She clung tight to the bag as the man dragged at it again, pulling her along the pavement and skinning her knees.

"Let *go* of it, you black bitch!" yelled the long coat, and kicked out at her. Ranjana cried out, seizing his leg and the man began to hop, lashing down and trying to break her grip. A hand tangled in her hair as she yelled for help, and twisted back savagely. The pain made her eyes fill with tears. The donkey jacket wrenched the bag from her arm at last, and all she could do was watch from the pavement as both men ran off towards the tower blocks.

An elderly couple were walking on the other side of the road. Ranjana held her hand up to them, but they continued walking as if they'd seen nothing. It was this more than anything that brought the tears.

Ranjana stood up, wiping the grime from her coat. She leaned against a wall, sobbing, and watched as the two men vanished down the road, finally turning into a side street before the tower blocks. She knew that she could never follow.

Trying to keep back the tears, struggling to regain her composure, Ranjana limped on ahead in the direction that the men had taken.All her money had been in that bag, all her belongings. What was she going to do now? Report it to the police? Not likely.

She had to find Anchorage Street – and Andrea.

Tears were still blurring her eyes when she passed the second tower block. Half an hour later, the relief was overwhelming when she saw the street sign up ahead, and had to stop to regain her composure. She had finally reached her destination. Taking a deep breath, wiping her face and steeling herself, Ranjana turned the corner into Anchorage Street.

"Oh, no . . . please . . . no . . ."

The street was derelict.

Ranjana began to walk quickly down the sidewalk looking into the houses as she passed. Their windows were boarded over. Grass grew from cracks in the pavement. She could see that some of the houses on the other side of the street were already in the process of being demolished, could see that roofs had caved in, that rubble had scattered into the street. Behind the houses on that side she could see a crane with a wrecking-ball.

Andrea's at number forty-seven. That's the other end of the street. It must be.

Ranjana was running now, feeling something in her throat and chest that was constricting her breathing. Something that tasted like the grief she had experienced when her father had died.

She checked for house numbers as she ran.

Fifty-three! That must mean that the next was . . .

Fifty-five. She had passed by Andrea's house.

Quickly, Ranjana hurried back, counting as she did so.

Fifty-one . . . forty-nine . . .

"Forty-seven," she said aloud – and stood looking at the door for a long time. The panels had been smashed in; a long time ago, apparently. Refusing to believe it, she stepped forward, biting her lip, and shoved the door. It opened with a screech, and Ranjana could now see the shattered bricks and rubble that lay in what had once been a passageway. There was a flight of stairs just ahead. Most of them had caved in. The house had no roof, only the bare ribbed rafters framing a grey sky.

Ranjana stood back then and looked around her.

The sense of desolation was overwhelming.

Still clutching the address book, fighting back useless tears, she turned and walked away.

She had no idea what she was going to do.

At the end of the street a black van cruised slowly past. Seeing her, it slowed down. But Ranjana, head down, kept on walking purposefully away. The driver floored the accelerator and the black van moved away.

It would be night soon.

18

It lies head-first in its resting place, where it has been thrown.

The clay and the soil are compacted tight around it. Its arms are jammed at its sides. Its mouth is open in a silent scream. Mud and dirt have been forced into that mouth, and living things have already found their way in there.

Something moves.

It is not one of the host of living, burrowing things that have already scented or sensed what is here with them in the darkness.

It moves again, down by the thing's left side.

It squirms, writhes . . . and begins to crawl spider-like down the thing's side, towards its chest. But it is not a spider – for this spider has only five pulpy-while legs.

Another movement on the thing's right side, and another white spider-thing begins to writhe through the mud and the soil downwards. Progress is not easy through the compacted soil.

Eventually, after long dark hours, they meet at the thing's face. They push downwards, past the head – like a swimmer – and begin clawing through the mud, burrowing down and away.

The thing's body begins to undulate like a snake; the head twisting, the legs writhing and pushing soil behind it.

The thing is burrowing.

It will take many weeks before it can emerge, but the thing has become as a foetus. It will be reborn in time. Clawing through the darkness towards the light.

Above all, it longs to be free.

Soon, it will join the others.

19

The morning was cold and sharp; bright early sunlight making the air seem cleaner than it actually could be. That sun hadn't been up long, but the market had been a hive of activity long before it had risen. Stalls had been erected, last-minute bargains with wholesalers agreed even as the first of the produce lorries had arrived. On the fruit and vegetable side, crops had been poor and the bargaining sharper than normal. In an attempt to remain "competitive", profit margins had been spliced even tighter than before. Everyone wanted to give the punters the best deal, which meant that the retailer/wholesaler battles were a great deal more heated than normal.

Norman Newell had three lorries. All of them had been travelling overnight, loaded down with vegetables. He'd bought them direct from the farm, and the old tosser with whom he normally did business had been harder than ever in his negotiations. There was no point pushing the codger too hard on any deal – there were lots of other freelance operators who'd be glad to step in and take over Newell's supplier if he was unhappy about arrangements. A deal with one of the traders at the market had been set a week before, providing that delivery was guaranteed by today's date. As a result, the stuff had been picked late afternoon and Newell's three lorries had been on the road all night.

Now, they were unloading. Tailgates down on the cobbles; crates being hauled out and transferred across the loading bays to one of the sheds. The trader himself seemed to have had some kind of problem in getting his unit fixed up for the day, and his boys were still erecting the stalls as the unloading took place. To Newell, it looked as if the old bastard had a hangover. What a way to run a business.

Newell employed five men: drivers and co-drivers, who also unloaded once they'd got to the market.

When he turned back to his own lorry to help Jordan with one of the potato sacks, he stopped in surprise when a young fella in denims suddenly appeared round the side of the lorry and picked up a sack from the van.

Newell moved forward, was just about to yell, *Thief!* when the young guy humped the sack up on to his shoulder and headed for the shed. Jordan had seen the guy now, too, and looked at Newell in puzzlement for instruction.

This wasn't one of the trader's lads. Not only had Newell never seen this fellow before, but he knew for a fact that the trader never allowed his own people to help with the unloading, regarding it to be part of the service he was paying for. Newell moved after the young man, who didn't seem to be wanting to make a break for it. He followed him to the shed entrance, watched as he walked inside and threw the sack down next to the others. Head down, without acknowledging Newell, the youngster walked back to the van, stepped on to the tailgate of the lorry and picked up another sack. He swung it on to his shoulder again and headed back for the shed. Jordan just looked,

"Making a mistake, aren't you, son?" asked Newell as the youngster passed by him, head down, lugging the next sack towards the shed. "My name's Newell, this is my load. You sure you got the right lorry?"

The young man ignored Newell, dumped the sack in the shed and returned to the lorry. He picked up a crate of apples.

The men from Newell's other two lorries had stopped working to watch.

"All right, all right!" snapped Newell. "You lot get on with it. I'll sort him out."

As the others resumed their tasks, Newell took off his woollen cap and rubbed his head. The young man passed by him again with the crate. "Look, son. There's no money in it for you here. Do you understand?" The youngster carefully laid down the crate and returned. "I've got my own boys, don't need any casual labour." The young man passed Jordan, carrying another crate. Again, no acknowledgment.

"You deaf, son?"

"Nope," said the young man, grabbing another sack.

"Then let me repeat. I don't need any extra help. And there's no cash in this for you." The boy passed him again. "So you might as well clear off."

"Don't want money," said the youngster. Now, Newell could see that the lad's face was grim, his teeth clenched. And it seemed to be something more than the exertion of lifting the crates and the sacks.

"So what the hell are you doing?"

"Just being useful."

Newell moved to the lorry, grabbing a sack himself. The youngster was at his side again, pulling out a crate. Some of the apples spilled. He carefully put them back again.

"What's your name?"

"Randall."

"You from Scotland?"

"Yep." Randall heaved the crate away, and Newell followed.

"Look, I'm serious, son. I can't afford to pay for any more casual labour. Don't need it. Why don't you try one of the other lorries here? There's a lot of stuff being delivered. Maybe one of the other operations needs a hand."

"Don't want money," said Randall. Newell could see that the lad was strong, knew how to handle himself.

"So what the hell do you want?"

"Just some self-respect."

The others began to laugh.

"Self-respect," said Newell, looking at him hard. Uttering a sarcastic laugh and waving a dismissive hand, Newell walked away towards the market, shaking his head, looking for his business contact.

Back at the lorry, Jordan tried to catch Randall's eye as they worked; spoke under his breath in case the others could overhear. "Listen, Jock. You can break your back here if you want to. But the man's right. You won't get anything for it. We've all been working for him for over a year and a half. Believe me, he's as tight as a badger's arse." Randall hoisted another sack and headed for the shed. Jordan followed close behind Randall, also with a sack. Inside the shed, Jordan said, "There'll be nothing in it for you at the end. And look – some of the others aren't as civilised as me."

This time, Randall looked at him as they walked back to the lorry. Now, he could see that the four others unloading Newell's other two lorries were watching him silently as they worked.

"They're hard," explained Jordan. "If they think you're muscling in, they might just want to use some muscle on you. After all, they've got families to feed."

"Only if I get paid," said Randall. "And like I said, I don't want his money."

Jordan sighed and shrugged at his companions.

The unloading continued.

Two hours later, the unloading was done.

By that time, Randall had moved to the other lorries to help out. There had been no hostility when he'd done so, just a certain wariness.

When they'd finished, the market was a seething mass of traders and customers. Newell had still to return.

91

"Where you reckon he's got to?" asked a short, wiry man with a Birmingham accent.

"Probably drinking with one of the traders, setting up another deal."

"What? At this time in the morning?"

"You know Newell."

Randall wiped the sweat from his brow and looked out across the market.

"You tried all the other lorries, didn't you?" asked Jordan.

"Yep," replied Randall, still looking out across the market.

"None of them needed paid help. Right?"

"Right."

"What you doing down here, son?"

"Not sure yet. Just arrived."

"It's a hard city. You've got to know your way around."

Randall laughed. "No harder than the place I've come from. Believe me."

"You been around?" asked one of the other men.

"Casual stuff. Government training schemes."

"When was the last time you had a proper job?"

"Never."

"So you're doing a Dick Whittington? Looking for the streets paved with gold, eh?"

"Plenty of stuff on the pavements round here," said Randall. "None of it glitters, though."

Jordan shuffled for a moment, then made as if to say something. But Randall had zipped up his jerkin and swung his holdall around his shoulder.

"See you."

He walked off in the direction from which he'd come.

The exertion had done him good. The physical exercise had filled him with renewed vigour as he walked across the cobbled street towards the main thoroughfare. He hoisted the holdall further back on his shoulder, wiped the sweat from his face again. That long walk to the first café after he'd been dropped off had been debilitating, a long monotonous walk, with nothing to show for it. Every one of the lorry drivers he'd tapped for a lift in the café hadn't been able to help him out, citing company regulations about picking up hitchers. He knew for a fact that at least two of the drivers he'd spoken to were independent operators, and that the only regulations were their own. Mulling over his third coffee and preparing himself for an even longer walk through the rain, a guy with an articulated truck had walked in and ordered an all-day breakfast. This time Randall had hit lucky. He was heading south, and he would be glad of the company.

Randall had been in the city for three hours or so when he'd found the market. But it seemed as if he'd have to try somewhere else to supplement the meagre cash in his pocket.

At the street corner, he stood for a while and deliberated which direction to take.

A hand tapped him on the shoulder.

Randall turned. It was Jordan.

"You were serious, weren't you?"

Randall just looked at him.

"About not wanting the cash. About just helping out for its own sake. For the sake of hard graft."

Randall nodded.

Jordan shoved something into his hand. "Me and the lads had a whip-round. Here's a tenner."

"Sympathy money?"

"No – you earned it, son."

Randall looked at the crumpled notes, then back at the men on the loading bay who were still standing around and watching him. One of them raised a hand. Randall nodded in return

"Wherever you're headed," said Jordan, "Good luck."

Randall nodded again, turned and walked off into the early morning sunshine.

Jordan watched him go.

"I'm glad you didn't say thanks," said Jordan after a while – and meant it.

20

Another fire had been built, but it was taking longer to get going. The rain that had drizzled over the city for the greater part of the day had soaked most of the wooden debris and garbage lying around on the streets or the building sites. One or two of the more organised of the street people had gone out with abandoned and battered prams and pushchairs, in some tattered travesty of a shopping expedition, returning later with whatever they had been able to find from building sites and abandoned houses. Anything that was dry and combustible. There was no great organisation about it, no great sense of comradeship. Just the need to congregate again, and keep warm.

No one knew or would be able to explain why they had gathered here down by the river. It had just happened. This stretch of the waterway was derelict and deserted – a good start, perhaps, since congregations anywhere remotely near to an inhabited or industrialised area were bound to draw complaints, and then the inevitable arrival of the police to move them on. There had been factories here once upon a time, but they were long gone, leaving only the cleared rough concrete patches where they had stood. Weeds and grass had sprung through these patches, cracking the concrete; as if trying to prove a point. This part of the riverside was due for reclamation eventually, but it was anybody's guess when.

Between two derelict jetties, which hadn't seen river-going vessels for twenty years, was a vee-shaped wedge of ground that might once have been some kind of slipway down to the water. It was too small to have been the slipway for any large kind of vessel, but large enough maybe for something of lifeboat size. The faint tracks of iron rail leading down to the dirty water were still slightly visible. And down here, between the two jetties and with that foul brown water lapping at the one-hundred-yard stretch of man-made shore, there was respite from the bitter wind which had blown up during the night. But it was still cold enough – and so another larger fire had been started to join the smaller fires in oil drums. At first, only clouds of billowing black, choking smoke filled the gap, driving the street people back, coughing and choking. But they had persevered, and when the latest "delivery" of combustibles arrived in a mini-convoy of battered prams and pushchairs it had all been thrown on to the heap. Bright orange flame had eventually begun to gout from the innards of that bonfire. When it finally took hold, the whole wedge of muddy ground between the jetties was lit with brilliant flickering light, the yellow-orange flames reflecting on the river water with its patches of oil and sewage.

There were twenty of them here tonight, perhaps twenty-five. Conversations and arguments shifted with the passing of bottles. Impromptu stagger-dancing was greeted with sporadic hand-clapping. Under the pilings of the jetty, a few were shooting up.

When the stranger appeared on the edge of one of the jetties, looking down at them, no one paid any heed.

After a while, he moved down and around – finally picking his way over the riverside detritus towards the fire. A long and tattered coat flapped around him as he moved. He wore a woollen balaclava, and the waistcoat had brocade buttons. When he sat on a stained crate, washed up God knew how long ago by the river, he lit a cigarette, pulled the coat around him and let the glow from the roaring fire lap over his body. Soon, someone had staggered to him and offered a swig from a bottle. The stranger took it, drank two deep mouthfuls – and returned the favour with a proffered cigarette.

Then his attention returned to the big man who was sitting down there, so close to the fire and the river's edge. Cross-legged and unmoving, with the orange glow of the fire lighting up his impassive, mask-like face. He looked for all the world like some carved wooden Indian from outside an American five-and-dime store. The stranger watched him for a long time.

"See him," said the man who had offered the bottle and taken a cigarette. The stranger looked back at his new companion. "Yeah, him. The guy down there by the fire."

The stranger nodded.

"There's some say that the Second Coming happened, and no one noticed."

"Come again?"

The man belched, staggered and took another swig from his bottle; then another drag on the cigarette.

"Jesus Christ," explained the man, "They said he would come back again, didn't they? After the first time. But there's some say that he *has* come back – only in this day and age, no one wants to know. Come

95

to save everybody, but the uncaring bastards just don't want to know. So he just walks the streets, and no one listens to him."

"What's that got to do with him?" said the stranger, nodding towards the unmoving figure.

"He saved my life. About three months ago. I was in a bad way – pneumonia, the docs said when they got me. He found me, carried me to the hospital. Wasn't for him, I'd be dead meat. Didn't stay there though, did I? The fuckers tried to tell me I had TB as well, wanted to take me in on a 'social admission'. So I said no way. I'm not gonna be beholding to the fuckers what put me there in the first place. Discharged meself, didn't I? Anyway . . . ." The man staggered away, heading back to the group of six whom he'd left sitting under the rotting struts of the furthermost jetty.

"So what's this about Jesus Christ?" called the stranger.

The man looked back over his shoulder.

"I've told you, haven't I?" The man staggered in a circle as he moved, looking back down to the figure by the fire. He paused, took a swig of the bottle, seemed lost in his thoughts for a moment. "Not the first time he's done it. Helped somebody. Him. I know people . . . people on the street . . . and from what they've seen, what they've told me . . . some of them reckon that he's . . ." The man drank again, staring down towards the fire. Then he shook his head and turned without saying anything further, heading back towards his companions.

The stranger finished his cigarette leisurely. There were no lights on the other side of the river. It was even more derelict than this side, if that could be possible. He looked at the others gathered around this fire, and then back to the man who was staring into it.

The stranger stood up, stretched . . . and then began to pick his way carefully down through the mud towards the fire.

When he drew level with the silent figure, he held his hands out to the flames. The heat was fierce on his hands and face.

"Hello, Mac," he said at last, without looking at the seated figure.

"Hello, Bernie," replied the big man, without looking away from the flames.

The stranger looked around him and found what seemed to be a car-seat cushion in the mud. He picked it up carefully, examined it, and decided that it was almost dry enough for the purpose. Carefully again, he huddled down and sat on the cushion, pulling his coat around him. For a long while he looked at the brown water lapping not ten feet from both of them. The bonfire seemed to be defying the water to rise and snuff it out. He wondered whether there was a high tide.

After a while, he turned to Mac and asked, "How come you don't burn down here?"

For the first time, Mac turned his face away from the flames to look at him.

Bernie laughed. "Sorry, stupid question." He threw a battered cigarette packet across to him. Mac caught it in a huge, scarred fist. He took three out, put two in his pocket, lit one, and threw the packet back.

After another long pause, Bernie said, "How's it been?"

Mac didn't answer.

"What about drugs for the pain?" asked Bernie.

Mac shook his head,

"Christ, Mac. You've gotta make sure you get the stuff. You'll get it free, won't have to pay. Fucking hell, they're *obliged* to give you the drugs after what you've been through."

Mac drew deeply on his cigarette, flicked the dying ember of the match out across the dirty water. "Comes and goes, Bernie. Comes and goes."

"What? The pain . . . ?" and Bernie watched as the big man looked down into his lap; realised that he wasn't talking about the pain at all. Realised that he was talking about himself, and the blurring that took place in his mind. Suddenly, Bernie didn't want to see any kind of weakness on that face; not on the face of the man who had dragged him back from his own personal pit of hell. As if sensing Bernie's concern, the big man looked up again. The movement of his head was mechanical, almost robotic. He was staring back into the roaring fire again. And there was no dismay on his face as he took another long drag on the cigarette.

"Been a long time, Bernie."

"Two years. Been travelling."

Bernie knew better than to expect an enquiry.

"Tried Newcastle. Fucking Geordies. Inverness, lot better. Folks there okay. Got back here maybe two, three weeks back."

There was an argument taking place somewhere behind them. A bottle shattered, but they ignored it.

"It's bad here, Mac. Worse than I've ever seen."

"Bad everywhere, Bernie."

"No," said Bernie grimly, shaking his head. "I mean something *bad* is happening here. It's hell on these streets."

The big man made a noise which might have been a small laugh.

"I mean it, Mac! The streets are turning into hell. Things have changed since I was here last. Weird things are happening. You mean to tell me that you haven't noticed anything?"

Something inside the fire cracked and a cloud of sparks gushed skywards. The sounds of fighting from under the jetty had died away into the distance as the aggressors moved off.

"The street people are changing," continued Bernie. "They're not the same. Christ, Mac, there are still people on the streets who I've known for years – but they're just not themselves any more. They just stand there and look. That's all. They just stand there, not begging nor nothing. They won't talk, won't answer me when I talk to them. They just *look* . . . as if they're waiting for something to happen. Haven't you seen it? I've never known so many people on the streets, just standing there and looking and waiting. And something else – they've all got the same bloody look on their faces."

"The same 'look'?"

"Like . . . like they're *hungry,* or something."

"You're not drinking enough, Bernie."

"Well if you haven't seen it – seen *them* – then you're fucking blind. Tell you something else as well. Something I overheard from some Salvation Army people the other day. There are more people on the street – more of what the bastards call 'Aye-tinny-rarants' – but the welfare people are scratching their fucking heads. Know why? I'll tell you why. It's 'cause their clientele is dropping away. What do you think of that? *More* of us on the streets, but *fewer* people spending the night in homeless hostels, or taking a handout, or being referred to hospitals, or turning up at the missions. Got them stalled, that has."

"So what's happening then?" asked Mac, and the uninterested tone in his voice angered Bernie.

"How the hell should I know? One thing I do know – I'm not staying to find out. 'Cause the other stuff I've seen is worse."

Bernie paused, waiting for Mac to ask another question. But the big man was simply staring out across the dark river again.

"I've seen some familiar faces back on the streets who shouldn't be there," continued Bernie. "And it's fucking scary. Remember Tosh and Fancy Graham? Well, I've seen them both out and about. Gave me a proper fucking turn, and I wasn't drunk nor high, neither. Tried to talk to them. But they looked right through me. Know what? Had the same look on their faces that those others have. That hungry look."

Bernie shivered despite the blazing heat of the fire. He stood up again.

"No, I'm not staying here," he went on. "Not after that. And if you had any sense, you'd get out of here too."

"Three, seven, four, oh-two," said Mac quietly.

"Oh shit," replied Bernie. He rubbed his hands in front of the fire and followed Mac's gaze out across the water, shaking his head. He'd lost him now. After a while, he turned and looked back up past the two jetties.

"See you in hell, Mac."

Bernie trudged back up the slipway and was soon lost in the night.

21

It senses that the surface is near.

For three weeks it has been burrowing, first downwards and away. At last, instinctively, its pulpy white hands claw to the side through the clay and the soil and the dirt. Its ragged, clotted body undulates and squirms as it moves forwards, clutching at the soil before its face and pushing behind, kicking with its legs.

On five occasions, it has crossed another burrowing hole, thrashed into a tunnel filled with soft soil. When that has happened, it has followed the route, following where others have gone before. But progress is still not easy, with the great weight of the earth pressing down from above.

It senses that the surface is near and claws upwards with renewed fervour.

It hungers to live.

Its body is upright now, the manoeuvre to do so taking four days.

It kicks down with its legs; kicks and thrashes. It tears at the soil with its claw hands.

And then a hand breaks the surface, thrusting into night air. That hand clutches greedily at ragged grass – and another hand claws eagerly to join it.

The body thrashes and squirms in a frenzy.

It is coming up.

A ragged, tattered head squirms twisting from the soil. That head is clotted with mud, the eye sockets compacted with dark clay, the mouth filled with soil. The head shakes, spraying dirt. As the arms emerge and the elbows give purchase on the surface, it claws at its eye sockets, gouging that clay away like a sculptor making and shaping his own face. It spits out the soil and the dirt and the living things.

And then it heaves itself out into the night.

A hundred yards away, by the abandoned cemetery wall, a vagrant sits with a bottle, watching. He has been watching for an hour now, ever since the ground over there started to heave and convulse. He has watched *it all happen impassively, with the blank and non-committal aspect of someone so completely immersed in his own delusions and fantasies that a sight such as this is not unusual. He watches as the figure claws from the ground to its knees, watches as it stands shakily to its feet. It stands there in the night like a scarecrow, weaving from side to side as if getting used to its legs and remembering about things like balance. It takes one tottering step and then stops. It looks around in the night.*

The watcher should be terrified, but remains blissfully unaware of the horrifying danger which his presence has put him in.

It does not see him.

It turns and staggers off into the night, each successive step becoming more confident.

Just another drunk, like me, thinks the watcher and returns to the bliss of his bottle.

The figure vanishes into the night to join the others.

22

Gerry was feeling good.

Not as good as he'd like to feel, but he was sure that things were going to get better now. Just before the others had dropped him off at his house, they'd heard the sounds of a fire-engine screaming off in the opposite direction. The sound of the clarion had begun to change his mood. The other cars had peeled off and vanished into the night. Gerry had made it known by his mood at the rave that he wasn't expecting any further "entertainment" that night. But Johnny and Harry had waited for permission to leave him and go on home to get high on the freebie crack that had been provided by Andreas. Gerry smiled when he remembered how Harry had sat at the driving wheel when they'd finally arrived at Gerry's house, nervously drumming his fingers. Johnny had given a superb impression of a guy totally ill at ease trying to look *at* ease. "Go on home, boys," Gerry had allowed at last.

Now, at home, Gerry sat on his bed again.

Waiting.

Next door, he had heard Sharon softly weeping.

"Shut *up!*"

The weeping had instantly ceased. Gerry looked around the former marital bedroom, checking to ensure that everything was unchanged. Everything was perfect. Even the semen stain. The Man Who Shines Black would return.

It was four a.m. Gerry had been waiting for more than an hour. But he was not impatient. He needed something tonight; needed a visit, needed something extra-special to compensate for that inner-ravening, that lack of buzz that was persecuting him so badly. He just knew that the Man was going to be pleased at his petrol-bomb incident earlier that morning.

I am, said the Man.

And Gerry recoiled against the headboard in surprise.

The Man Who Shines Black was standing in the middle of the room. The shimmering silhouette brought its hands together and wrung them in a gesture of earnest pleasure. Gerry couldn't believe that the Man had appeared so quickly this time. There had been no preliminaries; no whirling, giddy sensation, no bubbling lights, no slow approach down that long, reflecting tunnel.

That's because you're doing so well, Gerry.

"I am?"

Of course. The more you follow my teachings, the faster you allow me to come to you. It's a sure sign that you're doing well.

"Fucking great. That petrol bomb . . ."

Two are dead. The Fire Brigade were unable to save them. It was good – but tonight's incident was born from your discontent.

There he went again. Sounding like Gerry's English teacher. But again, Gerry was not intimidated. He just didn't . . .

" . . . understand?" said Gerry.

Very well, said the Man. *You've been unhappy all night, Gerry. You wanted – needed – to be happy. But something was preventing you.*

" . . . the buzz . . ."

The buzz eluded you. There are reasons for that. Believe me, I understand. You're discontented – the Man paused, looking for a better word for his charge – *too special, to be satisfied by the things that you see satisfying your underlings.*

Underlings. *That* was a good word. He'd looked it up in Sharon's dictionary when the Man had used it before.

I want you to think back. Back to the time when we first met.

"The canal."

Yes, think back to what happened then.

"That fucking hobo . . ."

Yes, him. Think back . . .

It had been a question of being in the right place at the right time. Or the wrong place at the wrong time. Purely a question of viewpoint. For Gerry and six of his gang, the right place. For the old vagrant who had wandered down to the canal, most definitely the wrong place.

The whole thing had started because of a problem with Gerry's self-image.

There'd been a lock-in at the Star: a local boozer paying protection money. At two thirty in the morning, Gerry had decided to move the lads on due to a potential problem in the cellar. Morry, who had always fancied the middle-aged tart behind the bar, had followed her downstairs when she'd had to change a beer barrel, and then the randy bastard had tried to give her one. It hadn't gone down well. Morry had persisted, and the old tart had started to scream blue murder. The landlord had stood at the bar listening to the screams, head down, while the other lads had laughed their socks off. But then, he had looked up – directly into Gerry's eyes – and said, "Just what the hell am I paying protection *for*?"

Gerry had been aware of the sudden silencing of laughter and the eyes on him. But he was also aware of the need for rationalising the terms of payment.

"You mean she doesn't like it?"

"*Of course* she doesn't like it!" The landlord was quivering.

Gerry smiled. He'd have to find a way to make this little runt pay for challenging him – at some future date.

"Johnny, Harry," said Gerry, eyes still fixed on the landlord. "The lady's not enjoying herself."

Johnny and Harry had ducked under the bar then. Quickly, they had vanished beneath the raised trapdoor in the pub floor. Gerry had been humoured to hear the sounds of the fight that had taken place when Morry had been reluctant to leave the object of his amorous attentions.

Gerry's crisis of identity had taken place after they'd left the pub.

Drunk as skunks, they'd staggered down the embankment behind that pub to the canal.

There were several barges and narrow boats moored there. Difficult to tell whether anyone was living on them or not. Gerry was walking ahead of the others. A cold wind was ruffling the black waters of the canal, streaming in Gerry's hair. He could feel the night *filling* him, felt sure that there were bigger, greater things ahead in his future.

Then Gerry had heard the shattering glass from behind. He whirled around to the sound of drunken laughter. Morry had picked up a chunk of rubble from the embankment and had hurled it directly through the window of one of the narrow boats. The others were howling with laughter. No lights came on in the boat, there were no cries of protest.

But Morry's action began to fill Gerry with a livid anger.

The feeling of a greater destiny had instantly dwindled and shrunk within him. He wanted more, so much *more* than the life he had on this estate. And the best that they could do for a buzz was throw fucking bricks through fucking windows. While Andreas and his mob were lording it around in their Porsches and their designer suits, all he was doing was running a street gang whose main ambition was spray-painting and window-smashing. Gerry's anger became a great, cold rage. In the darkness, the others could not see how he was reacting, could not react to the warning signs. Gerry whirled again, back into the wind, with the others still laughing. More broken glass, as someone else took Morry's lead and picked up another rock, putting it through another window. That cold rage possessed Gerry as he strode on ahead.

And then the old tramp had staggered down the rough stone steps up ahead, heading down towards the embankent. He was carrying something, struggling with its bulk as he manhandled it down the stairs. Gerry quickened his pace towards this shambling figure, anger speeding his movements. Now, the old man had reached the embankment and Gerry could see that he had a filthy, torn quilt cover – obviously retrieved from some waste tip. The man himself was about sixty years old, scruffy, with a coat torn at the seams so that the lining showed under his armpits as he struggled with his bed for the night.

"Hey you," said Gerry as he approached.

The old man turned. Gerry saw that the man was almost bald; thin wisps of white dancing around his ears and the nape of his neck in the night wind. His face was dirty beneath a yellow-white beard. Even in the darkness, Gerry could see the look of alarm.

Somewhere behind, someone laughed again as another window broke.

And then Gerry threw himself at the tramp. The old man fell at the first two blows to his face; right fist, left fist. His hands groped feebly up at Gerry as he kicked the old git in the ribs. The man folded, making a sound like a kid's doll when squeezed. The high-pitched, pathetic, terrified sound enraged Gerry with further disgust. Gerry kept on kicking, aiming for the old guy's head with each blow. The others were running up now. Johnny tried to join in, laughing – but Gerry shoved him back angrily.

"He's *mine!*"

Open-mouthed, with looks of wonder like the faces of children on Christmas morning, Gerry's gang stood and watched and made soft encouraging exclamations as their leader continued his assault.

When something *cracked* like the sound of plywood splitting, and the old man's hands began to quiver in the air, Morry laughed and said, "Fucking *hell* . . ." And when, breathing heavily, Gerry had stood back to look at his handiwork, the others had become strangely quiet. Gerry could see their white faces in the darkness.

"The only way," said Gerry, "is *all* the way."

He stepped quickly forward again, raising his foot.

He stamped down hard on the tramp's face, as if he was squashing an insect. The impact sounded wet and sickening. Morry staggered to the embankment and threw up into the water. The others stood, white-faced and silent. Watching Gerry. He straightened his tie.

"Remember that," he said and continued on along the embankment.

105

Slowly, the others began to follow.

The wind felt cleansing to Gerry as he walked.

Gerry, said a voice.

And Gerry looked out across the canal, in the direction from which the voice had come. It seemed very close, but definitely out there on the water somewhere.

You're special, Gerry, said the voice again. And this time, it seemed that the voice was coming from *under* the water. For a moment, Gerry halted in mid-stride. He hadn't heard one of these voices for a long time. Forcing himself to walk on, he kept his eyes on the glittering black water, waiting to hear it again. But the voice did not come again. Soon, the others had caught up with him and were walking alongside, talking excitedly, Gerry's leadership confirmed.

But the voice did not come again. Gerry tried to shrug it off. This voice was different. It sounded so much more powerful, so real. It seemed to resonate from his previous thoughts about destiny, about what lay ahead for him. Tonight, he had made an important step forward. His killing of the vagrant had proved that . . .

Proved that you were special, said the Man. *Proved it to me. The night that you killed the worthless one – I was able to come to you. Because you'd shown me that you were the one I'd been looking for. And I'd been looking for so long, Gerry.*

"You've been . . ."

Say it, Gerry. Don't be afraid to open yourself up to me.

"You've been like a father to me."

No one could have a better son. I've adopted you.

In that instant, Gerry remembered his former father – the man whose philosophy of turning the other cheek had got Gerry so badly beaten at school by the other kids.

Just as you remember this, said the Man. *I see it all clearly in your mind. Your father betrayed you, Gerry. He did not recognise the qualities within you, didn't see the real leadership that required such special tuition. You've come a long way, and all of it using your innate abilities.*

In Gerry's mind now, a playback. The fat kid who had beaten him in the schoolyard, twisting his arm up his back until he'd cried. Now Gerry in the empty classroom window above the alcove where the school dinners were delivered by special van; looking down to where the fat kid was smoking with three of his pals. Now, the window opening wider and Gerry dropping the length of rusted metal piping; seeing it whirl end over end on its way down. Hearing the dull, wet slap as it came down across the back of the fat kid's neck, slamming his wobbly body to the tarmac. Hearing the other kids screaming.

Then the visit to hospital. A bunch of kids bringing presents on behalf of the form. The fat kid lying comatose in his hospital bed when the kids brought in the chocolates and the Airfix aeroplane kit. The parents at the bedside, trying hard to control their emotions. Gerry there with them, having convinced the form teacher of what good pals they were. Seeing that the parents were just as gross and fat as the fat kid, wondering whether that fat git of a father also used to twist kids' arms up their backs when he was at school.

The fat kid lying there with the kids all around the bed.

And then Gerry's wonderful speculation on the doctors and nurses blaming each other for carelessness when that great purple bruise appeared on the fat kid's arm later on that day; not realising that Gerry had sidled up to the bed while the kids were singing their "Get Well" song, and he had secretly moved his hand under the sheet. He had pinched the kid's forearm between thumb and forefinger, really hard. Gerry had scrutinised that hateful, blank, fat face for any sign of a reaction. There had been none. How he wished he'd brought a penknife with him. Then he could *really* have stuck it to Fatso.

Yes, said the Man. *That's what I mean, Gerry. It was a turning point for you. The schoolyard comedians used laughs to avoid a beating. But you were better, more organised, more aware of your real potential.*

All these big words, like the English teacher. They made him feel so . . .

Important. You showed the others at school. Showed them that you were always prepared to go all the way. You organised the bullies, made them respect you, because not one of them – not ONE – was prepared to go as far as you. That's what you've done, that's what you are doing. You're the sole reason for the best, most organised street "management" that this council estate has ever seen.

"You've helped me . . ."

And I'm here to help you again. Tonight was good. The deaths were good. As a result, I've been able to bring you something. Something that will enable you to grow and become even bigger than you are. Much, much bigger than Andreas . . .

"All *right!*" exclaimed Gerry, his face a mask of rapture as the Man reached into his own dark-light shimmering silhouette with both hands. When those hands emerged once more from the dark folds, Gerry could see that he was holding two white bags. The bags were fist-sized, and both tied at the neck with some kind of rough twine.

The Man stepped forward to the bed, holding out his hands.

And then he dropped both of the bags. They fell to the bed. And as they fell from the Man's hands they seemed instantaneously to acquire solidity and substance. Gerry felt them hit the bed. He looked up again as the Man stood back. He tried to see if there was any kind of expression on that dark, blank visage. There was nothing to make out, but Gerry was aware of his guardian angel's eager anticipation.

Tonight I've brought you something very special.

"What is it?"

Open one of the bags and look.

Reverently, Gerry leaned forward across the bedspread and picked up one of the bags. It was heavy. Gerry carefully undid the knotted twine and eased open the neck. Now he could see that the bag was full of white powder, like flour.

"Drugs?"

Not any kind of drug. Not like anything that anyone's ever seen. This is the ultimate drug, Gerry. It's new, and nothing like it has ever been on the streets before. This more than anything will consolidate your leadership, put you in the position of power that is required to spearhead the great changes that are coming. This is a NEW drug, Gerry. It gives a better buzz than any of the others, has no side-effects, and never gives a bad trip.

"Does it have a name?"

It is called Nektre. And you will be its sole supplier via me. The influence of Andreas and his own organisation will be diminished once you begin to distribute this drug to the streets. They will react, of course. But I will show you how to deal with that. The drug cannot be reproduced, cannot be reconstituted from samples no matter how sophisticated the laboratory resources. If anyone wants it, they must come to you and you alone. But there is a condition, Gerry.

Weighing the bag in his hand with awe, Gerry looked back at the Man: "Yeah?"

I know that you want the buzz, know how dissatisfied you are. But you must not take the drug yourself. Do you understand, Gerry? This is vitally important. The pleasures of the drug are not for you, or for the lieutenants within your own organisation. There are reasons for this, which I will tell you later. I have much greater plans, much greater rewards for you – a buzz that will far outstrip the short-term measures that Nektre can afford. Tell me that you understand?

"I'm not to take it. Neither are my lieutenants."

This is vital. If anyone in your organisation disobeys, you are to deal with them as you dealt with the vagrant on the first night that I talked to you. Do you understand?

"Yes . . ."

You did well, tonight. Things will happen quickly now. It's important that you distribute the Nektre as quickly as possible. I will keep your supply steady. Very soon, you will have a stranglehold of power on the estate.

"And then will you tell me all about the great changes?"
Oh, yes. And of your part within them.
"When?"
Soon, soon . . .

23

Larry White adjusted his bow tie unnecessarily in the mirror, for the seventh time. He rubbed his face to make sure that he hadn't missed any patches while shaving and then began to brush imaginary dust from his lapels.

"You ready yet?" he called to his wife. She was still upstairs, still fussing with her hair, her dress and the "appropriate" jewellery combination for dinner tonight. Larry heard a distant murmur which indicated that she was still in the bedroom. Quickly then, he moved to the drinks cabinet and, careful not to let glass chime upon glass, downed a large vodka. Just enough to keep him sharp and one step ahead of the company tonight.

Larry owned a string of garages and had a Marina concession. Tonight's annual Businessman of the Year event meant that everybody who was anybody would be there. With luck, he'd be able to close at least three deals which he'd had on the back burner for some time. A few drinks, a little joviality, and he felt sure that his intended targets would be loosened up sufficiently by the bonhomie. Whoever said that you didn't mix business with pleasure was talking out of his you-know-where.

When someone knocked loudly on the front door, he quickly checked his watch. Seven forty-five. The taxi-driver wasn't due until eight. Angrily, he strode from the lounge into the hallway. As he passed the stairway, he heard his wife distantly ask: "Who is it?"

"Taxi," said Larry. "He's early."

"Make him wait."

"Well, get a move on, Audrey. I don't want us to be the last to arrive."

"Bollocks," said the distant voice.

"Charming . . ."

Larry pulled open the front door, and almost recoiled from the sight before him.

110

It was a taxi-driver all right, but not the taxi-driver he had been expecting.

Tony Dandridge was leaning in the door frame, breathing heavily. His hair was dishevelled and there was sweat on his face. His shirt front looked smeared with mud.

"Christ Larry," said Tony, gasping for breath. "You've got to help me."

Quickly recovering from his surprise, Larry grabbed him by the arm. "Come in, quick! Before anyone sees you . . ."

Closing the door and drawing Tony into the hallway, Larry kept his eye on the stairway for any sign of his wife emerging.

"What the hell's going on?" he whispered.

"Something . . ." began Tony. Larry hissed at him to be quiet. "Some*one*," he continued, "is after me." He wiped a trembling hand across his mouth. "I need help, Larry."

"Why the hell have you come *here*? For God's sake, we're just about to go out. If my wife . . ."

"What?" Tony's eyes flashed with anger. "Are you joking, or what? In case you've forgotten, you *owe* me one, Larry."

Larry held his hands up, wincing; another silent plea for him to be quiet. "All right, all right. Not here." He took Tony's arm again, pointing to what the Whites laughingly called the library. It was one of several large, expensively furnished rooms. There was one bookshelf in there.

"Larry . . . ?" queried his invisible wife as they made their way into the library.

"It's okay," replied Larry, still guiding Tony by the arm. "It's the taxi-driver. He'll wait."

Inside the library, Larry watched in puzzlement as Tony hurried to the French windows and peered out anxiously into the night. There was mud on his shoes, he'd trailed it over the thick pile carpet. Larry winced again, wondering how he was going to explain it away.

"What's happened?"

"Something's after me."

"Who?"

"Not who . . ."

"Come again? Look . . ." Larry checked his watch impatiently. "We've got a taxi coming at eight. I can't stay. So tell me what this is all about."

Tony returned to the French windows. For a moment, it looked as if he was going to explain. Then he halted in the middle of the room, hands falling to his sides. He sighed, wearily shaking his head. "Larry, I just don't know where to begin."

"Here." Larry moved to the drinks cabinet and poured a large

Scotch. "Take this. You look like shit."

Tony finished it in one swallow. "Someth . . . Someone's after me. I don't know why. It's got something to do with a punter I picked up in the taxi. Somebody thinks I know where they are, where she is. She's wanted for . . . something. Anyway, it's all one big bloody mistake. Mistaken indentity."

"What do you want me to do?"

"Isn't that obvious?" asked Tony angrily. "I want you to hide me."

"What, *here*? No way, Dandridge."

"Look, Larry. You were in a lot of trouble with the law. I gave you an alibi for that Thursday night, and I'm not proud of it. You said any time I wanted the favour returned, I just had to ask. Well, I'm asking."

"We're boozing buddies, Tony. That's all. The fact that we got to know each other hanging over the bar of the Portland pub doesn't mean anything. We don't really know each other from Adam."

"I gave you the alibi, Larry. When you and your heavies came knocking on my door, you made it pretty plain what was expected. I still don't know what you were up to that night."

"I told you it wasn't murder or anything heavy like that."

"And you said you'd return the favour. Now I'm calling in the debt."

"What the hell can I do? You can't stay here."

"I've nowhere else to go. It's . . . he's . . . out there somewhere hunting for me. I managed to give him the slip. But I know it's still out there and that he'll find me eventually."

Larry noticed the way that Tony kept veering in the description of his pursuer between "he" and "it", realised just how scared the man had become. "Okay, who is it? Maybe I can put some pressure on, put the frighteners on them."

"These aren't people in your line of business, Larry. Nobody you know – or would want to know, believe me."

"Larry?" Again, his wife calling from upstairs. That, and the knowledge that in a very few minutes, the *real* taxi-driver would be knocking on the front door and compounding his problems, decided Larry. Quickly then, he crossed to a mahogany bureau beside the door and opened a drawer, taking something out. For a moment he seemed to reconsider – and then threw the bunch of keys to Tony.

"You know the marina down by Blenheim Canal?"

Tony nodded.

"There's a narrow boat down there. I own lots of them. But the one you want is called the *Kestrel*. Can't miss it. It needs painting, but the undercoat is faded blue. A forty-footer. Get yourself in there, cast off, and away up the waterways. Engine's tuned, tank filled with diesel – and there are canal maps in there."

Tony weighed the keys in his hand. "Thanks, Larry. This will give me time to think. Get things sorted in my head."

"This means we're quits. Anything else happens, I don't want to know."

Tony shoved the keys into his pocket and headed for the door.

"And Tony?"

He turned back.

"If the police come sniffing around, or they catch up with you – then you stole those keys from me. Right?"

"You're all heart, Larry."

"Right?"

"Right. But believe me, police protection might be the best thing I could get."

Tony followed him into the hall and watched as he opened the front door. There was another man standing on the doorstep, just about to ring the doorbell. He started in surprise as Tony pushed past him into the night.

"Taxi?" enquired the newcomer, when he saw Larry in the hall.

Larry smiled tightly and nodded. Then he looked up the staircase again.

"Come on, Audrey! Can't keep the taxi-driver waiting all night."

The taxi-driver just stood on the doorstep and looked at him in puzzlement.

24

Tony felt too visible on the towpath of the canal.

He ducked into a space between shed-warehouses and crouched down in the overgrown tangle of weeds and dockleaf. He needed a rest. After leaving Larry White's house, he'd headed down to the canal, keeping in the shadows all the way. And all the way down there, through the cobbled alleyways and the narrow paths between warehouses, he had been consumed by that horrifying, skin-crawling feeling that the *thing* was somewhere behind him, following. Now that he was down here, on the canal embankment leading directly into Larry's marina, he had hoped that he would feel safer. But there was no respite from that terrifying feeling of being hunted.

Tony controlled his breathing; sat with his back against the cold metal of a warehouse wall. He scoured the darkness for any sign of movement, but there was none. Only the deserted towpath on both sides of the canal, the glittering black water between and the first of the moored narrow boats, silent and still.

"It's coming," he whispered. "I know it's coming . . ."

And Tony had run from his lodging house as if the Devil was behind him. At the end of the street, he had grabbed at a streetlight to slow him down; had swung around it to look back the way he had come.

Flames were licking from the top-floor window where he had made his escape, and although the sounds of screaming had stopped, he could hear a hubbub of other voices as the alarm spread.

Then the entire top floor seemed to judder – and all the windows exploded out into the night in a glittering rain of glass. Shattered window frames and masonry tumbled to the pavements. Tony had backed off then, still looking at the building in disbelief – and when the front door at ground level also exploded out into the street as if someone had detonated a bomb behind it, Tony turned and ran into the night again. A great wind seemed to have followed that explosion, gushing from the shattered door frame and into the street.

It was coming after him.

Tony turned to look back only once as he ran. He saw the gusting wind in front of the house making street debris whirl and fly before it as it came. And when he felt that cold, fetid wind on his back he knew without doubt that it was following. He hadn't looked back again. Tony had run, and run, and run . . .

The terror which he had experienced and tried to subjugate as a professional soldier in Northern Ireland and then in the Falklands was as nothing to the fear which gripped him now. There was no time to rationalise; no time to think; just the certain knowledge that something from hell was right behind him, at his back, and that its sole purpose was to find the girl and the baby – and if he did not know where they were, then it would kill him horribly in its quest.

Tony dodged and weaved down back alleys, careered around street corners, scattering sleeping pigeons into the darkling sky. The eaves of houses veered and swung at him as he hurtled on into the night, frantic breath burning his throat and lungs.

And down every street, and around every corner – the whisper of that horrifying wind at his back.

Until it had begun to rain.

A small, fine whispering spray of rain that quickly soaked him as he ran. Something within the twisting black canyons of clouds cracked and broke with a shuddering roar. The rain had lashed at him then, soaking him to the skin.

And that rain seemed to dissolve the wind at his back.

Tony continued to run, not believing that it was fading.

And then he had collapsed at last, exhausted, on a patch of waste ground. He lay there, face turned to the sky and the rain, chest heaving with exertion. It could take him now and he would have no strength to resist.

Somehow, he had lost the thing back there in the night.

But he knew with absolute inner conviction that it was still out there, still hunting for him, and that very soon it would scent him again, and would be following close behind.

When he'd staggered to his feet again and got his bearings, he'd remembered that Larry White's place wasn't far away from here – and that he owed him.

Now, crouched between two warehouses and with the fresh smell of rain still cleansing the air, Tony crouched and listened and waited.

Steeling himself again, he gripped the houseboat keys tight and ducked out on to the embankment again; this time keeping close to the darkness of the warehouse walls.

There were more boats now, moored at the canal side.

Faded blue, thought Tony, as he slipped through the night like a shadow. *Needs a coat of paint.*

Tony searched frantically as he ran, bent double, casting anxious glances behind him, expecting to see that nightmare whirlwind scattering newspapers and leaves on the embankment as it gusted towards him.

Somewhere, a siren mourned plaintively, like a distant banshee lost in the night. Tony shuddered. It sounded as if it was calling to the thing that was pursuing him, telling it where he ran and searched for sanctuary.

Forty-footer. How long would that look in the dark, for God's sake?

A dark fluttering of wind rippled the water in the middle of the canal. Tony froze – and then continued on when the wind whispered away. There was a cluster of boats just ahead and in the moonlight, it seemed that the paint on the stern of one of them was flaking away. Tony hurried to it, crouching low, and saw the stencilled sign on its side: the *Kestrel.*

Quickly, he steadied himself on the mooring rope and then stepped on to the aft deck. He looked back along the embankment. There was no movement, no wind. Quickly again, he ducked down to the double doors and fumbled with the keys to find the lock. The noise seemed preternaturally loud. He glanced around anxiously. Then the key had turned and in seconds, Tony slipped inside – into the darkness.

For a long time, he sat there on the steps leading below deck, unable to make out his surroundings. The windows had curtains, dissuading even the faintest light. His breath seemed loud in here, as if he was sitting in a cupboard. Could the sounds of his breathing be heard outside?

Tony sat and listened.

Listened for the sounds of wind.

25

"He has gone."

"How?"

"It began to rain. The Mechanic lost his scent."

"A momentary difficulty, as before. When the rain stops, it will find his scent again."

"We must find the girl and the child. The balance of the Serendip may change at any time."

"The Mechanic will find him – and make him tell us where the other two have gone."

"It has already taken other blood. How long can we control it?"

"Long enough . . . long enough."

26

It hadn't been as successful an evening as Larry would have wished. None of the three potential business contacts had made good, and the Businessman of the Year award had gone to someone who had crossed him once before in their dealings. He was sure that the bastard had fixed the jury.

Larry was also still simmering with anger at the fact that they had been the only couple to arrive and depart by taxi. All the others had used chauffeured cars. The point hadn't been lost on Larry's rivals. There he was – owner of several garages and apparently unable to find one of his own employees to drive them to what was, after all, *the* most important local business event of the year. No one had said anything directly, but the inferences had been there. Not his bloody fault that his own driver had the flu, was it?

Audrey hadn't helped his mood. One of the other wives had been wearing an identical outfit, and she had informed him repeatedly of how badly her evening was being ruined as a result. By the time that the taxi pulled up in the front driveway of their house, they weren't on speaking terms.

The rain had stopped when Larry paid the driver off. Audrey pushed roughly past him through the front door, stormed across the hall and up the staircase.

"Right!" shouted Larry, slamming the door behind him. "So let's get started on this argument, then! Believe me, I'm ready for it . . ."

But Audrey had reached the top of the staircase and vanished into the bedroom, slamming the door in reply.

Larry stood, hands on hips, looking up and silently raging. Then he stormed into the library, tearing off his so-carefully adjusted bow tie and flinging it behind him into the hall. Once inside, he poured a large scotch. He paced the room, downed his drink quickly, and then poured another.

It was Tony Dandridge's fault.

He nodded extravagantly while downing his third drink.

He didn't usually believe in such things as bad luck, but Dandridge's arrival on his doorstep had screwed everything up tonight. Larry thought about the *Kestrel*, wondered whether he shouldn't telephone for the police, or better still pay a few of his acquaintances to go down there and visit for a while.

Something tapped on one of the panes in the French windows.

Larry paused, glass raised to his mouth.

It came again. Three hard, brittle and deliberate taps.

Dandridge again!

Larry banged the glass down and strode to the French windows. He jerked the curtains away, reaching for the door handles.

There was no one there.

Larry had a clear view of the tiled patio just beyond the windows. No one could knock on the glass and hide quickly enough for him not to be seen. The only movement in the darkness was the swaying of the hanging baskets on the trellis just beyond the patio. Strange that he hadn't noticed a wind rising tonight. The baskets were heavy, could only be swayed by a really strong wind.

But there was definitely no one out there in the garden.

Larry turned away from the windows when the library door opened.

"And another thing," said Audrey from the doorway. "What gives you the right to interrupt me when I'm talking to someone?"

"Thought you'd gone to bed."

"Well I bloody haven't! How dare you just talk over the top of me like that when I was talking to Vera . . ."

"Because your stories are boring. Everyone's heard them all a hundred times before."

"You bastard!" Audrey stooped to take off her high-heeled shoe.

"Don't you dare!" snapped Larry, moving quickly towards her.

Audrey straightened, shoe poised ready to throw at him. Then Larry saw her stiffen in mid-throw, saw the sudden puzzled look on her face.

"Larry . . . ?" she said quizzically, and he realised that she was looking not at him, but *past* him – to the French windows and to something beyond them. Her expression of curiosity had become a wide-eyed look of alarm as Larry began to turn, following her gaze.

In the next instant, something like a bomb detonated on the patio with a shattering roar. The french windows imploded, curtains shredded and billowing. The blast flung them both to the floor. And then a great, howling tornado wind erupted in the room through the shattered windows.

Larry scrabbled to rise, pulled himself up against the wall; peering through the raging wind as it destroyed the room. The drinks cabinet toppled, bottles shattered and flew. Books fluttered and whirled like panicked, exotic birds. Ripped seat cushions span and bounced, their foam-rubber contents gushing and swirling in great clouds.

And in the middle of this nightmare wind, standing in the eye of this room-sized hurricane, was a figure.

Tall, somehow formless and barely discernible – but a living shape for all that.

"What the *Christ* . . ." Larry blundered across the room to where his wife lay. She grabbed frantically at him as he helped drag her to her feet. The wind sucked and tore at their clothes. Audrey's five-hour hairdo whipped and straggled in that wind like a Medusa's nest of snakes.

"*Where are the girl and the child?*" demanded the thing in the middle of the room.

Audrey began to scream hysterically at the sound of that voice.

"You fucking . . ." Larry's voice was sucked away by the wind. Still dazed from the blast, still not having time to rationalise what was happening, Larry broke away from his wife in an all-consuming rage. There was a vodka bottle rolling at his feet. He grabbed it, lunging forward.

And somehow, an invisible force had seized his wrist and the upraised bottle, preventing him from throwing it at the shape. He fell to his knees, arm still in the air. The pain in his hand was excruciating – and when he looked up at his hand, he could see that it was shuddering.

With a wet snap, his hand twisted *completely around.* Larry shrieked in pain as the bottle fell to the floor. Audrey shrieked from the doorway, both hands flying to her face.

"*For the last time,*" demanded the thing, "*where are the girl and the child?*"

"Go away," screamed Audrey over the storm. "Go away, go away, go *away!*"

Hugging his shattered hand, on the verge of unconsciousness because of the hideous pain, Larry twisted on his knees and tried to shout to Audrey, tried to yell at her to get away. Dandridge! The thing must want Dandridge, and he would tell it where he was, tell it about the *Kestrel* – but in that instant, Larry saw the pane of glass from the French windows lying on the carpet; saw it suddenly whip up from the littered carpet, saw it slice-spin through the air like some erratic, glittering frisbee.

Saw Audrey open her mouth wide to scream again.

Saw the whirling glass slash across her face.

Saw Audrey's red, red mouth open wider across her face than was physically possible.

Heard her scream become instantly silenced.

Watched her whirl backwards, hitting the wall and collapsing to the carpet.

"Where are the girl and the . . .?"

Roaring in rage despite the pain, Larry leapt to his feet and threw himself headlong at the shape within the storm.

27

Ranjana had no idea how long she'd been walking.

But the day had faded into evening, and she had no idea how many streets she'd covered. Every one of those streets could have been Anchorage Street; all deserted, all empty. The figures who passed her, the cars, the bicyclists, they were all phantoms. Perhaps they *were* real – and she was the phantom? These thoughts passed and sifted through her mind only randomly. Since her discovery of Anchorage Street, it seemed as if a vital link between her mind and body had been severed. The address in her book had been her only hope, her anchor. Now that it was gone, she was drifting aimlessly. She should be hungry, but there was a sick feeling inside which killed the pangs. She should be tired, but still she walked.

The image of her own face appeared before her. A three-year-old photograph, reproduced in a newspaper with the caption: *"Missing: Have you seen this girl?"* Was that what she was doing? Walking aimlessly, with nowhere to go, hoping that someone would eventually recognise her and stop her. But there was no recognition, no friendly hand on her arm.

She stopped. The paving slabs beneath her feet had become broken and rough. A drain had broken somewhere, and dirty water runnelled and furled in her path, the soil turning to viscous muck. When she looked up at last, she could see that the street ahead sloped sharply away down to a stretch of dirty water. The river? And now she could see that this street was not a street after all. There were no houses on either side of her any more. The grey and blank walls were the walls of warehouses and factories. Somewhere along the way, she had left the urban sprawl and wandered into an industrial area.

Ranjana moved to the nearest blank wall and leaned against it. She stroked the hair away from her face and breathed out heavily. She had to find her focus again, pull herself together and decide just what she was going to do. She rubbed her face, tried to force herself back into the here and now. Instead, the wall behind her seemed to give under her weight, as if made of paper. Ranjana pushed herself away from it with a startled cry. Her legs had become very weak, and there was a horrifying familiar feeling in the pit of her belly.

"Oh no . . . please no . . ."

The sound was in her ears again, the rushing sound, like wind – or the passage of traffic, when there was no traffic to be seen.

"Please . . . not now . . ."

Images flashed and jumbled in her mind. Her brothers, her mother, the leering face of Mr Gupta, which had now become the leering face of the young man reading the newspaper on the train. The headline. The faces of the two men who had mugged her and stolen her possessions.

She reeled, reaching out for some kind of support – but could find none. She was tilting and reeling, and tried to cry out.

It was another fit.

Smoke. Curling and drifting over the rim of a rough hill. A light on the other side of that hill; a cold blue, horrible light. And now, the man coming over that hill. The familiar silhouette. Now the man staggering towards her with his hands held out. The smoke curling and gushing from around his body. His hideously blackened face, and the uncanny blue of the man's eyes, staring from that ravaged face as his mouth worked soundlessly.

The man was burning.

Neither dead nor alive.

And as before, he was coming to embrace her. She could see his mouth working as he came, knew that he was crying out in agony, trying to tell her something.

The arms of the burning, dead-alive man swept around her.

"Come on, darling. Better fun when you're awake."

The dream had gone and Ranjana was filled with the same dreadful, sick feeling inside. The ground beneath her was hard. Her arms and legs ached and there was a pounding, sick pain in her head. She groaned and tried to rise.

Something slammed into her chest, knocking her back to the ground.

Was she still dreaming? Or was she awake? The pain always meant that her fit was over and that terrible debilitating feeling consumed her. Dark shapes loomed and swayed above.

"She awake yet?" said one of the shadows.

"Someone piss on her. That'll bring her round."

Ranjana pushed out at the pain on her chest. Someone laughed, and then she saw that it was a soiled boot. Despite the pain, she heaved out at it. The owner of the boot staggered to one side, laughing.

"Still got some fight left in her, then?"

Ranjana struggled to a sitting position, fought down the urge to vomit. At last, she could see where she was, and the owners of the taunting voices.

There were six of them. All late teens or mid-twenties. All white. They seemed better dressed than some of the street kids she was used to seeing. Their faces still seemed blurred even in the darkness.

"So what you been on? Glue?"

"Nah, too old for that, ain't she? Too sophisticated."

"Black tart."

"What do you think, Gerry?"

Someone at the back of the crowd stepped forward. He was obviously the ringleader. Short fair hair. A broad nose that seemed broader because of a bad break sometime in his youth. Small eyes, somehow too closely set together.

"Fuck her," he said calmly. "And then cut her up."

The one called Gerry walked calmly away.

The others fell on her.

28

Randall's luck had changed.

He hadn't been fully prepared, hadn't really given any thought to where he was going to sleep, but felt pretty sure that bed and breakfast establishments or even third-rate hotels were going to cut right into the little cash he had pretty quickly. He'd already slept rough twice, and had vowed that he'd try as hard as possible never to do it again.

He'd thumbed a lift again, another lorry. And the guy there had told him about the hostel. Randall needed a little time to think, time to work out some kind of ground plan. He had thumbed the lift to no particular destination, perhaps it just came as second nature to him now. Moving on, hoping that something would turn up. But the lorry-driver had said that he was passing close to the hostel. He couldn't take him all the way there, but he could drop him off pretty close.

Following the lorry-driver's directions, he had left the main road and walked up into the warehouse area next to the river. It was a quarter-mile or so on the other side of the industrial estate, and he shouldn't really have any problems finding it.

He hadn't been walking for more than fifteen minutes when he heard the screams.

They were coming from the other side of a great concrete and steel shed.

"Shit!" said Randall aloud, still walking in the opposite direction. Perhaps it was just kids larking about?

Then he heard the sounds of laughter. They were harsh, ugly, single-minded. Combined with the sounds of the girl screaming, he knew that this wasn't innocent horseplay.

"Shit!" he said again. He stopped, head down, jaw clenching and unclenching. What the hell did this have to do with him? Weren't things bad enough already? Didn't he have enough problems?

"*Shit!*"

125

Randall swung the holdall back over his shoulder and sprinted towards the shed. This time he heard the unmistakable sound of cloth ripping, followed by a coarse cheer. Maybe . . . just maybe . . . his very presence could dissipate whatever was going on behind that shed?

And then he had spun around the corner, gripping a drainpipe on the corner of the building. He came to a sharp stop, his feet kicking up loose gravel and detritus. The drainpipe came away in his hand – a three-foot length of it.

A crowd of kids – not, not kids – young men, were gathered around someone who thrashed and screamed on the ground. Three of them were holding the girl down, another – a skinhead – was astride her, and tearing at her clothes. His belt was already open, his trousers already on their way down as he knelt purposefully between her legs. The others, perhaps four of them, just stood and watched and cheered and clapped their hands.

For a moment, they all froze. Randall and the others, just looking at each other.

But the girl continued to scream and thrash. The one between her legs slapped her hard across the face and the girl began to cry. He returned to his task.

"Fuck off, you," said one of the young men.

"Leave her alone." *Is that MY voice?*

Another voice laughed. "Hey, Gerry. Look, it's the Lone Ranger."

Randall saw one of them standing apart, almost serene. Well dressed, like a 1960s Mod, very trendy.

Randall weighed the length of rusted drainpipe in his hand. "I said leave her alone."

The crowd made an exaggerated sound of pleasure, as if overtly impressed by this display of macho: a favourite trick – the audience of a TV show being shown Tonight's Star Prize. But the skinhead between the girl's legs jerked backwards to his feet angrily. He spat down on her, fastening his trousers – and then turned towards Randall. The other three still held the girl.

In moments, they would be organised. Randall had seen it all before. *But I'm fucking faster.*

He had to move now, move fast and hard and direct before they could organise and beat the living shit out of him. This was not going to be a "talk your way out of it" situation.

Randall stormed in fast, bringing the drainpipe round in both hands like a baseball bat. The skinhead had intended to get closer, for some hard face-to-face. He was completely unprepared for such a direct movement from one fella faced by eight others. The drainpipe took him across the side of the face with a hollow *thunk,* ripping his face from mouth-corner to ear. He screamed and fell to his knees, hugging his face.

"Gerry!" yelled someone.

And then Randall was on top of the three guys holding down the girl. The first got Randall's Doc Marten in the mouth. He made a *whumping* sound, as if he was trying to swallow his teeth, and went over backwards. Someone grabbed at him from behind, maybe one of the other watchers, but Randall whirled loose from the grip, letting one of the others holding the girl have it directly on top of the skull with the drainpipe. He was literally standing over the girl now as the third attacker darted quickly away. Randall remained there, holding the drainpipe with both hands. The skinhead was still on his knees, hugging his face and moaning. It looked as if he was grieving. Two of the others were lying on the littered ground, and weren't moving. But there were still five others, not counting the one called Gerry who stood back against the shed wall, watching and aloof. The five were moving around him now, getting into position.

Remember to breathe right, thought Randall. *Keep the act going. Get your breath before you speak. Don't let them hear any wavering in your voice, and for God's sake, when you do speak – say the right thing.*

"All right, boys." Randall surveyed each of the five quickly and carefully as they moved, keeping the drainpipe held in both hands as if he was going to break his batting average. "Who's next?"

Gerry remained detached as he stood against the warehouse wall, watching what was taking place. Since the visit of the Man Who Shines Black on the previous evening, he had been feeling good. Very, very good. Today was going to be the most important day of his life. He had been told what to do and where to go. He had gathered his lieutenants for an emergency meeting, had fixed where that meeting should be – a burned-out community centre that the local council hadn't got round to repairing yet. The venue was perfect, since Gerry had been responsible for its destruction in the first place. On their way there, through the industrial estate by the river, they had come across the black girl. Drugged to the gills, by the look of her. And a perfect diversion for the boys before they got around to the real meat of the business that day.

And now, the Lone Ranger had appeared out of nowhere and floored three of Gerry's gang.

This was even better. More diversion for the boys. Just the right way to start things rolling. Gerry knew that the others would be shitting themselves that they'd allowed this crackerjack to get the edge on them so quickly, knew that they would be keen to show off in front of him, keen to pound this stupid git into the ground and re-establish themselves in their leader's eyes. Yes, it was going to be a good day today.

Gerrry watched the newcomer as he stood astride the black bint, keeping the pipe raised. He was a stranger, all right. Gerry knew most of the faces on the estate, and this kid was new. He looked hard, had obviously seen some street action in his time by the way that he handled himself. Just a pity that he thought he had to be a knight in shining armour. Under different circumstances, Gerry could have used him. But the stupid bastard had dealt his cards, and now he was going to have to play his hand all the way.

Harry Bennet feinted a lunge at the newcomer. Gerry gave a slight, impressed nod when the newcomer didn't even react to it.

"Come on then, boys," said Gerry. "Just one hard man going to show you up?"

The newcomer looked him dead in the eye. "You in charge?"

Gerry didn't answer. The fella knew he was in bad trouble, now he was going to try and talk his way out of it.

"Well," continued the hard man. "Whatever happens here, *you're* going to get it. So don't think you're going to stand back and keep out of it." He hefted the pipe in his direction, before resuming his position. "You think you're hard, with all your pals here? Well, you're going down before I do, you skinny little bastard!"

Gerry pushed himself away from the warehouse wall. An uncontrollable rage had welled within him. With a face like a mask, he took a couple of steps forward. His hands began to clench and unclench . . .

And Randall willed him to step forward again, just to get within range. He had sussed out his chances here and they weren't good. Obviously, they were going to kick the shit out of him and just carry on where they'd left off with the girl. This gang was a great deal more dangerous than some of the aggro-merchants he'd been with and come across on the street. The first direct assault might normally have broken everything up, and they might grudgingly have gone on their way. Clearly, this wasn't going to happen here. The only other thing he could do was to try and taunt their leader into making a move. He would have to save face in front of the others. And even if he couldn't taunt the bastard into a direct move, just a couple of steps forward would be enough. Then Randall could leap away from the girl (hoping that the others wouldn't expect him to do that) and lay their leader out with

the pipe. After that, anything could happen. But Randall couldn't see
another way out. His greatest danger now lay in the deadening,
sickening fear in his gut which threatened to sap his strength. He had
to keep it at bay, had to follow through with the act. He watched the
storm of anger sweeping like a cloud over the mask-like face of their
leader as . . .

Gerry paused. He knew what this bastard was going to try on. He
smiled; a tight-lipped rictus. He wouldn't rise to the bait. Now, he would
just tell the others to move in and . . .

WHAT ARE YOU DOING?

The smile that was not a smile vanished from Gerry's face at the
sound of the voice in his head. He became rigid – and Randall stiffened,
weighing the drainpipe and waiting for the move.

*GERRY, WHAT ARE YOU DOING? WHY ARE YOU DIVERTING
FROM THE TASK I HAVE SET YOU?*

Gerry cleared his throat, aware that all eyes were now on him. But
the voice had punched in his brain like an electric shock.

It was the voice of the Man Who Shines Black.

"I . . ."

*I am disappointed, Gerry. Disappointed that such trivial diversions
are more important to you than the importance of the meeting, more
important than the Nektre.*

The sound of the Man's anger was alien to Gerry. It was more
terrifying, more stomach-churning than the admonishment of any
earthly father. This was the first time that he had heard the Man so
angry, the first time that he had ever incurred his wrath. Gerry could
feel the sweat trickling down the small of his back.

"Okay!" snapped Gerry, fighting to maintain his calm and struggling
to conceal any cracks in his authority. "Leave him alone."

"*Whaaat?*" said the skinhead as he staggered to his feet, clutching
the gash across his face. "You can't be fucking serious, Gerry." There
was an edge of tearful outrage in his voice, more like a child than a
man. "Look what he's done to me . . ."

That's the way out, that's the answer! thought Gerry. "You're bloody
hopeless. The whole fucking lot of you! Look at it. Quaid's had his
face done. Yosser and Ian still lying there." Gerry acted out his rage.
"Pick them up! Go on, pick them up!" The circle around the newcomer
began to disintegrate as two of them moved quickly to drag their
unconcious friends to their feet. "One fucking Lone Ranger! One bloke,
and he's got the jump on you with a piece of fucking *drainpipe*! What
the hell am I putting money in your pocket for? What the hell am I
organising you for . . . ?"

"Let me take him, Gerry!" snapped Harry Bennet. "Let me carve my initials on his . . ."

"*Shut up!*" Gerry stepped forward, carrying the act all the way. Quietly now, pretending to control an almost uncontrollable anger: "Shut up, Harry." He turned back to Randall. "Okay, you're a lucky man, Kimo Sabe. This is probably the luckiest day in your life. Because we're going to let you get away with this, and we're going to leave the girl . . ."

"Awww, Gerry . . ." said Johnny. A fierce glare silenced him instantly.

"Look on this as a . . . training exercise," said Gerry tightly. "For my people. You've got guts, son. After you've cooled off and you want to earn some money, come and see me. Maybe I could use you. The name's Gerry Tomelty. Ask anybody on the estate, and they'll tell you where to find me."

Gerry turned abruptly and walked away up the slope.

Reluctantly, grudgingly, the others moved away and began to follow. Those whom Randall had laid out were almost conscious, but still needed to be dragged by their fellows. The skinhead called Quaid was the last to move away. He pointed a bloody finger at Randall as he moved on up the slope, still glaring at Randall. The gesture and expression was not lost on him. This was obviously one score that would be settled at some future date, irrespective of his gang leader's wishes.

"Don't think about the police, sweetheart," he sneered. "It's just the two of you, and your word against the rest of us."

"Come on!" snapped Gerry from up ahead. Quaid grudgingly followed.

Gerry moved quickly on, thrusting his hands deep into his pockets and keeping his head down.

All right, Gerry, said the Man in his head. *That was good. You know that what we've agreed and what we've planned is the most important thing.*

Gerry nodded his head, like a chastened child.

Great things lie ahead for you, Gerry. You're special.

Inside, Gerry felt like crying. For the first time he had incurred the displeasure of his (father) mentor.

It's all right. This is the first time I've been able to speak in your head, Gerry. That's a sign that our strength is growing. I'll be able to speak to you directly, and to advise you.

Gerry nodded again and kept walking.

When the last of Gerry's gang had vanished over the brow of the hill, Randall stepped away from the girl and dropped the drainpipe to the ground.

For the first time, he saw that she was black.

One of her attackers had torn her blouse and jacket apart, and she had attemped to pull it together again with one hand. Her skirt had also been ripped. Randall held down a hand, but she didn't take it.

"You all right?"

"I think . . . think . . ." And then the girl turned over and vomited.

Randall stood back, looking up the bank to make sure that none of Tomelty's gang had decided to come back for a rematch. Then he moved to the warehouse wall, braced both hands against it and bowed his head. He sucked in lungfuls of air, controlled his nerves again. He began to shake, but managed to control it. The sounds of vomiting had ceased, so he turned back. The girl was struggling to rise. Randall moved shakily back to her. Clearly, her blouse and jacket were finished. He took off his jacket and then steadied her elbow as she finally managed to stand.

"Thanks," she said. Her voice seemed ridiculously calm and polite, given all that had gone before. Randall handed her the jacket. "No, I'll be okay . . ."

"Take it."

Randall watched as the girl pulled on his jacket and then zipped up the front. Her knees were grazed and bleeding.

"You live far from here?" asked Randall.

The girl managed a shaky laugh. "About one hundred and fifty miles north."

"Oh. Well, look – I think we better find somewhere to get you cleaned up. Maybe coffee."

Ranjana thought about protesting. But why? Where else was she going to go? She felt numb and dazed. Her legs and back were hurting. One of them had scratched her badly across the stomach, and this hurt more than anything. She didn't suppose that someone who had just stopped eight bastards from raping her was going to be any more of a threat.

"Okay."

"My name's Randall."

"So you're not the Lone Ranger?"

"Nope."

"My name's Ranjana. Listen, I just don't know what to say about . . ."

"Then don't say anything. Come on, let's find that coffee."

29

It is early morning. The sun has just begun to rise.

Somewhere, a milk float rattles and clatters on its early morning deliveries. A cat slinks across a cobbled alley, leaps up to the rim of an open rubbish bin and begins to rummage inside for an early morning snack. There is no other movement. It is too early yet for the hubbub of normal life.

The cat pauses in its quest.

It lifts its head from the rubbish bin and sniffs at the air.

Somewhere, a wind whispers. The cat's eyes are focused at the top of the alley. Has something moved? A rat? The cat drops to the ground again and begins to pad over the cobbles towards the top of the alley. It freezes again, slinks to a far wall and waits. An early morning pigeon, perhaps? Looking for scraps. The cat crouches low and begins to stalk.

The wind whispers again.

A newspaper drifts around the corner; twists and curls into the sky. The cat watches, unconcerned.

Then the hair begins to rise on its back. It begins to back away, jaws bared in a warning snarl and spray of breath. It screeches, like a newborn child; turns and darts panic-stricken down the alley.

And then the wind gusts around the alley corner like a blast from hell.

A whirlwind of paper and street detritus spins into the alley, howling like a miniature tornado. The rubbish bins in the alley whirl and fly, disgorging their contents. Is that broken glass whirling within the nightmare wind, or can it be the faint specklings of lightning, discharging into the cobbles and the rough brick walls of the alley?

This is no ordinary wind as it roars on down the alley. It is isolated and deadly. And it is moving. Apart from the garbage and the rubbish and the paper and the cartons that whirl and spin in this hellish wind, there are also the entire contents of a demolished living room. The magazines, and the newspapers, and the private papers and the letters and the cards, and the disembowelled stuffing of furniture from that room *whirl and toss in the centre of this whirling blast of air.*

No one is on the streets to witness this wind, but anyone who was might think that this wind is somehow sorting *through the whirling, ruined contents of that room as it drives on the wreckage before it.*

A photograph album flaps and tears through the air, disgorging a fluttering cloud of private memories into the sky. The wind sucks and grabs at the photographs eagerly as if snatching and examining every one.

One photograph whirls and spins above the others, and then falls to the ground. It is slammed flat there, as if an invisible foot has stamped it to the sidewalk.

It is a photograph of a narrow boat.

Larry and Audrey White are standing in the stern, waving at whoever has taken the photograph.

On the side of the boat is stencilled: the Kestrel.

The wind seems to subside. Torn paper, wadded foam rubber, feathers, torn cloth and newspaper begin to fall on the alley like some strange rain. A skinned cat, caught in this hell-wind, falls in a bloody mess to the cobbles.

There is a sound. Like some huge and dangerous animal. It seems to sniff and scrabble at the photograph, as if hunting for scent.

The wind roars into life again, sending the detritus spinning and flying once more. The photograph of the narrow boat spins and flaps at the centre of the storm. But the wind has changed direction. It is heading back in the direction from which it came.

Towards the canal.

30

Bernie needed to get out of this city as quickly as possible.

Since his conversation with Mac by the riverside, he had been feeling even more uncomfortable. On his walk back from the jetty, he had seen more faces in shop doorways, all looking out into the night with the same hungry expression that had so alarmed him on his return. There had been a gang of four or five hanging around a street corner at one stage, standing under a streetlamp and just, well . . . *looking*. And although he had been unable to see their faces or their expressions, Bernie had been filled with a dreadful feeling of apprehension. It was as if they *knew* that he was aware of the new breed of street people, *knew* of his conversation with Mac. He had crossed the street before he'd reached that weird bunch, had slipped quickly down a back alley. They had watched him all the way, in silence.

It was dangerous on the streets.

Bernie was adamant that he would leave this place just as soon as he could. But he felt vulnerable travelling at night alone on these streets. Far better to wait until day, when there seemed to be fewer of the hungry ones about. His best bet was to find a safe place to sleep, and to get out of there just as soon as the sun came up. He had some loose change, could probably get into one of the homeless refuges – but he felt sure that the hungry ones would be there, too. Felt sure that they would find his bed in the night.

There was a place nearby. A place that he'd slept in safely before. That would be the best thing to do until morning.

Bernie hurried to the concrete flyover, keeping a watchful eye on those who passed him. He didn't want any of the hungry to see where he was headed, felt sure that if one of them did, then the information would be passed on.

There was no traffic at this time of night, no passers-by, as Bernie climbed the bank under the flyover where two enormous concrete struts supported the motorway overhead. No cars passed on the road beneath, there were no shadowy figures on the small patch of waste ground across the way as he picked his way over loose rubble until he'd reached the apex of the arch. There was natural shelter here in the shadows, both from the weather and from prying eyes. Bernie examined the darkness carefully to make sure that no one else had found his hiding place. He laughed wryly when he saw the sheet of cardboard. It was from a box which had once contained a Slumberdown mattress. Flipping it over to make sure that no one was under it, Bernie pulled it around him as he sat in the concrete eave beside the enormous stanchion. He had a clear view from the darkness up here; the streetlights below on the roadside allowed him to see if anyone passed.

Satisfied that he was alone, he settled himself to sleep.

He dreamed of former times, and of former cities, and of former acquaintances gained and lost. Most of all, he dreamed of betrayal – and of the one woman in particular who had led to his life on the road. In his dream, she called his name.

And he was instantly awake.

Defensively alert, Bernie pulled back the cardboard sheet and bunched his fists. Had someone else found his sanctuary? One of the hungry?

No, he was alone. What had woken him then?

Down on the patch of waste land was a black van of some kind.

Two people were moving around the van, fiddling with its sides, as if unscrewing something.

Bernie settled back, content that there was no one up here, and watched.

Now the two figures were folding down a flap on the side of the van. Orange light spilled out from the interior, casting two long busy shadows behind the figures. There were three others inside the van, all busying themselves with something.

Hot dog stand, thought Bernie, and began to salivate. He hadn't eaten in a long while.

The figures outside opened two double doors at the back of the van and climbed inside to help the others. No, this couldn't be a hot dog stall. Too late at night, too out of the way and too many people serving. Bernie nodded. This had the feel of the "handout brigade". He shrugged, pulling the cardboard closer around him as he watched them preparing. Strange, this wasn't one of the usual patches where travellers congregated. And the vans normally stuck to the usual places, usually turned up where people would be expecting them, or vice versa. Still, he'd been away from this city for a long while. Things changed.

Even as Bernie watched, three figures were wandering into view from the direction he'd come earlier. Two men, one woman – all pissed. And from the long wrap around the woman's shoulders and waist, he recognised her as being one of the travellers down by the jetty where he'd found Mac. She had been the source of an argument going on under the struts of the jetty. Bernie watched them continue their argument along the main road, saw the woman spot the black van and motion to the others. They wandered over to it, and Bernie saw them getting a free handout from someone behind the flap-counter in the van. Two of the other figures were talking to them now. Someone laughed raucously, and one of the newcomers began to dance on his own. The woman joined him, carefully trying to avoid spilling her soup.

The hunger pangs stabbed Bernie into action. He'd seen these three before, knew that they were just three of the *normally* hungry people. He pushed the cardboard aside and began to move carefully down the overpass slope towards the main road. They wouldn't be able to see him, although he could see them, so his hiding place would remain secret. When he reached the main road at the bottom of the slope, beneath the flyover, he straightened his coat and crossed over, pretending that he had just happened along like the others.

An argument up at the van seemed to have developed. The ones inside the van seemed to be trying to talk to the newcomers, earnestly telling them about something.

Bible bashers, thought Bernie. *Give 'em something to eat and drink, then when you've got 'em, ram the Scriptures down their throat.* He shook his head; he'd seen it all before.

Bernie heard the woman tell the handout people to "Piss off!" and the other two men joined her as she flounced away from the van and back to the main road. He watched the three of them drunkenly wander off into the night, watched the people at the van stand and watch them depart. As he drew nearer, he could see the people at the van more clearly. There were three men and three women. All with earnest faces, all with the look of Salvation. Two of the women were in the van, behind the counter. One middle-aged, one teenage with long dark hair. Both ordinary-looking. The third woman leaned against the van and was sipping a paper cup of their own soup. Early twenties, very attractive. The three men all looked to be in their late thirties, or early forties; all wrapped up in overcoats and scarves against the cold night air. None of them wore uniforms, so they must belong to a voluntary organisation, and not the Salvation Army. One of the men seemed to curse softly under his breath at the departing figures, began to flap his arms around his waist, and then turned to see Bernie approaching.

Bernie watched him turn to the others, say something quickly. The others reacted in a way that made Bernie stop in his tracks. It was as if they'd spotted a policeman moving in to close down an illegal operation; as if they were street traders who'd spotted the approach of local fuzz and were shutting down straight away. Bernie saw the figures outside dart anxious glances all around, saw them dart back to the double doors at the rear of the van at the same time that the two women inside began to haul up the flap.

"What the bloody hell . . . ?"

The double doors slammed shut after the last figure had piled into the back. The flap at the side rattled home, snuffing out the welcoming orange light from inside. Bernie heard bolts being made secure on the inside of the flap. He could hear the sounds of scuffling movement. And then when two of the figures reappeared in the front seats of the van, and the ignition was turned on, anger flared inside Bernie.

"Come back here!"

Bernie ran forward, heard the engine being revved, and began yelling abuse. He slammed into the side of the van, slapping his hands hard on the panelling. He was hungry!

"What the hell's the matter with you, then? You all mental, or something?"

Bernie kicked at the van. Although the driver was revving the engine, the van still hadn't moved. He strode angrily to the front cab, twisted at the handle. The door was locked – and the middle-aged man who'd first seen his approach was sitting behind the wheel.

He was grinning at Bernie as he revved the engine.

"You giving handouts or what?"

The man continued to grin, and the stupidity of that grin fuelled Bernie's anger even further. He slammed his fist into the door, but the man's idiot expression remained constant. The bastards were taunting him! Bernie heard movement at the rear of the van, heard a door opening. Kicking at the driver's door again, he strode back towards the rear. The engine still revved, but the van did not move. When he rounded the rear of the van, he could see that one of the double-doors was open, but someone had switched off that welcoming orange light. The weirdos must be sitting in there in the darkness. Bernie dragged the door wide, ready to give them a mouthful.

And then someone hit him from behind.

The blow took him just above the right ear and Bernie went down to his knees. Instantly, strong arms had grabbed his own, and he was being hoisted into the van. Too dazed to react, Bernie saw his feet sweep over the ground as he was hoisted bodily into the back of the van. The doors slammed, and he was in utter darkness as the arms

137

dumped him on the cold floor in a heap.

The driver rammed the gears into first, and the black van took off into the night.

Bernie felt himself sliding on the floor as the van turned sharply on to the main road, felt a foot on his back holding him steady. No one spoke.

And then Bernie twisted over on to his back, grabbing the foot and yanking hard. The owner of the foot yelled in surprise – a man – and Bernie yanked again as he scrabbled backwards. The man fell heavily to the floor, someone else cursed and Bernie took another blow on the head. It wasn't enough to daze him. Consumed with rage, he grabbed out again and caught a wrist. Using it to pull himself up, he lashed out and fisted someone directly on the bridge of the nose – one of the women. She squawked, and then yelled, "Get him down!"

"Fuck that!" Bernie kicked out at the lumbering shape which reached out at him from the other side of the van.

Hands tangled in his hair, someone had him around the waist, and from the front of the van the driver yelled, "What the hell's the matter with you all? Hold him *down!*"

"And fuck you, too!" yelled Bernie back. The metal soup urn which he'd seen on the counter was directly in front of him. He lunged and swatted the lid from it with a clatter. One of the women raked her nails over his face. He brought his knee up against the person who was holding his waist, heard the *ooomph!* of air from someone's ribcage. Then he shoulder-charged the soup urn, let the weight of all those hanging on him fall against it. The metal canister juddered out of its socket. A wave of boiling soup splashed hissing over the combatants. Instantly, the van's interior was filled with shrieking. The soup had scalded Bernie's legs, but had done worse damage to some of the others by the sound of it. The hand was gone from his hair, the arms from around his waist. Kicking out, he lunged towards the front of the van.

"Stop him, you idiots!" shrieked one of the women.

Bernie grabbed a handful of the driver's hair and yanked his head back. The van swerved across the main road towards the pavement, tyres shrieking.He brought his fist down like a hammer across the bridge of the driver's nose, felt the bone crack. The driver screamed, and the van hit the pavement with a juddering crash. Plates and cutlery shattered, smashed and flew inside the van. Someone collided hard against the wall and rebounded on to his companions. Somehow, the driver jammed on the brakes and the van slewed to a halt on the pavement, catapulting Bernie over the seat and head down into the driver's lap. The man in the seat next to the driver lashed out at him.

Bernie sank his teeth into the driver's crutch and the man began to scream in a falsetto. Twisting, Bernie popped the lock on the door, kicked and lashed – and the door was open. He pushed himself hard, face down, and rolled out of the van, hitting the pavement. The pain in his shoulder was agonising, but he managed to roll and stagger to his feet.

Through blurred vision, Bernie could distantly see the flyover. They'd travelled perhaps a half-mile. He turned and began to run.

"Don't let him get away!" screamed one of the women, and Bernie heard the double doors at the back of the van flap open.

They were after him.

31

Mac couldn't recall leaving the riverside.

He remembered speaking to Bernie, who seemed to have disappeared just as mysteriously as he had arrived. He remembered dimly their conversation, and of Bernie's references to "hungry people". It didn't seem to make sense any more. Mac remembered returning to stare at the fire, and at the mysterious pictures that seemed to form and reform within the flames – and the next thing he knew, he was walking again.

It was late, but Mac wasn't tired. When he focused properly in the darkness, he could see that he had followed the river inland. He was on a canal embankment, a familiar stretch, perhaps two miles from the river itself, and from where he'd been sitting watching the flames. There were narrow boats moored along here. Dimly again, he seemed to recall that he had once slept in an abandoned boat down here years ago, when he had been caught in a bad thunderstorm late at night. He considered whether he should do the same tonight, but knew that sleep would not come easily. Far better that he just walk. Eventually, when he tired, he would find a place.

He remembered what he had seen in the fire.

First, the girl's face.

A good-looking face of a girl in her late teens, with large liquid eyes. She was black, perhaps Indian – and those eyes always seemed to be fixed on him, as if in puzzlement. And he too puzzled over that face. Was this someone from his forgotten past?

Then, the girl's face would vanish in the flames – and the *Other* would take place.

It played back to him like a movie, sometimes in puzzling fragments, sometimes complete. Tonight had been a complete show.

He saw a man in army uniform. It was night, and the man was bending over another who had been shot in the leg. He was never somehow able to see their faces, not of these two – or the others.

* * *

"Come on! Fucking move it if you want to get out of this alive. Come on, you bastard. All the others are dead."

"Dead?" said the wounded man weakly, and gave a small laugh.

"Come on!" The first man dragged the wounded man aloft. Now Mac remembered that the name of this first man was Cameron.

Another man was suddenly at his side, helping. Mac seemed to think that this one was called Willis. His face was indistinct and masked in blood, from a parallel bayonet gash across his forehead.

"Who's that?" said the wounded man, looking beyond them. "He been sent to clean up, then?" Mac watched the man called Cameron turn to look at another figure which was walking towards them through this hellish night. A silhouette, striding purposefully, carrying something that looked like a vacuum cleaner.

"JESUS CHRIST!" yelled Willis, letting go of the wounded man's arm and darting away, running low towards the mound. Cameron nearly lost his own grip on the wounded man, saw with horror that the silhouette was levelling the nozzle at Willis as he fled.

"Shit!"

Mac watched the scene in the fire, watched the man called Cameron leave the wounded man, saw him dodge and weave away as the night suddenly roared into bright orange flame. The scene in the riverside fire vanished momentarily. Now, there was only a blossoming cloud of black-orange fire – and someone was shrieking.

Then the man called Cameron had appeared again. He had flung himself behind a small hillock of straggling, tufted grass. He was clutching his automatic rifle tight. Waiting. Waiting . . . And now the man had flung himself to his feet again, aiming his self-loading rifle at the silhouette as it advanced on the wounded soldier with its dripping hose of fire. The wounded man was holding up an arm in a plea to ward him off.

The rifle was jammed.

Mac watched the man called Cameron run hard at that figure, heard him praying frantically inside his head that the man with the fire wouldn't hear, that he wouldn't turn. The wounded man was uttering hoarse cries of fear, trying to scrabble away. Mac saw through Cameron's eyes, saw the Argentinian adjusting the controls on the flame-thrower, saw a flower of orange-black erupt from the nozzle.

And then Cameron swung the jammed rifle and hit the Argentinian hard. They both went down in a thrashing tumble of limbs. Now, Mac was no longer in Cameron's body. He was somewhere above them, as they thrashed and fought on the ground.

"Use your gun!" yelled the wounded man, and Mac watched as he began to crawl towards them. Clouds of sparks gushed up towards Mac

where he watched. He watched them rolling in the sparks, heard the wounded man yell, "Use your fucking gun!" and wanted to shout, "He can't! The bloody thing's jammed!"

Cameron was on top of the Argentinian, throttling him.

But then the Argentinian had got his leg between them, and savagely kicked Cameron backwards. Mac cried out aloud when Cameron did.

"No!" yelled someone as Cameron hit the ground and struggled to rise. "No!" The flame-thrower nozzle was swinging around.

And Mac remembered that he had wanted to stop seeing this movie in the flames, had stood up on the river bank and tried to look away. But the horror was not to be denied, and Mac had been forced to watch as the orange-black cloud of fire leapt hissing from the flame-thrower's nozzle at the man called Cameron.

Mac had screamed then, silencing everyone else who had gathered on the river bank. He had turned from the fire and blundered madly up the slope just as the shrieking blazing marionette that had once been a man had blundered madly into the Falklands night. Mac had run and thrashed at his clothes, just as he'd once run and thrashed at the all-consuming, utterly hellish nightmare pain that had destroyed his mind and his reason.

Now, reliving the moment, Mac cried aloud again and collapsed to his knees on the embankment. He began to sob.

A series of fleeting images passed in his mind. He could not control their progress.

A soldier found with ninety-five per cent burns by Argentinian troops. No identification, the uniform burned from his body.

Awaking in a hospital bed where everyone around him spoke a foreign language.

Drifting in and out.

Hideous, nightmare pain.

Screaming and screaming for the pain to stop.

Masked surgeons and nurses.

The operating theatre light directly overhead.

Disembodied voices speaking to him in fractured English.

And now – Mac was in an office of some kind. Floating again, above two figures. One of them was dressed in a uniform of some kind. He didn't recognise the rank, but it was British. This man was sitting behind a mahogany desk littered with official papers. There were prints of historical conflict on the walls; the carpet was thick. Deep red. Stained with soldiers' blood? But it was the second figure who fascinated Mac most.

The figure was in a dressing-gown, but the entire head was swathed in bandages, like a mummy, with only slits for the eyes. The eyes were a startling blue, but seemed somehow dead. Even from where he floated, Mac could see that the skin around those eyes was hideously ravaged.

The hands were bandaged, each resting stiffly on the arm-rests. A door behind the figure opened, and a white-coated figure entered. Another man, carrying a file, which he placed on the officer's desk. The officer flipped through it, then looked directly at the bandaged figure.

"Is it worth trying?" asked the officer.

The white-coated man nodded, but seemed unconvinced.

The officer cleared his throat.

"Corporal Cameron MacKay Stevens of the 5th Battalion Parachute Regiment."

The bandaged figure nodded.

"Good," said the officer. Then, enthusiastically, "Good! You can understand me . . . well, Stevens. Where to begin . . ."

But Mac was whirling now, the scene shifting in and out of focus. The words of the officer and of the white-coated man seemed fragmented, making little sense.

". . . ninety-five per cent burns when you were found by the Argentinians . . ."

". . . thought that you were one of theirs . . ."

". . . process of confusion and – frankly – bureaucratic blunder, tied in with mistaken assumptions on your identity led to your being listed as 'missing in action' . . ."

". . . eight months of painful skin grafts after your eventual transfer home . . ."

". . . a charred, army ID tag . . ."

". . . to prepare yourself, Mackay. Your face has been reconstructed to the point where you will not recognise yourself any more. A remarkable job in the circumstances . . ."

". . . pain-killing drugs for the rest of your life. But you should count yourself lucky . . ."

Alarmed, Mac saw the bandaged figure suddenly leap screaming to his feet in the middle of the room. Saw him clutching at the bandages around his head, saw the white-coated man try to restrain him, only to be knocked to the floor; saw the uniformed officer cowering back behind his desk.

Another scene now. A hospital ward. A man quietly opening a locker door, pulling on the clothes he finds there. The man moves back to the foot of the bed and looks at the special army identification tag beside his medical chart. There are two photographs on this ID – one on the front and another on the back. He does not recognise the face of the man on the back, but knows the scar-ravaged face of the man on the front. The ID seems to be saying that the two faces are one and the same man.

Now, the same man is sneaking down a hospital corridor, hiding in a laundry room as two Military Policemen march past. Mac watches the

*man climb through a window at the end of a corridor, watches him sneak
quickly down a fire escape into the rain. It's night, and the man keeps to
the shadows as he escapes from the military hospital. At the rear gates,
in the bushes, he tears off the last remaining strip of bandaging from his
head. He feels the thick scar tissue on his face, then reaches into his pocket
for the army ID which he has taken from the bed. He looks at those two
faces again and reads the name aloud, tries to make sense of it but cannot;
tries to remember anything of his life before this hospital, but cannot. He
looks at his serial number.*

"Three, seven, four, oh-two," he says aloud.

And then Mac watches the figure vanish into the night.

Mac's hands came away from his face. There were no bandages there
and, for the moment, there was no pain. Still kneeling on the canal
embankment, he looked around at the night; at the narrow boats, and
at the ebony black, rippling water. When he looked at his hands, he
saw the rough scar tissue; flexed the fingers and felt as it they didn't
belong to his body. He felt his face again; the taut, rough skin. It
seemed as if he was touching someone else's face. The surface skin
and nerve tissue were dead. The pain, when it came, was from the
damaged underlying nerve tissue – on eighty per cent of his body.
And when that pain came, always without warning, his mind had
found the only way of coping with it. His mind was forced to
move out, to leave his body for as long as it took for the pain to
cease again. Not for the first time, Mac wondered whether he was
walking around in someone else's body. Already, the most recent
playback that he had seen in the flames was blurring and fragmenting
even further.

"Three, seven, four, oh-two," he said to the night, as if expecting
an answer.

Somewhere, a siren called in the night. Was it an answer? Mac
listened to it dying away; a police car giving chase. And by the time
that the night had swallowed the eerie noise, he had forgotten about
the Falklands and about the hideous fire-pain. It would come again –
the next time he stared into the depths of a fire. But for now, it had
gone.

Mac climbed to his feet, dusted off his trousers. Now, he was
suddenly tired and needed a place to doss. He looked again at the
narrow boats. Perhaps he could find one that was unlocked?

Then someone started to yell from further up the embankment.

Mac looked up. An indistinct silhouette was thrashing through the
bushes at the side of the canal a couple of hundred yards ahead. Mac
watched him pull himself through those bushes and up on to the

embankment proper. The figure began to run towards him. Was it waving at him as it ran?

Mac began to walk towards it.

And then four other figures erupted from the bushes behind the first. They too dragged themselves up on to the embankment. They seemed younger and fitter than the first – and now Mac could see that they were pursuing him. The first silhouette staggered and fell to the embankment, dragged itself up again and continued to run towards him. The others were gaining on him.

Mac hurried forward.

"Mac! For Christ's sake, help me!"

Mac froze in his tracks. The figure blundered on towards him, clearly in distress. At last, he recognised him.

"Bernie!"

Mac gathered himself and lunged on ahead.

But the first of Bernie's pursuers had reached him, seizing his shoulders. Bernie and his pursuer fell to the towpath. Now, the three others were on him; swooping down and seizing his arms and legs. Mac could see that they were all younger men. My God, were they *biting* him?

Mac roared as he ran.

The pursuers looked up in alarm, seeing him for the first time. The pursuer who had brought Bernie down quickly pulled something out of his jerkin pocket; something that glittered bright in the darkness. Bernie began to yell, thrashing and kicking.

"Nooooo!" yelled Mac.

The pursuer worked with the glittering object at Bernie's thrashing head.

Bernie ceased to thrash. His arms and legs began to twitch spasmodically. He screamed no more.

Still screaming, Mac could only watch as he hurtled on towards them, could only watch as the four attackers leapt to their feet and dragged Bernie's limp body to the concrete lip which separated the towpath from the canal. A dark pool glinted on the gravel where they dragged him. And suddenly Mac was engulfed in flames as he ran again, the horror and the sound of his own screaming instantly recalling that which he had forgotten again so recently. He was burning as he ran and ran and ran.

"Nooooooo!"

The attackers flung Bernie into the canal. Mac saw him twist and tumble, arms flapping; saw the splash of dirty yellow water. The attackers turned and fled back along the embankment.

Agony and rage were the flames engulfing Mac. He could not stand

145

the hideous pain, but had to rescue *(the wounded soldier)* Bernie. Mac kept running when he reached that dark glinting pool on the gravel, swerved and launched himself headlong from the concrete lip – straight into the canal after Bernie.

The face of the Indian girl, eyes flashing in alarm.

And then a darkness blacker than night crashed over him. Instantly, the flames engulfing his body were snuffed out. In that micro-second before he hit the water, Mac knew that the flames were only in his mind. But the water was colder than he could have imagined, despite the damaged nerve tissue on his body. It punched out the breath that he was holding in his lungs, but brought with it realisations of astounding clarity. He swallowed filthy water and choked, thrashing to the surface.

Mac thrashed and dived into the blacker-than-night, suffocating ice-darkness. Already his clothes were dragging him down. He crested again, treading water, and looked desperately for any sign of Bernie. He couldn't be more than a few feet from where those bastards had thrown him. He thrashed and dived again, clawing through the water, trying to hook an arm or a leg. When he crested again, Mac yelled Bernie's name aloud into the night. He knew that there could be no response. His sodden clothes dragged at him; again, his mouth filled with dirty water. This time, Mac lunged for the canal embankment. Grabbing a mooring chain fixed to the concrete side he twisted and looked back across the water, frantically searching for any sign of a drifting, sodden bundle.

There was none.

And Bernie's attackers had vanished into the night.

32

The body twists and rolls almost lazily in the night-black water.

Death did not arrive instantly, and the lungs have filled with water on impact with the canal; the last dying breath drawing it in. The weight of that water in the lungs keeps the body just below the surface of the canal as it drifts and turns.

There is a slight current here. The canal feeds directly into the river uninterrupted by a lock, and the tides of that river have a residual effect for at least half a mile. The body has been taken in that slight, swirling eddy of water and turns face down; arms drifting downwards as if searching for something on the filth-entangled, littered floor of the canal.

Another pair of arms are reaching upwards from the canal floor fifty yards ahead. They are ragged, spectral arms, waving lazily in the poisonous water. The owner of those arms has been bound tight, the gradually disintegrating corpse tied savagely with industrial copper cable to a filth-encrusted car engine; heavy enough to keep it down here for a long time. The gradual current has worked both arms loose from the wire. In time, the process of decomposition will rot the connective tissue and both arms will detach, as will the legs and the head, and eventually – in pieces too small and decomposed to be recognisable as human – the torso and the ribcage. The corpse has been here for three months.

And as the most recently deceased drifts over the watery prison of the canal's long-term denizen, their drifting searching hands almost meet.

The prisoner of the canal seems to reach out for its companion.

But the current carries the newcomer on towards the river, and thenceforth to the sea.

The decomposed skeletal face of the prisoner grins on in the blackness. It waits.

33

The girl walked in the rain, for the most part with her head down. She only looked up when crossing a road or turning a corner. The coat she wore was an old waterproof, at least three sizes too big. The hood enveloped her head, and it was impossible to see her face until she did look up – and that was exactly what she wanted. The coat hung down to her ankles, and the arms flapped empty at her side. Her arms cradled the baby, which was held tightly to her breast as she walked. It was asleep; safe, dry and warm within the coat. To a passer-by, it might seem as if this girl was eighteen months pregnant. The coat had been stolen from a bus station waiting room. In her former life, she might have felt bad about taking it. But not now.

As a child in Pennsylvania, USA, she had been told lots of stories about England, had read lots of books. The images had been strong compared to the steel-town environment in which she had grown up. Sherlock Holmes, fog, hansom cabs – and rain. Well, she'd seen nothing of the former but a great deal of the latter. And the city in which she'd ended up had more in common with her own steel-town than the Olde England which she had expected. She could laugh at her naïveté now, but laughter was something that she could not dredge up; not after the things she'd seen happening on these streets, or the things that she had experienced.

She was glad of the rain, hoped that it wouldn't end until she'd left this city. As long as it rained, she was safe. It would put the Mechanic off her scent. She'd already managed to buy herself two days and maybe the long-term rain might buy her that third, possibly a fourth. By then, she'd be well out of its reach and it would have lost her trail.

The girl stopped in an empty shop doorway. The posters on the window declared that the business had been relocated, giving a new address. The girl knew that address, knew that the entire building had been demolished. There was a pile of letters and leaflets lying on the mat beyond the glass front door. She adjusted the child, leaned back

148

against the door to take the weight off her back. The automatic pistol in her left pocket *clunked* against the glass.

It was four days since she had escaped, knowing that it would take them two days to conjure the Mechanic. Two days later, she knew that it was coming, had fled into the night when her protection had dissipated. She hadn't seen it, but the child had sensed its proximity. Almost exhausted, in the middle of God knew where, the taxi had suddenly appeared.

The rain that night had killed her scent, throwing the Mechanic away from her. When the taxi-driver had dropped her off, she'd fled to the nearby industrial estate, had hidden in one of the empty sheds there under a dirty sheet of tarpaulin. The rain drumming on the tin roof had been comforting. As long as it rained, the scent was dampened, and she was miles away from it by now. The following day, after she'd rested, she had taken to the streets again. She had no money, couldn't buy a ticket for a bus; had barely enough food crammed in her pocket to last her. And all the time, there was the knowledge that *they* were still out there, looking for her, even if she had managed to give the Mechanic the slip. Any one of the faces who passed her or stared at her from the shop doorways could be one of them – looking for her. At last, unable to stay out in the open any longer she had stolen the coat and taken to hiding again. This time it was a derelict house in a street due for demolition. Anchorage Street, the sign had read. The girl had crouched under a staircase in one of the houses, feeding and cradling the child. It never cried – had *never* cried. But during that time, she had rested, listened to the comforting rain, and had finally decided on her course of action. She would risk it – just head for the main station, jump on the first long-distance train out of the city, heading anywhere (it didn't matter) and get the hell out.

Get out of hell, she'd thought wryly, but again, couldn't smile.

She would dodge the ticket inspector if he came. Hide in the toilet, if necessary. Sneak through the barriers at the other end. Find a battered wife's refuge somewhere, make up a convincing story – and start again. Then, when she had enough cash, head for home.

Home. Another wry thought. Just where was that, exactly?

You can't do that, said the baby in her mind.

"What?" she asked.

Don't speak out loud, said the baby. *You might be overheard and draw attention. Just think it.*

All right, what?

You've got to find the taxi-driver again.

Are you crazy?

The Mechanic got your scent in the taxi. It went after him.

149

In that case, he'll be dead. He couldn't tell it anything.

He's alive. And you have to find him again.

Why, for Christ's sake? He's nothing to us.

That's the point! You still don't understand, do you? After all your time with the Sabbarite, everything you've seen with your own eyes, you still don't understand. I thought you would have learned something.

Don't lecture me, kid! It's not my fault about the taxi-driver. We had to get out of there. For God's sake, it's YOU I'm trying to protect.

But there's a right way and a wrong way.

Who the hell do you think you are, Jiminy Cricket? I'm your mother, remember.

A right way and a wrong way. Putting that taxi-driver in danger was the wrong way. In the long run, that will disadvantage us. I've told you before.

What was I supposed to do? It was right behind us. You were the one yelling at me, in case you've forgotten.

I've had time to think. You should have told him how to protect himself. That would have made things okay.

What about protecting us, kid?

You know what the Serendip is. You know about the scales and balances. We'll never get out of this city alive, unless you observe it – and make good. Find the taxi-driver, set the scales right, and then we might stand some kind of a chance to escape from what we're up against.

Okay, okay. So how do I find him again before the Mechanic gets to him?

I don't know just yet, said the baby in her head. *I have to dream.*

The girl sighed, and slid down the glass door until she was squatting. With one hand, she uncupped a breast from her brassiere, guiding the nipple to the child's nuzzling mouth.

It began to feed, with the same beautiful ecstasy of any child.

And it dreamed.

34

In the short two years since the community centre had been built, it had been burned out three times. On the first two occasions, the local council had managed to secure central government funds via an Inner City Aid programme to repair and refurbish the damaged building. But on the third occasion, the arsonists had performed a thorough job. The centre had been gutted. The fire-engines that turned up that evening to put out the blaze had been stoned by the very kids that the building had been designed to accommodate. This time, central government funds had not been forthcoming, and the council, strapped for cash, had been unable to do anything about it. The beleagured voluntary organisations on the estate had found themselves in the same position. And so, for three months, the burned-out shell had stood in the middle of the estate; windows boarded, covered in graffiti – and awaiting the day that the council could afford to send in the bulldozers to flatten it completely.

Gerry Tomelty picked his way through the charred litter in the centre of the building until he had reached what had once been a raised "stage" area. Most of it had burned and collapsed, but there were still four concrete steps there which had resisted the fire. He climbed them carefully, and looked back.

Two of Gerry's gang stood guard at the boarded door which had been pushed inwards. The others stood amidst the charred debris, waiting to hear what he wanted to tell them. Three of them had torches, and shone them at the steps now.

Gerry laughed. "I call this meeting to order."

The others shuffled uneasily.

"Okay, I'm still pissed off about what happened back there down by the river. One guy – and he made you all look like arseholes."

"Next time . . ." said the skinhead, still holding his gashed face.

"Shut the fuck up!" Gerry's voice seemed to bounce from the walls. He paused, calming himself. He knew that the Man Who Shines Black

151

was listening. Calmly then, he said, "All right . . . all right. This is an important day. Because what I'm going to show you now is the next big step. Andreas and the others think they're in charge on this estate, they think they call all the shots because they control the twinkledust supply. So far, they've been using us to stamp out all the small-fry drug dealing, making sure that they're the only source of supply. And so far, we've been letting that happen, because the backhanders have been good. But that's all going to change. Andreas and his people are going to get a very big fucking surprise shortly. Because we're changing the rules."

Gerry paused for effect. He watched the others shuffle uneasily. Laughing again, he reached into his inside coat pocket and took out the small bag.

"This is new. Never been seen on the streets before – *anywhere.* Not crack, not ecstasy, not acid. But it's better than all of them, and it doesn't give a bad trip, doesn't give side-effects. It's called Nektre. And I'm the only one who can supply it. Andreas and his mob will never have heard of it, and they won't be able to get their hands on it. I'm the sole supplier. Once this hits the streets, no one is going to want anything else. We're going to deal it, undercover."

"What if Andreas finds out we're dealing? Remember those first days? Things were pretty hairy."

"Don't worry. Yeah, I know we can't keep it secret for long. But there's something about this stuff which works in our favour. Something about the . . . chemicals in it. See, once you take this stuff, then it does something to your mind as soon as you've popped it. Look . . . no use my trying to explain. I'll show you. Come up here, Quaid."

"Eh?"

"I said come up here, you fucking moron. This is your chance to make up for letting that bastard down by the river get the drop on you."

Uneasily, the skinhead with the gashed face picked his way through the debris to the stone stairs. Gerry stepped down to meet him, opening the bag.

"Take some."

Quaid hesitated. "You sure about this stuff, Gerry. It ain't poison nor nothing, is it?"

Gerry grabbed him by the collar of his jerkin, and then grabbed his hand.

"Hold it out!"

Quaid held out a trembling hand. Gerry took a pinch of the white powder from the bag and dropped it on his palm.

"Go on then . . ."

Quaid sniffed at it. The others moved forward eagerly to watch. "Do I sniff it, swallow it? What?"

"Stick it up your arse," said one of the others from the darkness. They began to laugh.

"Shut it!" snapped Gerry. Then, turning back to Quaid: "Swallow it."

Apprehensively, face screwed up, Quaid raised his hand to his mouth. Then quickly, he licked it from the palm of his hand.

The others stood silently, watching.

For a moment, Quaid was silent, smacking his lips and looking around. Then his bloodied face creased into a big grin. "Good joke, Gerry. Good joke."

"What?" said one of the others.

"It tastes like *sherbet,*" said Quaid. "Just like kids' sherbet!"

The others wanted to laugh, but the look on Gerry's face prohibited it. He was still staring intently at Quaid, obviously waiting. Quaid hopped from foot to foot, still convinced that he had been the subject of a joke, and waiting for what Gerry was going to say next. When he saw the intense look on Gerry's face, doubt began to register again. "So what happens . . . ?" began Quaid, and then suddenly froze. His face had gone blank, but as the others watched in the gloom, they could see that blankness changing; could see the hint of amusement on Quaid's face, watched as it began to spread into a great, stupid grin.

"How do you feel, Quaid?" asked Gerry.

"Feel?" Quaid sat slowly on the blackened concrete steps. "Feel . . . ?" And then he began to laugh. *"Feel? I . . . feel . . . fucking . . . MARVELLOUS!"* Quaid hugged himself, began rocking like a small child in delight. "Yeah, yeah, yeah . . ."

"Quaid?"

Quaid was feeling his face now, feeling the gash on his face and the dried blood as if it was suddenly somehow a wonderful thing.

"Quaid!"

He looked up at Gerry, still with the idiot grin on his face. Gerry stepped down to him, crouched and looked directly into his eyes.

"Can you hear me?"

" . . . yeah . . ."

"See that wall over there? The one with the burned-out electrical wiring hanging from the ceiling."

" . . . yeah . . ."

"Go over there."

Quaid swung to his feet, still grinning. Arms held wide, he whirled across the littered floor like a child at play. When he reached the wall, he slapped both hands on it, then turned back to face Gerry.

"Feeling good, Quaid?"

"The best, the best. Like I'm coming all the time."

"That's good. Now, I want you to do something for me."

"Yeah?"

"Yeah. I want you to turn around and face the wall."

Quaid turned.

"Now . . . I want you to headbutt that wall, Quaid. I want you to knock yourself out . . ."

Quaid drew himself back, and then lunged at the wall, just as he had been told. Gerry's gang members winced as one at the sound of the wet smack. Soundlessly, Quaid slid down that wall, face first, tangling in the electrical wiring before sliding to the floor.

"Fucking *hell* . . ." said Harry. The others just stood and looked, their mouths open. The two guarding the door had forgotten their sentry duties and had joined the others in the middle of the burned-out room.

"And that's why none of us can use the stuff," said Gerry quietly, climbing the stairs again and turning to face his lieutenants. "It's the best. Gives the best buzz ever. But in the first five minutes that anyone takes it, while it's going into the system, it makes them susceptible to suggestion." Gerry used the Man's own phrase, then decided to rephrase it for the benefit of his gang. "Makes them do anything . . . *anything* you tell them in that first five minutes. So when we push this stuff, it has to be taken straight away. That's a condition of sale. No one gets to take it away and use it later. But I don't reckon we'll have a problem with that – the buzz lasts for eight hours. And no blacks get it. As soon as you get the cash for it, you tell them something. Something I'm going to tell you now."

The others had turned their attention away from Quaid's limp, bleeding form.

"And this is what you tell them. You tell them that Nektre is the only thing they'll ever want again. You tell them that they'll buy no more stuff from anybody else but you. Then you'll tell them to wait for the call."

"The call?" said Johnny.

"Yeah, the call. Because when we're ready, when we've got this stuff well and truly spread around the estate, we give the order. We tell them that they're going to make changes." Gerry's voice had begun to rise with passion. "We tell them they're going to blow the estate apart. We tell them to go out there and run the blacks off the estate. Torch the police stations, the rent offices. Wipe Andreas and his boys out. And I mean *wipe them out.*"

Gerry could see their eyes shining in the dark.

"The bastards think they've seen a riot? Well, they'll *never* have seen a riot like this one. We're going to take the estate. We're going to settle some scores and change everything around. *We* are going to be in charge! We can take anything and anyone we want."

"Jesus, Gerry," said Johnny. "Where does this Nektre stuff come from?"

"From me!" snapped Gerry. "And that's all you need to know. There's plenty of it. I can supply as much as we need. You come to me for it."

The others stood silent.

"But we can't take it?" said Harry.

"Not unless you want to end up like Quaid."

"So let's fucking . . . *do it!*" shouted Johnny.

His call was taken up by the others as they crowded around Gerry on the concrete steps. He held his arms wide as they slapped his palms.

The big buzz was coming.

Well done, Gerry, said the Man Who Shines Black. He had been silent throughout. *You haven't disappointed me. You've done everything as I advised. You're going to be big, Gerry. Very, very big. And you're going to get everything you deserve. You're going to get even. But now . . . now I want you to find someone for me.*

"Who?" asked Gerry in his mind as the others whooped and punched the air.

A young girl . . . and a baby.

35

When she had finished talking, Ranjana reached for her coffee cup and realised that it was cold.

"Two more please," said Randall, waving to the waiter.

It had been the first place they'd found. More like a corner store than a café, with frayed formica tables and the smell of frying bacon constantly hanging in the air no matter what was on the menu. There were only two others in there when they'd entered, an old man and an old woman. Now they were alone.

Ranjana suddenly felt swamped with a terrible feeling of anxiety. When they'd arrived, and this Scottish lad had introduced himself, she'd suddenly started talking; telling him everything that had happened to her. It was as if the attack on her had broken some kind of inner dam, and all the bad stuff inside had bubbled to the surface. She had been unable to stop. Now, after she had bared her soul to this complete stranger, she suddenly felt sick inside. Her hands began to tremble. She gripped them tight, hid them under the table.

"It's okay," said Randall. "Take it easy."

"I'm sorry, I don't usually . . . I don't know what made me tell you so much about . . . I'm sorry."

"Don't be. There's nothing to worry about. Look, you've had a bad shock. You just need a little time. You're going to be okay."

The waitress brought their coffee, gave a look which seemed to suggest that black and white didn't mix, and then went back to her tabloid behind the serving counter.

"We're in the same boat, you and me," said Randall, sipping his coffee.

"What do you mean?"

"You headed down here, not really knowing what you were going to do. So did I."

"I had my friend's address."

"Yeah, but even if she'd still been there, what were you going to do afterwards?"

"Stay a while, sort my head out. Try to get a job and . . . You're right, I hadn't really thought it through. But maybe if she'd been there I could have thought it through a little clearer." Still trembling, Ranjana asked, "So . . . what about you?"

Randall smiled. "Long story." When he looked up, he could see that she somehow *needed* him to compensate for the long story she had already given him. "All right," he said – and told her his story,

At the end, he said, "So you see, I was more vague than you. Still am. Got enough cash to keep me a few weeks. Maybe find some casual labour. Haven't got a trade, more's the pity. The only regular trade from my neck of the woods was professional thieving."

They sipped at their coffees. A long and heavy silence had descended on them. They had both told their stories, there was nothing else to say.

Finally, Ranjana said, "If you hadn't come along . . ."

"Forget it," said Randall. "Look, how are you fixed for money? I can let you have some if you . . ."

"No, thanks. I'll be okay for a little while."

"No you won't. You told me that those two bastards took your bag, and your cash was in it." Randall shoved a handful of notes across the table. Ranjana squirmed, so he took her hand and pressed the money into it.

"I'll pay you back," she said quietly.

"Listen . . ." Randall cleared his throat, drank more coffee. "If you want to tag along with me for a while until you've got your head sorted, I don't mind."

"Oh no, I don't think I could do that."

"No funny business or anything. Just until you're able to . . ."

"No, no thanks."

"Okay, then." Randall cleared his throat again, drank the last of his coffee. "More?"

Ranjana shook her head. Randall stood and made his way to the counter, paying the sullen waitress. As they both left the café, Randall heard her rattle the newspaper at them as the door closed.

On the street, Ranjana said, "Where will I be able to contact you? To pay you back?"

Randall laughed and shrugged. "Like I said, I'm even more vague than you. At the moment, I'm 'No Fixed Abode'. Look . . . there's enough money there to buy you a roof over your head tonight, maybe enough for your train fare home if you change your mind. I know you hate the idea of going back there, but frankly I can't see any other

157

alternative for you. You've already found out for yourself – these are bad streets for a girl on her own."

"But I can't just let you *give* me this money."

"Look, you said you needed time to think. Okay, well tag along with me for a while and give yourself that time. A guy on the streets told me that there are a couple of hostels around here. We could check in there – separate, like – and maybe think about getting a job."

"What kind of job?"

"Well, you can wash dishes, can't you? So can I. We'll find something. Then when you've had a little more time, you can make your mind up about what you want to do, where you want to go."

"I don't know . . ."

"Look, I can't be a rapist, can I?"

Ranjana laughed then. Despite the shock, despite the way she was feeling, it came involuntarily to her lips.

"Okay. Just for a while. Until I can think."

"Great. Let's get a move on then."

Three silent ragged figures with white faces watched them from the other side of the street as they moved on.

36

The fear of failing asleep, knowing that it was still out there looking for him, had finally driven Tony into action.

The exhaustion which threatened to overwhelm him at any moment had also put his fear at arm's length. After an hour listening for the sound of that wind, he had finally got used to the gloom inside the narrow boat. He had explored the interior then, rising from the double steps beyond the aft doors and pushing open the door at his left. It was a Portakabin-type shower, just big enough to stand in. Past this, on the left, another cubicle gave access to a chemical loo. Beyond that, still on the left, a double bed with chintzy curtains at the windows. Walking down the narrow corridor, Tony stepped into an alcove which served as galley. A sink, a refrigerator, two cupboards and a water heater. Beyond the galley, an open space with a battered sofa, two chairs, an ancient television and a stove standing beside the double doors leading up to the foredeck.

Doubling back, Tony pushed open the doors and looked out into the night from the stern. Dark, rippling water lapping at the sides of the boat. Another siren somewhere in the night. But no wind. Tony searched for the control panels, found the throttle inset in the cabin wall beyond the doors. Realising that he had never found time to ask just how you sailed one of these things, Tony pressed ignition and glanced nervously out into the night when the engine coughed into life.

Tony crept back on to the stern, looking around. The boat was still moored to the towpath by ropes at the aft deck and ahead at the foredeck. Quickly hopping to the bank, Tony ran to the foredeck and untied the rope. Keeping low, he darted back to the stern and untied the second, repeating the procedure. Back on board at the stern, he moved to the throttle and tiller. The operation seemed simple enough. Tony shoved the throttle forward and steadied the tiller with his other hand. Cautiously and awkwardly, the boat edged away slowly from the embankment, churning water at the stern. Cursing at the noise, he heaved the tiller over hard and the boat chugged out into the middle of the canal.

Cursing again when he realised that this boat wasn't going to do more than eight miles per hour, Tony jammed the throttle forward and cast anxious glances around him as the narrow boat chugged on into the night. Ahead was a stone arch, and when the boat finally turned slowly into it, Tony could see the outlines of warehouses and sheds on either side of a labyrinthine, twisting waterway ahead. There was no embankment here, only a concrete lip on either side where boats were moored.

Praying, and looking back every few seconds, Tony kept the throttle out, leaning into it as if he could force extra speed from the engine.

37

Mac staggered along the canal embankment, searching the water.

Dragging himself out of that icy water, up the mooring chain, had taken nearly all his reserves of remaining energy, the clothes hanging wet and heavy on his body. He had lain on the towpath, gasping for breath. Finally struggling to his feet, he had staggered back along the canal towards the river, scanning the dirty water for any signs of a floating bundle. When he had reached the small iron bridge giving pedestrian access to the industrial estate, he had crossed over to the other side and continued his search.

When the river came into sight again between the huddled silhouettes of sheds and warehouses, Mac knew that he had lost Bernie. He had no idea how long he had been staggering along this canal in the darkness, could not feel the wet sensation of the canal water on his nerve-damaged outer skin, but could feel the deep ice-cold seeping into his body. He knew then that he had to find somewhere to dry out, or he would surely die of hypothermia. Just ahead, the canal joined the river. Perhaps the fire down by the abandoned jetty was still alight? Mac staggered onwards, heading for the gap between the two warehouses just ahead.

Could he see two ragged shapes between the gap, two street people standing there and watching him?

Hungry faces, Bernie had said. What the hell was that supposed to mean?

A great weariness seemed to be overtaking Mac as he staggered on ahead towards the gap. The figures were moving slowly towards him now.

The cold inside Mac seemed to be freezing his legs. He had lost control of them; they were still walking, but it was as if some other engine was powering them. Mac reeled. The shadows in the gap began to hurry towards him.

Did they have hungry faces?

Mac's legs finally gave out. Blackness rushed to enfold him, like the ice-black waters of the canal. In that instant before oblivion, Mac was sure that time had looped around inside his head. He had not pulled himself out of the canal, had not gone in search of Bernie, had not staggered down to the river. He had plunged into the night-black water and it had enfolded him, had drowned him.

He was dead, at the bottom of the canal – with Bernie.

38

Tony had been travelling since the sun had risen, hoping that daylight would dissipate the dreadful nightmare of the day before. It was easy now to think that whereas something bad had happened back at his lodging house, maybe all that he *thought* had happened, hadn't happened at all. Maybe he'd somehow inadvertently taken a drug. What did you call them? Hallucinogens, or something. Maybe someone had put something into his booze. He had no idea who it could have been, or why, but surely this was the best explanation for what had happened? But the fear remained, even though the sun had risen. And the boat continued on up the canalways at its infuriatingly slow pace.He remembered idly reading a brochure a long time ago about the charms of a narrow boat holiday. The sedate pace, the calm and tranquillity. At the time, he had quite liked the idea of getting away from it all on his own, hiring a boat and cruising slowly away up the waterways. Now, all he wanted was a bloody outboard motor fitted to the back of this thing.

He had found the canal and waterway maps inside, just as Larry had told him. Ideally, he'd wanted a straight run – right out of the city and beyond. But the inner city canals were much more labyrinthine than he'd imagined, and he'd made agonisingly slow progress. There were too many bloody locks! The process of mooring the boat and opening and closing the bloody locks before passing through, had only served to fuel his anxiety. If he'd had any cash in his pockets, then he would have abandoned the boat and made straight for the nearest car rental agency, got himself the fastest model available and just got the hell out of the city, driving north until he hit John O'Groats. But he had left everything behind in the lodging house (or what was left of it). Maybe the place was untouched, maybe the fire and the explosions had all been part of this drug-induced nightmare. Maybe the best thing to do was to head back to the lodging house, check it out in the cold light of day.

The fear in his guts cancelled that thought immediately.

In the three agonisingly slow hours that he had been travelling, Tony had spent all his time at the helm, trying to rationalise and make sense of everything that had happened to him. Although the drugs option seemed to make the most sense, eventually it had become almost impossible to think about it all. As if his mind had decided that it would shut down on the whole business, crowd it out of his brain. Tony decided that the only way he would be able to sort this out was to find a bottle of malt whisky and consume it. Maybe then everything would click into place. For God's sake, he couldn't stay on this boat for ever! He had found some tinned food in the cupboard, had consumed it cold when he realised just how hungry he had become.

At four p.m. two things happened that brought the cold fear flooding back again.

First, it began to rain. At first only pattering into the canal, but finally sheeting down until a great grey-white mist seemed to rise from the canal to meet it. There had been no waterproofs inside the boat. Instead, Tony had wrapped himself in a spare blanket from one of the cupboards and stayed up top, steering. Soon, he had become soaked to the skin. The rain was unrelenting, making it difficult to see ahead through the twisting concrete canyons of dilapidated businesses and warehouses. The buildings on either side now seemed to tower over the boat as it passed; great, grey featureless monoliths in the rain. Tony began to feel claustrophobic as the narrow boat chugged on, the canal seeming to be an insignificant trickle in comparison. What if those warehouses suddenly shunted inwards? What if they slowly began to move in towards him? Eventually meeting in the canal, crushing the boat between them . . .

"Stupid bastard . . ." said Tony quietly to himself through clenched teeth.

And then the engine cut out.

Tony tugged at the lever. Nothing. He ducked down and pushed the ignition switch on and off several times. There was no response. The boat had slowed, if that was possible, and was drifting into the centre of the canal, which was already narrow here.

"Shit!"

Tony steered it in to the side, quickly leaning over to check that there were no other boats moored here. It was hard to tell in the grey hissing frenzy of rain on the canal surface and the thick grey canopy above. The narrow boat juddered against the concrete side of the canal. Cursing, Tony clambered on to the gangway rail running the length of the boat's side until he'd reached the foredeck, the canal edge almost parallel with the deck. Quickly hopping landward, Tony seized the mooring rope and ran ahead to the first iron ring he could see set into the ground. It was a difficult manoeuvre here. There was only three feet of walkway. Pulling the rope through the ring, Tony put his foot on it and held fast as the narrow boat slowly moved on past him. When the rope sprang taut, he held it tighter. The boat stopped. Springing back on to the boat's side and grabbing the handrail, he hurried aft and grabbed the mooring rope there. In moments, he had secured it to another ring and pulled the boat up close to the canal.

Back on board, Tony looked around but could see little detail in this concrete canyon. There were small alleyways between the buildings giving access to the canal. Could a gusting wind . . . ?

"Oh Christ . . ." The fear was real and alive as Tony yanked the aft double doors open and slipped inside. The rain sounded preternaturally loud on the roof of the boat; small hammer-blows by a horde of midget demons. The windows were fogged. Tony quickly wiped the canal-side windows. He wanted to see those alleyways.

There was a figure standing in the alleyway directly in front of him, rain forming a dense mist all around it.

The figure was bulky, wearing what seemed to be a waterproof coat and hood. It was just standing, watching him – although he could see no details of the face. Tony had never seen the figure before, but the horror of what he had been through, what he had seen and experienced, crowded in on him. He recoiled from the window.

Just a tramp. Or another boat owner come down here to check on their boat. That's all.

Tony saw the figure come on slowly towards him.

This wasn't the figure he had seen back in his flat, wasn't remotely like it. There was no horrifying, whirling wind. This figure *couldn't* be connected with any of it.

Using anger to try and swamp the fear, Tony blundered to the galley and pulled open the drawers. There was a breadknife in there; blunted but still pretty impressive. Tony grabbed it and hurried back to the aft doors. He yanked them open, admitting a blast of rain. Out on the deck, he turned and faced the cowled figure which steadfastly approached the boat, hooded head held down.

Bracing one foot against the rim of the boat, he steadied himself with one hand on the tiller. His heart was racing as he raised the breadknife in front of him.

"That's far enough!" he shouted.

The hooded figure stopped.

It made a strange, mewing sound.

Tony shifted uneasily, moving the knife to his other hand. Rain hammered on the roofs of the warehouses and the boat, raising a blanket of hissing white foam on the water. Tony saw a fog of breath emerge from the hood.

And then the figure's coat opened magically in the centre, and the hood was tossed back quickly from the head.

"Oh *shit!*" said Tony.

The girl was holding the child to her breast with one arm under the coat. She brought the other hand up slowly from inside that coat, empty sleeves dangling around her shoulders – and raised a familiar pistol in Tony's direction. Her face was white, but utterly impassive, and absolutely unmistakable as the same girl who had hijacked his taxi and started this whole nightmare rolling.

Tony could not move.

The girl raised the gun – and pointed it directly at his face.

PART THREE

THE SABBARITE

39

"What the hell do you *want* from me?" said Tony in bewilderment.

"Let me on board." That same American accent.

Tony backed away from the rail as the girl walked slowly towards him through the rain. The gun never wavered. Again, it looked much too big for her hand. Water began to drip from the end of the barrel. The child made a small noise against her breast, the mewing sound that had so unnerved Tony before. The girl reached the canal edge.

"Okay, throw the knife overboard."

Tony hesitated.

"I said *throw* it!"

Tony dropped it into the hissing water. The girl stood there for a while, trying to decide how she was going to make the difficult steps down on to the boat with a gun in one hand and a child in the other.

"I know, I *know*!" she snapped.

"What?"

"Not you. I was talking to the baby. Now, stand back against the far rail – and don't move an inch, understand? If you do, I'll just blow you off this boat. Understand?"

Tony nodded.

"Good." Tony watched the girl chewing her lip, as he stood back with both hands behind him on the far rail. If she bungled it, if she slipped, she would have to grab for the child and then he would . . .

But before he could really think it through, the girl had stepped quickly off the edge and had landed heavily on the deck. Her feet almost skidded in the rain, the too-large coat flapping around her and spraying water – but she quickly compensated, and the gun was still levelled at him.

"First the taxi," said Tony. "Now the boat. Listen, if you're running from somebody again, this thing only does eight miles an hour. You'll never . . ."

169

"Shut up and get inside." The girl motioned with the pistol towards the double doors.

"Bloody *hell*!" shouted Tony into the rain, anger swelling within him despite the gun. "I am sick to death of you and your bloody gun. Why the hell can't you just leave me alone? You turn up with your bloody kid and my whole world's been turned upside down. Look, just do yourself a favour and . . ."

Tony saw the girl exerting pressure on the gun, and his voice was snatched away. She twitched the barrel aside and squeezed the trigger. The gunshot was shockingly loud. A spray of water exploded from the canal three feet from where Tony stood, echoes of the gunshot ratcheting and clattering away down the concrete canyon of warehouses and sheds. Tony was shocked into silence. The child drew breath, was on the verge of squalling into shocked tears, and then the girl said, "It's okay, Sparrow. That was just a warning shot for him. He gets the next one between the eyes. Now – you – inside!"

Tony pushed himself away from the rail and down into the boat.

"Annie-Fucking-Oakley . . ."

"Shut up!"

Tony walked straight on in without looking back, heard the girl blundering into the boat after him, cursing as she barked her shins on the steps. He heard the doors being slammed shut.

"Someone will have heard that shot," he said without turning around.

"They'll think it's thunder. Haven't you noticed the rain? Listen, does that stove work?"

"I don't know."

"Well, is this your boat, or isn't it?"

"It isn't."

"Well, see what you can do about lighting it. We're both freezing to death waiting for you."

"*Waiting* for me?"

"The stove?"

Tony turned and saw that the girl was sitting on the sofa, carefully cradling the child but with the omnipresent gun still held where it could do him most damage if needs must. Tony moved to the stove. There was a pile of home-cut wood piled next to it; matches, newspaper and something that looked like a small bellows. He set about lighting the fire.

"All the comforts of home, eh?" said the girl at last.

"Are you joking, or what? In case you didn't know, I'm on the run. Running from something I'm starting to wonder I just dreamed about."

"You and me both. What?"

"What do you mean – 'What?' "

"Shut up, I'm talking to the kid."

Tony watched incredulously as the girl, still keeping a close eye on him, glanced repeatedly down at the child nestling at her breast – as if it was talking to her.

"I know, I *know!*" she snapped at it.

Drugs, thought Tony. *I was right all along. And I bet everything that's happened to me since I picked her up, everything I think I've seen and experienced, has to do with her. Somehow, she's managed to get those same drugs into my system. Maybe she jabbed me with a hypo or something in the taxi when I wasn't looking . . .*

"You think I'm a psycho," said the girl calmly. "Don't you?"

"No," said Tony sarcastically. "Why the hell should I think that?"

"Light the fire. Got anything to drink?"

"Tea or coffee."

"No booze?"

"I should wish."

"Okay, light the fire first. The reason we're reacquainted is 'cause of Sparrow."

Tony continued working at the stove. "Sparrow," he said.

"The kid, yeah. That's his name. If it wasn't for him, I wouldn't be here. Believe me."

"And if it wasn't for you . . ."

"Shut up and listen. There are a lot of things I've got to tell you, and we haven't got a whole lot of time. So now you know my son's name. My name is Lauren. Once upon a time I was called Lauren Morris. But when I got mixed up with . . . them . . . I lost my second name. Okay, so who are you?"

"Dandridge," said Tony. "Tony Dandridge. And before I got mixed up with you I had a—"

"I'm warning you, Tony. We don't have much time. And not enough for interruptions."

"So pardon the fuck out of me."

"Granted. Look, I'm sorry. I didn't want any of this to happen to you. I had to get away, and you were there. I didn't think for a minute that once we'd lost it, it would go after you."

"You mean that thing's *real*, and I didn't imagine it."

"Wait, wait! I'm not joking. Time's tight, and there's a lot to tell you. But yes – you didn't imagine anything, and frankly I'm surprised that you're still around. I don't know how you managed to get away from it but . . . What?" The girl looked at the baby again. "Oh yeah, the rain. It's rained a lot since then. That's the answer."

"What the hell are you talking about?"

171

"Okay, beginnings. You a religious man?"

"Is this going to be more riddles?"

"Nope."

"All right. No, I'm not."

"You should be. It's safer, believe me. Anyway . . . have you heard of The Latter Day Church of the Sabbarite?"

Tony grunted in the negative and continued with the fire.

"Okay, they were founded by one Pearce Ramsden back in about 1967 at the height of Flower Power. They're now highly organised. Strictly an English concern, but with international aspirations that they're working on at present. They're dedicated to the salvation of the forlorn. That mean anything to you? No? Well, basically they provide food and shelter and support for the homeless. For itinerants and tramps and hobos and runaways who find themselves on the streets of the big city.

"They've got churches and missions all over the place. Chances are that someone's probably waved a collecting tin at you. I was one of them – once."

Great, thought Tony. *A religious freak. With a gun.*

"I'm American," continued Lauren. "From Pennsylvania originally . . . look, are you *sure* I should be telling him all this?"

"What?"

"Not you!" snapped the girl. She looked down at the baby again, then sighed impatiently, looking out of the window and into the rain. "Okay . . . I got into some family trouble over there. You don't need to know about *that*. Bad things were happening to me, I didn't have anywhere to go, no one to turn to. So I used what money I could scrape together to buy a one-way ticket to England. Didn't have any real plans, other than to get away. Once I got here – about two years ago – it was literally a case of: 'Out of the frying pan, into the fire.' I ended up on the streets; homeless, starving. Then I came across one of the Sabbarite missions, went in there basically 'cause I needed a place to sleep and something to eat. There was a service going on, but like nothing I'd ever seen back home. The guy in charge, who was giving the sermon, took a personal interest in me. They took me in." The girl laughed bitterly. "Boy, did they take me in."

Tony had succeeded in getting a flame. He used the small bellows at the side of the wood-pile to fan it. There was a larger chunk of wood down here that hadn't been chopped up yet. It was heavy enough. Maybe if he let her go on, let her guard drop, he could fling it into her face . . .

"The guy up in that pulpit was preaching a different creed. No God, no Devil. No Heaven, no Hell. But definitely a higher force beyond understanding. If we asked no questions about this Benefactor, only pledged ourselves to the Sabbarite, then our hearts would be opened and we would 'Receive and Be Thankful'. I was tired, desperate – and maybe because of that I really did open myself up there in that church. I said, 'Okay, I'll take you on your word.' The guy in the pulpit looked straight at me – and believe me that church was *full* – and I felt it happen. *Something* seemed to . . . overwhelm me. I was engulfed in this feeling of well-being, of satisfaction, of . . . well, this is crazy, but there was a sex thing there, too. What he'd said would happen, had happened. So I stayed, and the Sabbarite took me under their wing.

"A lot of things happened after that. Know anything about religious cults and brainwashing and all that stuff?"

"Just what I've seen on television. Just what I heard about Waco, Texas."

"Yeah, right. Well, I was sucked right into it. There was more going on there than I could ever have imagined. I lost my own personality. The guy in the pulpit? Well, that was Pearce Ramsden himself, the founder of the movement. He took me as his wife. There were others. Like the Mormons. From that moment, everything in me just seemed to . . . glaze over. That's the only way I can describe it. Listen, can you imagine what it's like? People go to this church and listen to this guy, and they really do *feel* something. If you felt it, you'd want to know more, you'd want to be part of it."

Tony finished with the bellows, looked at the chunk of wood as he closed the fire-door.

"Okay," said Lauren. "How about some coffee?"

Tony stood up slowly, then turned and headed for the kitchen alcove.

"Look, mister. Don't get any funny ideas. Apparently, I have to tell you these things. But if you get any more brainwaves about things in kitchen drawers, or throwing hot water or cans of stuff at me I can easily splatter you with this gun. Believe me. So keep your actions slow and keep your hands in view. When the coffee's ready, leave it there and come back here. I'll go get it."

Tony plugged in the kettle and turned to look at her again, leaning with his back to the bench.

"Hands in front of you, please."

Tony locked his fingers in front of him.

"Ramsden made me pregnant. Deliberately. It wasn't his first child. I was living in this twilight world – and then one day I found out what the Sabbarite were *really* doing, how they *really* got their power. When they knew I'd found out, they couldn't get rid of me – because I was carrying Ramsden's special child – so they locked me up. For six months. They pumped me full of something to keep me quiet. Some kind of drug."

The girl was silent for a moment, her face a white mask of anger. Her reverie seemed to have been interrupted by something she'd heard. She looked down at the child again. "Yeah . . . all right. So this is what I found out, Mr Dandridge. You won't thank me for the knowledge, since it puts you even further into the shit than you already are."

"You mean it could be worse?"

Lauren laughed, a sound without humour. "Oh yes, Mr Dandridge. A whole lot worse. The Latter Day Church of the Sabbarite doesn't have God, or the Devil, or the good tooth fairy. It has the Benefactor. Like I said, no one questions who or what it is, that's the central core of the faith. That faith relates neither to good nor evil. The Benefactor must remain unknown and in return for the faith of its followers, it brings good health and wealth. But there are two separate layers of the faith – an Outer Circle and an Inner Circle.

"The Outer Circle are those who organise and operate the churches and missions, the street collections, the handouts. They're the ones, like me, who first come into the faith. They may remain simply as worshippers, may actually become involved in the organisation itself. They come from all walks of life, from the despairing to the curious to the disaffected to the idle rich. The Outer Circle acts as a kind of net where the funds are obtained and the recruitment begins. But the real Sabbarite, the real faith, the ones whom Ramsden chose to be the Elite with the Knowledge, form the Inner Circle. Kettle's boiling. Keep your hands in view . . .

"The Outer Circle is the upfront, Salvation Army-type operation. And the good vibes, the feeling of well-being that are conjured up and communicated to the brethren of that circle – yes, we're talking supernatural stuff here whether you like it or not – are conjured up by the activities of the Inner Circle. Now understand, only the people at the *top* of the Outer Circle know about the existence of the Inner Circle at all. When they've proved themselves, when they can be trusted, then they just might be accepted into that higher brethren."

"Like freemasonry . . ."

"Right. But this is something else altogether, this is . . . okay, okay!" Lauren was snapping at the child again. "I'll tell it in my own way. So . . . I found out about the Inner Circle, and what they do that generates this pleasure power, this wealth power, this fortune power."

"Which is?"

Lauren's face was grim again. She looked down and rocked the child gently. Tony looked at the scalding hot cup of coffee beside him.

"They kill people," said Lauren simply.

There was a silence then, broken only when the girl said, "Okay, move away. Come over here slowly and sit down." Tony did as he was told. Lauren watched him carefully all the way, rising stiffly and moving to the kitchen alcove. She put the gun carefully down on the bench next to her so that she could grab it easily if necessary. Then she picked up the cup and sipped at her coffee eagerly, never taking her eyes from him. "That's good . . ."

"So . . . they kill people."

"Uh-hmm. Mainly the very people that the Outer Circle seeks to help. That's all part of the sick plan, see? The Outer Circle draws them in, the Sabbarite soup vans go out regularly and find the regular pitches where vagrants and street people gather – just like the other voluntary organisations. But every once in a while, members of the Inner Circle take a van out, and when they can find someone alone, someone vulnerable – they'll kidnap them, take them somewhere . . . and kill them."

"Why, for God's sake?"

"Come on, can't you guess? It's easy. Sacrifice, what else. They've found that if they do it, if they go out and kill someone specifically for the benefit of the Benefactor, then the Benefactor rewards them. The act of killing like that *pleases* it, and it gives favours in return. It enhances everything for its Inner Circle members. Health, sexual prowess and satisfaction, wealth. Yeah, it can provide wealth too, it can manipulate people's fortune . . . I've seen it done. It can play the balance of the Serendip."

"The what?"

"The Serendip . . . oh, yeah." Again, another quick glance at the child. "Sparrow says that's too complicated for now. Forget it."

"What is it with the kid? Is it *talking* to you or something?"

"Or something," replied Lauren. "Yeah, I know it looks crazy. But he can talk to me – inside my head. Like I said, this is Ramsden's son. And Ramsden's kids always have special powers. He's the reason I'm here. He didn't like what we did to you, wanted things set straight, so the Serendip could balance out . . . but like I said, forget about that for now."

"So this Inner Circle – they kidnap people and kill them, sacrifice them. Because it gives them power?"

"Not just people. Vagrants, runaways, street people. People without connections, without family. People who won't be noticed. Who's going to miss someone who vanishes from the street if they've already gone missing once?"

"And they locked you up when you found out?"

"These people have special powers. That 'glazed-over' existence I was living had been conjured up deliberately for me. They kept it going with the drugs. So I wouldn't question, just do everything that was required of me. Give birth. Give him the son he wanted. All his other kids were female." Lauren laughed. "That was something even they didn't have control over. Eventually, they began to withhold the drugs – for the sake of the baby. That's when I heard and saw things. Then I found out what they'd got planned for my baby.

"Sacrifice is a powerful thing. Barbaric, but in return the Benefactor would give them everything. Ramsden was going to sacrifice my baby in a ritual to enhance his own power. Killing his 'own seed' had some kind of significance. He'd done it before. Six times. He had only one surviving daughter. I saw what she was used for. She should never have been born.

"So, I found out. They realised, and locked me away in a fucking cell in one of their missions. Four storeys up. The baby was born – and it wasn't easy. I thought they'd take him from me, but they didn't. They knew he had to be loved and fed and cared for. So they let me keep him. But they wouldn't let me give him a name. That was part of the ritual, part of that obeisance to the great Anonymous One. It was important that the child have no personality, see? It had to remain Ramsden's 'flesh'.

"The boy was about two months old. I thought I would go insane with fear,waiting for the time they'd come and take him away from me. Then one day, early evening . . . there was this noise beside the window. There was only one window in that room: a small window, with bars on it – naturally. And there was a bird sitting on the ledge, just beyond the bars. I swear, it was singing to me. It just sat there, with the sun going down and these big, long shadows creeping into the room, and the lovely orange light behind it. And it sang to me. And sang . . ."

Lauren seemed to have drifted away. Tony shifted in his seat. With astonishing speed, Lauren snatched the gun from the counter again, eyes flashing. When she saw that it was not a move towards her, she continued: "It was a sparrow. Just a sparrow. But it seemed so important. We were imprisoned there, waiting for death. Both of us. But even in that fucking hell-hole, something that was insignificant and small – but *free* – had found us and was letting us know what it was like to be free. That's how Sparrow got his name. His secret name. Between me and him." Lauren's face tightened. Tony could see the raw emotion there, saw a muscle twitch in her cheek where she clenched her teeth. "That sound like a stupid name to you?"

"Not when you tell the story like that."

176

Lauren relaxed. Slowly, she placed the gun down again and drank more coffee, eyes still steadfastly fixed on him.

"Know what it's like? Locked in for months and waiting for the moment they come for you? Every time the door opens? When they bring your food, and you're so sick with fear you can hardly eat. They force-fed me once, the bastards. For the sake of the child's milk. I vowed that would never happen again. Know what that's like, waiting for death?"

"I know what it's like to be chased by something out of a nightmare that just wants to tear me to pieces. Like it did to my landlord, by the way."

"It killed someone else?"

"Ripped him apart."

"Why didn't you know that, Sparrow? It's taken blood. Will that make a difference?" Lauren paused to listen. "He says he needs time to think about that."

"I can't believe I'm hearing this . . ."

"You'd *better* believe it, mister! That's why we're here. No other reason."

"What the hell is the thing that's after me?"

"It's called a Mechanic."

"A what?"

"Do you believe in Hell?"

Confused and angry, Tony made a helpless gesture with his hands. Lauren grabbed the gun again.

"Look, you're talking in riddles again," said Tony.

"You better believe in it, Dandridge. Because it really *is* a place. It exists. Ramsden visited regularly. And there are things there that I wouldn't want to believe about, but just trying to ignore it only makes us ignorant . . . and vulnerable. The Sabbarite had access to that place via the Benefactor. They could make use of its special resources. Good word, eh? That's the word Ramsden used all the time."

"Okay, what's a Mechanic?"

"It's a hit man. A hit man from Hell. Simple as that. They want to bump someone off for a special reason, someone they can't find – then they use some of the sacrifices, some of the power received from their ritual killings to conjure up a Mechanic from Hell. It's like a trade. So many deaths for the use of a Mechanic. They send it out to find and kill someone. Once it finds them and disposes of them, it goes back to where it came from. Back to Hell."

"A hit man from Hell," said Tony incredulously.

"Conjured up to hunt, torture and kill," continued Lauren. "Once it's conjured, it *must* have blood before it can go back. Know what it *really* is? It's a damned soul, suffering torment. The killing eases its hideous suffering for a fraction of a second while it's here, away from an eternity of pain."

"They conjured this thing up – and sent it after you?"

"I got away. Bad things happened to Ramsden. His bad luck was my good luck. I didn't know this, but Ramsden was getting out of control. His personal excesses began to worry the other members of the Inner Circle. He was in charge, was the founder of the movement, had first contacted the Benefactor. But even though the Inner Circle were in awe of him, they became afraid that these excesses would reveal the Sabbarite organisation to the world, would blow their real undercover activities. He began to . . . do things . . . that even the Sabbarite would baulk at. Know about Caligula? Never mind. They began to think that he had his own hidden agenda, that he was pursuing other goals apart from the Sabbarite, that he was losing control of the power.

"Round about then, Sparrow began to speak to me in my mind. Yeah, it sounds fucking crazy, I know. But I'd been through so much, seen and experienced so much it didn't seem unusual to me. I reckon round about then I wasn't in my right mind anyway. Waiting for us to die had turned my mind, or something. I didn't ask how he could talk to me like that when he was just a baby. But like I said, Ramsden's children all had special powers. Sparrow's power was even more special. Now I know why."

"Why?"

"Simple. Ramsden didn't want to die. Didn't want to have his soul eaten up by those things that live in the place you don't believe in. So it was vital that *this* child should have very special spiritual qualities, vital that he be able to give them a very special sacrifice if needs be. But in creating that child as an offering, he underestimated how the kid's power would give him the ability to think for himself. So Sparrow was able to tap into their minds, and find out what was going on. Then the big day came.

"Sparrow found out we had about three weeks before Ramsden was due to do it. But he wanted to bring the date forward. Wanted to do it straight away. Now, understand, he had been telling them all that they had to wait for a specific day and a specific time for the sacrifice if the Inner Circle were going to reap the full reward from the Benefactor. Now, he was changing all that, wanting to hurry ahead with our murder, the bastard. So they were nervous. They felt that he was up to something else. The hidden agenda again. There was only one thing they could do.

"Ramsden was their leader. Had set them up. Had shown them what to do. And they felt confident now in their dealings with the Anonymous Benefactor."

"So they killed him."

Lauren gave a matter-of-fact nod of the head, drank more coffee. The child squirmed at her breast.

"You still thinking, Sparrow?" continued Lauren. "Good . . . anyway, it must have been a spur of the moment thing. Like I say, they were still very much in awe of him. There was a gathering in the mission where we were imprisoned. Sparrow guesses that Ramsden had come there and then to take him away and do the killing. We heard the argument going on downstairs when someone brought our food. Something broke. Glass, I think. Then there was shouting. Sparrow told me to move quick when one of the two guys who'd brought me a tray of food dashed away downstairs and the other one went back to the door to see what was happening. Then I heard the sounds of a struggle – and someone started to scream. That's when I ran hard at this guy, threw myself at him. He hit the wall face first and went down like a thirteen-stone sack of bird shit. I grabbed the gun that this guy had dropped, grabbed Sparrow and then we took off. All hell was let loose somewhere downstairs. One of the Sabbarite women was screaming and someone else was telling her to shut the hell up. There was a fire escape at the other end of the corridor. I kicked out the window and we went down there. Nearly fell ass over tit more than once, but we hit the street and were away. What with all the screaming and everything, they never knew we'd gone.

"We'd been on the streets for maybe two days, hiding out, knowing the Sabbarite would be out there looking for us. Then Sparrow told me he'd tuned in to them and found out. They'd conjured up a Mechanic. To kill me and take him back. Ramsden was dead, so he couldn't do what he wanted to my son. But the Sabbarite still knew that sacrificing Sparrow – Ramsden's special flesh – would bring them enormous advantages from the Benefactor. So they had to have him back. We were on the run. Hiding in some burned-out slum building, when Sparrow told us that the Mechanic had found our scent and was after us. I'd seen what a Mechanic could do, wondered whether we shouldn't just end it for us both there and then.

"But we ran. It wasn't far behind us. And then I saw the taxi. *Your* taxi . . ."

"Thanks for choosing me to share your nightmares . . ."

"I didn't have a choice. It was right behind us."

"So why the hell did it come after *me*?"

"It lost us. But the Mechanic has a kind of telepathic link with the people who've conjured it up. It reports back. Can tell them what it sees. Obviously, it saw the taxi. Got the registration. By that time, we'd gone. All the Sabbarite could do was reconjure it and send it to you."

"What do you mean reconjure? I thought the thing had *your* scent, not mine?"

"Know anything about bloodhounds? The kid thinks it has something to do with water. Dogs can't follow a trail through water. For some reason, it seems that the Mechanic can't do it either. See that out there?" Lauren waved at the windows. Tony looked out into the hissing grey blur.

"Rain."

"Exactly. It had begun to rain that night. It wiped our trail, threw the Mechanic right off our scent. When that happened, Sparrow was able to use his power to keep the thing temporarily confused about where we were. All they had to go on was you. So they reconjured it on *your* scent. They couldn't believe that we'd escaped without any help. They were convinced you must be involved somehow. They had to find me, and especially Sparrow. You were their only lead. Now that the Mechanic has been reconjured, it's much more powerful."

"So that thing is still out there, still looking for me?"

"You couldn't have picked a better hiding place, Tony. On water. Where the Mechanic can't scent you, can't get to you. It can't cross a body of water. Did you know that?" Lauren laughed. "Just like a vampire."

"Now you're talking vampires . . ."

Lauren's laughter dried. "Believe me, there are far worse things out there. Stop worrying, Dandridge. You're on water – and look at that downpour. You couldn't be safer. Anyway, Sparrow and I are the ones it wants."

"So pardon me while I cry all over the floor. I don't want to be in this mess – and you're the one who put me in it." *Wait a second, wait a second – has she got me BELIEVING in all this?*

"That's the way it is," continued Lauren. "And that's why . . ."

Suddenly, she held a hand out to silence Tony. "Wait . . . what do you mean, Sparrow? What? The Serendip *isn't* balanced. Well, this was your idea, for crying out loud! What do you mean . . . what?!"

"What the hell is going on?"

"He brought me here because of the Serendip balance. Said I had to tell you what was going on so you could protect yourself. So now you know. Keep on the water and you're safe. Now he's saying there's more to it. Well, what . . . ? *What?*"

This is insane! thought Tony. *But keep cool, now that she's told you all this crap she might just disappear. Yeah?* said another voice inside.

180

And what about that . . . that Mechanic? Drugs, said the other voice. *Like you thought, you're on a bad trip. She got some stuff inside you somehow, and that's what this has all been about. Just stay here, let this crazy American woman and her baby let off steam and then go. After that, you can sleep it all off, get the stuff out of your system. Wake up to a normal world again, go back to your lodging house and start over again.*

"I don't believe this," said Lauren.

"Okay, what?"

"Sparrow says that he's found out more about the balance. Seems like you and I were made for each other, honey."

"What the hell are you talking about now?"

"Sparrow says that we have to stick together. The three of us. You're here to help us. That's what the Serendip says."

"*I'm* here to help *you*?"

"That's the way it is."

"Look, you've found me and you've told me your life story. Now why don't you just take your kid and your cannon and get the hell off my boat?"

"You sure about this, Sparrow? Sparrow . . . ?"

The child was squirming uncomfortably at her breast.

"What is it, baby? Something else?"

The child made one small sound. A very ordinary, child-like moan of discomfort. Lauren shifted so that she could hitch the child further up into her arm. When she looked at Tony again, he could see that her face had somehow changed colour. The blood had drained from her face, her skin was putty-coloured.

"Oh, Christ . . ." she moaned.

"What? What is it?"

"The Mechanic is coming."

Now instinctively thrown into the logic of the nightmare again, Tony said, "How? You said the canal and the rain would confuse it, keep it away . . ."

Lauren paused again, as if listening to the child. She moved quickly to the window and looked out into the hissing blur of rain. "I know . . . I know . . ."

"How close is it?"

"Sparrow says close. Very close. And moving fast."

"But how . . . ?"

"Oh God, I can see what's happened. Yeah . . . it's lost the scent in the rain. Can't find you because you're on water. But it followed your scent to the canal, *knows* that you took a boat. Even though it can't scent you or see you, it knows you're somewhere on the canal. So it's been *following the canal*."

Tony stood up quickly. This time, the gun didn't swivel in his direction, and Tony didn't think about taking advantage of it.

"Can it still find us then?"

"No . . . no . . . it can't. It'll be blind. Like I said, the canal and the rain. It'll just go straight on by. Yes, that's right. It'll be okay. It'll be . . . oh *Christ!*"

"What?"

"The boat's moored to the side of the canal. By those ropes."

"So?"

"We're still *tied to the land*! We've got to be afloat in the water, Dandridge! For God's sake, get out there and cast off! If it reaches us while we're still tied up there, it'll scent you for sure! It'll be able to get us! For God's sake, cast off!"

Tony stood, uncomprehending. The chunk of wood that he had managed to hide behind his back all this time fell forgotten to the floor as he moved to the window.

"Go on, go on!" Lauren gave him a hard shove, and Tony blundered to the double doors again, swinging them wide and admitting a spray of rain.

"But the bloody boat won't start!" snapped Tony. "The engine cut out . . ."

"Sparrow did that, you idiot! It'll start okay now!"

"The kid . . . ?"

"Go on!"

Crazy, this is all too crazy to be true! This was his chance.

Tony whirled and kicked the nearest of the double doors back in the girl's face. As they slammed, he heard her cry of pain and alarm, and jumped awkwardly from the deck to the concrete lip of the canal. His feet skidded, but he quickly regained and dashed down the narrow alley ahead, where the girl had first approached. Behind him, he heard a curse, and the sounds of the doors being flung open as she regained her balance and clambered out on to the deck. Tony ducked low and dodged from side to side, from wall to wall.

"Come back, you idiot!" yelled the girl.

And then something exploded up ahead in the dense rain-mist.

The gun! The girl had fired at him, the bullet ricocheting against the corrugated metal warehouse walls. Tony threw himself from side to side with greater speed, his heart hammering. Please God, he'd soon be lost to sight in this hissing, enveloping rain,

"For Christ's sake, look up ahead!" screamed the girl.

And this time, he did look up when a roaring wind seemed to explode into the alleyway. The blast was cold and fetid, bringing with it a familiar, instinctive terror. Somewhere, a window exploded with a

182

coughing roar of broken glass. Tony froze in his tracks, hearing a clanging cacophony of steel pipes being rended and hurled to the ground. Somewhere, masonry cracked and tumbled. The walls on either side of him seemed to tremble with the vibration. Old newspapers and street litter suddenly engulfed him, a centre-page wrapping itself around his head. He tore it away . . . and saw something up ahead in the rain-mist.

A blurring movement, a dark silhouette – striding towards him through the hell-wind.

The sight of it threatened to rob him of the strength to move.

"*Come ON!*" screamed the girl from the deckway. Her shout galvanised him.

Tony turned and darted back the way he'd come. He could see that she was struggling with the mooring rope aft.

Now she could see him dashing out of the rain-mist straight towards her.

She raised the gun at him.

"*For Christ's sake . . . .!*" Tony staggered and weaved. He could never avoid the bullet.

The gun erupted, spitting a deadly yellow spark above his head.

Heart pumping, Tony ran on, realising that she had been shooting at the thing which advanced down the alley. Another blast of air from behind seemed filled with anger at this weak and hopeless act of defence. It served to fling him forward and he saw the girl's feet skid on the deck. She regained her balance, and had almost slipped the mooring rope free when Tony all but fell onto the mooring pin on the canal edge.

He had a flash-view of her white, terrified face – knew that she could see the thing right behind him. There was no time.

"*Start the engine!*" he screamed into her face. "*The ignition button!*"

Lauren followed the motion of his frantically stabbing finger, saw the red ignition button and jammed it hard. The engine coughed into life.

Tony dragged the rope free and flung it hard out across the canal. Leaping to his feet, he kicked at the boat-rail hard, shoving it only a few feet from the edge. Lauren wrestled awkwardly with the tiller, but Tony had no time to explain. Behind him, something howled in the hell-wind. He could feel its breath on his back.

Tony launched himself towards the second mooring rope, saw that the narrow boat was beginning to swing out away from the edge and into the canal. If the last mooring rope pulled taut, with the engine straining to be away, then he would never be able to untie it from the pin. They'd remain moored, and that thing would—

Something screamed with hellish ferocity and hate, directly behind him.

Tony screamed too when something that seemed to be made of glass sliced down his back from neck-collar to waist, clean-slicing his shirt and jacket apart and carving a deep furrow in his flesh. Tony fell away from this horrific, clutching grasp, kicked and rolled on top of the mooring pin – and yanked it free. Refusing to look at the horror which he knew must be right on top of him, Tony kicked hard with both legs against the concrete lip, hurling himself backwards over the edge, still gripping the mooring rope.

Ice-cold darkness enveloped him. A great roaring filled his ears. The roaring of the hell-wind, or the roaring of his own blood in his veins. Light swirled and flashed, and then – as his head broke water – the agonising pain in his back threatened to overwhelm and cripple him. His back arched, he spasmed in the hideous pain, his mouth filling with rank water. He struggled with the pain, knew that he must drown if he did not swim – and felt himself being dragged inexorably through the water.

The thing had him. It had grabbed him and was hauling him out of the canal.

Please God . . .

Tony turned in the black water again, face down, struggled to hold his breath and then crested again. Now, at last, he could see.

Through the hissing spray of torrential rain on the canal surface, he could see that the narrow boat was chugging away from him down the centre of the canal. He was still gripping the mooring rope, and was being dragged along behind it through the water. The pain was eating him alive. He cried out in agony and rolled over in the water as he was dragged on. Looking back to the canal embankment, he could see an incredible sight through the hissing rain-blur.

Something was destroying the warehouse where they had been moored only seconds before.

A hellish whirlwind was spinning on and around the concrete landing stage. As he watched, a corrugated metal wall was punched inwards and ripped apart as if made of cardboard. A huge section of the roof burst out and slid roaring down into the alleyway between the sheds. Something inside the warehouse seemed to explode with a shattering roar. Was that the sound of an explosion, or was it the sound of something else? Was it the angry, raging sound of something from Hell howling at the fact that it had been thwarted? A compacted, twisted mass of tubing, wiring and bent metal-sheet suddenly whirled into the water. As Tony watched, a deadly rain of torn metal and glass and shattered masonry began to rain into the canal, exploding in hissing sprays of dirty water on the spot where the narrow boat had been. The thing was blind, had lost their scent, but it was still trying to get to them in its hideous killing rage.

The canal edge and the mist-shrouded warehouses were suddenly swallowed in the rain. The noises of savage destruction continued, and Tony could still hear the splashing of detritus in the canal. He twisted again, trying to pull himself hand over hand towards the narrow boat as it continued erratically onwards.

Then the engine cut out.

Tony tried to cry out, but then saw the silhouette of the girl as she began to clamber back along the handrail at the side of the boat.

The boat began slowly to turn in towards the bank.

"Get . . ." Tony swallowed more water. He gagged and choked. "Get back and keep your hand on the tiller. Don't let it hit the bank . . ."

The girl seemed to hesitate, then nodded furiously and hurried back the way she had come.

The narrow boat was hardly moving now, but Tony saw its slow course being steered back into the centre of the canal. With agonising slowness, Tony began to drag himself hand over hand towards the stern of the narrow boat.

When he reached the side, he tried to reach up for the rim, but couldn't make it. There was no strength in his arms. There was only pain.

And then a hand had taken his, was trying to pull him on board.

With a last despairing effort, Tony hauled himself up on that hand – and was able to seize the handrail on the boat. A blackness greater that the canal water enveloped him.

He was aware now that he was lying face down on the deck, and that he was vomiting.

He could hear someone cursing. An American accent?

The coughing roar of the ignition.

The shuddering of the engine as the narrow boat got underway, churning water.

That sound was the most wonderful thing he had ever heard.

His mind could take no more nightmares.

Tony slipped away into a safe place.

40

Randall stopped Ranjana at the first clothes store. The shops on this particular street seemed a little rundown, a little seedy, but this was the first halfway decent place he'd seen since they'd left the café.

"Okay, let's go in here."

Ranjana looked at him in puzzlement.

"Your clothes," he said by way of explanation.

Ranjana held the collar of his jacket close around her throat, nodding in embarrassment. Randall pushed open the door and ushered her inside.

While Ranjana chose a new skirt and a blouse, Randall looked around the shop pretending to look interested in the clothes hanging on racks and sharing a fractured smile with the middle-aged lady in charge.

"Are these two okay?" asked Ranjana at last.

"Yeah, sure. Great."

"No . . . I mean from the money point of view."

Randall insisted that it was fine. While Ranjana was paying at the till, using the cash that he'd given her earlier, he looked out through the window into the litter-strewn street. Checking from her reflection that she was not looking his way, he checked on the remaining cash in his pocket . . . and grimaced. He watched her reflection as she vanished into the changing rooms – actually a barely adequate curtain across a small alcove – and changed into her new clothes. When she finally pulled back the curtain and came over to him holding his coat, he quickly changed his expression, took back his coat, and within seconds they were back on the street again.

"What kind of place is this hostel you were talking about?" asked Ranjana at last.

"Yeah . . . I've been thinking about that," said Randall, head down. "I don't think it's the place for us . . . I mean, the place for you."

"What do you mean?"

"Well, it's a place for . . . you know, the homeless."

"Oh . . ."

"That would be okay for me. But I don't think you'd like it much. I've got a better idea. Tonight I think we should find somewhere decent. A bed and breakfast."

Ranjana looked at him as they walked. From the corner of his eye, he saw her uncertainty.

"Just for tonight, I mean. Then we set about finding somewhere to work, so we can get enough money."

"I'm really not sure . . ."

"Look, there's a place up ahead."

Ranjana followed Randall's pointing finger, saw a side street off the main road; a row of terraced houses. The first house on the corner had a "B & B" sign in the garden with a "Vacancies" card beneath it. The house seemed respectable enough.

"It's getting late," said Randall. "And we don't want to leave it too late."

Ranjana nodded, again uncertain – and Randall led the way across the street.

The front door needed a coat of paint. It flaked when Randall rang the door chime, as if that one musical note had loosened it. Randall struggled with a hopeful grin, saw the "Come Right In" sign, and followed its advice.

The hallway inside was dark, but Randall moved on ahead, checking that Ranjana was following. Around the corner was a reception desk. A man was reading the newspaper he'd spread across it. He was in his late fifties, early sixties; mainly bald but with straggling tufts of yellow-grey around his ears. If the pince-nez were meant for effect, it was difficult to ascertain just what that effect might be. Randall noticed that there was a soup stain on his ancient waistcoat – the only remnant of a long-gone three-piece suit.

"Room for two, I suppose?" he said, looking up as Ranjana joined Randall.

"What?" Randall shifted uneasily, looking back at Ranjana.

"I said, I suppose you want a room for two."

"No," said Randall tightly, and now he could feel irritation beginning to turn to anger. "Two separate rooms. Singles."

The man looked over the top of his spectacles. "With baths, or without?"

Randall was conscious of the crumpled notes in his pocket. "With. In both rooms." Could he feel those notes shrinking?

"Payment in advance," said the man, looking down at his newspaper and holding out his hand.

187

Randall fought to control his anger, fumbled for the money in his pocket. When he placed it in the man's hand, the man looked up in distaste and then moved to the cash register, holding the cash as if it might somehow be contaminated.

"Breakfast at eight a.m. sharp. Rooms vacated by noon, please." He dumped the money in the register and brought back the change – only copper. Randall grimaced when he put it in his pocket. "Sign here."

Randall half turned, realising that he didn't know Ranjana's second name. Clearing his throat, he said, "Maybe we should sign separately." He signed his own name and former address, noticing that the man was leaning forward and trying to read it upside down. Randall handed the pen to Ranjana. She signed a completely different name: Ansis Singh. She had barely finished signing in a fictitious address when the man swivelled the register back again, and dropped two keys on to the counter.

"Rooms forty-seven and forty-nine on the fourth floor. *Not* adjoining, I'm afraid."

This was too much. Randall leaned over the counter, staring into his face.

"You got a problem, mister?"

The man stood back, startled. "You'll . . . you'll have to carry your own bags. I haven't got the help."

"Did you see any bags, apart from the one on my shoulder?"

The man tried to look over the counter without getting too close to Randall's face.

"No?" said Randall. "That's 'cause we don't have any others. Right? And I can carry this one *without* any help from you. Thanks."

"Randall," said Ranjana. "Don't . . ."

Randall followed Ranjana to the staircase. There was no sign of an elevator. The carpet was frayed, and so was Randall's temper. He turned to look back at the man again on the stairs, but Ranjana caught his arm and led him away.

When they'd gone, the man said, "Fucking disgusting . . ."

"George," said a woman's voice from the dingy room behind the counter. "That girl."

"What about her?"

"Come and look at this . . ."

The rooms were dry – and that was all that could be said about them by way of compliment. They checked Ranjana's first, and Randall's turned out to be identical, even down to the faded quilt covers and curtains. He wondered now whether they shouldn't have gone for the hostel after all. It couldn't be less spartan, and would certainly have been cheaper. Not for the first time, he cursed himself for a fool. Every time a decision had to be made, it seemed that he made the wrong one.

Ranjana sat on her own bed in her own room.

"Right, then," said Randall, standing in the doorway and feeling a little awkward. "I'm just across the way . . ."

"You want some coffee or tea?" asked Ranjana. "There's a kettle here."

"Oh . . . right . . . yeah. Tea would be great."

He shoved the door gently closed and sat on a battered wooden chair as Ranjana went to plug the kettle in and make the tea.

"Look," said Randall after a while. "You don't *have* to marry this guy, do you? I mean, it's your life – they can't just make you do it if you don't want to."

"You don't know what it's like. Being in my family."

"No, I don't. But I can't believe they can force you to go through with it."

Ranjana was silent for a long time. When she spoke again, Randall had to strain to listen to her: "They betrayed me, Randall. That's what hurt so much. I just had to get away from them. It was more than misleading me, or lying to me. It was a betrayal."

Betrayal.

Randall remembered the way he'd felt as he was walking out of his bedroom, away from his father. He remembered the sight of that family photograph on the mantelpiece. The sight of his mother and the smiling faces. He had felt betrayal then, too. Suddenly, he realised that both he and this strange girl had so much more in common than he could ever have realised.

"I understand that," he said simply.

They were silent again as Ranjana made the tea.

Then Randall said, "Don't understand how anyone could marry someone by arrangement."

Ranjana laughed. "What makes you think the other way's any better? I've got nothing against the principle of an arranged marriage. I'm not as westernised as my brothers make out. And they use that term as an insult, by the way. No, if it's done properly, if it's done in the proper manner – then it's usually a damn sight better arrangement than the usual English way."

"I can't believe that."

"Look, you don't believe in love at first sight, do you? Think of all the thousands, the millions of people all out there looking for a partner. It's just a great big lottery. How do you know that you're going to be compatible with one man or one woman you meet purely by chance, when there could be thousands and thousands of others out there who may be better matched to you? No, the Sikh and Hindu way is better. Ideally, the family is involved. Your partner is carefully screened. The courtship is – should be – carefully handled. Over time, love can grow. If it's properly handled."

"I'm not sure I understand you at all."

"They knew what I wanted. Knew my wishes, my plans. They didn't take account of my feelings, were going to *force* me for family business reasons. That should never have happened. My father would never have allowed it."

"Still seems – I don't know – too *organised*."

"One in three English marriages breaking up and you believe it's still the best way?"

Randall laughed then. "Yeah, okay. Maybe there's something in what you say."

"Are you . . . were you . . . ?"

"Married? No." He laughed again, "A man with my prospects doesn't want to be tied down." He opened his arms in a gesture which took in their whole crazy situation. Ranjana laughed then, too.

They talked and finished their tea, tension melting away.

Maybe tomorrow would bring them better answers.

Randall knew what was going to happen before it happened.

He had been dreaming. A nightmare flashback to that night when his father and his drunken girfriend had come back, kicked in his bedroom door and dragged him from bed. He woke from that dream sweating, with the replay sounds of the dream-fight still ringing in his ears. Those sounds refused to vanish when he awoke. They had resolved into a scuffling sound in the passageway beyond his door. That scuffling sounded like someone travelling fast, and when he heard a hoarse male voice grunting some unintelligible instruction, he *knew* that someone was coming through that bedroom door.

Randall had been sleeping on top of the bed still fully clothed. He flipped from that bed, landing upright, just as the bedroom door crashed inwards against the wall and two silhouettes blundered into the door frame.

No longer sleep-blurred, but with the distinction between reality and his dream-fight confused, Randall was not going to let whatever was coming go the same way as the last time. When the first black figure moved quickly towards him, Randall lunged forward head down. He headbutted the oncoming figure in the midriff, knocking the breath out of him with a *whump!* of air from the lungs. The figure crumpled against the wall, but the other figure was on him – and another had

190

emerged from the corridor. Randall went down under both of them. Somewhere, another door crashed against a wall and Randall heard screaming. He twisted under the weight of the two men on top of him, saw that Ranjana's door was open and that she too was struggling with a figure. Randall braced a leg beneath him and heaved himself upwards. The action threw the two men on top of him over to one side.

"Cuff him, Bob!"

And now, Randall could see that Ranjana was the girl who had screamed, and that she was struggling with a uniformed policewoman in her room. The door flapped shut again as Randall sank his teeth into a bare arm. A man screamed and fell aside, allowing him to scramble sideways out of the tangle and lever himself upright against a wall.

"Shit!" Now, in the dim light of the corridor, Randall could see that he was struggling with two policemen, one uniformed and the other in plainclothes. The plainclothes man lunged at him. Randall sidestepped and kicked him on the kneecap. The policeman yelped and fell back on his companion.

"You're under arrest!" yelled the man at the bottom of the pile.

"No, I'm fucking not!" Randall kicked open Ranjana's room and lunged inside. The policewoman was still struggling with Ranjana, but had her back to him as he entered the room. Randall shoved her hard and she cartwheeled over the bed. Grabbing Ranjana's hand, he pulled her back into the corridor and past the struggling mass on the floor. A hand tried to grab her ankle as they passed. Ranjana kicked out and in the next moment was dragged past them to the top of the staircase.

Randall and Ranjana blundered and half fell down the stairs.

Behind them, the sound of the policemen finally getting to their feet. The thunder of heavy boots on the frayed carpet.

"Come *on*!" yelled Randall, and Ranjana could hardly draw breath as they reached the last small flight of stairs leading into the reception.

Poised with one foot on the bottom step, the owner was in the act of ascending. He looked up in alarm as they rounded the corner and hurtled down towards him.

"It was *you*, wasn't it?" yelled Ranjana. "The bloody newspaper!"

The man's face had turned grey, he seemed unable to move out of their path. Behind the reception counter, an elderly woman with a coiffure like a dead poodle on her head began to shriek. Randall placed his hand on the man's face as they hit the bottom of the staircase – and shoved. The man staggered backwards as they passed, sitting heavily on a potted plant and snapping it in half.

The woman was still shrieking for the police when they burst out through the front door.

Ranjana saw the panda car parked outside, saw the driver's door begin to open as Randall hauled her down the pathway. She hesitated, but Randall was still dragging at her arm. They blundered out on to the pavement just as the policeman inside the panda was in the act of clambering out. Randall released his grip on her arm and dived at the panda door, jamming it back against the policeman, trapping him there with sickening impact, half in, half out of the car. Then he dragged the door open, seized the dazed policeman and dragged him out on to the pavement. Somewhere behind, the boarding house door slammed open.

Raised, angry voices.

The police driver rolled on the pavement, groaning in pain – his helmet rolling on the driver's seat.

Then Ranjana yelled, "The *car!*" as Randall made to run on past. Instead, he staggered in mid-stride, looking back in astonishment as Ranjana skipped over the policeman on the pavement and dived into the driving seat, kicked the helmet on the floor and slammed the door. Randall dashed around the front of the car and clambered in as Ranjana twisted the ignition keys and gunned the engine.

"You're under *arrest!*" yelled a voice from the boarding house.

"Get away from that car, you bastard!" shouted another.

And Ranjana still had to fight for her breath as she looked back and saw the police blundering down the path towards them, only a second away. Then she thrust the car into first gear and the panda car lurched forward.

Ranjana crouched down over the wheel, as someone began to smack their hands on the back window,

Then the car had picked up speed and they were roaring away down the street, leaving the silhouetted figures running and gesticulating in the distance.

"Randall . . ." She gasped for air as the car screeched down on to the main road. "What . . . what are we doing?"

"You're in the driving seat," said Randall, still astonished.

The car screeched across the street, narrowly missing another car. Randall screwed his eyes shut. Now they were heading down the main street at top speed.

"It's okay," said Ranjana, as if trying to convince herself. "It doesn't matter what the newspaper says. The police have got no right to arrest me, or you. I haven't been kidnapped . . ."

The car screeched from the main road and down a dimly lit back alley. Ranjana prayed that no one would step out of the darkness.

If they did, they wouldn't stand a chance.

"They've got no right . . ."

"Look," said Randall tightly from the passenger seat. "How old are you?"

"What's that got to do with it?"

"How *old* are you?"

"Fifteen."

"Then use your head, Ranjana. You're still below the age of consent. Of course they can take you back."

The car swerved again, down another side street, also badly lit.

"Oh God . . . I'm sorry, Randall. I'm making you a part of this."

"Hasn't been boring since we met, I'll give you that."

"*Cars six-seven and one-nine-seven,*" crackled the car radio. "*Report that police panda four-zero-seven has been stolen. Repeat, stolen.*" More static.

"Knew it wouldn't take long," said Randall tightly.

"Hang on!" shouted Ranjana, seeing at once that the road they were on led steeply downhill, saw the familiar warehouses and sheds from the riverside where she had been attacked.

"What are you going to do?" asked Randall, shifting uncomfortably.

Ranjana remained silent as the car screeched down an alley between warehouses and dipped sharply downwards until she could see the glittering black water of the river. Now they had passed the warehouses and were on a concrete jetty, a loading bay for the warehouses, Ranjana stopped the car and then reversed out of the light back into the night-shadow of the last warehouse.

She switched the car engine off.

"What now?" asked Randall in the darkness.

Ranjana drummed her hands on the steering wheel. She turned to look at him with an expression of utter confidence. Then she looked back out through the windscreen. Confidently again, she said, "I don't know."

"Okay, get out," said Randall, suddenly deciding.

"What?"

"Get out. Quick!"

Ranjana clambered out of the car and looked anxiously back the way they had come. How much distance had they covered? Surely it couldn't have been far?

"What are you going to do?" she asked as Randall climbed out of the car and hurried around to the driver's side.

"This," said Randall, jumping in and twisting the ignition key again. He shoved the car into first gear, and the car moved off down the jetty.

Towards the water.

Randall leaned down, jammed the policeman's helmet on to the accelerator and then kicked open the door.

Ranjana was holding her hands to her mouth in shocked surprise as Randall appeared merely to *step* out of the car. It was an act of exquisite calm and grace. He even managed to close the door again gently just before the panda reached the rim of the jetty.

The car continued smoothly on, straight over the edge and into the river.

Ranjana stood frozen, hands still at her mouth, as a foaming wave of dirty yellow water crested over the edge of the jetty. Randall skipped quickly away from it and then moved quickly back to the edge, looking down.

"Glug, glug," he said. "All gone."

"I don't believe you just did that," said Ranjana when he joined her.

"Come on." Randall took her sleeve again, and pulled her into the shadow of the warehouse. "They'll never believe we got rid of it so quickly. They'll still have their cars out looking for it."

"I don't believe you just did that."

"You just said that."

"I don't believe . . ."

"Okay, Ranjana. Change the record. Come on, we've got to move."

"Where?"

"We'll follow the river. Find a place to hide."

"Then what?"

"Let's just find a place, first," said Randall.

Still pulling at her sleeve, he led her off along the riverside and into the night.

41

Fire.

Orange blossoms of flame licking at the night. Black-grey, curling clouds of smoke unfurling into the darkness. Mac's eyes were drawn to the flame, as they always were. But there were no pictures in there, no matter how long he looked. No pictures of dripping, fiery hoses and of man-shaped figures in flame, screaming in agony. Mac's eyes blurred. Beyond the flame, he could see black glittering water. A siren sounded mournfully, and he knew that he was dreaming of the river.

Mac shifted, and looked down.

He was wrapped in a blanket, sitting in front of the fire that he had left earlier that evening, Someone had kept that fire alive. Not only the fire. The blanket was oil-stained and heavy. It smelt badly of human urine, but he was warm beneath it. The damaged nerves on his skin gave no clue to what he was like under that blanket. One hand explored while the other kept the blanket tight at his throat. He was naked.

Mac looked up.

There were several familiar faces sitting on the mudbank around him, all looking at him now that he had awakened. An old woman wrapped in several layers of clothing and wearing a tattered man's cap smiled a toothless smile at him. Because of this shape, the others called her Michelin Man. Some of the others smiled, too, when Mac looked around and saw that someone had taken off his clothes. They were hanging on an improvised drying apparatus beside the fire: a broken scaffolding pole jammed into the ground and bent over at forty-five degrees towards the fire.

A figure that Mac had never seen before pushed himself up from the bank and began to walk slowly towards him. A young man, in his mid-twenties, perhaps; reefer jacket and wild hair. He was holding a bottle out before him as he came. He stopped beside Mac, held the bottle out further. There was an expression of wonder on his face.

"They've told me about you," said the young man. "The others."

195

Mac shifted, reached out and took the bottle. The young man stood back, as if in awe, and watched as Mac took a long swig. He had no idea what was in the bottle, and it tasted foul, but he could feel it burning all the way down into his gut – and it felt good. He offered the bottle back, but the young man shook his head and smiled. Slowly, like a courtier before a king, he backed off and returned to his place on the bank. Mac drank again, and the Michelin Man began to sing "If I Ruled The World".

Mac looked back into the flames. He had been dreaming, hadn't he? Everything seemed so confused again. Something about Bernie down by the canal. Something about hungry people. None of it seemed to make sense. Why had he taken his clothes off? Why were they hanging on the pole? Even as he thought these things, an older man had tottered through the mud to the pole; began feeling the clothes. He nodded extravagantly, deciding that they were dry and warm. He began to slide them from the pole, staggered to where Mac sat and began carefully to place them on a slab of dry concrete beside him. Mac watched, drinking from the bottle. When the old man had finished, he laughed, gave something that looked like a salute and went back to join the others on the bank. Mac reached out and felt the clothes. Groaning, he shrugged off the blanket, felt the ice cold air invading, felt it sweeping over his body.

No one commented as he stood up straight and naked. He reached down and began to put on his clothes. Trousers, two shirts, ragged woollen socks and boots. Finally, his greatcoat, still damp around the hem but gloriously warm on the inside. He turned to look at them, silhouetted against the fire. The stuff in the bottle (was it booze or something even more flammable) had filled him with another great warmth. He smiled on them, held his arms wide and stretched.

"Jesus Christ . . ." said someone quietly from the bank.

From the abandoned jetty overlooking them came a muffled cry.

The street people turned as one to look up there, and Mac turned to follow their gaze.

There were two figures standing up there. A young girl and a young man. Mac supposed that it was the young girl who'd cried out. She was holding a hand to her face in alarm, and it looked as if she had nearly fallen – because the young man with her had seized her arm, apparently preventing her from falling off the edge of the jetty and down into the slipway with them.

For a long time, they all stood and looked at each other.

42

They had followed the river.

For a long time, Randall and Ranjana walked in silence, keeping to the gigantic night-shadows of warehouses and sheds, looking at the oily reflections of the occasional security light in the water. Once, when they had heard the distant sound of a police car siren, they had hurried deeper into shadow, standing with their backs against the cold metal of a warehouse wall. But the siren had faded into the night. They continued walking.

After what seemed a long, long time, Ranjana said, "This is hopeless."

Randall had been doing a lot of thinking since their long walk had begun. He had arrived at roughly the same conclusion. When the police had burst into his room like that, he hadn't been thinking straight. He had still been dreaming of the fight with his father, was still charged with the nervous energy that had enabled him to confront that street gang. Reacting instinctively, he had been laying into his new attackers without any thought – and once the ball had started rolling, there was nothing he could do about it. He was in enough trouble already. Now, it seemed he had inherited the troubles of a complete stranger.

The sounds of their footsteps changed beneath them. Randall looked down to see that the concrete ramp on which they were walking had given way to what seemed to be a wooden jetty. The river was no longer a few feet from the edge. As they'd walked, the river bank had sloped upwards or else the river bed itself had sunk lower. Whatever, the surface of the river was now about twenty or thirty feet below them.Some way ahead, perhaps fifty yards or so, orange light was spilling out from beneath that jetty, across the oily water.

"Wait a minute." Randall moved carefully to the edge of the jetty and looked over the edge, trying to see what the source of that light could be.

"What is it?" hissed Ranjana.

"Can't see. Look, we'll have to get a little closer. There's no way we can walk around it here."

"What if they're workmen or something?"

"Then we'll have to backtrack a little way."

Still keeping to the shadows of a vast steel door on the riverside front of an indeterminate warehouse, they kept walking. When they reached the end of the warehouse, Ranjana could see that this was the last building in its block. The jetty continued onwards to what seemed to be a slipway into the water. That slipway stretched back off the riverside and into darkness. The jetty beyond the slipway also vanished into the night.

"Stay here." Randall crept forward across the jetty until he'd reached the edge overlooking the slipway. Ranjana watched him look carefully over the edge, down to where the light was emanating from. He straightened then and waved back to her that she should come. There was obviously no need for caution any longer. Before she reached him, Randall turned again and said, "It's all right. They're only tramps."

Ranjana looked down into the abandoned slipway.

A figure was standing silhouetted against an improvised bonfire.

His arms were held wide in a cruciform pose.

The fire danced and flared behind him.

"Oh no . . ." Ranjana reeled, clutching at Randall's arm.

He seized her, felt her swaying on the edge. "What is it?"

"Not again," said Ranjana weakly. "Not now . . ."

It was the man from her dreams. The Running Man from the sickening visions that had so afflicted her these past months. She was having another fit.

"Oh no . . ."

The remaining strength left Ranjana. Her legs crumpled beneath her.

As the tramps in the slipway finally caught sight of the commotion and looked up at them, Randall was holding her in his arms. She was unconcious.

Below, Mac lowered his arms, looked up – and then beckoned at them to come down and join them.

43

Tony awoke with a start, automatically clawing aside whatever it was that constricted him. Still blurred, he suddenly found himself on his hands and knees on the floor of the narrow boat. He had been in bed, in the section amidships, and had flung himself out. He was naked.

"You all right down there?" called Lauren from somewhere above.

Tony pulled himself upright, braced his hands on the window frame and sucked in several deep breaths. His stomach felt cramped, and there was a slow-burning pain in the middle of his back. He tried to touch his back with one hand, but couldn't reach the site of the pain.

"Dandridge?"

"Yeah . . . yeah . . . I'm okay." Struggling to regain focus, Tony stooped again and looked out of the window. It was no longer raining. The weather seemed relatively clear, and the narrow boat was chugging along at a steady pace in the centre of the canal. He could see other boats moored on the bank. They seemed to be in open country now. How long had they been travelling?

The thought of what had happened back there, of the thing finding him again and of their desperate struggle on the concrete ramp – all of this suddenly swamped Tony. He bent double and gagged, feeling the fear inside. There had been bad times in the past; in Northern Ireland, in the Falklands. There had been the dreams of that dripping hose of fire and the certain knowledge that he was going to die just as horrifying a death as Cameron – but none of it compared to the instinctive fear generated by the thing that Lauren called the Mechanic. Struggling to pull himself together, Tony looked out again across the canal, looking for any sign of a gusting, destructive wind following them along the canal towpath. At last, he reached back and grabbed one of the blankets from the bed, wrapping it around his waist. Pushing open the double doors he could see Lauren at the helm. She was holding the tiller with one hand, still with the child in the crook of her elbow. For the first time, Tony could see exactly what the child looked like. He was about eight months old, fine fair hair blowing in the breeze. He was looking around in curiosity, and stared at him when his head emerged from the shadows below deck. The child's eyes were a startling green.

"So you're awake at last," said Lauren. "Hey, this is pretty good. I've really got the hang of it . . ."

"How long have I been out?"

"About two hours. Listen, do you know how difficult it is to open canal locks with a kid in one hand? Jumping off, tying up, opening the lock paddles, shutting them again. First couple of times, I had to come the helpless little woman routine until a couple of guys helped me out."

"You tied up at the side?" said Tony in alarm. "With that thing behind us somewhere?"

"I tied up on the *other* bank, stupid. It can't cross water. Didn't I tell you that? The only way for it to get us if we tie up there is for it to follow the river around, find a bridge, or a place where it bends and goes underground or something. Anyway, it gives the bastard a headache trying to figure it all out. Right now it doesn't know where the hell we are. We're okay, believe me."

"My clothes . . . ?"

"Apart from all the crap and sewage and effluent in this canal, you threw up all over yourself while I was pumping the water out of your lungs. I took them off. Your shirt and jacket have had it – slashed right down the back. But your jeans and other stuff are okay. Haven't been able to wash them, I'm afraid. No time – and I don't do laundry. They're back there in the kitchen. You'll have to handwash them in the sink or something."

Tony fumbled with the blanket around his waist.

"My waterproof is back there too," continued Lauren. "Better put that on for the time being. Listen, Dandridge – I thought it had you back there. I really did. It was right behind you, almost on top of you. Christ knows how you got away."

"Just call me Mr Lucky. I've had nothing but luck since the day you walked into my life. All of it bad."

"You've got a nasty slash down the middle of your back. I washed it out, cleaned it with some stuff I found in a medic kit back there. Bandages are a bit rough and ready, I'm afraid, 'cause I don't . . ."

"Yeah, yeah. Let me guess. You don't do bandages."

"Don't think it needs stitches, but we'll have to wait and see. Dandridge, you're going to have to listen to what I say in future. Making a break for it like that was just dumb. Dumber than me trying to put a shot in the fucking thing. Should have kept that bullet for when the Sabbarite come sniffing around. And they will, pretty soon. Believe me . . . Lock coming up."

Tony looked around the double doors and up along the canal in front. The concrete buttresses of a lock loomed about two hundred yards away. The huge wooden doors were closed against them.

"I'll get my jeans," said Tony.

"Forget it," said Lauren. "Come up here."

Still dazed, Tony clambered awkwardly up on deck, holding the blanket tight around his waist. Before he could react properly, Lauren had shoved the child into his arms. Tony tried to protest, but Lauren moved quickly up on to the side of the boat, grabbing at the handrail and pulling herself away along the landward side of the boat. Tony sat awkwardly on the rail, hitching the baby up to the crook of one arm, using his elbow to keep the blanket in place as he sat. Quickly grabbing the tiller, he began to steer the boat slowly into a parallel course with the towpath embankment. The boat passed two elderly men, fishing in the canal. They watched in open curiosity at the strange sight of the semi-naked helmsman holding the child.

"We're trying hard to add to the family," said Lauren as the boat passed them. "He's a lousy lover. But he's a wonderful father."

A hundred yards further on, Tony steered the boat tight to the side and killed the engine. The boat glided slowly into the side, fifty feet from the great wooden doors. Lauren skipped nimbly from the boat to the canal side.

"Make sure you tie up . . ." began Tony.

"I know, I know. Lots of slack when I tie up, otherwise when the lock opens and the water level here goes down, the boat's going to be left hanging on the side of the canal." Tony watched her expertly tie up fore and aft.

"You sure you haven't done this before?" he asked, as she finished tying up aft.

"Done lots of things in my time, Dandridge. But this is a first. My little girl act back there learned me a lot. Believe me, I've learned *more* than a lot since I arrived in your country. Most of it I'd rather not know."

He watched her move quickly and nimbly up the rough path on the embankment until she had reached the swing-beams; watched her begin to wind down the windlass to open the lock paddles and lower the water level for the next stretch of canal. Beyond, he could hear the wooden doors on the other side begin to close. How old was she? Early twenties?

He looked down at the child he was holding. He seemed completely unconcerned about being left with a stranger. The baby sat quite comfortably in the crook of his arm, watching his mother as she moved

201

to the other paddles when the outside doors were closed.

"Is it true, kid?" asked Tony, as Lauren closed and opened the lock gates.

The child looked at him curiously.

"You talk to your mother? In her head?"

The child smiled. A gossamer strand of spittle drifted delicately from his lower lip on to his arm. Then, still holding his eye, the baby laughed and turned his attention back to his mother.

"Was that an answer?" said Tony. He shook his head. The nausea inside him engendered by raw fear and two pints of effluent-tainted water was still cramping his stomach.

When Lauren had completed opening and closing lock doors, she returned quickly to the narrow boat. The water level had dropped by twenty feet, but there was a green-slimed ladder at the side of the boat and she climbed carefully down before dropping on to the deck. The child held his arms out to her and she took him, resuming her place at the helm with an impatient wave of her hand when Tony tried to assist. In seconds, they were under way again – and Tony still felt like a bloody idiot in his blanket. There were many more questions to be answered, but Tony couldn't think about posing them; about deciding just what the hell was going to happen next, until he'd got something more to wear than a blanket. Back inside the boat, he found his jeans in a basin in the sink. He scrubbed them by hand, rinsed them and then laid them across a chair directly in front of the wood-burning heater. Rummaging through the drawers beneath the bed, he found an old pullover and a ragged pair of cut-off shorts that had once been denim jeans. He pulled them on. They were too big, but his belt kept them in place. Returning to the helm, he climbed out on deck and stood next to Lauren at the rail.

"You won't get any prizes for best-dressed male."

"Thanks for pulling me out back there."

"Like you say, I'm the bad luck fairy. It was the least I could do. And don't forget, I've got an ulterior motive now."

"What do you mean?"

"Like the kid said, it's been decided that you're going to help me out."

"By who?"

"The Serendip."

"And who the hell are they?"

"Not they – it. Explaining it would take longer than we have. But it's something that the Sabbarite became aware of through Ramsden. You won't believe . . ."

"Look, after what happened back there, I'll believe anything you say.

There was a time when I thought . . . well, I thought that I'd been drugged or something. Maybe by you, without my knowing. I was ready to believe that's why my world got turned upside down and I started to see that . . . the Mechanic. But druggie dreams don't come to life and rip a hole in your back. No, I believe everything you've told me. More than anything else, I just want out of this bloody mess as quickly as possible. So . . . what's the Serendip?"

"The Sabbarite teaching of the Inner Circle was . . . *is* . . . based on the creed that there are no absolutes. No such thing as a God or a Devil, no such thing as pure good or pure evil. There's only the Benefactor – the Anonymous One. And they don't ask questions about morality, about what it is – they just do what it wants, and they'll get things in return. But it's a smokescreen, Dandridge. You see, there *is* good and there *is* evil – although probably far removed from our limited understanding of it. Look . . ."

Lauren looked out across the canal away from him, so that he couldn't see her face any more. But Tony could see that the muscles were working in her cheek; she seemed to be chewing at her lip.

"I was looking for things, Dandridge. Something that made sense out of life. Out of what I was doing here, what we're *all* doing here. It led me to the Sabbarite, and I felt those vibes that they gave out. I thought at last that I'd found something that made sense of it all. If Ramsden hadn't seen me, hadn't chosen me, hadn't . . . hadn't . . ."

She was quiet again, and Tony moved around because he wanted to see her face. Her head snapped back, and it was the same hard face as before.

" . . . hadn't just wanted to *fuck* me, then God knows where I would have ended up. But I was chosen. To bear his child. And that opened me up to insights you wouldn't believe. So believe me when I tell you that . . . the Benefactor is evil. I've no doubt about it. There *is* a Hell – and the Mechanic is from that place. Is there a Heaven? Well, it seems to me there must be something – because of the Serendip.

"The Serendip is a separate thing from good and evil. It's not an . . . what do you call it? It's not an entity. Doesn't have a personality or anything. But it's like . . . a scale or a balance. Someone once described it to me as the balance holding the fabric of reality together. It's the reason that we have good and evil in this existence. It's the reason why one has never won out against the other over the centuries. It's like fate – but it's much more than that. If you could key into it, then you could weigh up the pros and cons of a particular kind of action . . ."

"What, you mean like astrology or something?"

Lauren sighed. "Yes . . . and no. I'm sorry, it's so complicated I couldn't begin to explain it properly. It's like . . . a *barrier* between good and evil. The Sabbarite have a bare understanding of it, have used its ebb and flow to determine their key actions, used it to decide when and where to move. Because sometimes the balance between the two shifts, and when it's to evil's advantage to act, then they can make their move.

"But it's the same with good, whatever that may be. And those who think they're on its side. All those who were supposed to be divinely inspired over the centuries were supposed to have had a psychic link with it. The saints and the holy men."

"You're saying that *you've* got a link with it?"

"Not me. Sparrow." Lauren stroked the child's head. "You hungry, baby?" The child looked at her and smiled. "Okay, maybe later."

"The child . . ."

"Pearce Ramsden's son, remember. And, like his father, he's special. Actually, he's *more* special. Has a much greater power. Including insight into the Serendip. Sparrow told me that I had to come back and try to protect you. It evened up the balance, set certain things right. Chances are if I hadn't come back, we'd be finished right now."

"So all we have to do is let the kid listen in or something," said Tony, "and we'll be all right?"

"Wrong. Like I said, the Serendip is neither good nor evil. It's only a balance. It doesn't *care*. We can use Sparrow's insight to help us, but it doesn't guarantee us a happy ending. He's told me that something about our being together – the three of us – has given a big swing in our favour. But God knows how many chances we've already used up. Sparrow says the luck is still against us, and we'll be lucky to get out of it alive."

"Thanks for the good news."

"There are worse things than being dead. I've told you that before."

"Such as?"

"Hell," said Lauren.

They were silent then, as the narrow boat continued on its way. After a while, Tony said, "So what do we do next?"

Lauren held a hand up for quiet as the boat continued on its way. When Tony saw the way she was looking at the child, and the way that he was staring up at her, he knew that they were in communication again and were not to be interrupted. Tony leaned on the rail and looked out across the canal. They were still in open country, but he had no idea where they were or how far they had come. He stretched, groaning again at the pain between his shoulders. Refusing to accept what he was being told, or the evidence of his eyes had already nearly got him killed. He was past all that now, quite prepared to accept that this woman was able to communicate telepathically with her eight-month-old son. Why not? He'd heard and seen crazier things in this nightmare already.

"Dandridge . . ." said Lauren, at last.

Tony looked up to see that she was nodding at the child, as if agreeing with something it had said. She held the baby to her breast and sighed.

"What is it?"

"Tie the boat up somewhere. I've got something to tell you. And you're not going to like it."

"You mean it gets worse."

"Maybe. Maybe not."

"What about the Mechanic?"

"We're safe for the moment. Sparrow can sense it, and he says it's miles and miles away, heading in the wrong direction."

There was a long stretch ahead with wild country on either side of the canal. There were no mooring pins in sight. Tony ducked down into the narrow boat and retrieved the small hammer and pegs he had discovered in the cupboard on the previous day. When Lauren brought the boat slowly into the bank and cut the engine, he jumped off the stern, grabbed the mooring rope and pulled it landward. In minutes he had secured both ropes fore and aft by hammering the pegs into the ground and tying the ropes to them. Back on board again, he sat back against the rail and crossed his arms. Lauren and Sparrow were just looking at each other. Lauren's face was grim. She nodded again.

"Well?" asked Tony. "Let's have the bad news."

"It's good and bad," said Lauren. "Like I told you, Sparrow can tune in to things – to the Serendip, to the Mechanic. He's been trying to tune in to the Sabbarite, find out what they're up to. But that's harder for him. Seems they've done something to keep him tuned out."

"You mean they've 'cast a spell' or something?"

Lauren smiled grimly. "Or something."

"So?"

"The Mechanic is in telepathic contact with the Sabbarite. It's already told them that it's lost us again, but it's also told them we're down here on the canal. It won't be long before they come for us. When they find us, they'll certainly take Sparrow and use him for the ritual they originally had planned. As for you and I – they'll either kill us outright, or leave us to the Mechanic."

"Great. So much for the bad news. What about the good?"

"Sparrow's found a way to stop the Mechanic. The only way to send it back where it came from."

"Why is it that I think this good news is going to be worse than the bad news?"

"The Mechanic was reconjured to hunt for you. You're the only one who can stop it."

"And how do I do that?"

"You have to have a photograph of yourself. When the Mechanic comes for you, when it's within striking distance – when you can see it – you've got to pin that photograph to another living thing. The Mechanic will be forced to switch targets, then. It'll go for the thing that bears your photograph and destroy it instead of you. Don't ask me how it works, but Sparrow says it will. It's the only way. Afterwards, the Mechanic will have tasted blood and will go back to Hell."

"A photograph of me?"

"Yes."

Tony turned and stared out along the canal.

"You haven't got one with you, have you?" asked Lauren.

"Nope."

"Well – you're going to have to go and find one."

"You mean leave the boat. Leave the water?"

"There's no other way. You've got to find a photograph."

"All my personal possessions were back at the lodging house. When I left it, the place was burning."

"What about family or friends? Maybe they'll have something . . ."

"No," said Tony firmly. "I'm alone."

"Maybe we could get a camera, buy one, steal one. Take a photo of you now and . . ." Lauren was suddenly silent, looking at the child. "No, sorry, it won't work that way. Sparrow says it has to be a photograph taken before the conjuration of the Mechanic."

"And it's the only way?"

Lauren nodded bleakly.

"Then I'll just have to head back to the lodging house. Hope it hasn't burned to the ground. I've got some photos and stuff back in my flat. But even if I do get back there and find a photograph, it means we've got to find someone to take my place, someone to stick it on when the Mechanic finds us again. That means *murdering* somebody . . ."

"Not somebody," said Lauren. "Sparrow said a 'living thing'."

"So it doesn't have to be human?"

"No. It can be anything, just as long as it's alive. A rat or a cat or a dog, maybe."

"Okay. Supposing I do find a photograph back there. Suppose I do manage to get back here in one piece without the Mechanic picking my scent up again and tearing me to pieces. Supposing I *do* manage to paste it on to some poor bastard's pet cat when it shows up? What's to stop the Sabbarite just conjuring up another Mechanic, or another, and another . . . ?"

"Their powers are limited. This will be the second time they've conjured a Mechanic. It would be months before they'd have the power to reconjure another. Believe me."

Tony stood against the rail for a long time, looking out over the reeds. Finally, without saying another word, he vanished below deck. When he re-emerged minutes later, he was wearing his dried-out jeans and his shoes. He returned to the rail again, head down in thought.

"Okay," he said at last. "Don't suppose there are any other options?"

"None," replied Lauren.

"What does the kid say about the odds of my pulling this off?"

"Slender," said Lauren. "I wouldn't be doing you any favours by lying to you."

"Be nice. Try lying sometimes."

"Do you want the gun?"

"No, you keep it. I've seen what effect it has on the Mechanic. And you might need it if the Sabbarite come sniffing around."

"All right. We'll take the boat back the way we came. May as well give you as much cover as we can, still being on water."

"Can that thing *see* us, if we pass it?"

"No, the water will blind it. Last time, when it almost got you, we literally vanished from its sight as soon as we cast off the last rope and you jumped in. We could cruise right on by it and it would never know. The Sabbarite are our biggest problem."

"Okay, I'll cast off and we'll head back."

Lauren pushed the ignition switch again and the engine chugged into life.

"Lauren?"

"Yes?"

"I want to know if anything changes. If the kid tells you anything else, anything about that Serendip balance, I need to know. Even if the odds get shorter than they are. Understand?"

"Okay," said Lauren, watching as he jumped off the boat and untied the mooring ropes. *How much shorter could they be?*

44

This time, the flames were real.

They twisted and curled before her eyes; wreaths of smoke unfurled like tattered night-black flags. She could smell the smoke, see the glowing orange embers at the centre of the fire. But there was no running, burning man here, screaming in the night. There was no Christ-like silhouette against the flames, holding his arms wide.

"You okay?" said a familiar voice beside her, and Ranjana realised that she was not in another dream, realised that she was awake. She half turned to see Randall next to her. He had taken off his jerkin again and wrapped it around her shoulders. Now she could see that they were sitting on a ragged piece of tarpaulin spread out on a muddy bank – the slipway, where the vagrants had gathered.

The man!

"Where is he?" asked Ranjana in alarm, and saw the look of bewilderment in Randall's eyes.

"Who?"

"The man who was standing in front of the fire. The big man."

"Do you mean me?" said a voice in the darkness.

And then Mac stepped around in front of them. He had been standing behind them both, watching the fire.

Ranjana shrank back, and Randall – not knowing what he could do to reassure her – simply put a hand on her shoulder.

"No need to be scared," said the big man. "No one here's going to hurt you." His voice was so calm, so controlled. But even the man's reassurances couldn't quell the feelings that were engulfing Ranjana. Randall could feel her trembling.

"It's okay, Ranjana. I've been talking to this guy a long time. While you were . . . out. He's okay."

"He's not okay, Randall. He's *not!*"

"What do you mean?"

"I've seen him before."

"Where?"

"I just have . . . and he's . . . well, he's *not alive.*"

Mac just stood apart from them and listened. The expression on his face did not change.

"What do you mean 'not alive'?" said Randall. "He's standing there, isn't he?"

"No, I mean . . . he's not alive . . . but he's not dead either. Oh, I don't know. It's just that . . . that . . ."

"I know what you mean," said Mac. "Even if he doesn't. No need to worry, though. I've seen you before, too."

"We've never met before . . ." said Ranjana.

"But you said . . ." began Randall.

"Oh, we've met before," continued Mac. "No offence meant – but I've seen you in my dreams. Plain as day." He spoke as if this was somehow the most ordinary thing in the world.

Randall saw the look on Ranjana's face, saw her eyes glaze in shock or surprise. Anger began to rise inside him. Was he trying a come-on? Randall bunched his fists, started to rise – but then Ranjana had taken his arm and pulled him back. Randall sat down again.

"Yeah, that's right," continued Mac. "Not very nice dreams, either. What's your name?"

"Ranjana . . ." The voice that came out of her mouth sounded more like Ranjana aged ten years old.

"They call me Mac. Know what I think?" Mac squatted down in front of them, on his haunches. "I reckon that means something. Don't you? Both of us seeing each other in our nightmares – and now meeting up like this? I nearly died tonight. Wonder if it's connected . . ."

"That's just about enough, mister," said Randall through gritted teeth.

"You nearly died once before," said Ranjana. "A long time ago. When you were a soldier . . ."

Randall gave her a hard look. "What the hell are you *talking* about?" he snapped. "Do you know this fella or not?"

"You're not listening," said Mac. "We've only met in our dreams. Cue for a song, eh?"

Mac stood up and walked slowly over to the fire. He held out his hands to the flames. Randall turned back to Ranjana, could see the firelight reflected in her widened eyes.

"So what's going on?" said Randall at last. "Where do you know each other from?"

Ranjana swallowed hard. He could see that she had been badly shaken.

"Look, it's all right," he continued. "I know that your seeing him back there was a bad shock, but like it or not, we're both in a mess together now, Ranjana. And I need to know what's going on."

Ranjana looked at him. When she spoke, her voice was quiet but firm. It didn't waver, but contained only the certainty of truth.

"For the past three years, I've been seeing various doctors. I've got this . . . condition. Nobody knows what it is, but the popular consensus is that I'm subject to fits. But they're not like any fit that any doctor I've been to has ever seen before. And they've tried to prescribe drugs for it, but nothing works. The thing is, Randall, when I pass out like that, I see things. At first, the things I saw were stupid, ordinary things about people I knew. Like video-action replays in my mind's eye. I saw my brother have an accident in his car. Nothing serious. Just someone shunting him from behind and wrecking the bumper. Then the next day – it happened. Just as I'd seen it. It scared me. Scared me badly. Then, whenever I had another of these fits I would see something else – and whatever I saw always happened.

"The doctors said it must have something to do with my age. A whole load of patronising shit about 'girlie stuff'. But I knew that there was something more to it. I kept quiet about it all. Having these turns was bad enough in my family, but telling them that I could *see* things, things that were going to happen . . . well, they might have done something about it. You don't know my brothers . . ."

"Yeah, I wouldn't put it past them to do something. Particularly with this marriage thing in the offing."

Ranjana looked at him hard for what seemed a long time. "You mean you believe what I'm telling you?"

"Of course I believe you. Why should you lie?"

"One day," continued Ranjana, "I saw my father die." She paused and looked down into her lap. When she looked up again, the reflections from the flames were bright and luminous in her eyes. "I didn't know what to do. He seemed well, hadn't been ill, wasn't suffering from anything. But I saw him die. Quietly, in bed. I *knew* that it was going to happen, Randall. But there wasn't anything I could do about it. If I'd told him, can you imagine . . . ? Can you imagine what it would be like if someone said you were going to die tomorrow?"

"I'd be terrified," said Randall calmly.

"So I said nothing. Knew there was nothing I could do. Next day, in the morning . . ." Randall held an arm around her, waiting until she had found the strength to continue. "The doctor said it was a heart attack. Right out of the blue. He'd never had heart trouble in his life."

"There are worse ways to go than dying in your sleep," said Randall quietly. "That's what I'd prefer, believe me."

Ranjana nodded. "At least I was able to tell him . . . I loved him."

Randall watched as she forcibly pulled herself together, wiping her eyes.

"Afterwards . . . well, afterwards the dreams came less frequently. It's as if my father's death had done something to keep these visions at bay. Not so much the fact of Dad's death, more to do with the way I reacted to it. Emotionally, I mean. From then on, I began to have different dreams . . . or, I should say, the same dream. I still had the turns, though less frequently – and I saw the same thing each time."

"What did you see?"

"Him," said Ranjana, looking to where Mac held out his hands to the flames.

"You mean someone that looks like him."

"No, I mean him. Not a look-alike. The dream is always the same. I dream of fire, of horrible orange-black clouds of it. Petrol flame, giving off clouds of thick black smoke. That's all I can see. Then I see someone running towards me out of the fire. He's screaming – because his body's on fire. Like he's been sprayed with petrol or something. And I can see the clothes . . . the clothes burning and shrivelling and falling away . . . see his skin burning and bubbling." Ranjana halted for a moment, her body trembling violently. Once again, Randall watched as she controlled herself, and then continued: "He can see me as he comes. And it's as if I'm the only one who can help him. His arms are wide as if he wants to embrace me. And then – just before he does, just before that fire engulfs me – that's when I wake up. I've had that dream about two dozen times, and it's always the same. The same fire. He has a different face, but it's the same man. What did he say his name was?"

"Mac, or something," said Randall.

"Mac," repeated Ranjana. Then she called out loud to the big man beside the fire. Mac turned at the sound of her voice. Slowly, he walked back to them.

"You going to beat me up then?" Mac asked Randall, and smiled.

"Not unless you start something."

"Okay, son."

"Mac," said Ranjana, "would you believe me if I said I can see what's going to happen in the future sometimes?"

Mac looked at her for a long time. It was impossible to read his expression.

"You can see the future?" he said, without intonation.

"Sometimes."

"Okay. I've heard crazier things. Seen crazier things. Like you, for instance, in my dreams."

"What have you seen? I mean, what have I been doing in your dreams?"

"Just your face, looking at me. How did you know I'd been a soldier?"

"I don't know. That's just the feeling that came across. Like this other feeling that I can't make sense of."

"What other feeling?"

"The feeling that you're dead *and* alive."

Mac laughed. It was a quiet and bitter sound. "Sometimes I don't know myself."

"Mac. You've got to keep away from fire. That's what I see in my dream. You've got to avoid fire. In my dream, I see you dying . . ."

"Got your wavelengths mixed up, Ranjana."

"What do you mean?"

"What you're seeing in your dream is what *happened* to me when I was a soldier. Not what's going to happen."

"Oh God . . . Oh God . . ." Ranjana's eyes seemed fixed on some inner point now, not on the man who stood before them. "Yes, I think . . . I think I see . . . Your whole body, your face were badly burned. You look completely different now."

Mac squatted down again, smiling.

"You died," said Ranjana at last.

"That's right," replied Mac, as if it was the easiest thing in the world to understand.

"You *died*?" echoed Randall.

"Three times, son. So they tell me. On the operating table. I saw . . . saw the tunnel of light."

"Tunnel of light? What the hell is going on here?" said Randall in exasperation, hanging his head and sighing in weariness.

"That makes you special," said Ranjana, again concentrating on that inner place. She blinked rapidly, as if suddenly rising from that secret interior. "For some reason, that makes you special."

"Not as special as you, Ranjana," said Mac, standing again. "Not as special as you."

"What do you mean?"

"Well, how the hell have I seen *you* in *my* dreams? What does that mean?"

"I don't know . . ."

"Something to think about, eh? Something to . . ."

They watched as a cloud of doubt seemed to pass over the big man's face. He raised a hand to his face, touching his lips and forehead gently as if it was a stranger's face.

"Are you all right?" asked Ranjana.

Mac looked down at them both, still deeply confused.

"I need . . . need some time. Some things have been happening . . ."

"Sit down here."

"Bernie . . ."

"What? Who? Look, I'll make room for you here. We need to talk."

"Three, seven, four, oh-two . . ." said the big man, and turned away. They watched him move awkwardly back to the fire, holding his head. Then he sat, oblivious to everyone around him. After a while, he took his hands from his head, raised his face and began staring into the fire.

When Ranjana and Randall looked around at last, they could see that all the eyes of the other vagrants were on them, had been on them since their arrival. Silently watching and listening. Their faces all held one expression, and it was an expression that at once disturbed and disquieted them both as they huddled together for warmth.

It was an expression of awe.

"Looks like we're here for the night," said Randall at last.

One of the vagrants, a man of indeterminate age, moved to the fire and threw more tattered wood on to it. Sparks swirled high.

"Something's happening, Randall," said Ranjana. "I don't know what it is. But something's happening, or going to happen. And it involves all of us. You, me – and that man over there."

Randall put his arm around her.

They watched the rippling reflection of the fire on the water.

45

Gerry pushed the key into his front door lock, turned and looked back the way he'd come. He looked at the curtained windows and the lights of the houses behind, thought of them all sitting in those rooms, watching television or stuffing their faces with convenience shit-food. He listened for the sounds of police sirens, but couldn't hear anything tonight.

Big changes coming, he thought, stabbing each word out across the housing estate. *Big fucking changes.*

He thought about the others at the community centre, remembered with a laugh how Quaid had finally come around; the pain in his head dulled by the ecstasy of Nektre, not understanding why everyone was laughing at him as the blood streamed down over his face. He had touched that blood, smelled it, laughed – and then tasted it, laughing, laughing, laughing. The others had gone out on their first errands, spreading the word – spreading the Nektre. All of Gerry's supply had gone.

I can supply as much as you need, Gerry, the Man had said. *You will be the sole supplier.*

Gerry smiled, and let himself in. The smile soon faded when he closed the door. He was still feeling deeply uneasy about what had happened that day. When they'd stumbled on the black tart lying spaced-out down by the warehouses, it had seemed like an opportunity dumped in their laps; something to help the boys' morale. He'd felt sure that the Man would approve. Then that stupid bastard had arrived and done his knight in shining armour bit – another chance to give the boys a bit of practice. But when the Man's voice had exploded in Gerry's head, it had seemed somehow even louder than a shouted voice heard normally. The words had stung Gerry. He could still feel residual pain throbbing in his temples. But worse than the pain had been the strong essence of displeasure in the Man's voice. It had disturbed him deeply – was still disturbing him now.

"Have I done right?" he whispered, still standing in the hallway. There was no reply from the Man. "With the Nektre, I mean?" Still nothing.

Head down, Gerry took off his jerkin, threw it over the banister rail and pushed open the living room door.

Something shrieked and flung itself at him from within.

Gerry cried out in horror, hands flying to his face as he staggered back into the hallway.

He saw the kitchen knife held in the figure's hand. That knife was held high, and the manic shrieking figure screamed directly into his face as the knife came down.

The blade sliced across the palm of his hand.

Gerry fell back against the hallway wall, and then flung himself forward with no time for thought, grabbing the thrashing arms of the thing that had attacked him, seizing the wrist that held the knife. And the figure shrieked, and shrieked, and shrieked.

"*Sharon!*" he screamed back into his wife's face as he forced her back into the living room in an awkward stumbling dance. "*Sharon, you stupid bitch!*"

But Sharon was flinging her head from side to side like a madwoman, her hair lashing her face. She kicked at him, lunged forward, tried to bite him . . . and the sheer savagery of her attack forced Gerry backwards. His feet stumbled against the sofa and he fell on it, dragging Sharon on top of him as he held tight to her wrists. She brought a knee up, planted it on his chest – and the fact that she had got the better of him, the fact that she had *dared* to raise a hand against him, brought a great, cold and furious rage on Gerry. He released his grip on one hand. Instantly, she seized a handful of his hair. Yelling in pain, Gerry clenched his teeth and grabbed at the knife-wielding hand with his own free hand. Sharon shrieked again as he tore it from her, flinging it across the room with a clatter. He seized her own hair then, yanking back her head.

Her shrieking was instantly cut off when he punched her full in the mouth.

The second blow made her stagger back from him on her knees.

When Gerry pushed himself off the sofa, he could see that her face had instantly changed colour to a sick marble-white. Then the blood came from her nose and mouth, and all Sharon could do now was to kneel there on the carpet, and look at the blood as it spouted on her hands. When she looked up at Gerry again, her face was completely blank.

"You *bitch!*"

Gerry lunged downwards, taking Sharon by the throat with both hands.

215

She made no sound as he forced her over backwards on to the carpet. Her teeth were clenched, the blood still came – but her eyes were far away.

Do it! Do it! The Man again, in his head, urging him on.

"I . . . thought . . . you'd . . . gone . . ." Gerry was sobbing as he throttled his wife, each word a strangled gasp of his own.

Never, Gerry. I'd never leave you. I told you that everything was all right, didn't I? A father sometimes must chastise his son. Isn't that right?

"Yes . . . yes . . . yes . . ."

Do it, Gerry. That's right. Do it. Do you see? Do you feel the power? Use this, Gerry. Use it to kill everything that's ever been done to you in the past. This is the first part of your revenge . . .

Sharon made a noise like a drain unplugging.

"What have I done . . . ?"

Gerry slumped backwards away from her. He was on his knees now, still astride her, looking at his hands. The knife had sliced deep into his hand. The blood on her throat was mainly his own. Sharon was still staring at the ceiling, her eyes seemed to be bright with tears. The blood from her nose and mouth had stopped. Her struggling had stopped. Everything had stopped.

A great thing, said the Man. *You've done a great thing. Something to make a father proud of his son. That's what I am to you. You know that, don't you?*

"Father . . ."

There was movement at Gerry's right, from the direction where he'd thrown the knife. He looked up slowly.

The black silhouette of the Man Who Shines Black was there. But this time, there was no bubbling light, no transparency, no shifting aura around that figure. He was as real and substantial as a man dressed from head to foot in black velvet. Gerry could still see no features. The Man was tossing the knife end over end in his hand.

You see what your further act has done? You see how closer I am to you now? There are no more barriers between us. In that act, you've drawn us nearer than flesh. I can reveal all. All my plans.

Gerry's head was spinning. He couldn't seem to function properly. His limbs felt heavy and awkward.

"Why did she do it?"

She was mad. And you did what anyone should do to a mad dog, a mad bitch.

"Yeah . . ."

You're not finished, said the Man.

The knife thumped to the carpet, next to his bleeding hand.

The act is not complete.

"Complete . . .?"

The knife won't be enough. Do you have other tools?

"In the garage," said Gerry faintly. "Some stuff in there."

A hacksaw?

"Yes."

Good. I'll tell you what to do, show you how to do it. And with each moment, you'll be consolidating me.

"Consolidating?"

The garage, Gerry.

And afterwards, when it is all over, the dawn light is seeping through the curtains of the bedroom.

Gerry is kneeling on the carpet, leaning against the wall. And the voice of the Man Who Shines Black is still speaking in his head, even though the figure of the Man left him again two hours ago, when he was tying up the last of the black bin bags and dragging them into the garage. The taps are still running, the shower attachment still sprays hot water into the bath. Clouds of steam wreath the bathroom and creep across the landing towards the bedroom where Gerry kneels.

Gerry's eyes look the way that Sharon's eyes looked, at the last.

I was dead, Gerry, said the Man. *They killed me. Now, I'm neither dead nor alive – but everything you've done, everything that you've done here tonight, has made me more whole and brings me closer to the life that I crave. From the first, on that night by the canal, I knew that what was within you would help give me back life. I have already set plans in motion for revenge, Gerry. Revenge against those who killed me.*

Listen to me, Gerry. Those who killed me KNOW that I am on the verge of returning. They don't know how or where, but they know I'm planning my return. They know how strong I'm becoming. What they don't know is that I'm using the very things that give them power, the very things that give them their own life's blood – against them. We will have an army, Gerry. Do you understand? An army! Not yet. Oh no, not yet. But soon. When the time is right.

But there is something else I need. Something that those who killed me are also searching for. Something that will give the ultimate power, everything I need truly to return. You and your gang, your people, must find them for me. They are still here. Close at hand. I can sense it. The young woman called Lauren – and her baby.

"We're still looking . . ." says Gerry and his mouth fills with vomit. He grimaces and swallows again, his eyes still glazed and staring. A tear rolls down his face but his expression does not change. "Do you . . ." he begins again. "Do you have a name? I mean, a real name?"

Gerry hears the Man laugh inside his head. It is a gentle, comforting, fatherly sound.

A name, my son? Yes. My name is Ramsden – Pearce Ramsden.

46

The narrow boat cruised slowly down a concrete canyon.

On either side towered the featureless grey-blank walls of factories, most of them derelict and boarded up. There had been a petrol leak somewhere, and dark rainbows of liquid curled and twisted around the prow of the narrow boat as it came slowly on. The two figures standing on the deck at the stern were quiet and watchful. Watching the narrow towpath on either side and scanning the great concrete walls. As if any sound too loud would bring those walls crashing down on top of them.

There was no wind.

The narrow boat moved to the canal side, slowed as it came parallel. The two figures moored the boat to the side as if they had been doing it all their lives. Then Lauren cut the engine and leaned back against the rail. Tony hopped back down on to the deck beside her.

"So what do you reckon?" he asked.

"This is about as far as we can go," replied Lauren. "Safely."

"What about the Mechanic? Where is it?"

Lauren held the child up and looked into his eyes. After a while, she said, "He doesn't know."

"That's great . . ."

"But it's not close. If it was, Sparrow could sense it."

"That thing can move fast."

"Don't we know it. But you'll be okay if you keep moving yourself. How far is your lodging house?"

"A mile and a half, I think. Hard to tell on this waterway. Some of the industrial stretches look all the same. Think I know this place, though. Look – you're sure about this, aren't you?"

"You mean about the photograph?"

"Yeah."

"Sparrow's sure. And he's never wrong about stuff like that. We've kept alive on his hunches so far."

"Hunches?" exclaimed Tony. "He'd better have more than a bloody 'hunch'!"

"Take it easy. Okay . . . wrong word. He *knows*. All right?"

"All right . . . but one sign of that bloody thing, and I'm coming straight back. Maybe you'll still be here."

"What do you mean by that?"

"Doesn't it occur to you that I'm taking everything on trust? The whole lunatic situation. A thing from Hell that tears people apart, a bunch of crazy religious nuts who sacrifice down-and-outs, an eight-month baby who can speak to his mother but only in her head?"

Lauren smiled. It looked grim and purposeful. She stepped slowly forwards to the rail where he was standing half turned away from her. Then suddenly, she leaned quickly forward and slapped him hard on the back. The pain was excruciating. Tony cried out, arching his back and staggering away from the rail.

"Feel that?" asked Lauren calmly. "Does that feel real enough to you?"

"Christ." Tony composed himself again. "If it didn't need stitches before, then it might need them now. Okay, point taken. But you better be here when I get back."

"Would we leave you treading water in a canal, trying to keep away from that thing for the rest of your life? Think about it, Dandridge. Where else are we going to go?"

Lauren paused, listening to the child. "Okay – whether you're able to find a photograph or not, the Mechanic is bound to pick up your scent eventually and follow you back here to the canal. I'm mooring here on one rope. Any sign of that fucking wind or the Sabbarite, I'll cast off and keep the boat in the middle of the canal. I'll have the engine running and be moving up and down the centre. There's room to turn two hundred yards either end of this stretch."

"You were born to be a sea dog. What about the Sabbarite?"

"Sparrow thinks that the Mechanic hasn't been able to tell them where we are yet. But they'll find out soon. They're trying."

"*Thinks*, Lauren?"

"He's doing the best he can. The Mechanic's tasted blood. Your landlord. That always makes it slightly harder to control."

"So . . . a photograph. And another living thing."

"What are you going to do about that?"

"God knows. Swipe some poor old lady's pussycat from her front step. Catch me a dog. Something."

Tony moved to the rail, looking out along the towpath for any signs of movement.

"If it was anywhere near," said Lauren, "then Sparrow would know, believe me. But Tony . . ."

He looked back at her.

"As soon as you step off the boat, it'll sense that you've returned. It won't know where straight away, but it'll begin hunting until it picks up a trail. Remember that."

"How could I forget?" said Tony, and stepped up from the deck rail on to the towpath. He pulled the waterproof tight around his neck and looked back.

"Keep your eye open for your religious friends. Anyone pokes their nose out, shoot it off."

"Have a good day at the office, dear," said Lauren and tried to smile.

Tony nodded awkwardly, like a man receiving confirmation from his doctor that he had only hours to live.

And then he hurried off down an alley between warehouses. He did not look back.

Soon, he had vanished from sight.

47

They stayed on the abandoned slipway, by the fire, all night.

Randall had dozed in fits and starts, still with his arm around Ranjana. She had fallen asleep almost immediately, and Randall supposed that after everything they'd been through in a day – everything she'd been through – she was still in shock. Exhaustion had taken its toll on Ranjana, but there was too much spinning around in Randall's head to allow him to slip into a deep sleep. Every time he awoke, the big man called Mac was still sitting there, staring into the fire. Didn't he ever sleep? One of the other vagrants would occasionally wander over to that fire and throw more detritus on it to keep it going. It was a bitterly cold night, but that fire was keeping the chill at bay.

In the moments of sleep, everything that had happened to Randall whirled around in his head like a crazy action replay. When he awoke, the bigger questions that he hadn't had time to ask himself came crowding in. What the hell had he let himself in for here? He was in enough trouble already. Now he appeared to have inherited Ranjana's problems, too. If the police caught up with them *(when* the police caught up with them – who was he kidding?) they were bound to pin the panda car bit on him. Whatever happened to Ranjana, he was going to end up doing time. He'd ignored common sense and gone running right in when he'd heard those screams, had played his hand then whether he liked it or not. But afterwards he should have moved on and left her to her own devices. What the hell had got into him? So, he'd saved her from those yobbos, prevented the police from taking her back to her family. Gave her money, bought her clothes. What the hell else did he have to do? Wasn't it time to move on?

But . . . but . . .

Something was preventing him. Despite all the common sense he could muster, he believed the hare-brained story that she had told him. On the face of it, she might have seemed looney-tunes, telling such a crazy story. But he remembered the look on her face, and the way that she told it. Randall had grown up with lies, could smell one a mile away. And this girl wasn't lying. And she wasn't out of her head, either.

There was something else.

Something about their meeting with this strange man called Mac had affected him profoundly. He had never felt like this before. It was as if that meeting was connected on long, invisible rubber bands, to the time when his father had drunkenly pulled him out of bed and tried to smash his head in with that poker. From that moment, it was as if the whole journey from that dingy, ill-kept flat on a no-hope street in a no-hope slum to this abandoned slipway God-knew-where had been predestined. The journey wasn't over – whatever the nature of that journey might be – but something important had happened when they had met the big guy. Ranjana's reaction, nearly keeling over and falling off the jetty. The talk of dreams – of Ranjana's and Mac's. All of it seemed connected, and Randall knew that he must stay and see this mystery through. He was not a bystander, the way he had been a bystander in most things all his life – he was part of whatever in hell was unravelling here, and he would have to stay and wait to see what his part in this thing could be.

The sun was coming up. Randall could see a faint orange line on the crooked industrial skyline beyond the river. The clouds there were stained with a vermilion tint. A gentle movement off to his right caught his eye. When he turned to look, Randall could see that one of the street people was shambling through the mud towards him. He walked like an old man, his hair was awry, the seam of an indeterminate jacket split from hem to armpit, but he couldn't have been much older than Randall. He had the same look on his face that the others held: respect, even awe. He held out a bottle to Randall. It was a lemonade bottle, but the contents were purple-coloured.

"Something to get the day started," said the man.

"No," said Randall. "No thanks."

The man nodded extravagantly and backed off to where the others slept or watched. Ranjana stirred at his side at the sound of his voice. Something else moved, this time beside the fire. Randall watched the big man slowly stand, noticing how all the others on the slipway turned their attention to him. He stretched, turned and slowly began to pick his way through the mud to where Randall and Ranjana slept. Mac stopped when he was still several feet away.

"Still here?" he asked.

"Still here," replied Randall.

Now, Ranjana began to awake. She felt beautifully warm against Randall's side. Mac looked out across the river. "The ship that took me to the Falklands was built here."

223

"You were in the Falklands?"

"Yeah, 5th Battalion Parachute Regiment. I was a corporal."

"That's where you were burned," said Ranjana, now fully awake.

"Just as you've dreamed it. Skirmish at Mount Longdon. I was reported 'Missing in Action'. Know what's really funny? I spent nine months in intensive care, undergoing plastic surgery. They didn't know who I was. The Argentinians had me, see? Then when they found out their mistake, when England and Argentina were trying to come to some sort of 'arrangement', I became an embarrassment. I was ... hushed up. Now ... well, now I'm on the streets."

"What about your family, what about friends?"

"Records said I'd not got family. Apparently my father died while I was still missing. As to friends, who knows? Lost my memory, see? Can't remember anything before I was burned."

"Is the pain bad?" asked Ranjana.

"Yeah ... pretty bad sometimes."

"What about drugs?" asked Randall. "Surely someone can help you."

"I can't. They find out who I am – chances are they'll lock me up to avoid embarrassment."

"That can't be right. Not from what you've said. Who cares a toss about ... ?"

"Look!" snapped Mac. His voice was powerful. "There's something you've got to understand about me. Chances are this is the only time you'll get anything out of me – first thing in the morning. My body was damaged – but so was my mind. Sometimes I remember things, most of the time I don't. I ..." Mac looked out across the river again, as if searching for the right word. "I ... drift. See? So bear that in mind. While I'm still ... while I'm ... look, anyway, *you're* here now. Right, girl?"

"What do you mean?"

"This dream thing. You recognised me as soon as you saw me. Right? Well, it's the same for me. Soon as I saw you up there on the jetty."

"But I don't understand," said Ranjana. "What does it all mean?"

"Something's happening," replied Mac. "Don't know what. But something *bad*'s happening. My mate Bernie started to tell me about it, but he didn't make much sense. Now Bernie's dead and gone and I can't ask him any more. He was murdered."

"Bernie?" asked Randall.

"Okay," said Mac, ignoring the query. "Let's go."

"Where?" asked Ranjana.

"Aren't you hungry?" Mac turned from them and began to trudge up the slipway.

Randall looked at Ranjana ruefully. "So what else are we going to do? Let's follow him."

He helped her to stand. Their joints were stiff and awkward after an entire night sitting down there, but Mac was making no allowances as he strode away up the sliproad. Randall noticed how the other vagrants were beginning to rise and drift away, as if they had somehow been an audience at some strange open-air play. Now that the performance was over, they were on their way again.

They followed Mac as he strode on ahead, up to the top of the slipway and on through the rusted and abandoned sheds that had once been part of a thriving industrial area. Rusted chains swayed and screeched from skeletal cranes. Unlocked factory doors banged in the wind. Now that they were away from the fire, they were both suddenly aware of the bitter chill in the air.

Half an hour later, they passed under a flyover. Beyond it, off to the right-hand side of the road, they could see a patch of cleared ground – as if someone had decided that it was a good spot for a car park, but then after clearing all the weeds and the soil and the detritus away, had changed their mind and left it. Beyond, Randall could see the first line of houses on a council estate. Half a dozen people were already standing in that "car park", flapping their arms and stamping their feet to keep warm.

They followed Mac on to the waste ground. When he reached the mid-spot he stopped and turned to face them. None of the others who were already there made an effort to communicate.

"What happens here?" asked Ranjana when they finally reached him.

"This is one of the places where the street people can eat. There's usually a van here, first thing. Salvation Army, maybe. One of the voluntary organisations. Get something hot to eat and drink. There are other places like this."

Even as he spoke, a van was coming down the main road towards them. Randall watched the others on the waste ground turn towards it as it came. They were no longer flapping their arms, no longer stamping their feet.

The van slowed, and then turned in their direction. It came on towards them, bumping over the rough ground. Mac turned and clapped his hands. When the van driver sounded his horn once, he smiled and said, "Breakfast."

The van swerved around and stopped as the street people moved briskly towards it. Randall followed close behind Mac as he also moved towards it. The driver jumped out of the cab and exchanged a few words with the first two people nearest to the van: a wiry old man who looked like a scarecrow, and an enormous bag lady wrapped in several dozen layers of clothing. Randall couldn't hear what was said, but it elicited a howl of laughter from the woman. Smiling, the young man moved to the side of the van and unfastened a series of clasps in the bodywork. He was in his mid-twenties, smart and fresh-looking. Immaculate white shirt, clean new jeans. Someone else was inside the van and Randall watched as a flap in the side of the van was lowered and the young man pulled out a couple of struts, so that it formed a high bench. Inside, he could see a soup urn and sandwiches already piled. Suddenly, he realised just how hungry he'd become.

"Don't know about you, Ranjana," he said, "but I could eat a . . ."

When he turned, Ranjana was no longer at his side.

She was standing back at the original spot they'd been in when the van had first arrived.

"Come on!" he shouted. "Aren't you hungry?"

In reply, Ranjana shook her head – too vigorously. There was something wrong. In puzzlement, Randall looked back to the van again, and to Mac, who was already moving forward as the young man skipped back into the van again. The others were crowding around the flap, eager to eat.

"What's wrong?" he asked, turning back to Ranjana. She shook her head again. Cursing, Randall left the van and strode back to her. As he drew nearer, he could see the expression on her face at last. She was terrified. She was standing, straight-backed and staring at the van. Her hands were clasped in front of her. "Ranjana . . . ?"

She didn't answer him. It was as if all she could see was the van and the people around it. Randall looked back there. Could one of the street people be one of the yobs who had attacked her yesterday? No, these were all a lot older, and certainly not so well-dressed.

"What's the matter?" he asked again. "Is there someone . . . ?"

"It's the van," said Ranjana in a tight voice.

"What about it?"

"I don't know. It's just . . . just . . ."

"Look, come on and get something to eat." Randall could see that Mac was eating. "We haven't had anything since yesterday."

" . . . just . . . *evil.*"

"What do you mean, 'evil'? For God's sake, Ranjana, it's just a van."

"It's not just a van!" Ranjana's voice had risen. Randall could see that she was trembling. "It's not just a *van!*" Ranjana was backing off now, and Randall did not know what to do. He moved forward, tried to calm her, but Ranjana suddenly turned and began to run.

"Ranjana!"

Randall ran after her, cursing again under his breath. He was

226

hungry, needed to eat. And how could a bloody van be evil?

He caught her on the main road, just beneath the flyover. Grabbing her arm he spun her around to face him.

"Why are you running away? What the hell's wrong with you?"

"Leave me alone!" snapped Ranjana, her voice echoing under the concrete buttresses of the flyover. Randall stood back when he saw how distressed she had become. Tears were in her eyes. "Just . . ."

"Okay, okay . . ."

Ranjana took a deep breath, tried to calm down. She wiped the tears from her eyes with the back of one hand.

"Look, Randall. I'm sorry. But there's something . . . something about that van. Something not right. I don't know what it is, but I just know that it's dangerous to be near it, dangerous to be around it."

"Have you seen anything? You know, like those – vision-things you see."

"No, I can't see anything." She moved closer to Randall, put a hand on his arm as she looked back at the van. "It's just a feeling, that's all. Just a feeling."

Randall turned to look back and saw that Mac was making his way towards them, eating a sandwich.

"Okay," said Randall, trying to keep her calm. "Try and analyse your feeling. Is it the van itself, or the people, or maybe something about the food they're giving out?"

Ranjana stood in silence as Mac drew nearer. Randall watched her face. It was tense as she concentrated inwards, trying to grasp the essence of her fears.

"No, it's no use. I can't isolate it. But what I'm feeling is real, Randall. It's *real*."

Mac finally reached them.

"What's wrong?"

Randall explained, and Mac stood watching them both carefully as he finished his sandwich. When Randall finished, he said, "Nothing wrong with the food?"

"No," said Ranjana. "Not the food – but *something*."

"Good, well, as long as I haven't been poisoned" – Mac pulled out two cellophane-wrapped sandwiches from each jacket pocket – "you may as well have these."

Randall looked at Ranjana. She nodded, and they both took a sandwich each, ripping open the cellophane eagerly. Mac looked back at the van.

"Let's walk."

They turned and walked back in the direction of the river, away from the van.

"What makes you think there's something wrong with the van?" asked Mac eventually.

"You better tell him everything," said Randall. "But it's going to sound crazy."

"Probably no crazier than two complete strangers dreaming about each other," replied Mac.

As they walked, Ranjana explained everything about her precognition. Mac listened in silence as they walked. And Randall found himself examining this strange man closely as Ranjana told her story. There was something intriguing about him. He had the look of a vagrant, with his wild hair and his beard, the very way that he walked. He looked shabby, but his clothes weren't dirty. Something about Mac's face intrigued Randall. Then he remembered the plastic surgery and guessed that his face had been completely remodelled. It seemed that Mac was wearing a life-like mask, but the startling blue eyes behind that mask seemed to belong to a different face altogether. It was a curious and unsettling effect. Again, Randall found himself wondering at how he had got himself mixed up in this bizarre jigsaw. They had been walking for some time, following the main road. At last, they had reached a shopping centre, with greengrocer's, convenience stores and newsagent's on either side of the road. The traffic was busier here as the world began to wake up, and they received more than one curious stare from the early morning pedestrians as they walked.

"What about the two thirty at Doncaster?" said Mac at last. "Who's going to win it?"

"This is *serious*," said Ranjana sharply.

"Yes, I think you're right," continued Mac. "But there's more going on here than—" He stopped suddenly, his hand going to his face. "More going on than . . ." He moaned then and reached out with his other hand to steady himself against a wall.

Randall moved to him. "What is it? What's wrong?"

" . . . Three, seven, four, oh-two . . ."

"What? What did you say?"

Mac pushed himself back from the wall.

"All right . . . all right . . ."

He motioned that they should keep walking. Randall and Ranjana had gone on ahead for several yards before they realised that Mac was not following them. This time, he was simply standing, hand at his temple and staring directly across the street.

"*Now* what?" asked Randall, as they moved back to join him.

As they drew level, they could both see that something was disturbing the big man.

" . . . don't believe it," he said, as they followed his gaze.

There was a furniture store just across the way. The steel shutters on the windows had yet to be removed for the day's business. Red and black graffiti covered the metal. But it wasn't this that had drawn Mac's attention. Between both windows was a recess, leading to the store's front door.

There was a man standing in there.

His shoulders were hunched as if he was frozen with the cold. His hair was wet and awry, his face white and bloodless. His clothes were torn and shabby. From this distance, he looked wet through. He was staring fixedly at Mac.

Before Randall or Ranjana could ask, Mac stepped forward to the kerb and shouted to the man across the street.

"Bernie? Is that you, Bernie?"

The figure did not respond. It remained motionless in the shop doorway, arms hanging at its side.

"Bernie? For the love of Christ, *is that you?*"

Mac stepped off the kerb. Instantly, a horn blared – and Randall just managed to pull Mac to the safety of the pavement as a van hurtled past. There was more traffic behind it, and Mac pulled roughly away from Randall, looking for a break so that he could cross the street. Finally, there was a gap and Mac dodged quickly between two cars, vanishing from sight.

When the stream of traffic had passed, Randall and Ranjana crossed over to see what was going on.

Mac was standing in the shop doorway, his back to them and blocking the stranger from sight. As they reached him, Mac turned – and now they could see that the shop doorway was empty. All that remained was a dirty pool of water.

"He's gone," said Mac in a voice that suddenly sounded very hollow. "By the time I got here, he had gone."

"Bernie?" said Ranjana. "Wasn't that the man you said you saw murdered?"

Mac turned and looked up and down the street for any sign of the stranger. There was none.

"It can't have been him," said Randall.

"It was him, all right," said Mac.

And then he remembered what Bernie had been telling him last night. Mac remembered Bernie's story about the newcomers on the street, the street people with their terrible, blank and hungry faces. He remembered Bernie saying something about people whom he knew were dead – but were suddenly turning up again on the streets.

"Whatever in hell is going on," said Mac, "Bernie's joined them now."

229

"What?" said Ranjana.

"Dead people are coming back," said Mac simply, and walked on ahead up the main street.

Ranjana and Randall looked at each other, and then followed after him.

48

The ground beneath Tony's feet felt alien to him. As if he'd touched ground for the first time in years.

Now that he was away from the narrow boat, Tony felt vulnerable in a way that he had never experienced before. As he ran quickly down deserted alleys, looked furtively around corners and kept watching and listening as he moved for any sign or sounds of wind, it was like being back on the Shankill Road, like being back in the Falklands. Back in Ireland, the fear was generated by the unseen presence of a sniper's gunsight. Moving from street corner to street corner, knowing that you would never hear the shot before it hit you. All this bullshit in the movies about hearing the gunshot and then dodging in the nick of time before the shot bounced off a convenient rock, was just that – bullshit. One moment you would be there, weaving from side to side, dodging from street corner to street corner, and the next your head would be gone in an instant, like an exploded melon. In the Falklands, he had judged all of his fears by the ultimate experience of all – by that dripping hose of fire, and the knowledge that hideous, agonising death was seconds away.

But the fear now was somehow much, much greater than then.

As soon as Tony had stepped onto dry land, an instinctive, almost animalistic fear had returned. It was an instinctive fear of anything human hunted by a Mechanic. That fear threatened to rob his strength as he ran, and Tony knew that he had a long way to go yet.

When he finally reached the first main street where people were going about their daily business, he felt alienated from them in a way that he'd never experienced before. As if somewhere along the way, he had turned the wrong street corner and walked straight into the Twilight Zone, where the normal rules that govern life and existence no longer applied. He'd turned that wrong street corner on the night that he had picked up Lauren and her child. From that moment, he'd somehow ceased to be in the real world. The people he saw now were

231

a different breed, had nothing to do with him. They could not help him. Unlike them, he was being . . .

Hunted.

Again, instinctively, he knew that the Mechanic was aware that he had moved away from his sanctuary on water and was back on land. Instinctively, it knew he was back – and, wherever it was, it was trying to find his scent.

Tony skipped across a main street and narrowly avoided being flattened by a taxi. The horn blared at him as he passed, and as he darted down another alley, he wondered if that taxi-driver had been one of his colleagues in a previous life. He blundered into a dustbin overflowing with rubbish, left in the alley for collection. He hopped over the spilled garbage and continued on his way. Already, his energy was flagging. The pain in his back was excruciating and he had still not fully recovered from all the liquid crap he'd swallowed back there in the canal escaping from the Mechanic.

When he reached the side street which led up to his lodging house, around the corner, his heart began to pound. He had been running too hard for too long, must stop. He braced his hands on his thighs and bent over, trying to catch his breath, unable to hear any first signs of a whispering, deadly wind because of his own ragged breathing, and the pounding in his head. He continued walking after a while, face red with exertion, sweat trickling down his back and further aggravating the pain in the wound there.

At the street corner, he leaned against a streetlamp and looked around to where his lodging house stood, over a hundred yards away.

At least it was still standing.

But even from this distance, Tony could see that it had been badly damaged. All the windows seemed to have been blown out. There were black smoke stains on the upper brickwork edges of each window. The ground-floor doors and windows had been boarded up. There was a ribbon of red and white tape right around the site, held in place with workmen's metal spikes jammed into the ground at regular intervals.

Tony began to walk towards the lodging house. There was no one else on the street, and it seemed to him as if he had walked on to a vast movie set. No extras were going to be allowed to wander into this scene – this stage-managed nightmare was for Tony Dandridge alone. As he moved, he kept looking for any sign of a wind, a gust, a sound. Eventually, he could make out more detail of the damage done to the building since he'd fled. Now, he could see the window from which he'd escaped. The drainpipe had fallen away.

Christ, look how high up it is . . .

Something white and rustling flew up from a garden hedge. It hissed, dropped low and skimmed the pavement towards him.

"Bloody *hell!*" Tony leaped back in panic, kicking out at the thing. It flapped at his feet and wrapped itself around his shins. Tony kicked it away in horror – and saw that it was a newspaper. It flopped into the gutter and remained still. Heart hammering, Tony whirled in the street, looking for the direction from which the hell-wind would erupt, the wind which had flicked this newspaper at him.

But there was no breath of air, no whisper.

Tony wiped his face, and continued on towards the lodging house.

Part of him was desperate to run away, desperately afraid and only wanting to get away from the horror. But another part of him knew that he must stay. He had accepted the logic of this nightmare; knew, crazy though it was, that he had no alternative other than to accept that logic if he wanted to stay alive. Knew that he must force himself not to think too closely about what he was doing, because if he did, then he might begin to question everything, just as he'd questioned everything before – and again instinctively he knew that doing this could only lead to slow reactions and to his death. Or worse.

Hell is a place, Lauren had said. And those words seemed to echo in his head.

At last, Tony drew level with the front of the house, but kept to the other side of the street. In all this time, no one had passed him. The whole building, in its semi-derelict state, just seemed to confirm his inner plight. Once, this place had been his home, his refuge from bad memories and evil streets. Now it stood like some kind of monument to his former world, his life and his beliefs – all of which had been turned upside down. How many people had died here as a result of his encounter with the Mechanic? But Tony killed this thought before it debilitated him.

Somewhere in the distance, a car passed. The sound of its tyres on gravel made Tony freeze again, looking back and forth along the street, waiting for the wind to explode around a corner, coughing forward an explosion of street rubbish and detritus before it.

Again, nothing. The sound of the car disappeared into the distance. Looking back, he wondered what had happened to his taxi. If it hadn't been smashed up by collapsing masonry or that bloody hell-wind, maybe the firm had taken it back. The no claims bonus on that taxi was the least worry on his mind.

Tony steeled himself and crossed the street, walking towards the lodging house. As he walked, another thought came to him, one that made him weak with fear. What if the Mechanic was still here? What if it was still in the building, just waiting for him? Could it know that he *knew* there was only one way to stop it – ridiculous though that way seemed? Just as Sparrow was supposed to be able to sense things about its movement and its action, could it also sense things about Sparrow and know that he had told Tony what to do? Instead of prowling the waterways, not knowing when and if he was going to set foot on dry land, wouldn't it just be better to stay here – in the lodging house – and wait for *him* to come to *it*?

It was a long way back to the canal. Even further to any other stretch of water.

"Shit!" Tony yanked one of the metal spikes out of the ground in front of the building and tore off the red and white tape. What was he going to do after all – just stand outside and pee his pants? He stepped forward to the boarded-up door and jammed the point of the spike between the board and the brickwork. Using fear to fuel his anger, he pushed hard and then began to lever the board away from the door.

The board ripped away easier than he would have expected. Dropping the spike, he was able to get his fingers in the crack that he had made, and after several hard tugs the board came away in his hands. He flung it to the ground – and heard the sound echo inside.

As he grabbed up the spike again, part of Tony prayed that the reason for the echo was that the staircase had burned through and collapsed. The other part – the part that had accepted the nightmare – told him that if it had, he was as good as dead. This was his last chance. Unless he wanted to spend the rest of his limited life floating in a canal. A crazy rush of images came to him as he stood on the threshold, waiting until his eyes became accustomed to the gloom. Images of him somehow coming to a deal with Larry White, of staying on that narrow boat and keeping one step ahead of the religious freaks who were after Lauren and her baby. Occasional ventures onto dry land to steal food. Then, another thought: once they got the girl and the child, they surely wouldn't be after him any more. Angry at the fact that this thought should have intruded, angry at everything that had happened to him, Tony strode into the hallway, holding the spike as a weapon. He nearly stumbled on the loose rubble at his feet.

"All right, you bastard!" he shouted into the darkness. "I'm here!"

The only replies were the echoes of his voice, as if he had shouted in some dark cathedral. Despite the fact that the place had been burned out, he could *still* smell that bloody damp in the hallway. Just beyond him, he could see the staircase looming. Carefully, struggling to keep the terror at bay, Tony moved forward and began to climb.

The darkness seemed all-enveloping. He could barely make out more than the staircase in front of him. And the higher that he climbed, the darker it seemed to become. Somewhere up ahead, through a

234

crazy criss-cross framework of burned and shredded flooring, he could see isolated shafts of light stabbing into the interior of the building from the burned-out windows of the upper storeys, but that limited light gave no clue to the extent of the damage.

He climbed, holding the spike like a spear.

There were gaps in the stairs beneath his feet, making it almost sensible to hang on to the banister as he moved. But Tony remembered that loose banister further up and he concentrated carefully instead on the individual steps, testing each one before putting his full weight on it. The smell of burned wood and fabric was now overpowering. It tasted sour in his mouth, just like the taste of fear.

He reached the first landing and paused there, breathing hard, still holding the spike defensively. The spears of light up ahead illuminated ragged patches of scarred plasterwork and an occasional fallen timber but still gave no clear idea of how safe it was to continue. He strained to look right and left along the corridors that gave access to the first-floor boarding room, but it was impossible to see whether the floors even existed in this darkness. Tony continued onwards, each testing and careful tread of his foot on the creaking stairs enormously amplified.

Something hissed softly up ahead.

Tony's stomach lurched, his mouth filled with bile. Jabbing the spike instinctively upwards, he froze on the stairs.

A thin cloud of plaster dust drifted down over his head and shoulders. There was no further sound. A pigeon maybe, dislodging something higher up. Tony swallowed hard and continued.

There were gaping holes in the second landing. Warily stepping around them, he reached the next flight. He knew from memory just how high up he was now. If this staircase decided that his weight was too much for it, or if something he'd rather not think about suddenly came rushing down from above . . . ? Tony ascended. The stairs here seemed more solid somehow, less fragile. The landing itself was also pretty solid. But on the next flight was the wobbly banister of old. How much had that been weakened or burned? After that, a final flight of stairs leading to his own floor. Tony still tested each step, but these stairs did not creak. He was going to make it after all . . .

And then his foot came down where there was no step.

Tony shouted out involuntarily, his cry loud and echoing, as his leg went straight through a ragged aperture. He twisted as he fell, his right arm hooking on the banister rail which he already knew was loose. Something crashed away beneath him, the iron spike spinning from his hand. He heard the crashing explosions of plaster far below, heard the ringing clatter of the spike as it bounced and shivered all the way to the ground floor.

All of his weight was on that banister.

Oh sweet Jesus, Jesus, Jesus . . .

Tony braced his left leg on the step below and felt the banister creak under his weight. He paused again, gasping for air. He knew what was going to happen now. When he took his weight on his left leg and used the banister for a brace, the whole thing was going to collapse and send him hurtling downwards, following the spike.

There was no other way.

. . . sweet Jesus . . .

Tony pushed down with his left leg and began to raise his right from the ragged hole in the stairway.

The banister groaned. Then the wood gave a terrifying *crack!* It was going. The whole damn thing was *going . . .*

And then his foot was out of the hole and back on the previous step. Gasping in exertion and disbelief, Tony leaned away from the banister and stepped down several steps. He stood like that for a long time, not believing that the whole damn thing hadn't just collapsed and sent him spinning into the stairwell.

"You little bastard," he said aloud to the banister. "You were fooling me all along . . ."

And then something up ahead groaned, cracked and fell away with a shuddering roar. The staircase juddered violently. Caution gone, Tony skipped backwards on to the landing, poised and waiting for the whole structure to fall apart. Light suddenly flooded the stairwell from above, momentarily blinding him. He shaded his eyes with one hand, still prepared for the worst.

The crashing and rumbling slowly stopped. The staircase ceased to judder.

Waving away the clouds of plaster dust, coughing and spluttering, Tony looked up ahead.

Crashing through the stair that didn't exist had set something into chain reaction here. A huge chunk of masonry had come apart in the far wall, dropping away into the interior of the building. At last, he could see what had happened in here. And he thanked God for that missing stair.

There was nothing beyond the staircase he had been climbing. At the top, where there should have been a landing and a further flight of stairs leading to his floor, was a great, vast nothingness. The entire top floor of the lodging house had burned, including the two flights of stairs leading down from it. And the staircase, and floor, and every single room that had once been there, had burned and collapsed into the building's interior. He could see the vast scene of destruction below him now through the holes in the staircase that he had just ascended. Now, he could see just how lucky he had been. The staircase was even more riddled that he'd imagined. The missing step, and the banister that should have snapped but didn't, had saved him.

Tony didn't know whether to laugh or cry.

Any prospect of finding any of his material possessions, least of all a bloody photograph that he may or may not have had, was gone. He would never find anything in that chaotic, jumbled mass of brickwork down below.

Carefully again, but now more sure of his step, Tony descended.

Now that he could see more clearly, now that it seemed less dangerous – was this when the staircase would decide to collapse?

Tony was soaked in sweat.

Two flights from the bottom, he could take no more of the tension.

He jumped down both flights, hopping from one apparently firm footing to another. The sounds of his descent echoed and rattled loud, but he kept on going. Halfway down the last flight, he flung himself forward in a leap that seared agony across his back. Clouds of plaster dust enveloped him as he hit what had once been the hallway floor. The staircase screeched in protest as Tony hurtled towards the front door.

Outside, in the daylight and on the sidewalk, he turned to look back, expecting to hear a great shuddering crash as the entire staircase finally collapsed into the stairwell. It failed to oblige him.

Tony staggered away from the doorway, coughing and spluttering, catching sight at last of a council notice that hung from the red and white tape.

This building is unsafe.

"Thanks for the warning," said Tony out loud.

What the hell was he going to do now? Lauren had been precise about the photograph. Now that his entire personal possessions had gone, what was he going to do? Not for the first time, he knew that he was in one hell of a predicament.

Hell is a place, Lauren had said. Again, that bloody phrase, repeating in his head.

Lauren's last words to him when he'd left the narrow boat, meant as some kind of grim joke.

Have a good day at the office, dear.

And Tony wondered just how stupid a man could be. Probably as stupid as someone called Tony Dandridge who had just risked his life in a dangerously burned-out building, when he'd no need to. Just as stupid as a man called Tony Dandridge who had given the Mechanic extra time to find his scent by wasting time in the same burned-out building.

Cursing himself as he shook off the plaster dust from his head and shoulders, Tony ran to the other side of the street.

Somewhere, maybe somewhere close, he heard the soft keening sounds of a wind.

"Oh God, no . . . just a little more time, just a *little* more . . ."

Tony spun around on the pavement, getting his bearings.

" . . . a *little* more time . . ."

This really was his last chance, one that had been given to him. After that, he wouldn't be able to run any more.

Tony looked back in the direction he'd come. An empty beer can rattled and rolled across the street. Turning quickly, he tried to ignore the pain, and ran again.

49

Gerry sits in the darkness, looking at the crackling blue-white storm of nothingness on his television screen. It is the only illumination. The curtains have never been drawn since Sharon went away. Transmission closed down over two hours ago, but he still sits watching the screen.

Earlier that day, he called a special meeting. Again, at the ruined community centre. The Man tells him that the venue is almost poetic. The Man is with him always now, they are never apart. Sometimes when Gerry speaks, it is as if the Man himself is speaking. Like today, at the centre.

The Nektre distribution is proceeding even more speedily than the Man could have hoped for. It's all over the estate – and Andreas and his boys are furious. Their own trade is not so much "dropping off" as disintegrating and they're on the lookout for the suppliers and peddlers. They've made it known that whoever's dealing will have their balls cut off, so Gerry's people are being super careful. So fast is the new drug burning out the opposition, that the kids on the street have already rechristened it – Wildfire.

The identity of the supplier – Gerry – can't remain a secret for long. The Man had told him so. All Andreas has to do is make a guess, and there could only be two, possibly three names on the suspect list. The drug hit the streets four days ago, and the Man tells Gerry as he sits staring at the hissing screen that they've probably only got a couple of days before Andreas puts two and two together, or catches one of Gerry's lieutenants Nektre-handed. But by that time, it won't matter. Hundreds of kids will have taken the drug by then, and that's all that matters. Gerry nearly asks why, but the thought hardly forms in his mind before Pearce Ramsden's reassuring voice tells him not to worry – it's all part of the great plan, all part of the great revenge which will give him all that he's ever wanted.

Gerry knows that things have changed in his mind.

It's a strange feeling, a feeling of not really being in his body, but of

239

being outside it somehow. Like now – he sees himself sitting in the armchair looking at the television screen, as if he was standing on the other side of the room. Today, at the community centre, he seemed to be standing with his own gang, looking up at someone who looked like him standing on the steps of the ruined stage. The voice that came from that figure sounded like his voice, but the words were the words of the Man.

That feeling started when Sharon had tried to kill him.

The Man tells him that the changes in his mind are all part of the plan. He must embrace those changes, do as the Man says – and it will all come right.

But most of all, Gerry's gang must scour the estate and the city to find the girl and the baby. This is the most important thing of all. Gerry listened to the Man's voice coming from his mouth today, reinforcing this point. A vital part of the strategy.

Gerry turns his attention from the blue-white flickering of the screen to that which rests upon it like an ornament.

Sharon had such lovely hair, took such great care of it. He wonders if he should comb it.

The black bin bags are all over the living room, dragged back in from the garage at the Man's behest. The contents have been arranged in the living room; on the coffee table, the dining table, the sofa. The Man tells him that this is necessary to maintain the changes taking place in his head.

Gerry wonders if he'll be allowed to kiss Sharon goodnight before he goes to bed.

"Of course," says Ramsden indulgently. "What kind of world would it be without love . . .?"

50

Lauren!

The call of her name brought her instantly awake.

At first, she had tried to settle down below in the narrow boat, keeping watch through the windows. But those windows were too narrow, and too low. She could not possibly keep a close watch on the area to which they were docked; the view was much too restricted. So she had settled Sparrow down on the double bed – he was clearly worn out, and had gone straight to sleep. Then she had returned to the aft deck, throwing open the double doors and sitting on the top step, cradling the gun in her lap. She could see most of the surrounding area from here; more if she simply stood up. It was quiet here. There were no sounds of distant traffic, only the gentle lapping of water. She hadn't meant to sleep, had been unaware that it was going to creep up on her like that.

But sleep had finally ambushed her.

And the sound of Sparrow's urgent voice had awoken her.

Lauren stood up quickly, grabbing at the gun in her lap. And then fear crested and plummeted inside her.

Four people were standing on the canal towpath, looking at her.

They were standing calmly and quietly, and as if they had suddenly appeared from nowhere. Each figure stood apart from the others by about eight or nine feet, in a crescent shape – and looking for all the world like some human net.

They had caught up with her. The Sabbarite.

Lauren raised the gun in two hands and pointed it at them, gunsight moving slowly from one figure to the next. Her hands began to tremble violently.

"Stay where you are!" she shouted.

In response, the figures simply smiled. She knew each of them.

Fletcher: in his mid-twenties, wearing a business suit and looking as if he'd just come from a car salesroom. Blond hair, spectacles, hands

241

clasped comfortably in front of him. Smiling.

Bradford: a woman in her mid-forties. Power-dressed in a black trouser suit. Dark hair down to her shoulders and framing a face that seemed bleached of colour. A string of pearls around her neck that looked like a necklace of human teeth from this distance. Smiling.

Ernest: middle-aged, wearing a tweed jacket that looked too small for him and the wisps of hair usually carefully parted over his balding pate ruffling in the breeze. *Eyes like a pig*, Lauren remembered.

Terri: early twenties, slender-framed. Short dark hair and raincoat. Lauren knew that she worked in an expensive fashion shop, and was working her way up as the "good vibes" of their activities manipulated fate and fortune.

Sparrow! Why didn't you tell me?

I didn't see them coming, Lauren. They must have done something. They "cloaked" themselves. They know I can sense them.

Shit, shit, shit, shit!

"Hello, Lauren," said a young woman's voice from somewhere behind the silent figures on the towpath. The others inclined their heads only slightly in the direction of the voice, and then Lauren saw an all-too familiar and horrifying figure step around the corner of a warehouse wall and walk slowly towards her.

The figure was a young woman, nineteen years old. Her red hair was braided and hung over her shoulders, like something out of *Little House on the Prairie*. Her dress was more like a nineteenth-century smock, hanging down to well below her knees. There were stains on the front of that smock. Food stains – and other stains.

But the girl had no eyes. Only empty, black sockets.

She smiled as she came on, walking through the crescent of four and on towards the narrow boat.

"Stay where you are, Lorelei!" Lauren gripped the gun hard to prevent the trembling, aiming it dead centre at the approaching figure. The girl with no eyes stopped.

She knows that we can communicate, knows when we're speaking, said Sparrow in Lauren's head. *But I don't think she can actually hear what we're saying.*

"What a clever child you have," said the girl, holding her hands wide, cocking her head to one side in a hideous child-like parody, and smiling the horrifying smile that Lauren remembered from her drug-soaked, twilight existence.

Lauren grabbed the deck handrail and pulled herself closer to the quay. They were going to try something. The sooner she could cast off the better.

"Stand back! All of you!"

The five figures remained unmoved.

"I said stand back!"

They still remained unmoved.

Lauren pulled the trigger. The shot made a *ratcheting* echo, the bullet ploughing into the grass between the blind girl's feet. She did not flinch, and the smile remained constant. But neither did she move forward.

Carefully, Lauren stepped up on to the quay. Kneeling, she began to unwind the mooring rope from the stanchion. She kept the gun pointed at the others.

"I should just put a bullet in you anyway," she said grimly as she untied the knot.

"You couldn't do that," said Lorelei. "Think about the Serendip. The scales and balances. Shooting one of us would be *evil*, wouldn't it, Lauren? It would be a *naughty* thing to do. And the balance that has worked in your favour so far would turn against you."

She's right, said Sparrow from inside the boat. *If you've got to shoot, make sure it's self-defence.*

"Shut up!" shouted Lorelei, face twisting into a snarl. "I wouldn't listen too closely to everything your little bastard says, Lauren. I don't know what advice he's giving you – but look at all the trouble it's got you into already."

"You take one step forward towards me, Lorelei," said Lauren calmly, "and I'll take that as an aggressive action. Then I'll put an extra hole in that face of yours."

Again, the smile returned and the blind girl held her hands up in a mocking gesture of surrender. Still facing them, Lauren finally managed to untie the mooring rope. Without looking back, she threw it on to the deck, stood and carefully walked towards the stanchion at the fore deck.

"This isn't like the girl we remember," said Bradford.

"Not at all like our own sweet Lauren," said Fletcher.

"Maybe because the Lauren you knew was pumped full of fucking drugs twenty-four hours a day."

"How ungrateful," said the blind girl. "Those weren't just *any* old drugs. Daddy had to pull all sorts of strings to get them. And you won't find drugs like that in any pharmacy, my darling. They helped the baby inside you to develop the way it has . . ."

"And kept me like a zombie."

"Give the child back to us and we'll let you go," said Lorelei suddenly and sternly.

"You can all go to Hell," said Lauren, reaching the mooring rope.

243

"Once you had the child from me, you were going to kill me anyway. You want us both dead. I know it, you know it. So don't waste your breath."

Lauren began to untie the rope again, quickly checking behind her to make sure that the unmoored stern of the boat wasn't drifting out into the canal.

"Hell," said Lorelei. "Nice place to visit. But I don't think we'd want to live there."

Lauren, something's happening!

What? Lauren yanked at the mooring rope. It had been double-looped and seemed stuck fast. She darted anxious glances around. *What is it?*

I don't know. It's blurred.

What do you mean, "blurred"?

Blurred, Lauren! As in "blurred"!

The blind girl began to laugh.

"Don't get testy with me, you little son of a bitch!" snapped Lauren, still struggling with the rope.

Call me that, you're calling yourself a bitch . . .

"Sparrow! Cut it out!"

Okay, okay . . . I'm trying . . . trying . . . to sort it out in my head. But there's danger, Lauren. Coming close.

At last, Lauren was able to yank the mooring rope loose. Standing, she threw it backwards on to the roof of the narrow boat. Then she turned to jump down on to the foredeck.

And then the narrow boat's engine coughed into life.

Lauren! Help me!

Lauren saw water churning from around the stern of the boat, knew that someone – impossibly – had got to the controls on the aft deck. She made ready to jump – and then someone hit her hard from behind. She fell heavily to the concrete quayside, the weight of a body on top of her, a hand clawing into her hair and dragging her head back. Lauren screamed and twisted. The gun discharged, sending a plume of dirty water spraying upwards from the canal.

And then someone hit her hard again, on the back of the head.

Blackness.

Convinced that they'd thrown her into the black water of the canal, and with Sparrow's cry for help still ringing in her ears, Lauren clawed through the blackness. Strong arms seized her.

"Calm *down*, you stupid bitch!" Someone hit her across the head again, and Lauren fell back. Grey, shifting shapes began to form in the blackness. There was pain at the back of her head, and when she

244

clasped a hand there she could feel a raw wound, and blood. Finally, her vision came into focus.

She was back in the narrow boat, in the small cabin. And the others were there, too. Bradford stood back, and Lauren realised that she had been flung on to the small sofa. Bradford had delivered the blow that had knocked her back down when she'd finally come round from her daze. Ernest was busy opening and shutting cupboard doors in the kitchen area, hunting for something. Terri had her usual blank expression and was sitting on the kitchen bench itself, letting her legs dangle like a child. She was chewing gum, and examining her fingernails. Ernest was looking out of the narrow boat, landward. And a stranger was standing next to him, naked from the waist up and towelling himself dry. He was about Ernest's age, dark hair – and wearing rubber suit bottoms like a skindiver.

"Welcome back," said Bradford. Lauren watched her toy playfully with the gun. "Never would have taken you for an Annie Oakley."

Lauren!

"Sparrow!" Lauren lunged from the sofa. Bradford grabbed her hair and tried to force her back, but Lauren shoved back hard, tore free from her grip and lunged down the boat towards the sleeping area. Bradford cursed and stumbled as the boat began to rock violently from side to side.

"What the *hell* . . . !" exclaimed Ernest, slamming a kitchen door as Lauren rushed past him.

"Stop there, Lauren!" yelled Bradford, recovering her balance.

"No!" said the blind girl, suddenly stepping into view from the sleeping area in front of Lauren. "Let her come, Bradford. Everything's all right."

Lauren pushed roughly past Lorelei and looked down on the bed. Sparrow was lying still and calm.

"If you've hurt him . . ."

"Hurt him? Oh no, my darling – not *him*."

Lauren scooped up her son and cradled him close, sitting on the edge of the bed as Lorelei calmly joined the others.

I'm all right, Lauren. She's been . . . talking to me.

"Are you sure? Just talking? That's all?"

"What else could I be doing?" said Lorelei, her back still to them.

"I've seen all sorts of things you're capable of, you fucking monster!"

"Now that's not nice, Lauren. If you're mean to me, I'll have to be mean back."

"Let me slap her around . . ." said Bradford, moving forward.

"No!" snapped Lorelei, turning at last to "look" back at them. "Sit down."

Bradford readjusted her hair angrily, stuck the gun in the belt of her trouser suit and turned to the window. She gestured for a cigarette, and Ernest moved forward to oblige.

Can she hear us, Sparrow? Lauren asked her son.

She just knows we're talking. But she doesn't know what we're saying.

"Don't whisper,' said Lorelei. "It's not nice."

She was just asking questions. About what we'd done. About Tony Dandridge. Trying to communicate.

"And she didn't hurt you?"

No, she never touched me. It's okay, Mother. Take it easy.

"I feel like shit," said the stranger, towelling his hair.

"Never mind," said Terri, still sitting on the kitchen bench and examining her nails. "We'll kill two or three more and you'll feel much better."

"Who's he?" asked Lauren tersely.

"Bolam," replied Lorelei. "He's a new recruit. He's seen the way, Lauren. Knows what the Anonymous One requires, and what he'll get in return. While you were watching us, he swam around the boat and climbed aboard. Very athletic. I think I might let him fuck me tonight."

Bolam ceased to towel his hair and looked up in genuine alarm.

Lorelei laughed. "Just joking, my sweet. Just joking." She turned back to Lauren. "You've caused us a lot of trouble. Two Mechanics conjured? That means a lot of recompense."

How are we going to get out of this, Sparrow?

I don't know. We have to stall for time. That's all we can do . . . Lauren, watch out!

Lauren whirled just as the blind girl reared into vision, delivering a back-handed slap across Lauren's face.

"I said *stop whispering!*"

Lauren shoved at her with both hands, sent her staggering back. Bradford and Ernest crowded close behind her, anxious to get past and teach Lauren a lesson.

"No!" Lorelei held them back. "No . . ."

They won't kill us here, hissed Sparrow quickly. *They'll want to do it at one of their churches to give them extra power in the sacrifice. If they do it here, they'll be wasting their power.*

"I'm warning you," said Lorelei. "If you don't stop whispering, I'll let them past and I'll let them hurt you badly. They won't kill you, but – oh, darling – how they'll *hurt* you."

Stall, Lauren. I'll be quiet for a while until I can get something figured.

"How can you do it, Lorelei?" asked Lauren, cradling Sparrow. "How can you kill your own brother?"

"Appealing to family loyalty?" laughed the blind girl. "That's rich.

We share the same father, that's true. But we were bred for special purposes. Surely you remember that? I was bred for the killing. I was the only one of Daddy Pearce's children allowed to live. Surely you remember some of that, even through the drug haze that Father kept you in all the time. As to killing my brother – well, why not? It will give us power. I killed Father, after all."

"*You* killed him . . ."

"He had to be killed. Poetic justice that I should do it. Didn't he conceive me for a specific purpose? And Lauren, you won't know this, but it's even more poetic that we should find you down here."

"Why?"

Lorelei laughed, relaxing now. The others moved back to the sofa and the windows. "Because, my sweet, your beloved 'husband' and our beloved 'father' is now lying at the bottom of a canal about five miles from here, tied to a car engine block and with his lying, egotistical throat cut. Maybe you've actually sailed over him in your little floating love nest."

"What about Dandridge?"

"What about him?"

"He had nothing to do with any of this."

"It doesn't matter whether he did or not. He's a loose end, sweetie. The Mechanic will take him very soon now, and that little loose end will be neatly tied. Oh, and it's a lot closer to him than your child might have sensed. We've discovered a new little trick. We can mess up his wavelengths, feed him wrong information."

Is that true, Sparrow?

Stall for time, Lauren. Stall! Let me think . . .

Lorelei wagged a stained finger at them both.

"No more whispering, children. Or you'll be *punished* . . ."

"Call the Mechanic off, Lorelei. Let Dandridge go."

"So humane, Lauren. Probably your biggest failing. But impossible I'm afraid . . ."

"It's not impossible. Dandridge told me it killed his landlord. It's tasted blood, so it *can* be returned."

"Oh it can . . . it can . . . and it's tasted *more* than the landlord in its search for you. But it's too late now, my sweet."

"Too late?"

Lorelei giggled like a school child. "Too late for Dandridge. You see, my darling – he's already dead!"

51

The front door of the taxi office burst open, and a wild man blundered into the room.

At the switchboard, Doreen shrieked and fell back in her chair. It swivelled away from the board on its castors and she narrowly avoided being tilted on to the floor.

A drunk! was her first thought. Sometimes, after the pubs were closed, there was trouble with late-night punters who'd missed their last bus home and needed a taxi. Frustrated at not being able to flag one down on the street in their less than stable condition, they'd sometimes blunder in here and make a scene. But this was the middle of the afternoon and Doreen was on her own. No other drivers sitting drinking coffee in the small waiting room next door to help out. Heart hammering, she grabbed at the only available weapon – an empty coffee mug – and raised it threateningly as she staggered out of the swivel chair to face the intruder.

It was Tony Dandridge.

Now leaning against the filing cabinet by the door and fighting to get his breath.

"Tony! What the *hell* are you doing . . . ?"

Tony tried to speak, but couldn't find the breath. He waved a placating hand at her as he leaned against the cabinet. Doreen stood up from the switchboard and moved towards him, mug still in her hand.

"You're in big trouble, Tony. The boss has been going wild. You're going to be in for it when he gets back."

Tony nodded his head at her impatiently, still unable to speak.

"They took your taxi, you know. After the fire."

Tony's eyes registered wild fear.

"My *cab!*"

Doreen took a step back, afraid of that look. "The rental on the cab's overdue and they're talking about revoking your licence, you just

248

buggering off like that. Of *course* they took your cab away."

"Where . . . where did they take it?"

"I don't know. Just away. It ain't here any more."

"Something . . . I need . . . in it."

"That's as may be. But you won't find it here, I'm telling you."

Tony threw his head back, banging it in hopelessness and frustration against the plasterboard wall. Doreen winced.

"What do you need?"

" . . . photograph . . . on licence . . . in the front of the car."

Doreen shrugged. "Like I said, it's not here."

Behind her, the telephone began to ring. She turned towards it – and then Tony grabbed her hand. There was still a wild look in his face, but this time not fear – more a grim determination.

"Give me . . ." gasped Tony. "Give me . . . the keys to the personnel cabinet."

"What? I can't do that."

"*Car 22 here. Doreen, where are you . . . ?*" The switchboard Tannoy crackled into life.

"Oh bugger!" Doreen pulled her hand free, banged the mug down angrily on the cabinet next to Tony and returned to the switchboard to take the call.

"Control here, Car 22. What's the matter?"

"*Been sitting here for fifteen minutes outside 23 Cartwright Terrace. Went and knocked on the door, and nobody's ordered a taxi. What's going on, Doreen?*"

"Get your head screwed on proper, Car 22. That was 23 Cartwright *Road*."

"*What do you mean, Road? You told me Terrace, you silly bint . . .*"

"You call me that again, Billy, and you'll be back on the hackney carriages. It's logged in as Road, and I *told* you Road . . ."

Tony pushed himself away from the cabinet and strode across the office towards a fluted glass door. There was a novelty card pinned to the door: *Boss Man: Don't Do As I Do, Do As I Say*. Tony flung it open and entered. Behind him, he heard Doreen shout: "Tony! Get out of there. You know he doesn't like people . . ."

"*Control? Car 27 here . . .*"

"Oh bugger! Control . . . ?"

Tony moved quickly across the cluttered room that served as the boss's office, around the scarred desk and shoved the boss's seat to one side as he reached the filing cabinet. He yanked at the top drawer. It was locked. Turning around in a frustrated circle, hands held aloft, Tony stood with head down – and then marched back towards Doreen. A telephone rang.

"Hello, Handley Cabs, can I help? Yes, we'll have a cab free in ten minutes." Tony reached her and tried impatiently to interrupt. She slapped at him as she continued. "Where to? And the address? Thank you. And the name? Thank you. Ten minutes." Doreen reached for the switchboard, and Tony caught her hand again.

"I need the keys to the personnel cabinet, Doreen."

"Have you been drinking? Look, I don't know what's the matter with you, but you better get all your answers sorted out before he—'

"The *keys*, Doreen!"

"You want me to call the police?"

Tony turned from her and stormed back into the office.

"I mean it, Tony. You go anywhere near that . . ."

"*Control? Car 24.*"

"Bugger!"

Tony snatched up the chipped letter-opener from the desk and jammed it into the top drawer. He leaned on it with all his weight – and the door juddered open at the same moment that the letter-opener snapped in half with a brittle *crack!*

"Hey!" yelled Doreen. "No, not you . . . now Tony . . . look, you just can't . . . no, not you, Car 24 . . ."

Tony's fevered fingers groped through the alphabetical folder-index, found "D" and yanked the entire section out of the cabinet, throwing it down on to the desk. In seconds, he had found his own folder. Inside, his tax details, National Insurance number, council licence clearances . . . and a copy of the photograph that was attached to the ID in the front of his cab. Tony snatched it up triumphantly and kissed it savagely.

Juggling several calls at the switchboard, Doreen watched Tony stride out of the boss's office, jamming something into his pocket.

"No, you *don't!*" Doreen slammed down the telephone, disconnected her Tannoy call and, as a furious taxi-driver berated her in crackling static, she shoved back her chair again and launched herself at Tony. "Whatever it is, Tony – you put it *back!*"

"For Christ's sake, Doreen." Tony grappled with her in the middle of the office as she tried to get the photograph out of his pocket. "I haven't stolen anything!" Doreen had both hands in his pocket now, and Tony dragged her across the room towards the front door.

"If I . . . let you . . . get away . . ."

"Doreen! Listen . . ."

" . . . with anything . . . then I might as well . . ."

"Doreen, for God's sake? Can you *hear* anything . . . ?"

" . . . say goodbye to this job . . ."

"*Doreen!*" Tony seized her wrists, dragging her hands from his pocket. She struggled furiously in his rough grip, but when she looked at his face, she could see that he wasn't looking at her but at the open front door. That look of fear was on his face again. Suddenly realising just how much of a chance she was taking by grappling with someone who could have lost his mind, she tried to pull away. Tony held her hands tight.

"Let *go* of me, Tony!"

"Listen . . ."

"Let *go*!"

"Is that a wind? Can you hear a wind?"

Doreen raked her high-heeled shoe down Tony's leg. He cried out in pain, but his eyes didn't leave the front doorway.

"Okay, okay." His voice was trembling. "It's time to go."

"What the hell are you talking about?"

"Come *on*!" Tony dragged her away from the front door, and back across the office. Both telephones on the switchboard were ringing. Several lights were winking on the switchboard, and now another angry taxi-driver was berating Doreen over the Tannoy. She struggled furiously to be free, and saw that he was dragging her towards the back door.

"Tony, if you're thinking of any funny business, I'll scratch your fucking eyes out . . ."

A flurry of rubbish swept into the office through the front door on a gust of cold wind. Empty milk cartons, crisp and cigarette packets, torn newspaper.

Doreen saw another cold gust scatter papers from her desk. She tried to scratch Tony's face, kicked at his shin again – but his grip was unrelenting. His face seemed to have gone grey as he finally reached the back door and tried to drag her through. Doreen was not going to be a victim, was not going to be a column in the tabloids.

Another cold gust sent the scattered papers and rubbish whirling into the office.

Doreen whirled, and kneed Tony between the legs.

His grip was instantly gone. He collapsed to his knees, hugging his groin. Doreen grabbed for the glass water pitcher on a table beside the back door and raised it high to bring it down on Tony's head.

A savage, howling, ululating wind exploded into the taxi office.

Doreen's cry of shock was snatched from her mouth by the noise of the hell-wind. The glass pitcher flew from her hand, shattering against the wall, spraying them both with water. The cabinet by the front door tumbled over, drawers flying open, disgorging more paper into the spinning maelstrom. The windows by the switchboard exploded with detonating roars. The light fitting spun, flapped and exploded. The fluted glass door of the office cracked and splintered apart.

Doreen staggered against the wall, peered through the twisting, spinning blur of shattered glass and wood and paper that formed the insane whirlwind in the middle of the office – and thought she could see a shape step through the front doorway. The movement was impossibly calm, impossibly measured in this nightmare wind. And even though the shape was no more than a silhouette, ragged and blurred, it reminded Doreen instantly of something.

It looked like a monk, or a priest. In a cowl.

It stepped calmly into the office.

And now it looked like one of those horrible insects.

A praying mantis, with its forelegs held before it. There was hideous, insectile movement around the thing's face. When it moved towards her, Doreen screamed. It was a silent sound in this insane bedlam of noise.

She screamed again when something seized her arm. She lashed out at it, looked down and realised that it was Tony. Using her arm, he hauled himself aloft, then dragged her to the back door. He shoulder-charged it in one fast, lunging movement. The weight of their bodies, and the ferocity of the wind in the office, flung the back door wide open and they staggered out into the back yard, followed by a gale of shredded paper and detritus.

Before Doreen could properly get her breath, Tony dragged her across the yard towards the double gates at the rear of the property. There were piles of black bin bags out here, awaiting collection by the council's waste disposal people. Doreen staggered in her high heels.

"For God's sake!" yelled Tony. "Kick them off!"

The shoes were gone in an instant, and they were both at the double gates when the whirlwind exploded through the back door. Doreen shrieked again as the bin bags stacked around the door exploded, spilling out their garbage into the howling, twisting wind. Now at last she realised that the sound made was not like a wind at all. It was the sound of some hideous and predatory animal. Dimly, she saw the same horrific shadow suddenly step into view in the back door – and then Tony dragged her through the double doors and into the alley. They began to run. Behind them, it sounded as if the back yard of Handley's Cabs was being torn to pieces.

Tony suddenly halted, and Doreen collided roughly with him.

"*Christ*, Tony . . . what *is* that thing?"

Tony did not answer. He was staring now at a rubbish skip in the alley. Someone nearby must be having building restoration done, because it was almost full with wooden beams and torn linoleum. He looked quickly back to the double doors from which they'd just escaped, as if weighing something up.

"Tony, what are we . . .?"

Doreen's voice was suddenly cut off as Tony swept her up into his arms, lunged towards the skip – and then roughly threw her inside. She began to protest.

"Stay down, Doreen! For God's sake, stay down and cover yourself over! It may not see you! Stay with me and you're as good as dead. Believe me!"

He turned and ran then. Doreen had only a split-second to decide her course of action. To protest, and climb out – or to do as she was told. Instinctively, she ducked and pulled a roll of linoleum over her head.

Just as the double doors at the rear of Handley's Cabs exploded into the alley, with a clattering, rending roar. The wind erupted into the alley, a great blur of garbage at its centre, and the silhouette of something that stood for a while, looking away down the alley in one direction – and then in the other direction. To see Tony, as he flung himself around the corner.

It came after him.

Tony swung around the corner, grabbing in his pocket as he ran.

The photograph was still there.

Pin your photograph to another living thing while the Mechanic is within striking distance.

An elderly couple out shopping recoiled from him as he almost collided with them. Was this the answer? Just stick the photograph in the top pocket of the first stranger who came his way? Let the Mechanic take them, instead of him?

No, I can't! I CAN'T just do that!

A keening sound of fear came from Tony's lips as he dashed across the road, leaving the couple to stare after him in alarm. As he ran, he prayed that he had done the right thing by throwing Doreen into that skip. He had seen what the Mechanic had done to his landlord and knew that, given the chance, it would do the same to her. Maybe, just maybe, it was so close to him that it would overlook her. Behind him, the elderly couple were enveloped in a howling blast of wind. They fought their way across the mouth of the alley from which the wind had come and scurried away as fast as they could.

Tony blundered across the road towards the fruit and vegetable market. The stalls had been erected in the main thoroughfare since early morning. There was a bustling hive of activity here, of traders and punters. The rattle and clatter of lorry gates and deliveries and traders yelling their latest bargains and a calliope organ somewhere on a novelty train ride for the kids and Madonna singing her guts out from someone's ghetto-blaster. There was sanity here; people and movement and reality. Something as unreal and hellish as the Mechanic couldn't possibly exist in a situation as *real* as this market. Tony staggered towards it, praying now that the nightmare would end.

And a horn blared angrily off to his left.

Tony whirled, arms flung out to protect himself. The lorry-driver slammed on his brakes, and the air was filled with the sound of screeching tyres. The radiator grille loomed large, like a row of metal teeth and Tony fell backwards to the ground. A tyre shuddered to a halt inches from his head. Tony scrabbled out of the way, heart hammering. He kept running, aware of the frozen and startled expressions of traders and customers at the nearest stalls. A lorry door swung open behind him, and a man's voice yelled obscenities. His words were suddenly drowned by another noise: a rushing blast of air, a roaring, juddering sound. Tony felt the blast of wind on his back, saw the nearest people to him suddenly wince and cover their faces, saw the canvas sides of the nearest stalls billow and flap, saw traders diving over their goods to stop them blowing away. Tony turned as he ran, and looked back.

A miniature tornado enveloped the lorry which had almost run him down.

Tony saw the spinning hell-wind engulf the vehicle, saw it shaking madly on its suspension. The sign on the cab roof – "Newell" – blew apart. And then the driver who had flung open his door to yell abuse dived away from it, hit the ground hard and rolled, scrabbling to get away – just as the windscreen imploded.

And now people were yelling and screaming and running in all directions as the Mechanic came on, straight after Tony. He turned and ran again, plunging into the crowd. They scattered before him, as if sensing that he was the quarry. Far from saving innocent bystanders from the hell-wind, it seemed as if now he was going to be responsible for leading it straight to a crowd of victims. Tony collided with someone, a young man, and sent him sprawling across a hardware stall. Over the sound of the cyclone and screaming, Tony could hear the sounds of breaking crockery, shattering glass and ripping canvas. Up ahead, he could see the entrance to the indoor section of the market, a huge renovated nineteenth-century building.

Scent. The thing has your scent.

Most of the traders in there dealt in meat, poultry and fish.

Tony pushed through a tangled knot of people, jumped over someone who had sprawled in front of him – and ran into the indoor market. Those nearest to the entrance were already standing alarmed and amazed, wondering just what the hell was going on out there. Further and deeper into the market, the yelling of traders and the crash and clatter of crates had drowned out any other noise. There was a fish stall just ahead of him; rows and rows of fresh catch, all stacked in boxes filled with ice. Tony staggered against the stall, fighting for breath.

"What the hell's wrong with you, mate!" said the small, elderly man who owned it, adjusting his cap and taking out his cigarette. "Devil after you, or something?"

"Something . . ." gasped Tony, and ran on, just as the hell-wind erupted into the market.

The fish – all this fish – and the meat – maybe it'll be put off the scent.

Tony heard the stalls nearest the entrance begin to blow apart, heard the shouts and the screams and the sounds of destruction, felt the cold blast of hell on his back.

Something live . . . there must be something LIVE in here . . .

Tony blundered into a rack of pigs' carcasses, ignored the yells of the man who was pushing it across the market and frantically looked around.

There was nothing live in here, nothing to which he could pin his photograph. Everything in here was dead meat.

Dead meat.

Just like him.

He saw the Mechanic come on, saw the horrifying blurred silhouette at the centre of the cyclone calmly walking in the eye of the storm towards him. He saw the destruction that it wreaked as it came on, knew that it could not be put off the scent, knew that it was ignoring all the other human beings who came within reach.

It *had* him.

Fifty yards from where he stood, he saw the silhouette open its arms in anticipation of an embrace.

"God in heaven . . ."

Tony threw the rack to one side, turned and blundered on into the market.

52

The walls and floors of the shopping precinct had been tiled in primary colours, like the basic colours from a child's Lego set. The intention had been to give a psychological feeling of child-like warmth, security and cleanliness. But those colours had faded on the floor because of the constant pedestrian traffic, and the maintenance of the area did not apparently extend to the walls, where graffiti and indeterminate stains seemed to suggest that the children in charge of this adult Legoland had been allowed to run amok. The planners' attempts to suggest a bright fairyland in the centre of an area of urban blight seemed to suggest naïveté at best, cynicism at worst.

Mac, Ranjana and Randall sat on one of the tiled alcoves surrounding a plastic fountain and pool which had not seen water for five years. Instead, it was gradually filling with litter. The pool and fountain were set in a square, the centre of a crossroads for shoppers, with four separate corridors of shops leading to it. Shoppers swarmed past them as they sat, drinking coffee from paper cups.

Mac talked of people who should be dead, but were not.

Randall and Ranjana listened as he recounted what little he remembered of Bernie's visit at the slipway. It was blurred. But his account of what had happened at the canal was not. Every detail of the attack on Bernie, and Mac's struggle in the water, was burned vividly into his mind. When he finished talking, they were quiet for a long while, watching the shoppers bustle past them.

"Funny thing," said Mac at last, changing the subject. "But when you've spent time on the street like me, it's as if ordinary people – I mean people like this – become the strangers."

"What do you mean?" asked Ranjana. There was a cold knot of fear deep inside her which even the hot coffee could not melt.

"They get *blurred*. As if they're not real. I suppose you feel the same way about street people. How many times has someone come up to you for a handout? A tramp, or some kid smacked out of his mind.

And how many times have you just walked on and ignored 'em? Dozens of times, I bet. Hundreds. After a while, it's like . . . well, like they don't exist any more. They're *there*, all right. On the streets, sleeping in shop doorways, lying in cardboard boxes, but to people walking past, it's like they're just shadow people. People who aren't really there. Well, the funny thing is – it's like that for street people as well. We see each other, know each other, sometimes try to help each other. And it's the ordinary people who pass by that are shadows. They and their world have nothing to do with us. After a while, you don't see them – unless you need a handout . . ."

"I feel as if I'm slipping in and out of the Twilight Zone myself," said Randall. He sat forward and ran a hand through his unruly hair. "I'm asking myself just how the hell I've got into all this . . ."

"I'm sorry," said Ranjana. "It's me . . ."

Randall waved at her impatiently to be quiet, finished his coffee and screwed up the paper cup. "Part of me says walk away. Let's face it, Ranjana. This is a seriously loony situation. A runaway girl who has visions, a guy on the street who's not alive or dead and says that he's seen dead people walking around. Complete strangers seeing each other in their dreams. A street gang who are going to beat the living shit out of me if I ever come across them again. Not to mention a police panda car at the bottom of the river—"

"All right!" snapped Ranjana. "That's enough! If you feel like that – walk away. Like you said. I owe you for what you've done for me, Randall. Probably more than I'll ever be able to pay back. But don't start treating me like a millstone around your bloody neck."

"You didn't let me finish," continued Randall. He threw the paper cup neatly into an overflowing waste basket. "There's another part of me, a part I don't understand, that says I've got to stay and see what happens. Despite the fact that this is all looney-tunes, I've got to see it through."

"Don't do me any more favours." Ranjana finished her own coffee. "Something's happening, all right. Something I don't understand, but it's . . ." Ranjana froze, coffee cup raised to her face.

"What's the matter?" asked Randall.

Ranjana did not answer. Instead, he followed her gaze.

A man was standing in the doorway of the greengrocer's just opposite them. He was wearing a long coat of indeterminate colour, one white-knuckled hand keeping the collar tight around his neck. His hair was lank and unkempt, his face white. And he was staring at them. Randall looked back at Ranjana. She seemed hypnotised with fear, the way she had looked back at the food van.

"What is it?" Mac was looking at her now.

257

"Him," said Randall, and Mac looked over at the stranger. "Do you know him?"

"No. Never seen him around before."

"Hi, you!" said Randall aloud. The stranger never took his gaze from them. "Yeah, you!" he continued. "Get lost!"

The figure remained unmoved.

Randall leaned across and touched Ranjana's arm. She started, dropped her coffee cup, and looked anxiously around.

Another figure was standing in the doorway of a MiniMart. A woman in tattered anorak and torn jeans. She seemed to be soaking wet, her hair also hanging lank across her face. Her attention was also riveted on them. Ranjana stood slowly.

"Oh *no* . . ."

"What?" Randall joined her, holding tight to her arm. "What's wrong?"

"The man you said you saw killed . . ." said Ranjana in a small voice.

"That's not him," said Mac, also standing.

Both Randall and Mac watched Ranjana look around the precinct square, and saw what was alarming her so much.

There were other figures in the shop doorways.

Other ragged street people, standing amidst the continual flow of shoppers, unseen by them and with their attention fixed on the three people standing beside the plastic fountain.

They were surrounded.

And, at last, Mac knew what Bernie had meant when he talked about the new people on the street and their terrible, white, *hungry* faces.

"They're . . ." Ranjana cleared her throat, tried to rid her voice of the sound of terror. "They're all dead. All of them."

"Jesus *Christ*," hissed Randall. This might still be looney-tunes, but there was no mistaking the unhealthy interest that the unmoving figures displayed in them. People moved and bustled past them, and Randall knew at last what Mac had meant about street people being shadow people, unseen by the crowd. He counted the figures. Mac saw what he was doing.

"How many?"

"Twelve – no, thirteen."

And as he spoke, each one of the figures slowly turned their heads away to the left to someone who was approaching down one of the precinct corridors towards the square. Another ragged figure was coming to join them, shambling amidst the unseeing crowd which passed on either side of him. The figure reached the square and stopped, looking up at them. Mac knew who it was even before he raised his head.

"It's him, isn't it?" said Ranjana. "It's your friend, Bernie."

Mac nodded, his throat dry.

Bernie's white and hungry face cracked into the parody of a smile: a hideous rictus of a grin, but the eyes were dead. Behind him, he had left a trail of water on the faded tile floor.

"Dead people," said Randall in disbelief. "You're telling me that these are all dead people?"

"Yes," said Ranjana.

"What the hell do they want?"

"Us," replied Ranjana. "They want us dead, too."

"What the hell *for*?"

"Because we know they're dead," replied Mac, his eyes fixed on Bernie. "That's all."

"No . . . no, this has gone far enough . . ." Randall broke away from Ranjana and strode across the shopping mall towards Bernie. He would confront this threat in the only way he knew.

"Randall, no!" Ranjana tried to follow, but Mac caught her sleeve and held her back.

Randall fought down the fear as he approached the man called Bernie, fought down his instinctive dread of that horrible white face and its deathly smile.

"All right, pal." Randall stopped a few feet in front of him, looked around to make sure that none of his companions had moved in. They remained still, their eyes still fixed on Mac and Ranjana. "Come on then," continued Randall, holding up his hands in a beckoning gesture. "Start something."

Bernie's death mask grin widened.

"Dead, but still with a sense of humour, I see," said Randall. His stomach felt knotted. "Well, what about it, Bernie? Make the first move."

Slowly, Bernie's hand moved up towards his face. Randall took a step back and bunched his fists. Shoppers continued to stroll by them, uncaring and unaware. When Bernie's hand reached his neck, the thin white fingers fumbled at the soiled cravat that was tied there – and pulled it loose.

Randall took an involuntary step back.

"Christ . . ."

Bernie's throat had been cut.

The gash ran from ear to ear, a glinting red-black morass within. Randall could see the sickening white network of severed cartilage in that horrifying, glutinous wound and needed no further convincing.

He backed off, never turning from Bernie but casting anxious glances from side to side to make sure that none of the other monstrosities had crept up behind him. When he reached Mac and Ranjana, she moved to him quickly and held him tight.

"He's . . . he's . . . God, Ranjana. What are we going to do?"

Slowly, at an unheard signal, the figures began to move in.

"What else?" said Mac. "We . . . *run!*"

Mac seized Ranjana's arm and dragged her with him as he lunged away from the concrete seating area, Randall following close behind. The sudden lunge of activity made the nearest of the pedestrians passing by rear back in alarm. An elderly woman snapped an unladylike expletive at them as they dashed past her. In that one sudden move, Ranjana caught sight of the ragged figures also bursting forward towards them like suddenly animated scarecrows, themselves pushing people aside as they surged forward. Mac ran for the nearest of the mall corridors, and for a moment it seemed as if they all might make it without being caught.

A dark, ragged figure reared from a shop doorway and seized Mac's sleeve with both hands. It was a figure that none of them had seen. That lunge took the figure – a man with wild hair and a stained parka – to its knees, and his weight on Mac's arm dragged him off balance. Mac stumbled and also fell to his knees as the man clung tight to his sleeve, scrabbling to rise. Mac twisted, trying to get a better position to fend off his attacker, saw his attacker's hood flap back to reveal a wild white face ingrained with dirt, saw the chunk of scalp that had been torn or eaten away, saw the mad staring eyes and champing teeth.

And then Randall's size ten Doc Marten boot came down on the attacker's arm, stamping it on the tiled floor. Mac heard the snap of the bone, saw the hand fall away – but there was no expression of pain on his attacker's face. That arm was broken and useless, but the wild and feral look on his face was unchanged and even now he scrabbled with the other hand to hold on as Mac twisted free and clambered to his feet. Someone close by screamed.

"Come *on!*" yelled Randall into his ear, and Mac ran after him and Ranjana as they continued on down the corridor. Behind him, Mac heard someone else scream and yell *"Police!"* as the oncoming figures blundered into a knot of passers-by, knocking someone else to the floor in their rush. Randall almost collided with a young couple pushing a pram. The woman screamed, and the husband took a defensive swing at him. Randall ducked under the roundhouse right and grabbed Ranjana's arm as they continued to run. Behind him, Mac could hear the rush and scuffle and movement as the dead ones came on. He turned back to look as they ran, and saw the scarecrow figures bursting through the crowd and into the corridor. They'd gained thirty or forty yards, but the figures were moving fast. When he snapped his head back to look, he saw Randall perform an ungainly twist to one side, as if avoiding another shopper – then saw that a figure had lunged out and tried to seize him.

It was another of the dead.

Randall couldn't avoid it. The figure was another man, impossibly thin in something that might once have been a business suit but looking as if it had been buried with his corpse months ago. The figure had nothing beneath the jacket and Randall had a flash of a prominent ribcage beneath a covering of thin, white stretched skin as the figure took him by the throat with both arms, forcing him sideways across the corridor towards a greengrocer's window. Beyond the window, Mac saw the alarmed customers shrieking and scattering away as the twisting figures lunged towards them. Then Ranjana was on the man's back, trying to pull him off.

Mac reached them in a couple of strides, pushed Ranjana aside, and gripped the man's own throat from behind. Pushing down hard in one fierce movement, he forced the man to his knees, tearing one of his hands away from Randall's neck. The other remained fastened, and Randall cried out as the fingers dug into his flesh.

Mac pulled the man's head back as hard as he could.

The attacker made no noise.

Not even when Mac heard the man's neck snap and stood back to see the head loll impossibly on to his shoulder.

He did not have to see the thing's face to know that the expression of feral hatred would be unchanged. Randall tore the remaining hand off and twisted away from the shop window.

Mac stepped back, braced his foot between the man's shoulder blades and shoved hard. Inside the greengrocer's, the customers screamed again as the emaciated man dived head first through the store window. It shattered, drowning out the screams, and the man flailed beneath sheets of jagged, shattering windowpane, scattering vegetables everywhere. His unstable head lolled and rolled on the shoulders like a badly designed Guy Fawkes' dummy.

"*Run!*" yelled Mac again, breaking Randall and Ranjana out of their shock.

The scarecrow figures were right behind them.

Shop doorways reared and loomed crazily at them as they ran.

How many of those things were there in here? They could be *anywhere.*

The exit lay ahead, out on to the main street. The pedestrians ahead of them had heard the screaming and crashing, and scattered out of their way as they came on.

"*Run!*" yelled Mac again.

Randall threw a look back over his shoulder. "Yeah, man! But where *to*? Those fucking things are all over . . ."

"How can we *stop* them?" cried Ranjana, the first words she had uttered in that nightmare dash.

Two ragged figures staggered around the corner of the exit and came towards them. A man and a woman. One of them was carrying a bottle, and for a fleeting moment it seemed that they were just a couple of drunks. But in the act of turning into the mall corridor from the main street, it was as if their act was over. Both silhouettes straightened at the sight of the running figures – and came on with the same relentless and horrifying intent of those who followed behind. The man smashed the bottle almost casually against the mall wall, holding the broken neck like a jagged knife.

With a yell of rage and defiance, Randall crouched low as he ran and flung himself straight at the man. The man tried to swing the broken bottle, but Randall headbutted him in the midriff. The man made no sound, but the impetus of Randall's move sent them both hurtling out into the main street. The woman was swooping on Ranjana, tattered hair flying like a banshee as Mac drew level, caught an outflung arm and sent her spinning away. Beyond, Randall and his attacker crashed into an iron pavement barrier leading on to a pedestrian crossing. Passers-by scattered and moved on, not wanting to be involved.

Ranjana ran to where Randall struggled with the scarecrow at the traffic barrier, and Mac moved to join them – but suddenly the banshee woman was on his back, sharp fingernails gouging for his eyes. Mac cried out, clutching at those claws on his face. They whirled in a mad circle and Mac had a fleeting image of a bus stop at the pavement, saw the shocked and astonished people who were standing there suddenly scatter as they whirled amidst them.

Randall tried to break free from the thing at the barrier. It gripped him tight around the waist, trying to push its face into his own. God, was it trying to *bite* him? Ranjana raked a hand across its face, dragging three parallel gashes across its forehead. There was no blood from the wound, and the expression on the face was unchanged. They twisted against the barriers again and Ranjana fell heavily to the pavement. But Randall had managed to get the heels of both hands under the thing's chin and pushed that face away from his own. His breathing was laboured, the breath being squeezed out of his body – but the thing that held him was not breathing at all. At last, Randall could see that he was grappling with a man aged sixty-five plus. Ranjana clambered to her feet again.

And then two figures slammed into them both, jarring them back against the barriers.

Oh, Christ! thought Randall. The pursuing Dead from the mall had caught up with them.

But then one of the figures yelled, "Okay, that's enough! Break it up!" and Randall's attacker was suddenly dragged away from him. He fell back against the barrier, gagging for breath and watching as two blue-uniformed security men from the mall dragged the vagrant back. The old man thrashed and struggled as they dragged him back over the pavement. Ranjana's breath was coming in sobs as she held Randall at the traffic barrier. The sound of a woman screaming drew their attention back to Mac.

The woman on his back was still trying to reach his eyes.

Suddenly lunging backwards, scattering more shoppers, Mac slammed her into the outside mall wall. The impact dislodged her and she fell to her knees as Mac staggered away from her, turning ready for another assault. The two security men had their hands full as the old man lunged and reared, trying to get back to Randall and Ranjana.

"Oh God, *look* . . ." hissed Ranjana, and Randall followed her gaze to the mall entrance.

The vagrants who had pursued them were standing back in the entrance, watching the security men struggle with the old man. They were not coming on.

The banshee woman threw herself at Mac again. He sidestepped just before her outstretched arms could connect again, caught her ragged coat and flung her on past him like some awkward matador. Mac fell to his knees and the impetus of his dragging lunge sent the woman staggering out into the road.

Directly in front of the bus which was just pulling into the stop.

Someone somewhere screamed again as the woman was slammed to the ground with a shivering *bang!* The bus went straight on over her, and Mac saw passengers inside the yellow bus jerk forward in their seats as the driver slammed on the brakes. The bus shuddered and lurched – and from where he knelt, Mac saw the woman disintegrate beneath the wheels and chassis, saw her body bounce and pitch, saw the flesh compact and mangle. He bowed his head and dry-heaved on the pavement.

A hand grabbed his shoulder.

Mac lashed out and struggled to rise, almost too weak to fight back against another attack.

It was Randall and Ranjana. Beyond them, he saw the security guards let go of the old man in shock as they stared at the stationary bus and what lay beneath it. The double doors of the bus hissed open and the driver staggered out, face white. He turned and vomited into the gutter. On board the bus, children were crying and dazed passengers were trying to rise. Mac saw the old man who had attacked Randall lurch back towards the mall entrance, saw him vanish past the shadows of the undead scarecrows who were standing there watching.

In the front of that silent and ragged crowd, Mac saw Bernie. His dreadfully white face was fixed on him, his eyes like glittering marbles. And with that same horrifying look of *hunger* that he shared with the others on either side. Silently, as if at an invisible signal, they stepped back in unison, into the shadows of the mall corridor, turning away and melting into the darkness.

And then they were gone.

Unable to speak, Mac allowed Randall and Ranjana to haul him to his feet.

Arms around each other, and with shocked and sickened passers-by keeping well out of the way, they staggered off down the main street.

No one tried to stop them.

53

"It's time," said Lorelei.

The others had grown restless and impatient while they had talked; anxious to be away from the narrow boat and to get on with the business at hand.

Still sitting on the bed in the centre of the boat, Lauren hugged her child tight.

Sparrow!

He had been silent in her mind for what seemed a long time now.

"He can't help you," said Lorelei, sensing Lauren's attempt to communicate. "And he can't do anything to help himself, either." Lorelei laughed. "Since you're family, I'll do you both a favour. I'll make it as painless as I can. Honestly, I will. I won't protract it."

"You'll have to kill us here," said Lauren grimly. *Sparrow!* "You're not using us to give yourselves power."

"I've told you, Lauren," continued Lorelei. "We won't kill you here – but oh, how badly we can hurt you."

I need a little more time, hissed Sparrow in her mind. Lorelei's blind face darted in the direction of the child. *Just a little more . . .*

"Lorelei, you can go to Hell."

Bradford pushed past Lorelei, stepping into the galley and pulling open a drawer. "Let me," she said, taking out a Stanley knife. "I've been wanting to change that expression on her face since we got here. I'll carve her name on her face with . . ."

Lauren put both hands quickly around Sparrow's throat, balancing the child on her lap. Quietly and simply, she said, "I'll kill him."

"What?" sneered Lorelei. "Your precious little baby?"

"I mean it. I'd rather that he died here and now. Quickly, by my hand. I'll never let you have him, never let you do what you've got planned for him."

Bradford moved forward, but Lorelei quickly grabbed her arm, without even turning her head in Bradford's direction.

I'm sorry, baby, thought Lauren.

Good, good! said Sparrow. *It's okay, just a little longer . . .*

"Stop *whispering!*" screamed Lorelei. The sound of her voice even made Bradford recoil.

"Back off, Lorelei!" snapped Lauren. "I mean it – I don't care what you do to me. But you're not getting Sparrow."

"You stupid fool!" hissed Lorelei. Behind her, the others were shuffling uneasily. "Your child isn't even human. It was bred for a purpose, nurtured by the drugs we gave it. What kind of child do you think it could ever be? It can never be human, *never* be what you want it to be. Ever! Lauren, give him to us, and we'll let you go."

Lauren's laughter was grim and bitter.

"I mean it," continued Lorelei. "We want him more than you. Give him here – and you can go."

"Get off the boat," said Lauren. "All of you."

"She's bluffing, Lorelei!" snapped Bradford. "Can't you see that? Let me . . ."

The narrow boat rocked in the water, making them all stagger. Lauren steadied herself on the bedpane with one hand, quickly moving that hand back to Sparrow's neck as the others righted themselves.

All right! exclaimed Sparrow.

Lorelei heard the torrent of excited whispering that followed between Lauren and her child.

"He's begging for mercy, Lauren? Isn't he? Look – darling. You could never forgive yourself if you hurt him. I promise that we'll make it as easy and as gentle as we can. Death doesn't have to be a painful thing. I promise . . ."

Lauren looked directly at her with a grim smile as the whispering stopped.

"Thought you were clever, didn't you, Lorelei?" said Lauren. "Finding a way to cloak yourselves from Sparrow when you found out that he was listening in. Well, it's a trick that he's learned now."

"What do you mean?" spat Ernest.

"While we've been talking, he's been doing a little cloaking of his own. He's found out how you were able to do it, Lorelei. And he's been able to use the same technique to cloak the vibrations being received by you. In fact, he's *changed* them."

"What the hell are you talking about?" Could that be a note of fear in Lorelei's voice?

"Where's the Mechanic, Lorelei?"

"The Mechanic? It's gone. Dissipated. It killed Dandridge, and it's gone back."

"Wrong. It didn't kill Dandridge, and it didn't go back."

"You're stalling for time, Lauren!" Lorelei moved forward.

"Dandridge is still alive, and it's still hunting for him."

"Impossible!"

"Is it? Sparrow cloaked your vibrations, fed you the wrong signals, just the way that you did it to him. Made you think the Mechanic had found Dandridge, killed him and gone. But it hasn't. Here, Lorelei – Sparrow wants you to feel this."

Lorelei halted.

"*Feel* it!" hissed Lauren.

The child turned his head and looked straight at Lorelei.

"Is she right?" hissed Fletcher in alarm.

Lorelei began to moan, clutching the narrow boat wall.

"It's coming," said Lauren. "Isn't it, Lorelei? Dandridge is heading back here to the boat – and the Mechanic is following."

"For fuck's sake!" snapped Terri, jumping down at last from the kitchen bench. "Tell us she's bluffing."

The narrow boat rocked again, as if another boat had passed. But there was no other vessel on the canal.

"Tell them, Lorelei. The Mechanic is almost here."

"*Lorelei!*" Bradford's voice had risen hysterically. "Tell us it isn't true."

Lorelei twisted until her back was against the narrow boat window. There were beads of sweat on her brow. Ernest took her by the shoulders and began to shake her. "That thing is *indiscriminate*, you stupid bitch! If it comes back here, it might take *us!*"

Lorelei lashed out at him and he staggered back towards the others. The boat began to pitch and toss. Beyond the narrow boat windows, the water had begun to swirl and foam as if a great wind was coming. It splashed and misted the glass.

Ernest could take no more. He lunged at the double doors behind him, bursting them open. A cold wind blew into the narrow boat. He lunged out on to the deck and the others began to follow.

"You idiots!" screeched Lorelei, her shock broken at last. "What the hell are you doing?"

"Didn't you hear?" shouted Bradford, clambering after Fletcher. "If that thing is headed back here, I don't want to be around."

"You're safer *here!*" shouted Lorelei. "Safer on water than on land . . ."

"Fuck you!" snapped Terri, and followed the others.

Lorelei looked back at Lauren, her face a mask of rage and hate. For a moment, Lauren was sure that she would hurl herself on them both. She braced herself, taking Sparrow around the neck again.

"I'll never let you have him, Lorelei. Even now. I'll kill him first."

Then Lorelei looked back to the double doors through which that chill wind was gusting, and listened to the sounds of the others clambering from the deck back on to the quay. At last, she darted quickly after them, catching Bolam by the arm before she could reach the quayside.

The narrow boat tilted.

"Give it to me!" It was Lorelei's voice, screaming above the sounds of the growing wind. "*Give* it to me!"

Lauren ducked down to look and see what was happening. The boat pitched again, nearly throwing her on to the floor. And in that instant, she saw Lorelei slip and fall on the deck, heard her cry out in pain. Heard Bradford shout, "Leave it for now, Lorelei. We can get them later. Leave it – it's *coming*!" And then Lauren saw Lorelei squirm for balance on the deck, saw her raise the gun that Bolam had taken from her in the struggle on the quayside, saw Lorelei level and aim that gun directly at her.

Lauren threw herself back across the bed, clutching Sparrow, just as Lorelei pulled the trigger.

The sound of the shot stabbed an agonising blast in Lauren's eardrums. A great chunk of woodwork from the panelling on the frame of the bed – where Lauren had been crouching a moment before – exploded whirling and splintering into the air.

More scrabbling on the deck. God, was Lorelei coming back into the narrow boat? Lauren risked another darting glance, saw with overwhelming relief that she was gone from the deck – and then remembered the windows facing quayside; the windows looking directly into the sleeping area.

Sparrow!

Lauren clutched Sparrow tight, rolled on the bed and threw herself from it on to the floor.

Just as Lorelei fired her second shot through the narrow boat window. The window exploded, showering them with glass. Outside, Lauren heard Lorelei scream in rage and frustration. Lauren hugged Sparrow close, pushing herself up tight against the wall beneath the window, lest Lorelei should try again. Wind gusted through the shattered window.

And on the quayside, Lorelei turned from the narrow boat in rage and saw the others milling in confusion. The only approach to this section of the quayside was down the narrow alley between two warehouses, the route they had originally followed when Lauren and her child had finally been tracked down. But now, that cold and gusting wind was blowing directly down the alley on to the quay, pushing before it a cloud of dust and litter.

The Mechanic was coming that way.

And if it was coming, then Dandridge must surely be coming as well, running before it. Lorelei saw Fletcher and Ernest turn and look back at her, saw them both decide what to do, saw them both gather themselves, ready to run and throw themselves into the canal, into the safety of the water. Crazed, Lorelei fired a shot into the ground at their feet. Bradford, Terri and Bolam span around in fear, saw Fletcher and Ernest frozen to the spot, saw the mad look on Lorelei's face as her red braids twisted and writhed in the wind. Bolam began to yell something at her, looking frantically back to the mouth of the alley, but his voice was lost in the wind. Ernest took a step forward, hands held wide, and Lorelei waved the gun at him again.

"Wait!" yelled Lorelei above the wind. "Just *wait*, you cowardly fucks! The Mechanic will take him . . ."

And then a figure hurtled around the corner, freezing in his tracks when he saw them. Lorelei laughed: a wild manic sound that cut through the sounds of the wind.

The others followed her gaze.

Tony Dandridge put one hand against the nearest warehouse wall and looked back the way he had come, gasping for breath. Even from that distance, they could see the deathly white of his face, the look of fear at what followed close behind him. He looked back towards them, nodded grimly – and then began to walk slowly in their direction.

"Lorelei!" shrieked Bradford. "Don't let him come over here. Not with that thing behind him."

The Sabbarite scattered and ran.

"You make me sick," smiled Lorelei, and raised the gun at Tony.

Instantly, Tony ducked low and ran for the cover of a pile of rubble. Lorelei fired, the bullet hitting the warehouse wall in a screaming ricochet as Tony flung himself behind the tumbled bricks. Tony twisted to look back down the alley. There was a whirlwind of litter and debris back there, about a hundred yards away, and as he looked, he saw something vaguely man-shaped turn a corner and begin walking slowly down that alley in his direction. Tony twisted again. The quayside was about thirty feet beyond this wall of rubble, past a pile of old and rotting packing crates. Even now, the bizarre woman with the gun and the other figures – the Sabbarite, he guessed – could be striding towards where he lay. He had no time to ponder what had happened to Lauren and her child. Perhaps they were already dead. His only safety lay thirty feet away, beyond the quayside edge. The safety of the water. Tony struggled to his knees, the taste of fear bitter in his mouth as . . .

Lauren squirmed low on the aft deck, found where the mooring rope

STEPHEN LAWS

was attached to the deck rail – and began to saw at it with the knife that Bradford had wanted to use on her.

Lorelei had been moving towards the mound of rubble with a ghastly smile on her face, "sensed" movement back on the narrow boat and whirled screaming. She fired again, and the shot *spanged!* from the tiller. Lauren snatched her hand away, rolled across the deck and threw herself through the double doors and back into the boat as . . .

Tony scrambled into a crouching position behind the rubble, tensed – and then ran like hell for the quayside. The hell-wind blew fierce on his back, and Tony waited for the sound of the next gunshot. In that split-second, he remembered his soldiering days, knew that you never heard the shot that killed you. The packing crates loomed on his right, the edge of the quayside lay twenty feet beyond, the dark water troughing and rippling below in the wind. Just one lunge and . . .

Ernest stepped out from behind the packing crates, where he had fled just seconds earlier. As Tony passed, he swung a rubbish bin lid like one half of a huge corrugated cymbal, smacking it hard across Tony's head. The blow slammed him to the ground. Tony writhed in agony as Ernest stood back and threw the lid down hard on top of him. In that moment, Tony recognised his attacker. It was the man who had looked like a bank manager or an estate agent; the man who had come to his flat, pulled a gun and said, *Something will come.*

That same something was coming now, down the alley.

Ernest backed off, eyes wide, chewing his bottom lip. He looked up the alley into the hell-wind and saw the shape within. Still backing off until he had reached the warehouse wall, Ernest pointed to Tony as he lay on the ground. The look on his face was still fearful, but now contained something else – an expression of eager and hungry anticipation at what was to come. He was laughing now, the sound swallowed by the wind as . . .

Lorelei whirled back to the narrow boat, stooping low and darting glances through the shattered window, trying to "see" where Lauren had gone. Still crazed, she fired a shot through the window anyway. Somewhere inside, glass exploded as . . .

Lauren jerked back out of the aft double doors again and threw the wrench that she had found on the floor. It spun end over end through the air, hitting Lorelei on the shoulder with bone-jarring impact. She doubled up in pain, falling to the quayside. The gun whirled from her hand to the ground – and Lauren dived at the mooring rope again, slashing hard. The fibres parted, and the stern of the boat began to drift from the quay, pushed by the raging hell-wind. Lauren ducked back below decks again, grabbing Sparrow from where she had laid him as . . .

270

Tony grabbed for the bin lid, saw Ernest grinning back towards the alley, and knew that the thing was almost upon him. Bracing one arm, Tony flung the lid hard at Ernest like an oversized frisbee, praying that the wind wouldn't carry it away. The lid wobbled in the air, and Ernest jerked back to look at what was hurtling towards him – just as the lid hit him hard in the face, smashing his teeth. He dropped instantly to his knees, clutching his face. Tony scrabbled towards him on hands and knees, half turning to see . . .

A blurred figure in the eye of a hellish hurricane. A praying mantis, opening wide its claw-arms as it swept down to take him.

Tony seized Ernest by the neck and jammed the photograph down his collar, stuffing and crumpling it deep.

Something seized Tony.

And in the next instant, he was somehow lying on the ground again, twenty feet away from where Ernest still knelt. The pain in his back and head was crippling and hideous. He had been flung away. Tony saw Ernest scrabbling frantically at his collar, saw black-red blood painted on his nose and chin, saw even from that distance the look of insane terror on his face as the hellish, spinning wind engulfed him.

Ernest began to scream then, a noise even louder than the hell-wind.

Tony rolled to his knees again, sensed movement to his left and twisted to see Lorelei also kneeling by the quayside, clutching her arm. The narrow boat had been unmoored at the stern and was drifting away, still anchored at the foredeck. Lorelei groped forward – and Tony saw the gun lying on the quayside. He lunged forward, still crouched as . . .

Lorelei's scrabbling hand found the gun. Still kneeling, she raised it toward Tony, her eyeless face a mask of rage.

And then Tony hit her hard, still crouched. The force and impetus of his body tackle swept Lorelei backwards as he took her around the waist. The gun discharged over his shoulder, and in the next moment they both plunged over the quayside, twisting and turning. The thrashing black water engulfed them.

Ernest fell out of the whirling nightmare and its hideous shape.

His clothes had been shredded from his body in seconds, his flesh slashed and torn. His scalp was ripped, a flap of skin hanging down the back of his neck. An eye was gone, swallowed in the wind; three fingers had been bitten away, his penis severed. But the instinct to survive was still paramount despite his terrible injuries and the shock and terror which had descended upon him. Screaming, in a ruined and bloody blur, he flung himself at the narrow boat. His bloodied hand fastened on the foredeck rail. His feet left the quayside and he scrabbled and thrashed at the side of the boat looking like a butcher's side of beef as he clambered aboard, leaving a massive bloody smear. There was a wild and triumphant look on his ruined face as he staggered to the deck and looked back with his one remaining, glittering eye into the twisting cyclone-pillar.

"*Water!*" he screamed at the monk/mantis shape within the storm. "*I'm on WATER!*"

But the boat was still moored to the quayside.

And Ernest's look of grim triumph dissolved into a screaming rictus of terror as the hell-wind suddenly swept aboard the narrow boat.

Below decks, Lauren hugged Sparrow tight as the narrow boat began to judder and lurch as never before. A great roaring sound filled the cabin and Lauren screamed out aloud when something *cracked* and juddered not far from where she crouched. Water began to pool around her feet. She screamed again when something above seemed to explode screaming into the air. With a great ripping and rending, the roof of the boat tore apart. Lauren saw daylight above as a huge chunk of the roof blew away into the hell-storm. The wind was in here now, swirling and shrieking and destroying everything it touched. The bedclothes were whipped into the air, spinning and twisting like great cloth banshees. The remaining windows imploded with a shattering roar.

And above it all, the sounds of a hideous screaming. Like something that was being skinned alive.

Oh, Christ, thought Lauren. *I'm so sorry, Tony. I'm so sorry* . . . He must have made it back to the boat, but the Mechanic had followed.

Lauren scrabbled across the cabin, keeping low and shielding Sparrow from flying glass, cutlery and shattered furniture. She knew that she could not stay here. The Mechanic was tearing the boat to pieces. Reaching the double doors leading to the foredeck, knowing that they were still moored and that she must get off this boat before the Mechanic sank it, Lauren ducked when another chunk of roofing split and whirled upwards into the maelstrom. Then she lunged for the double doors again, knowing that Lorelei must still be out there somewhere on the quayside, waiting with the gun. Praying that the severity of the wind must affect her aim, Lauren burst out on to the deck. Without looking back, she flung herself at the quayside in a great stepping-leap. Her legs did not collapse beneath her, and Lauren staggered, righted herself and began to run. There was no sign of Lorelei.

She kept running until she had reached the pile of rubble behind which Tony had sheltered. Collapsing behind it, cradling Sparrow, she looked back.

Her decision to get off the boat had come not a moment too soon.

Something had torn the handrail and mooring rope away from the quayside. Already, the boat was drifting away from the quayside.

The boat itself was engulfed in a twisting, spinning vortex of wind. Lauren could see the hell-wind ripping the boat to pieces. The water all around it was thrashed into a frenzy as great chunks of boarding and shattered wood rained into it. The boat began to spin slowly in the water, right at the centre of this hellish cyclone. The screaming had long since stopped and Lauren knew that Tony was dead at last. Somewhere deep within that devastating tornado, something exploded. Lauren saw a gout of flame. The engine . . .?

In the next moment, the petrol tank ruptured and detonated like a bomb.

The narrow boat was engulfed in flame, the detonation raising a cloud of water from the surface of the canal. Lauren ducked as burning debris hurtled and bounced over the quayside. A great roaring, even greater than the hell-wind, filled the air.

When Lauren looked up again, the hell-wind had vanished.

The Mechanic had fulfilled his task, and had returned to Hell.

And the remains of the narrow boat were sinking. The prow was raised in the air, the hull shattered and splintered in dozens of places. The canal water had rushed in eagerly; pools of burning petrol lapped and surged around it as the boat turned in the water. The hull juddered, keeled over on to its side – and was still. The water here was only twenty feet deep, the wreck of the narrow boat still jutting from the surface of the canal, the shattered starboard side plainly visible. Burning wreckage bobbed on the surface. Stinking black smoke wreathed the devastated remains and drifted in great clouds towards the quayside.

"Tony," said Lauren quietly. "I'm so sorry . . ."

"Not as sorry as you're going to be,' said a voice behind her.

Lauren, look out! snapped Sparrow in her head, the first words he'd uttered since the nightmare descended on them.

Lauren crouched as she turned.

Bradford stepped forward and slapped her hard across her face, just as Fletcher and Bolam seized her. Terri tore Sparrow from her grasp and when she tried to resist, Bolam kneed her in the stomach. Lauren doubled over in agony, the breath knocked out of her body. Bradford slapped her again with the back of her hand, then looked out across the canal to the burning wreck of the narrow boat. She smiled grimly.

"All right, Lauren," she said. "Let's begin again where we left off."

Lauren was hauled to her feet.

And then they dragged her away down the alley.

There was no breath of wind.

273

54

The city streets had become strange and menacing places.

They kept their distance from each shop doorway, turned each street corner with nervous care – and they shrank from each shambling figure in the night, searching puzzled and equally frightened faces for any signs of that dreadful hunger.

Mac led the way.

He knew the warrens of alleys and shopping malls and side roads by heart, tried to assess which way was the best way. They were in an impossibly vulnerable position. Too much in the open, and they might be spotted by a cruising police car who may or may not have been advised about the horrific scene back there at the shopping mall entrance, and be on the lookout for maniacs who had thrown an innocent woman – a vagrant – in front of an oncoming bus. Too much off the beaten track, in the quieter, secret places, and the dead things that masqueraded as vagrants might be lurking there, waiting for them.

Ranjana and Randall hadn't spoken since the shopping mall. Both in shock, they followed silently behind Mac, trusting him implicitly. They had no idea how long they had been following the big man, had no idea where he was going, but did not question him. Mac hissed brief directions as they crossed roads or moved quickly through abandoned buildings. Once, he pushed them back against the wall of a burned-out building, and they stood like that for what seemed a long time – just listening. When he was satisfied that they had not been followed, they moved off again.

They reached a steep, grassed embankment and Mac held them both back while he checked. The area leading up to this bank was open.

"Quick!" he hissed, and they broke from the cover of a litter-strewn alley and ran for the embankment. There was a rough stone wall at the top, but Randall and Ranjana had no idea what lay beyond. Just before they struggled to the top, they heard the sound of a train whistle. There was a break in the wall about twenty yards to their left. Mac obviously knew that it was there, had obviously been this way before, and he swerved towards it as they reached the top. Randall and Ranjana followed quickly, as he staggered over fallen stones.

Beyond the wall, they looked down on to a railway goods yard and a vast criss-cross network of railway lines and sheds. The embankment leading down to that area was overgrown and wild and whereas the railway lines several hundred yards out into that great web of rails were well used, the lines closest to the embankment seemed to have been overgrown with weeds and dandelion. There was a cluster of sheds at the bottom of the embankment – all of them derelict.

"Come on," said Mac simply, and began to stagger down the embankment.

Again unchallenging, they followed.

Near the bottom, Randall almost tripped and fell. Ranjana grabbed his arm and steadied him. Mac strode on ahead, stepping over the overgrown railway lines and heading for the dilapidated buildings. Obviously, this was going to be their hiding place for a while.

When they reached the unkempt buildings with their shattered windows, Randall tried to assess which one Mac would head for. Through the broken windows of an old signal box, he could see that someone had been there in the past. There was obscene graffiti on the walls. But Mac veered around the signal box, looking back briefly to make sure that they were still following. There was another building next to it. The door swung open, and inside Randall could see more graffiti-smeared walls and what looked like the remains of an old mattress. It looked less than inviting, but at this juncture he supposed, quite literally, that beggars could not be choosers. But Mac veered around this building too, and at last Randall could see what Mac had in mind.

Behind the abandoned British Rail buildings was another stretch of overgrown railway line. Sitting in the middle of that stretch, and screened from the embankment by the buildings, was a single railway carriage. It was obviously old stock, shunted on to this stretch of line many years ago and forgotten about. Mac hurried towards it and they followed. When he reached the side, he looked back quickly, then stretched up, grabbed a handle and pulled hard. A door in the side slid back and Mac quickly hopped up. Kneeling in the doorway, he waited until Randall and Ranjana had reached him and then held out his hand. Ranjana was first, quickly lifted up and into the dark interior. When Randall held out his hand and Mac took it, he realised for the first time just how powerful this big man was. Randall weighed twelve stones, but Mac lifted him by the arm as if he was a child, quickly swinging him inside. Randall grabbed at the aperture and slithered quickly after Ranjana as Mac slid the door back into place, leaving only a small gap so that he could look back the way they had come.

Another train whistle mourned somewhere in the distance, and Mac remained frozen in that crouched position for a long time, making sure that no ragged, shambling shapes were staggering down the embankment in their direction. Eventually, he moved back, leaned heavily against the railway carriage wall and slid down on to his haunches, breathing out a great sigh of relief.

It was impossible to tell what this carriage had been used to transport all those years ago. The floor wasn't clean, but at least it wasn't littered with the unpleasant debris that they'd seen in the buildings beyond. It was obvious that Mac had used this place to sleep in the past. In the darkness, Ranjana could just make out a tattered sleeping-bag in one corner.

They were silent for a long time, heads down – thinking.

Randall's voice sounded cracked when he broke the silence at last. "Those people were *dead* . . ."

It was a simple statement of protestation that such a thing could happen, that reality could be inverted in such a sickening and demonstrable manner.

"What the hell is happening?"

"Something out there is killing people," said Mac simply. "And after they've been killed, they're coming back."

"But why?"

"It's to do with the vans," said Ranjana. "I felt it back there, remember?"

"What, you mean the people who bring the vans out? They're the ones who are doing the killing?"

"Can't say for sure," replied Ranjana. "I'm not getting anything specific, not seeing pictures in my head. But it's to do with the vans. I'm getting some things – strange impressions that don't make any sense."

"What kind of impressions?" asked Mac.

"I don't understand them. They're jumbled. Like I say, I'm not getting pictures. But apart from the vans – how dangerous they are – I'm getting an impression of a child. A baby boy. But it's crazy, as if the baby has a voice and he's trying to talk to me, trying to warn me. And something to do with water. Dirty, poisonous water. None of it makes sense."

Mac stood again and moved to the railway carriage door. Night had fallen and the straggling sodium lights that were British Rail's excuse for security down here on the railway tracks gave no illumination of the goods yard beyond the intense blue arcs of light directly around the battered and stained poles from which they depended. Mac peered out through the gap.

"Oh no . . ." he said quietly.

"What is it?" hissed Randall.

Ranjana shuddered, holding herself tight with arms criss-crossed on her chest.

"It's them, isn't it?" she said.

Randall joined Mac at the door and peered out across the goods yard, back towards the embankment.

Figures were shambling through the night in their direction. They were picking their way over the railway lines in a great crescent formation, about twelve or thirteen of them. All shambling and moving slowly with their heads down, but all unmistakably heading in their direction.

"What the hell do they *want* from us?" said Randall.

"They just want us dead," said Mac. "Because we know they've come back."

"What do we do?" Ranjana joined them. Randall could feel her shivering, and struggled to control the feeling of sick fear inside. "We can't go on running for ever. There must be something we can do."

"Like go to the police?" said Mac grimly. "Excuse me, Constable. Dead people are trying to kill us."

"Then what *are* we going to do?" snapped Randall.

"Follow Bernie's advice. Advice he gave before . . . before they got him. We've got to get out of this city altogether. These things are only here. Nowhere else. That's what Bernie said. We've got to hop on a train or something and get as far away from this city as we can. Maybe even leave the country if we can do it."

"And how do we . . .?" began Randall.

"No time," said Mac, and fiercely swung the railway carriage door back.

Before Randall could continue, he dropped quickly to the ground. Randall followed, holding up a hand for Ranjana and helping her carefully to the track. Mac had moved quickly to the end of the carriage, looking behind. The shambling figures came slowly on from the embankment, heads still down as if following their scent.

These were no slow-moving, shambling extras from a zombie movie. They could move horrifyingly fast, as all three knew from their nightmare experience in the shopping mall. Randall clung to Ranjana, keeping a close eye on them – waited for them suddenly to throw back their heads, spot them and begin to bound across the railway tracks in their direction.

"Come on, then," said Mac when he returned. "The good news is that they're not behind us as well."

They hurried around the carriage and paused while Mac worked out which direction to take. He pointed out across the goods yard towards another embankment about three hundred yards to their right, beyond a cluster of carriages and the silhouettes of other huddled British Rail buildings. When Mac charged off into the night, Randall and Ranjana followed close behind.

The criss-cross network of railway lines made it difficult to move fast, resulting in a hop, skip and jump over the rails as they moved. Randall kept darting glances back, but from this new angle, the railway carriage in which they had been hiding screened the vagrants who were approaching. With any luck, they could reach the night-time shadows of the other rolling-stock and buildings before they found the carriage.

"How . . ." gasped Ranjana as they ran. "How . . . did . . . did they *find* us? Can they . . . scent us . . . ?"

"Save your breath!" snapped Mac. "Keep heading for the embankment. I know . . . know another place we can hide."

Randall swallowed his protests as they clambered on ahead over the lines. If the street people had found them in the railway carriage hideout, what was to stop them finding any other place that Mac knew about? A train whistle sounded again, and they looked off to their left to see a slow-moving goods train. It was heading slowly in their direction, but there was no way of telling whether the driver had actually seen them in the darkness and was giving a warning signal, or whether he was just blowing that whistle for the hell of it.

They had almost reached the stationary carriages in front of the embankment. When Randall snapped his head back again, he could see that the shambling shapes behind had investigated the carriage, found nothing, and even now were moving around it and heading across the tracks in their direction.

And then, as Randall turned back again, he collided with Mac – who had suddenly come to a halt with Ranjana. He steadied himself, heard Mac say, "*Shit!*" and then looked on ahead.

There was movement beside the railway carriages.

That dark movement became more solid as they watched.

Several dark and shambling figures had stepped out from that deeper darkness, and were heading across the tracks toward them.

"Maybe it's British Rail workmen, or something . . . ?" began Randall hopelessly.

"It's *them*," said Ranjana.

And then the shambling figures raised their heads, saw them – and began to lope across the railway tracks towards them like horrifying, uprooted scarecrows.

They were surrounded.

Randall looked around for some kind of weapon, but could find nothing. Mac just stood watching the Dead run towards them. Ranjana was frozen, both hands to her mouth.

"What are we going to *do*?" she yelled.

"The train!" hissed Mac, and Randall looked over to their left again, towards the slow-moving goods train heading in their direction. It was still a good hundred yards away.

"Right!" Moving fast, Randall grabbed Ranjana, and in the next instant they were racing along the railway track on which the train was travelling. The Dead on either side of them made no noise; the only sounds of tortured, ragged breathing were their own.

"We'll never make it!" shouted Ranjana.

"Shut up!"

The train whistle sounded again. This time the driver of the train must surely see them. They skipped to the left of the track again, kept running. The train rumbled and clanked onwards like some dark night beast.

And then they were in its night-black rumbling shadow as it passed them. They kept running. Behind them, something hissed and rattled – and when they twisted to look back, they could see that several figures had jumped across the tracks on their side to join their original pursuers.

Mac grabbed at a passing carriage door, cursed when it was locked – and then fell away again. They kept running. Mac jumped and grabbed again. Another locked door. But there was no time to keep trying doors. On his next jump, Mac seized a rail and hauled himself up on to a ridge at the foot of the carriage. Ranjana lunged to follow him, caught the rail and stood up alongside him – but the train was carrying them back towards their pursuers. Randall staggered on loose soil, regained his balance and made ready to leap up to join them.

"Look out!" Ranjana's warning pierced the night.

Randall instinctively ducked low as a ragged silhouette swept down on him, arms held wide. The first of their pursuers was upon them. The arms closed on empty air. Randall seized a ragged coat-tail as it flapped by, was enveloped in a choking, stinking smell of decay and then he dragged the figure on past him. It tottered and fell. Jerking upright again, he saw Mac and Ranjana climbing up the side of the freight car towards the roof. A horde of ragged, flapping night-shapes were only yards away from him now. He could never escape. From the roof of the freight car, passing on past them into the night, he heard Ranjana yell again, *"Randall!"*

And knew that he must soon join the Dead.

Another figure launched itself through the air at him, as if it could fly. Randall saw the white malevolent face, the glittering marble eyes, the bared teeth.

And in that instant, a cold and furious rage engulfed him. Everything that had happened to him in the last few days seemed to imprint in his mind, in one cold and clear instantaneous montage. His father. The desperation. The anguish. His rational world turned upside down. The violence and the death and the horror. In that one moment, dying in itself seemed unimportant. But dying at the hands of these monstrous and hungry things was something else altogether. He would die by his own hand if necessary. But he would not let these things take him. And he would not let them take Mac and Ranjana.

If he had to die – then it would be by his own hand.

Randall stood his ground and delivered a right-handed piston-punch to that furious white face as its body embraced him. The blow sent shock-wave shivers up Randall's arm. It was a punch that he had learned on the street, but he had never in his life hit anyone or anything as hard. The thing's nose was destroyed, smashed back into its leering face. It whirled backwards in a jerking, thrashing tangle of limbs. But Randall knew that he could not fight the horde of ragged figures behind it.

Randall dashed for the train, head down. One of the vagrants landed on his back, claw-hands raking. Randall lunged on and the figure fell away.

Before him now, grim and relentless – the wheels of the train.

Behind him, the scrabbling horde of dead vagrants, intent on bringing him down.

The rumbling, crunching, unstoppable momentum of steel on steel; the juddering of the rails.

A claw-hand raking in his hair.

Randall threw himself at the wheels, unable to judge the gaps between them, and knowing that he was going to land across a rail and that in one hopefully brief but agonising moment, a wheel would pin him and cut him in half.

Something dragged at his legs as he lunged forwards.

The smell of engine oil and darkness. The stinging impact of dislodged gravel and dirt beneath the train. The suffocating darkness.

And the brief but hideous *shriek* instantly cut off by the horrific *crunch* of an immense steel wheel slicing through his flesh.

But he was not dead. He was still in one piece as he instinctively hugged himself tight into a ball beneath the train. He frantically rubbed at his legs, unable to believe they were still there. And then something that twitched and clawed feebly dragged past him. Randall recoiled with a cry of fear and disgust. The severed upper torso of the vagrant who had tried to grab his legs, but who had in that act been dragged beneath the wheels just as he himself had feared, bumped and rolled away from him, snagged in a projection from underneath the train. The silhouetted head jerked from side to side. Randall saw a spray of spittle. The arms waved feebly and the silhouette was carried away from him down the centre of the track. Randall flattened himself to the gravel track. How soon could it be before just such a projection under the train snagged his own flesh and dragged him off? Beyond the flickering black and white light of the wheels on the rail, he could see the lower torso of his attacker being dragged away in a liquid mess; could see the shambling, staggering legs of the other vagrants. There was no time for revulsion or fear. If he had come this far, could he chance his luck again? There was no time to think about it. How long would it be before this slow-moving freight train passed right on over him and left him lying exposed on the track?

Randall jerked his head to the other side, watched the wheels moving and began to count.

"One! Two! Three! One! Two! Three! *One! Two* . . ."

Randall brought his legs up tight into a ball again and flung himself over the rails, rolling fast.

"*Three!*"

Miraculously, he was out on the other side.

He staggered on the gravel track beyond the rail, part of him refusing to believe that he had come out of that hellish place alive. His limbs were trembling and he needed to vomit. But there were only five, perhaps six carriages left to pass on this track – and then the train wouldn't be a barrier between him and the street people any more. And there was no way that he could risk clambering aboard the train as Mac and Ranjana had done. Perhaps the other street people had clambered after them and dragged them down

Fear, desperation and relief were a potent cocktail, fuelling Randall.

He turned and ran into the night, moving faster than he could dream possible.

Was he really dead? Was this dashing frantic blur really happening? Had the Dead claimed him? Or was he pulverised and mangled beneath the train? Would he wake up?

The train whistle sounded again in the night, like a banshee rallying the Dead, telling them where to find him.

Randall ran . . . and ran . . . and ran . . .

55

Tony crested from the dirty water again, coughing and gagging. He kicked and lunged for the side, grabbed a rotting timber beneath the quay and clung tight, hauling himself and Lorelei under the rotting superstructure of the quayside.

They had drifted on down past the point where the narrow boat had been moored, past the reinforced concrete quay to a forgotten and dilapidated stretch sixty feet from where they had plunged into the water. Once, this had been a wooden jetty, about twenty feet above the canal and giving access to a forgotten factory. Now, the timbers that supported this rotting structure were slime-green and on the verge of collapse. But Tony was grateful for it as he clung there, keeping Lorelei's head above the canal surface.

The fight had gone out of Lorelei on impact with the canal. That twisting, tumbling fall had at first separated them. But when Tony had crested for the first time, he had seen her weakly thrashing in the water. She had swallowed lungfuls of it, was on the verge of unconsciousness. The gun was gone.

And then all hell had been let loose on the narrow boat.

The Mechanic was somehow on board. That horrifying, spinning vortex that looked like a miniature tornado could not be mistaken for anything else. And it was tearing the boat apart. Tony saw that it had been untied at the stern, that it had drifted in the hellish wind so that the foredeck faced the quay, still tied there. He knew that Lauren and Sparrow were still on the boat, and that knowledge made him strike out through the filthy water towards it; not knowing what he could do, but desperate nevertheless to try and get them away. Through the blurring of wind, he heard the agonised screams – and struck out even harder. There was movement on the foredeck. A figure. Lauren? It was almost impossible to tell, looking through that hell-wind. The figure jumped on to the quayside, and in that fleeting moment he knew that it *must* be Lauren, clutching Sparrow tight.

And then something on board had buckled and snapped, the handrail at the side had split and fallen away. The mooring rope snapped and the boat began to drift out into the canal.

Tony had ducked beneath the surface again when something on board had exploded and the narrow boat had drifted to the centre of the canal. When he surfaced, he had been carried away down the canal, away from the quay and the nightmare whirlwind which was tearing the narrow boat apart. Somehow, the Mechanic had *not* been stopped when Tony rammed his photograph down that bastard's collar and had rampaged aboard. Could Sparrow have been wrong about what could stop the thing?

And then the boat exploded, the impact stunning Tony, spinning him in the water. His mind was instantly blurred, water filled his mouth. He kicked and thrashed, coughing and gagging, knowing that he must not lose consciousness lest he drown.

At that moment, Lorelei had all but drifted into his arms. She was semi-conscious, clutching feebly at him. Tony grabbed her without thinking, and struck out for the canal side. He could see the narrow boat, see its shattered hull and watched as it turned in the water like some great beast, wreathed in smoke and flames. The whirlwind was gone and he knew instinctively that the Mechanic had returned to Hell. The very fact that it had gone seemed to loosen something inside Tony, something that had been gnawing at his guts like a raw wound. Instinctively, his terror of it had always been there, even when it had been miles away. But its conjuration had resulted in a deep-rooted and primal *knowledge* that something which defied description and by rights should not exist was out there somewhere intent on hunting him down and killing him horribly. Now it was gone – and with it had gone that dreadful soul-destroying terror.

Now, clutching at the timbers, Tony watched the pools of burning petrol drift and snuff out.

Lorelei moaned, and then was racked with coughing. She clung to his arm. For the first time, Tony saw her face and remembered the way she had looked at him just before he had rammed into her and sent them both spinning into the canal. Now, he could see those empty eye sockets up close. How could a blind woman *see* the way that she was so obviously able to see? How could she shoot at him with such hate and precision? No matter, Tony had learned in the last few days that all kinds of things he had once thought impossible were incontrovertible facts of life. This woman was vile and dangerous.

"Sabbarite?" he hissed at the blind girl.

She twisted in his grip. Tony looped his arm around her neck, so that he was still holding her above the water-line, but had a stranglehold as well.

"*Sabbarite?*"

"Go to hell . . ." gasped Lorelei.

Tony tightened his hold on her windpipe. Lorelei gagged.

"You tried to kill me up there," continued Tony. "Been trying to kill me all along. Just remember, I don't owe you any favours. You answer my questions, girl. Or I'll choke the bloody life out of you. Do you understand?"

Lorelei thrashed in his grip.

"*Understand?*" He tightened his grip again, ducking her head momentarily beneath the surface of the canal. When she crested, she shook her head furiously, clinging to Tony's forearm.

"Sabbarite?"

Lorelei nodded. "This won't . . . won't . . . do you any good, Dandridge. We've taken Lauren and the little bastard. Let me go now – and I promise we'll leave you alone."

"She got away," coughed Tony. "I saw her . . ."

"No!" Lorelei struggled again, but Tony held fast. "She got off the boat, but they were waiting for her up there. Believe me, Dandridge. They've taken her. The best thing you can do is forget her and . . ."

"*Forget!*" Tony held tight. "Are you bloody joking? After everything I've been through, after everything you've done? Not a chance!"

"You've been lucky, Dandridge. Let me go, and you'll come to no harm."

"Where are they taking her?"

"Forget . . ."

Grimly, Tony held Lorelei under again. Her legs kicked and raked at him. When she surfaced, she coughed and gagged again, frantically shaking her head. "Look . . . look . . . listen. There's more going on than even Lauren has told you. More at stake."

"What do you mean?"

"The child has to die." Tony made a move as if to choke her again. "No, wait! Not just for our purposes. Not just a sacrifice for power. The child has to die – because Ramsden wants him."

"Bullshit!" said Tony. "Pearce Ramsden is dead. Lauren heard him killed. Told me all about why the Sabbarite wanted him dead."

"He's dead, all right. I killed him. But he's on the verge of returning, of coming back to life."

"What the hell are you talking about?"

"Listen! Listen to me. I'm his daughter. Do you understand? I can sense things the way that Lauren's child senses things. That's because of the way I was conceived, the way that the child was conceived. I

285

was bred for . . . I was bred for the purpose of killing. Ramsden has had other children by other women. But none of the others except me has been allowed to live. He's bred and sacrificed them all. He told us that Lauren's child was going to be the same. But he was lying . . ."

Lorelei paused to retch out water. Tony tried to strengthen his grip on the slime-covered strut – and she sank her teeth into his arm.

Tony cried out, and Lorelei was able to thrash free from him.

She didn't get far. Tony surged through the water and seized her hair. In the next moment, he had anchored himself against another strut and had Lorelei around the throat once more.

"I'm not joking!" snapped Tony. "I'll *kill* you!"

Lorelei stopped squirming, wiped straggling red hair from her eyes.

"Now, what do you mean he was lying? And how the hell can a dead man come back to life?"

"He only told us part of the story," continued Lorelei. "The drugs which he'd obtained were feeding the child psychically and spiritually in ways that far exceeded anything he was telling us. He didn't want his bastard to die! Had no intention of letting us sacrifice him."

"What the hell are you talking about?"

"He was creating a new body for himself! He had bred the child, was giving it enormous psychic powers. Was going to tutor it, constantly develop it with the talents he'd acquired. Somehow convince us at some stage that it should *not* be sacrificed. Maybe by killing *me* – and letting it take my place. Then, at the appropriate time, when the boy had reached maturity, he was going to transfer himself into the child. Rid himself of his own body, embody within his own child. He'd have a new body, be younger and more vital, would inherit the enormous powers that he'd bred within the child . . ."

"So you killed him?"

"Of course! He'd forgotten that I had sensitive powers. He'd tried to cloak his motives from me, but he underestimated me. He *always* underestimated me! He was becoming more erratic, was threatening by his behaviour to expose us. He *had* to die."

"So he's dead. How can he be coming back?"

"Get me out of here . . ."

"Tell me!"

"Get me *out*! If you do, I'll tell you everything that you want to know."

Tony tensed, thought about dunking her under again. But his actions, however justified, were sickening him. And his grip on this slime-covered stanchion could not last for ever. The sodden weight of the girl was also becoming unbearable.

"Everything?" he growled at her again.

"Everything . . ."

Tony clung tight to the girl, and pushed himself out into the canal again.

"Don't struggle. Just relax . . ."

The girl allowed herself to be pulled along behind him as Tony moved out from under the jetty, looking for any way that they could return to the quayside. There was no way to climb up this dilapidated wooden jetty, and the floating, smoking detritus from the shattered narrow boat up by the concrete mooring made it too dangerous to even think about swimming up there. Tony headed in the opposite direction, still keeping tight to the side in case his strength should give out and he might need to grab for any kind of support there. Past the wooden structure was another length of reinforced concrete wall. Tony looked up. The top of that wall was level with the wooden platform of the jetty, fourteen or fifteen feet above, but as they floated he could see that the wall was sloping downwards towards the canal. There was a bend ahead, and Tony continued on, still pulling Lorelei with him. When they rounded that bend, with factories on either side, he saw with immense relief that the water level here was only two or three feet from a towpath.

They drifted into the side and Tony aimed for a rusted metal ring set into the canal side. The factories here were also deserted; presumably no chance of anyone rushing to their rescue after hearing the narrow boat explode like a bomb. Grabbing the ring, he pulled them into the side, gulping in air for several seconds. Lorelei was limp in his grasp, showing no sign that she was going to attempt another escape. Finally, he relaxed his hold on her, took her hand and made her hold on to the concrete lip of the canal. When she was steadied, Tony put his foot in the ring, grabbed the side with both hands and hauled himself out of the water. He groaned as he slumped on to dry land, feeling as if he weighed twice as much because of the sodden clothes. Again, he lay there breathing deeply, finally rolling over and crawling to the edge, taking Lorelei's hand and pulling her out of the canal. She lay beside him for a long time.

"Everything . . ." said Tony at last. "You said everything."

"It won't . . . won't . . . do you any good in the long run, Dandridge. The Sabbarite will come back for me."

"Everything!" Tony rolled over and seized Lorelei's shoulder. He began to shake her. "All right, how can a dead man come back to life?"

Lorelei laughed then, the laughter abruptly choking away as she retched again. When she recovered, she said, "I stabbed him, the others beat him – they picked up anything at hand, a walking stick, an iron bar, and they beat him until they broke every bone in his body. Then we took him" – Lorelei laughed again – "and we tied him to an engine block, threw him into a *canal*. We wanted to be thorough. All of that – but he's still on the verge of coming back."

"How?"

"If I was to ask you . . . ask you if you believed in Hell . . . ?"

"Then I would believe you. Lauren's told me all about it. It exists. It's a place – another dimension, or something."

"What, no questions? No protests . . . ?"

"Get on with it!"

"Father – Ramsden – had made contact with those who dwell there. Not nice people, Dandridge. But we established contact. We could do things for them, if they did . . . things . . . for us. What none of us realised was that Father's contact with them was much more intimate than he'd let on to us. He established" – Lorelei laughed and retched again – "established *trading links*. There are drugs over there, can you believe it? Drugs that a physician would tell you cannot physically or chemically exist. But they do exist. And we were able to obtain them for our own use. Drug trafficking with Hell – but something more was going on than Ramsden allowed the Sabbarite to discover. We still don't know exactly what he was planning, but he had become too dangerous, too absorbed in the development of his *own* power. That's why he had to die."

"You're still not explaining how he can come back . . ."

"We don't *know*! His body is still in that fucking canal – but I can sense that his presence is still active. He's up to something, has come to some kind of arrangement with those he contacted in Hell. An arrangement that will free him from that place in exchange for something he will be able to do for them, free him to return, to be *reborn*."

Lorelei lay silent, her outburst robbing her of strength. Tony pulled himself up into a sitting position.

"What about Lauren and Sparrow?"

"They're going to die. What do you think? Sparrow must die to prevent Ramsden returning. The child is a vital link in his plan. Once the child dies, Father will never be able to return – no matter what he's got planned."

"Where have they taken her?"

"Leave it, Dandridge. Just walk away. We'll leave you alone, I promise . . ."

"And let you set another Mechanic after me? I don't think so."

"You're in above your head," said Lorelei.

"Then so are you!" shouted Tony, scrabbling to his feet. Grabbing Lorelei by the shoulders, he dragged her back to the canal edge, forcing her head over the side. "I'm not joking! You tell me where they've taken them, or I'll drown you here and now!"

Lorelei struggled in his grip, but was still not strong enough to resist. Frantically, she began to nod her head.

"All right . . . all right . . ."

Tony stood back, throwing her down.

"I've seen and heard some vile things," said Tony. "Done some pretty bad things in my time. But I've never come across anything like you and yours. You're filth, just plain filth . . ."

"Sticks and stones," said Lorelei.

"Tell me!"

"To one of our churches," gasped Lorelei. "For the killing."

"Which one?"

"The nearest."

"What's your name?"

"Snow White."

"I should just wring your neck."

"Lorelei. My name is Lorelei."

"Very well . . . Lorelei. Let's go and say our prayers."

56

"Where *are* you taking me, then?" asked the girl in the back seat of the car.

"Like I said," replied Harry from the driver's seat. "You don't need to know." He checked on her again in the rearview mirror, watched as she blew a gum-bubble and then checked on the bundle that lay next to her on the seat. The bubble popped and Harry saw the obvious look of distaste on her face for what was in that bundle.

"Should dump him," she said.

"What?" asked Mark.

"The kid. Should just dump him. On me mother, I mean."

As if in answer, the baby began to squall. Impatiently, the girl pulled a comforter out of her leather jacket and shoved it into the baby's mouth. Harry could hear the kid furiously sucking, even from the front seat.

"Some fucking mother you are," said Harry.

"Who sent you, the social services? Look, you've got to make a living in this life."

Next to Harry, Mark began to laugh. "Good, that. Nearly a joke. Gotta make a living in this life . . ."

Harry looked at him, looked at the great stupid grin on his face. That grin had been there since they'd met earlier in the morning – and Harry was not happy about that grin at all. It was too much like the grin he'd seen on the stupid fuckers who'd been taking Nektre.

"You sure you haven't taken any?" asked Harry, turning the car into the council housing estate.

Mark laughed again. "Just 'cause I'm happy, you think I'm on a false high."

"If you've been on that stuff – you know what he'll do."

Mark laughed again.

"Don't go in for James Bond stuff," said the girl from the back. "Like to know where I'm going."

"You'll know when we get there," replied Harry.

"It's twenty quid," said the girl. "And I mean *each*. I'm not into this group thing, though. One at a time, not altogether."

Harry hit the brakes hard, and the girl snapped out an expletive as she jarred into the front seat. The baby squalled again when the comforter was dislodged.

"We're here." Harry climbed angrily out of the car, and stood there with one hand on the door frame watching as Mark climbed out from the passenger side. Across the roof of the car, Harry said, "I'm serious, Mark. If you've been taking that stuff, he'll *know*. Christ knows what's happening to him recently, but if he sees that stupid grin . . ."

"Ah, bollocks!" exclaimed Mark, slamming the door. "You're like my mother. You worry too much."

"Nobody ever learn to open a door for a lady?" said the girl, clambering from the back of the car.

"Show me a lady first," said Harry.

"It's going to cost *you* thirty quid!" snapped the girl.

"I wouldn't touch you with a barge pole."

"Keep your money, pal. Spend it on wank magazines. What about the kid? Do I leave him in the car, or what?"

"Bring the baby," said Harry.

The girl took the bundle from the back seat and followed them to the cul de sac.

At the front door, Harry paused to look at Mark.

Mark made a big joke of wiping the smile from his face.

Harry shook his head, and rang the front doorbell. At his touch, the door opened.

"Gerry?" Uncomfortably, Harry tried to look inside. It was pitch black in there. "Gerry . . . ?"

"Shit," said the girl, standing back from the doorway. "What's that smell?"

Harry knew what she meant. On the last two occasions that he'd been here, it seemed as if the house was permeated with sickening perfume. Not an expensive brand you might buy at the Boots perfume counter. This was a pungent but indefinable "flowery" smell – like the kind of cheap freshener his own wife might use in the toilet to disguise the other, more horrendous smell generated by ten pints of bitter and a home-made curry. Except that this smell seemed to be worse than the smell it was meant to cover up. Harry held a hand to his mouth and stepped into the hallway, trying to peer into the darkness. "Gerry?"

" . . . come in . . ."

The voice was distant, but unmistakable. He must be in one of the other rooms.

Harry stepped in, and Mark shoved the girl in the small of the back, making her follow. Mark reached for the light switch.

"Leave it!" snapped Gerry from somewhere in the darkness.

"I think we've found her," said Harry.

At last, he could see where Gerry's voice was coming from. It was the living room, a little further down the hall. The door was ajar. It was dark in there, too. Gerry had drawn the curtains – just like the last time that Harry had been here for instructions – and now he could just make him out, sitting in that old armchair. It had been turned to face the door. Harry could see the silhouette of Gerry's head above the headrest, looking out into the hall at them.

Gerry did not answer.

"The girl and the baby," continued Harry. "The ones you're looking for."

"What makes you think it's them?" said the silhouetted head.

"Couple of the boys caught her stealing some old girl's handbag at a bus station. Said she and the kid needed to get out of the city for a while."

"Who is this?" said the girl, looking around the darkened hallway, wrinkling her nose in disgust at the smell. "Howard Hughes?"

"I'd watch your mouth if I was you," said Mark, smiling.

"Doesn't matter to me. Been fucked by worse."

"It's not her," said Gerry from the darkness.

"Are you sure?" asked Harry.

"*It's not HER!*"

Harry held his hands wide in supplication. "Look, Gerry. We're doing our best, but this is a big fucking city, man. And to be honest, you haven't given us much to go on."

"So are we doing business, or what?" said the girl.

"Shut *up!*" shouted Harry, whirling on her, allowing his own deep anxiety in Gerry's presence to focus on her.

"It's still twenty quid . . ."

"Get her out of here!" snapped Harry.

Mark seized her from behind and dragged her to the front door. The child began to cry in her arms.

"Take your bloody hands off me! Dragging me out here, promising me . . ."

"Here." Mark stuffed a ten pound note in her hand and shoved her through the front door, watching as she staggered out onto the drive. Screaming another expletive, giving a two-fingered sign, the girl turned and tottered away, shoving the ten pound note into her pocket and then yelling at her child to be quiet, making it cry all the harder. Mark stood at the door and watched her go.

"Like I said," continued Harry, turning back to the silhouette. "There's not much to go on, Gerry. We're all out there, looking. But looking for what? I mean, what does this girl look like, how old is she? How old is the kid? What about the . . . ?"

"Quiet, Harry!" hissed Gerry.

"What?"

"I'm listening . . ."

Harry turned to look back at Mark in bewilderment. Mark was still standing at the front door, looking through the crack in the door at the departing figure and her baby. He was still smiling.

"All right," said Gerry at last. 'She's about twenty-two. Blonde, shoulder-length hair. She's got an American accent . . ."

"That's more like it. American, eh? That's going to narrow it down a lot . . ."

"She's attractive. He says, 'very attractive' . . ."

He says, thought Harry. *What the hell is that supposed to mean?*

"The child is . . . a boy. Eight months old. And it's . . . it's more important that you find the child than his mother. But we need to find him. We *need* to find him, Harry! There's not much time left."

"All right, all right. I'll get the others on to it straight away . . ."

Somewhere beyond the door, something crashed – and Mark laughed. The crash resolved into a brittle clattering of broken glass. Harry whirled around.

"What the hell was that?"

Mark laughed again, eyes sparkling. "It's that stupid bint we just threw out. Oh dear, oh dear . . . Harry, you're not going to like this at all."

"What . . . ?"

"She's just put a plant pot through the front window of your car." Mark laughed loud, as if this was the funniest thing that he had ever seen. "She's . . . she's pulled your fucking wing-mirror off, as well."

Harry made to move forward – but was halted by the sound, and the horribly dangerous tone, of Gerry's voice.

"What are you *laughing* at, Mark?"

"Like . . . like I said. Harry's car. The poor, fucking . . ."

"Last time you were here, you were so scared you could hardly talk. Isn't that right, Harry?"

"He's pissed," said Harry defensively. "That's all. Just pissed."

"Is that all, Mark?"

"Yeah." Mark snorted back tears of laughter, still looking out through the front door. "That's it. Had a couple of pints at lunchtime." His words dissolved into a giggling fit.

"Mark!" snapped Harry. "Shut the fuck *up*!"

"No," said Gerry calmly. "Let him laugh. I like to think my . . . my employees . . . are happy in their work."

"Really, Gerry. He's just had a few . . ."

"Goodbye, Harry. Don't come back until you've found the girl and her baby."

"Yeah. Right. Okay. Well – now we've got something to go on." Harry edged towards the front door. "Come on, Mark."

"No," said Gerry, still calm. "You go on ahead. Leave Mark here. I want to have a talk with him."

"But . . ." Harry's voice dried as he reached the door. He looked long and hard at Mark, who was still almost bent double with laughter. He tried to will him to stop it. Then, looking anxiously back at the half-open living room door and the silhouette beyond, he pushed roughly past him. It seemed as if Harry's leaving the house was the second best joke that Mark had ever heard.

"Shut the door," said Gerry – and Mark nudged it shut with his hip.

Outside, Harry marched grimly away from the house towards his car and its shattered windscreen. When he reached it, there was no sign of the girl and her baby. Wiping the shattered glass from the driving seat, Harry flung himself into the car, gunned the engine and swung the car away from the house with a screech of tyres.

"You stupid, *stupid* idiot . . ." he said as the car turned on to the main road, and away from the housing estate.

Inside the house, in the darkness, Mark stood in the hallway trying to control his laughter.

"Come here," said the silhouette in the living room.

Mark staggered across the hallway to the door. He leaned on the door frame.

"Sorry . . . sorry . . . to tell you this, Gerry. But this house . . . this house . . . fucking *stinks*!" It was another huge joke, and Mark bent double again with laughter.

"You think maybe I need to decorate," said the silhouette calmly. "Clean the place up?"

Gerry's response fuelled gales of laughter in Mark.

"Come on in then. Let me show you the new furnishings and fittings I've got in here."

Mark stood again, tears of laughter streaming down his face. He stepped through the living room door as the silhouette began to rise from his seat.

"I'm sure you can make a personal contribution."

57

The streets were empty and desolate, just like those end-of-the-world movies that Randall used to watch when he was a kid.

He should be too exhausted to walk, but he was walking. His mind and body seemed numb, as if he was in a dream – and he could not believe that he had managed to escape from those things back in the goods yard. Then the thought came to him that perhaps he really was dead, after all. Maybe that would explain the numb way that he was feeling, explain away why he hadn't collapsed with exhaustion. He *had* been caught by the Dead and torn apart. Or perhaps it *had* all finished beneath the wheels of that train. That horrifying sound had not been the train wheel crushing the vagrant – it had been the sound of his own death. He had never survived, and never rolled out from under the train and escaped.

The street ahead seemed unsteady, rolling from side to side; crazy angles shifting and looming, just as if he was drunk and staggering home.

Then they stepped around a corner – a dozen of them. Street people. And this time, they did not turn their hungry gaze on him and then give chase. This time, they turned and smiled when they saw him. There was no hunger there now, no dreadful longing. Their night-wreathed smiles were smiles of welcome, smiles of recognition. He was one of them now. Of course, he was dead, had staggered away from the goods yard unsure of his new status, of his passage from life to death. He could join them at last. Still numb, drawn on towards them, Randall kept walking. The street was no longer tilting like a bad booze dream. They held their arms wide to greet him.

And then Ranjana and Mac stepped around the corner to meet him.

"Welcome to the club," said Mac. His voice sounded as if he was gargling. And that was because his throat had been cut.

Ranjana smiled, and Randall saw that her teeth had been smashed out, leaving only a hideous broken smile framing the jagged shards that remained embedded in her gums. Her blouse had been torn away at the front, and someone had carved something there in the flesh.

"We're the shadow people," said Ranjana, her voice horribly distorted. "Mac and me – and you. Real people don't exist. Only us . . ."

The shock of it woke Randall instantly.

He thrashed to his feet, clutching at the brickwork beside him. For a while he stood there, swaying – and then finally realised where he had fallen asleep. It was a shop doorway, somewhere in the middle of the town. He vaguely recalled his flight from the goods yard, vaguely recalled reaching a high street. But there was no one around – no *real* people – to remind him of the real world in which he thought he'd been living up until that point. And then the thought had come to him – what would he do if he saw another vagrant, another down-and-out? Would it be one of *them*, one of the hungry ones? How long could he keep running? Exhausted, still in shock from his experience down on the railway line, Randall had found the shop doorway, had slumped in the darkened alcove. All he wanted was rest. Falling asleep was probably the most dangerous thing he could do in the circumstances, particularly if those things could sniff out their prey. But sleep had crept up on him unawares; one moment he was watching the street, anxiously looking for any sign of movement, any sign of slow, shambling figures – and then he was walking in his dreamscape.

He had no idea how long he had slept. Randall looked furtively around. Just staying here until daylight was no protection. Getting out of the city – perhaps heading home – was probably his best bet. He thought about Ranjana and a sickness jammed solid in his innards. Maybe she and the big man had managed to escape after all. There was no way of finding out, and a return to the goods yard was pointless. If they had managed to stay on that train, perhaps they were miles away by now. If they'd been dragged off it and torn apart, what good would it do?

Randall stepped out of the shop doorway, turned up his collar and moved quickly into the night.

A police station . . .

Could that be a way out? Find a police station somewhere and turn himself in? Maybe he could find protection there? After all, he had dumped one of their panda cars into the river. Then the thought of being stuck behind bars while a crowd of the Dead gathered outside the station came to him. He could see them moving in . . . No, that wasn't the way. Randall kept moving.

He was still trying to decide whether it was best to find a place to hide out until daylight, or whether he should keep moving. When the early morning traffic began again, he might be able to flag down a lorry.

Out in the open, he was vulnerable, could be spotted. But staying in the same place was equally dangerous. Still trying to weigh up the pros and cons, he suddenly realised that he had reached the edge of the shopping area. The street veered sharply uphill, and there were no longer shops, stores and buildings on either side to provide cover.

"Shit!"

Randall looked back. The multicoloured lights from television rental shops and department stores lit up the main street and would show anything that moved down there. The traffic lights kept a silent vigil, constantly changing as if in the hope that traffic would be attracted by their action. Randall hadn't seen a car, van or lorry all night. He turned back to look up to where the street vanished overhill and into darkness. There was waste land on either side there.

Darkness or light?

Randall chose – and began to run uphill into the night.

There was no guarantee of safety anywhere.

As he ran, he stooped and picked up half a housebrick lying by the side of the road. Jamming it into his pocket, he kept running. It wasn't much of a weapon, particularly against things that Ranjana had said were dead – and which therefore felt no pain. But the act was an act of aggression on Randall's part and he knew from bitter experience that aggression was often the only thing he could use to get himself and others out of bad situations. He imagined confronting a crowd of the street people, once he'd run over that hill. They would be standing there with arms wide, just as in his dream. What other options would be open to him?

Can't we talk reasonably about this?

Randall laughed with bitter derision and melted into the night.

At the top of that hill, he staggered to a halt, breathing heavily.

Someone was down there.

The street itself wound downwards again. The streetlights on either side were in a poor state of maintenance. Some gave faint blue light across the tarmac, but the bulbs in others had either burned out or been vandalised, giving only ragged illumination to the entire stretch, which seemed to vanish completely into the night. The distant flickering of neon on the night horizon gave the added impression that this wasn't a road at all, but a black river, flowing out into the night to meet a distant and poison-glittering sea. There were dark and crowded buildings on either side, probably factories, although it was impossible to see. But on the right-hand side, about two hundred yards on, there was a ragged patch of waste land. Randall could see piles of broken bricks scattered randomly. A demolition area?

But what really drew his eye was the van.

297

And the two figures who were standing with their backs to him, illumined in the harsh light of the serving hatch. A woman was serving them both, and Randall could hardly believe his eyes.

It was Ranjana and Mac.

Surely he couldn't be mistaken?

Mac paused on the brow of the hill and looked back to the silent shopping area. There was no movement back there, no suddenly converging crowd of shambling figures stepping out of shop doorways and around corners. Just the silent winking of the traffic lights on the main street. When he turned back to look down on the van, Mac and Ranjana were still there. He watched Ranjana take a paper cup of something hot from the aproned woman behind the serving hatch, saw her head become wreathed in steam as she bent to drink from it. But hadn't Ranjana been the one who had felt that the vans and the people who drove them and served from them were evil? How could she have changed her mind so completely?

Had they been caught by the street people after all? Had they been dragged from the freight car, and converted to the new cause?

Without consciously deciding, Randall found himself staggering down the hill towards them.

If they'd been caught, it would explain their lack of fear. But if they had, why in hell was he walking down to join them instead of running away?

Because you're still dreaming. Because you didn't really wake up in that shop doorway after all. Don't you see that?

Randall nodded and kept walking.

Mac turned from the serving hatch with his own paper cup and saw him coming.

Yes, Randall was right. It was them. Mac was waving at him now, beckoning for him to come forward. He was saying something to Ranjana as Randall came, and now she too had turned and waved.

Even if this was a dream, was it really so bad to be dead?

After all, there was no pain. No need to worry about dying if you were dead already. No need to be anyone or go anywhere. No need to keep that little boy inside hidden any more; the little boy in the photograph on the mantelpiece with his forced black and white smile trying to hide the pain of two broken ribs and trying to imprint his love for his parents on the camera. No need to run away, no need to hitch-hike to unknown destinations searching for an adult happiness which would always be withheld from him. When you joined the dead, you became a part of their select society. You could walk the streets unseen by the real people. Join all those others who had no family and had said goodbye to all their pain. You could become part of a new family.

A family that didn't need money, didn't need a roof over their heads, didn't need roots. Didn't need food.

. . . food . . .

Why were Mac and Ranjana drinking from those cups if they were dead?

It's a sham, came the voice in his head again. *Of course they don't need food. But they have to act the part, don't they? Have to keep it secret, not give the game away.*

Twenty feet from the van, Randall halted – and the expression on Mac's face changed.

Because it wasn't Mac, after all. This was a younger man, but with the same powerful build. He seemed disappointed now.

"Sorry, pal," said the stranger. "Thought you were someone else."

The girl turned to look at him. She was white, about twice Ranjana's age, her hair hanging long and unkempt.

"Told you it wasn't Johnnie," she said in a Birmingham accent. "Never fucking listen to me, do ya?"

"Shut up," said the man, and lifted the cup to his lips again.

It wasn't Mac or Ranjana, but it wasn't those dead street people either. Randall strained to try and get a good look at the woman behind the serving hatch. She was middle-aged with white hair tied tight in a bun behind her head, for all the world like a school dining hall supervisor. It was hard to see her face in the darkness as the light in the van backlit her features to a silhouette, but she seemed to be smiling.

"Get away from here," said Randall simply.

"You what?" said the man.

"I said get away from here, if you know what's good for you."

"Who the hell do you think you are? Don't fucking own this van, do you?"

"I don't mean that!" snapped Randall. "I mean it's dangerous for you to be here . . ."

"Threatening us as well," said the girl, turning to the woman in the van. "You heard him. Should get the police . . ."

"I'm not threatening you, you idiots! I'm just telling you that it's dangerous here. Somebody I know . . . somebody who means a lot to me . . . knew . . . *knows* that these vans are dangerous, and so are the people who drive them and who give out the food. They kill people like you . . ."

"He's drunk," said the girl.

"So am I," said the big man, and began to laugh. "But I don't go around threatening people, do I? Don't need a drink to be big."

"*Listen!*" Randall's shout seemed to reverberate with shocking clarity in the night. And Randall suddenly knew with a strange and blinding insight that what he was about to say, something entirely unsubstantiated and without reason, was absolutely true. "These people. They're killers. Get away while you can."

The girl took the big man by the arm and began to guide him away from the serving hatch. The big man was still laughing, but the girl was clearly disturbed by the arrival of this crazy man. Randall kept a careful eye on the figure behind the serving hatch. She seemed unperturbed by what he was saying. Unconcerned, she continued to wipe the bench. As the girl dragged the man slowly away and the big man continued to laugh and be led, Randall shifted position to watch them – and also keep his eye on the van.

"And be careful out there," he continued. "There are things out there in the night. Dead people."

"Right," said the big man. "Not to mention the pink elephants and the blue crocodiles."

"I'm telling you! Keep away from these vans. I don't know why they're doing it, but the people who run them just want to kill people like you."

"Maybe they're social workers," laughed the big man. "You know, like South-fucking-America. Cleaning the cities up by killing off the fucking vagrants. New government policy, eh?"

"Yeah," said Randall. "Maybe something like that."

"You need treatment, you!" shouted the girl, now feeling safely out of range as she dragged the big man across the badly illumined road and deeper into the night. "Too much fucking meths, that's your trouble."

"Or not enough!" laughed the big man.

The night swallowed them up.

"Be careful!" yelled Randall after them. "For Christ's sake be careful."

"You're ruining our business," said a quiet voice behind Randall.

He turned, flinching.

But he could not avoid the plank of wood that was laid across his head.

In this sleep, there were no dreams.

58

The freight car rumbled on into the night.

And Ranjana could still not believe that they had managed to escape.

Mac had pulled her on to the roof of the carriage, and she had looked back frantically as the first of the street people staggered along the cinder track below towards Randall. Only one had tried to leap up on to the side of the train in an attempt to reach them, and he had fallen back very quickly as Mac braced himself on the roof, ready to fight. For some reason, they seemed to have lost interest in them both, concentrating instead on the one who had been left behind. Ranjana had called Randall's name long and loud as the train trundled on into the night, until Mac had been forced to take her by the arms and shake her until she stopped.

Randall was dead. And there was nothing they could do about it.

Climbing down from the roof again after they had left the goods yard had been infinitely worse than climbing up. Mac had gone first, had balanced himself precariously while he worked on the freight car door, had finally managed to prise it open and swing it wide. But Ranjana had been too afraid to descend. Eventually, he'd had to climb back up and drag her with him, inch by perilous inch. The train still travelled at the same pace, and if they'd fallen they might have managed to make it without breaking any bones, but Ranjana had been mesmerised by the sight of those great steel wheels and the sound they made on the rails.

Finally reaching the ledge on to which they'd first jumped, Mac had all but thrown her into the freight car. There were wooden packing crates in there, but in the darkness it was impossible to tell what was inside. The smell of cow manure was strong. Ranjana had found a place to sit, had watched as Mac swung himself into the carriage and then pulled the door closed, leaving a two-foot gap through which he could see where they were going, and also allow what little illimunation there might be from the outside into the carriage.

Then he'd staggered to the carriage wall, stood there for a while with his hand on his head – and then sat heavily beside the door, staring out into the night as the train clattered on. Ranjana sat between two of the packing crates, watching him. For a long, long time neither one of them spoke.

"Three, seven, four, oh-two," said Mac at last.

"What?"

Mac mumbled something else, lost beneath the sound of the train on the track.

"What are we going to do?" Ranjana asked. Mac did not reply. Was he smiling in the darkness? Ranjana braced her hands on the packing crates and pulled herself to her feet again. Stepping carefully in the darkness, nose wrinkled at the disgusting smell, she moved to join him.

"Three, seven, four, oh-two," said Mac under his breath again.

Ranjana knelt down beside him and looked directly into his eyes. "Wake up."

Mac laughed, his eyes still fixed on the gap between the doors.

"Wake up, damn it!' Ranjana slapped his face.

But Mac did not respond. His flesh felt cold to her touch. She slapped him again – and felt terribly guilty when he still refused to respond.

Tears were coming, God knew why at this moment in time after everything that she had been through beforehand. She bit her lip, took Mac by the frayed collar and began to shake him.

"Wake *up*!"

Still no response. Ranjana let him go and he slumped back against the carriage wall. Had he lost it completely now? Still fighting back those tears, cursing herself for trying to retreat into being a little girl again, Ranjana stood up and moved back to the packing crates.

What the hell was she going to do?

"Are you all right?" asked a calm, resonant voice behind her.

She spun around. Mac was looking directly at her, still sitting in the same position.

"That's what I've been asking you, damn it!" snapped Ranjana. "What the hell's the matter with you?"

"You mean you don't know?" asked Mac. There was no hint of reproach in his voice. He wiped his face with a huge, scarred hand.

"Just . . . just don't do that to me again."

"Sorry," said Mac, and in the darkness she thought she could detect a wan smile. "I told you, sometimes I drift."

"Do you think" – Ranjana coughed, clearing the choking sound from her voice – "do you think Randall got away?"

302

"I don't know. You're the one who can sense things. What do *you* think?"

Ranjana braced her hands behind her on the tops of the packing crates and screwed her eyes shut. After a while, she let out her breath in an angry, impatient hiss. "No, just the child again. And the vans . . . and maybe something about somebody who can't . . . who can't *see*. But nothing about Randall."

"Maybe you can't feel anything because he's dead."

"No, I won't believe that. Not after everything we've been through."

"Face it, he's probably dead."

"No! We've . . . we've got to go back for him."

"And I thought I was the crazy one. Look, there's nothing we can do for him now. The best thing we can do is stay in this train. Let it take us as far from the city as possible. Like I said before."

"Aren't you forgetting something?"

"What?"

"The dreams. The fact that I saw you, the fact that you saw me! And then both of us coming together like that."

"Maybe it means that we're supposed to be doing what we're doing right now! Saving each other's skins and getting away from this nightmare."

"No, it means more than that. Much more. Don't tell me you haven't felt it. We saw each other, we met up the way we did – for a *purpose*. And running away isn't what we're supposed to do. The only way we can really fight this nightmare is to follow it through. Find out just what the hell is going on. And we have to find Randall."

"Forget it, he's dead."

Ranjana was silent then, and Mac tried to see the expression on her face. Maybe he had at last convinced her. Then she seemed to wilt, to lean back against the packing crates.

"Are you . . . ?" began Mac.

"*They've taken him*," said Ranjana.

"What? Who . . . ?"

Ranjana's hand flew to her mouth. She seemed to be struggling to stop herself from vomiting. She swallowed hard, and when she spoke again, her voice was hoarse and breathless.

"Now I know. I *know*, Mac! It's never . . . never happened to me like this before. Normally, I'm ill. I faint . . . or something. But I know."

"Take it easy . . ."

"It *is* the vans. People who are pretending to be voluntary workers. They're taking vans out. They're finding street people on their own. And then they're killing them . . ."

Mac had a sudden and vivid mental flashback. He saw Bernie

303

struggling on the towpath with his pursuers. He heard Bernie yelling for him, saw the flash of a knife. He saw Bernie's body tumbling over the quayside and into the night-black water. He saw himself diving over the side – and the sudden recollection of the shock of icy water jerked him back to the present.

"They've taken Randall," continued Ranjana. "I just felt it. And they're going to kill him."

"But what the hell can we do?"

Ranjana strode towards him across the carriage. Mac tried to rise. But suddenly she had placed her foot squarely on his chest, and she shoved him down hard to the carriage wall again.

"I know what I can do," she said calmly, and in the next instant Ranjana swung open the carriage door.

"Don't be a bloody fool!" yelled Mac.

But he was too late.

Ranjana gathered herself and leapt through the gap into the night.

Cursing, Mac braced both hands on the doors and looked back after her.

Cursing again, he followd her out on to the cinder track below.

59

The car was still at the bottom of the alley where they had left it, but it had been pushed aside by the hellish whirlwind which had passed over it. It stood at an angle to the kerb now, and both wing-mirrors were gone. The bonnet and roof were stained by the detritus which the wind had carried.

"Thank God for that," said Terri as they hurried out of the alley.

"Who?" snorted Bradford, and pushed Lauren on ahead of her.

Bolam reached the car first and fumbled at the lock. Suddenly, he pulled his shaking hands away and slammed them down on to the roof of the car, lowering his head.

"Did you see?" His voice sounded cracked. "Did you see what happened to Ernest? Did you see what it *did* to him . . . ?"

"Open the car!" snapped Bradford, shoving Lauren up against the bonnet.

"How could that happen?" continued Bolam. His hands were plainly shaking. "I thought you said we were protected against that thing. It should have taken Dandridge, not Ernest."

"The *car!*"

"But how . . . ?"

Terri pulled him around, snatching the car keys from his hand. She was half his weight, he was two feet taller, but it looked as if she could tear him apart if necessary.

"We don't know how. But it doesn't matter. Dandridge is dead, and we've got the child." Terri threw the car keys to Bradford as she pulled him away from the door.

"But it wasn't supposed to . . .'

Bolam's words were suddenly slammed out of his body as Terri placed both hands on his chest and shoved him hard against the car. It rocked on its suspension.

"Listen, you fucking wimp!" Terri's expression, so far placid and blank, looked like the ferocious snarl of some animal. "You knew what

305

you were getting into when you joined us. You've been at killings before. You've had the *benefits!*" On the last word, Terri seized Bolam by the balls. He cried out and crumpled against her. Terri slammed him back against the car. "Remember?"

"That thing . . ."

"It was a mistake bringing him," said Bradford, shoving them both aside as she opened the car door. She turned and gave Lauren a look laden with menace as she pulled open the back door, nodding that she should climb in with the child. Lauren considered whether or not she should make a run for it.

No! shouted Sparrow in her mind. *I'm thinking. We need more time. Just go along with it.*

Lauren climbed into the car.

"We needed him," said Terri. "He was the only one with the wet suit and stuff. And he was supposed to prove himself tonight. Remember that, Bolam?"

"Yeah . . . yeah . . . okay." Bolam was beginning to recover, a slow anger beginning to take over now that he had allowed this slip of a girl to rough him up. "But that shouldn't have happened to Ernest. That's all I'm saying."

"Get in the car," said Bradford. "The others will be waiting for us with the third."

"Well, it shouldn't. If it happened to him, then maybe anything can happen to us. Maybe we're not as protected as Lorelei told us."

"Get in the fucking car!"

"Lorelei was wrong . . ."

"Lorelei is *dead!* So get in!"

Reluctantly, Bolam clambered into the passenger seat as Bradford climbed into the driving seat. Terri crushed Lauren and Sparrow in the back next to Fletcher on the passenger side. He had remained strangely silent throughout, his face white. The car started on the first turn of the key, to the surprise of everyone.

"What now?" said Lauren – and felt the point of a stiletto knife in her side. She turned to see Terri's child-like grin.

"Now we carry on with what we had planned," said Bradford as the car swung away from the kerb.

"Without Lorelei?"

"We don't need her. Not for the killing. We've killed before without her. You know that."

"But isn't this special? Ramsden's baby. Don't you need her for . . ."

"You're stalling for time," said Terri. "I guess the baby is telling you to do that."

"No, I'm just . . ."

306

"We can make it hard or easy, Lauren. But you know you have to die. And the child most certainly must die. Lorelei told us what was required. The mother, the child . . . and an innocent."

"Innocent?"

"Some of the others have been out on the streets. Looking for a third. An innocent. They'll be waiting for us – with him or her."

"You don't have to . . ."

"But we *do*," said Bradford. "The child must die to prevent Ramsden from coming back."

Sparrow, for Christ's sake what are we going to do?

Let me think, let me dream. I'm close to all the answers. And I think there's someone out there who can help. An empath. I'm trying to contact her, trying to reach her . . .

But Sparrow . . . ?

Mother, be quiet! I'm juggling with all kinds of stuff. I need time, that's all. Just time.

Whatever you're up to, you'd better make it fucking quick!

Mother!

Lauren was silent.

The car sped on into the night.

60

Stanton was a ghost town.

A slum clearance plan had begun in the area, but seemed to have been interrupted halfway through the programme. The entire district had been composed of council house tenants, the narrow twisting streets of terraced property originally built to house workers in the then thriving engineering and shipbuilding industry. But that industry had long since vanished. Now, the tenants had been moved out and relocated in other housing estates and the first square mile of demolition had begun. But ten months ago funding had run out; central government had withdrawn funds from various projects as part of a vitriolic battle of words with the local council, run by the opposition party. The remaining three square miles of abandoned property remained abandoned, and in time those houses had been stripped by local "entrepreneurs" of their plumbing and heating systems for sale on the back-of-the-lorry market. This part of the city had been called Stanton after a long-dead local politician, whose dreams and plans for the area had long since crumbled to dust with his bones.

Now it was a ghost town.

And in the centre of that abandoned slum stood Stanton Methodist Church, long since abandoned even before the clearance programme had begun, due to falling attendance. A monument to the abandoned spiritual hopes of the people who had once lived there. *Lift up Your Hearts* said a tattered poster on the sign-board at the church gates; a forlorn entreaty.

Lauren recognised where she was as soon as the car rounded the bend and the ruined church came into view. She could not remember Stanton from her 'twilight' days with the Sabbarite – but she would never forget that ruined church and what had happened there.

Sparrow had been silent since the car had pulled away from the canal area, and they had been driving for well over half an hour. Lauren struggled with her fear, desperate to 'speak' to Sparrow, desperate to

308

know if he had learned or could do anything to help them.

The car swung past a row of terraced houses. The headlights swept over shattered windows and open doorways, making gigantic shadows loom and rear across the cobbled street. Lauren felt panic rising as the car juddered over those cobbles towards the church entrance. There were two cars parked by that entrance. The other Sabbarite with their third-party innocent were already there and waiting.

Sparrow, for Christ's sake!

Nothing.

Look, as soon as this car stops and Terri opens the door to climb out we're going to make a dash for it.

The car rolled to a halt outside the battered iron gates. Lauren realised that this was a side entrance and not the main entrance after all. By the light of the headlights, she could see the main drive up ahead, but it was impossible to take a car up there. At some stage, the steeple had collapsed; a great tumbled mass of masonry filled that driveway.

All right, Sparrow? That's what we're going to do. All right . . . ?

Terri threw open the door, reached back and took Lauren by the collar.

"Don't think about it, Lauren." The stiletto was jammed harder against her side. Lauren felt sure that it had pierced the flesh. Gritting her teeth, she let herself be dragged across the back seat as Terri stepped outside, still holding her collar. The temperature had dropped, but Lauren did not know whether it was the cold night air or the sick feeling of fear inside that made her tremble. She clenched her teeth to stop them from chattering. She looked down to where Sparrow was cradled in her arm as the others climbed out of the car; looked at his face. That face was just as blank and untroubled as the face of any eight-month-old child. His mouth was slightly open. She held him tight as Bradford took her arm and the two women dragged her through the side entrance and up the ragged bank towards the church. Bolam followed sullenly in the rear, casting anxious glances around for any sign of movement.

Lauren was led around the grime-encrusted side of the church. Slates and roofing tiles had fallen to the walkway here, and a rusted drainpipe clung miraculously to the stone without visible support.

Sparrow, for God's sake . . .

Although the steeple had toppled forwards into the main entrance, the Gothic arch which fronted the building had remained untouched. The huge pile of shattered rubble provided a perfect barrier as Bradford pushed Lauren around the corner and into the dark entranceway. Now, their footsteps were echoing in the darkness as they entered the church. The cold in here was much more intense than outside, seeming to emanate from the very brickwork of the building.

Lauren tensed as she walked in this darkness. Maybe this was the place where she could make a break for it?

Sparrow . . . ?

She gathered the child tight in her arms.

The stiletto jabbed into her back again.

"I *said* – don't think about it!" said Terri through gritted teeth. "Remember?"

They emerged from the complete darkness into semi-light. Now, Lauren could see the extent of dereliction. The roof had partially caved in and stars were visible through the timber-splintered gaps. Rubble had fallen into the church, shattered pews lay crushed beneath old blocks of dark, mould-encrusted stone.

Yes, Lauren remembered this place.

She remembered that she had been brought here by the Sabbarite and left to sit on a shattered pew in her twilight state while Ramsden and the others had vanished somewhere in the church to carry out their "business".

Ramsden had eventually returned, those dark eyes glittering.

He had made her lie down in the ruined aisle.

And he had taken her.

Nine months later – Sparrow had been born.

"On ahead," said Bradford. Despite the fact that the roof was gone, there still seemed to be an impossible echo in here. "Down the aisle."

Lauren walked on ahead, listening to the echoing footsteps of those behind. Were there any gaps in these walls? Somewhere she could aim at when she made her break for freedom? Huge piles of rubble and broken beams seemed to block every possible exit.

The altar ahead had also been crushed under tumbled masonry. Was this where they were headed?

"On the left of the altar," said Terri, as if in answer to her thoughts. Bradford pushed past her and headed for an arch on the left of the altar. In the dark recess, Lauren could just make out a heavy door with massive iron studs and a black ring-handle.

Sparrow!

Lauren cried out aloud when Terri jammed the stiletto hard into her back. This time, she knew that the point had broken through the flesh, could feel the warm dampness of blood between her shoulder blades.

"Careful, Terri," she said through gritted teeth. "Not sure if the others would be happy with you damaging the merchandise."

310

"I hate your fucking wisecracks," replied Terri, shoving her forward to the door as Bradford swung it open. "Hate your American accent, hate your fucking face."

"So tear up the fan club card." *Sparrow, unless you've summoned up the police, or an army, or thunderbolts from heaven – this is it! We've had it.*

Just wait! snapped Sparrow at last. *Stop interfering with my head!*

There was a faint illumination beyond the door, and Bradford stepped through. Lauren heard echoing footsteps on rough stone stairs as she descended. Terri pushed her on ahead, and now they were all descending – to a place that was colder still.

There were others waiting down here. Lauren could sense them even though there was no noise. The staircase was not deep, perhaps twenty feet below ground level and Lauren also knew what the source of that illumination would be before she saw it. That light was faint but flickering, casting large and undulating shadows. Candles.

"They're here," said an unnecessary voice as Lauren followed Bradford through another heavy door.

They were in an underground chamber, perhaps forty feet square. Water glistened on the rough stone walls in the candlelight, and Lauren could see that the candles were made from black wax and scattered apparently randomly. Some of them had been placed on an ancient stone sarcophagus in the corner, the only "furnishing" down here. That candlelight also glinted in the scattered pools of black wax on the rough soil floor of this underground chamber.

There were four other people here, and Lauren recognised all of them. Three men, one woman. All respectable people, all in respectable lines of business, all members of the Inner Circle and all reaping the rewards of their Sabbarite membership.

"You don't look the part," said Lauren. "You should be wearing hooded cowls and be chanting the Latin Mass backwards, or something."

"Shut your fucking mouth," said one of the men, stepping forward. He was in his early sixties, with immaculately combed hair and wearing an expensive three-piece suit. "You've caused us all a lot of problems." Lauren knew that he was the head of a thriving construction empire: Collins.

"And I'm sure," said the woman, "that most of us would rather *play* with you before you die. But needs must, I suppose." The woman was in her mid-forties, with horn-rimmed spectacles and a long overcoat buttoned severely at the neck. A headmistress: Weldon. The remaining two men were younger, perhaps in their thirties. She remembered the one with the moustache. His name

311

was Sutton, and in a drug-blurred dream, she remembered vaguely that he had come into the room where she was sleeping during her early days with the Sabbarite and had tried to rape her. Ramsden had intervened, had put him in hospital for interfering with his "great plan" – his own impregnation of her. He nodded extravagantly at the use of the woman's word *play*.

"What, no welcome home cake then?" said Lauren, trying to control the tremble in her voice.

"Funny," said the fourth man. His names was James, whether first name or last she had never been sure. He hardly spoke, but was obviously a man who took his pleasures seriously. Stocky and well built. The blank look on an essential cherubic face looked all the more disturbing; a promise of sickening violence.

Behind her, Fletcher closed the chamber door.

Christ, Sparrow. We have to do SOMETHING!

"Where's Lorelei?" asked the older man.

"Dead," said Bradford. "The Mechanic followed Dandridge back to the boat when we were still there. Somehow, the child was able to block out the fact that it was headed back after Dandridge. It destroyed the boat, and Lorelei was drowned. Ernest's dead, too."

"And *how!*" said Bolam from the door.

"Shut up!" snapped Terri.

"What does he mean?" asked Collins.

"The Mechanic took him, instead of Dandridge."

"Dandridge is still *alive*?" Weldon's voice rose a pitch, as if she was admonishing the children in her class.

"No, of course not," rejoined Bradford. "He's dead. He went into the water with Lorelei."

"But the Mechanic took *Ernest*,' said Collins. "How could that happen?"

Someone's coming, said Sparrow in Lauren's mind. *I don't know who, or how or why. But someone's definitely coming. Maybe it's the one I've been trying to contact. Someone who can help us. Play on their fears, Mother. Confuse them. Tell them about how I found the way to stop the . . .'*

"You've got good reason to be confused – and scared," said Lauren, struggling to keep her voice calm.

"Shut up!" snapped Terri and Lauren stepped quickly forward before she could jab her again with the stiletto. "Let's get on with it, Bradford."

"Hear that?" asked Lauren. "She's scared . . ."

Terri lunged forward. "I should just fucking *stick* you . . ."

Bradford caught her arm and stopped her. "No!"

"What the hell's going on here?" Collins was disturbed now. "Why did the Mechanic take one of us?"

"You tell me," said Bolam, voice wavering.

"Because there's more going on than even the Sabbarite know about," said Lauren.

That's it, Lauren. Keep going. Keep them frightened. Someone IS coming . . .

"The child stopped the Mechanic. Told us how to divert it to another target. He's special – you all know that."

"Lorelei's dead?" Weldon was now also clearly worried.

"Yes, but it doesn't *matter!*" snapped Bradford. She strode angrily through the half-light to the sarcophagus and shoved aside the lid. The grating sound of stone on stone filled the chamber. The candles wobbled on its surface, casting leaping shadows in the chamber.

"But this is different," continued Weldon. "Lorelei always told us that a Mechanic couldn't be stopped. We've relied on her, relied on her perception, her ability to see the other side."

"And now she's gone," said Lauren. "And you're lost."

They're close, Mother. Very close – and looking for us.

"She's playing for time!" snapped Terri. "We don't need Lorelei. Ramsden showed us what to do and how to do it. We've made our own contacts with the other side, made our own deals. We don't need her any more. You've said as much yourself, Collins! Sutton! James! Hold her – and let's get on with it."

Lauren watched the two younger men push forward, forced herself to remain relaxed and calm.

"The mother first, then the child," said Bradford. "Let her hold the baby while it's done. Remember what Lorelei said."

Lauren forced herself not to flinch as the two men took her by the arm and shoulder.

"And last, the innocent," said Terri. "Where is it?"

"He's over here," said the young man called James. Lauren looked at the foot of the stairs, and the bundle that lay there. For the first time, she could see that it was an unconscious human figure. A young man with tousled hair. His face looked the colour of melted candle-wax in the half-light. This was to be the third victim, another poor bastard picked up from the streets. Another vagrant who had foolishly accepted the offer of something to eat and drink from one of the black vans.

"Killing us is the worst thing you can do," said Lauren. "Believe me."

They're here, Lauren. They've found the church.

Bradford's hand emerged from the sarcophagus. Inside, was a myriad pattern of shattered stained-glass shards. The window had once been a blessed feature of the church in the days when the faithful had prayed here. Now the remains of that window were hidden in the stone coffin. One shard for each killing. Just as in the other deconsecrated and derelict churches of the Sabbarite in the city. All part of the killing ritual. Bradford turned, and the candlelight seemed to spark on the six-inch glass shard in her hand.

"What do you mean?" Again the fear and uncertainty registered in Bolam's voice.

"Shut *up!*" screamed Bradford.

"Because it's what Ramsden really wants. Killing us like this really *will* bring him back. It's what he wants."

"She's lying!" screeched Terri. "Can't you see that? She doesn't want to die."

"Of *course* I don't want to die. Neither does Sparrow. That's why I'm telling you the truth. Kill us and he'll return for sure."

They're nearly here ... nearly here ...

"Didn't you think it was a little too easy getting me here, Bolam?" continued Lauren. "Did I try to run away? Did I beg you for mercy?"

"Well ... you said ..."

"Sparrow is special. Lorelei told you as much. You knew that the child was bred to be special. Well, he's *grown*. He has special powers, even more special than Lorelei. She was afraid of him."

"We need another council meeting," said Collins. "Even if she is lying we can't take a chance that she's telling the truth."

"They have to die now." Bradford moved forward. "Hold her still."

"Collins is right," said Weldon. "We can't take a chance. We have to reconjure, check that everything is all right, that we won't be making a mistake. All it means is a delay, that's all."

"Oh yeah!" snapped Terri. "A delay for you, and that's okay – because you've all had your benefits from the last killing. Now that it's *our* turn to benefit – me and Bradford – you're quite happy to have a delay."

"You see," said Lauren. "That's what this is all about. They're just greedy to get their rewards from the Anonymous One. They're afraid they'll miss their turn ..."

"Bitch!" Bradford strode forward, holding the shard before her.

"Wait a minute." Sutton suddenly pushed Lauren behind him, standing forward to meet Bradford as she came. "It can wait. Like Collins said, if Lorelei is dead then the other council members need to know. Lorelei was our main defence against Ramsden. She was the one who sensed he was trying to come back. And if she really is gone, we don't want to make a mistake now."

"Out of my way, Sutton."

"No," said Sutton simply, and Lauren felt James's grip tighten on her arm, a sign that he was taking Sutton's side.

"She's *lying*," said Bradford, turning to appeal to the others. "Can't you see that?"

It's done, said Sparrow. *At last it's done.*

What? For God's sake, speak to me, Sparrow!

I know what's happening, Lauren. Know what Father has done, and what he's planning to do. Something about the tone of Sparrow's 'voice' seemed strange. He sounded strained, and ill.

"You won't miss out," said James. "We'll readapt the rota. Make sure you get your share."

Terri shuffled uneasily, passing the stiletto from hand to hand nervously.

Tell me, Sparrow. Tell me what's happening.

The others – the ones who are nearly here. I don't know who they ARE, Lauren. Something's not right there, something's cloaking them in a different way than before. It's not the one I've been trying to reach. This is something, someone else . . .

For Christ's sake, TELL ME WHAT YOU KNOW.

And when Lauren spoke, it was Sparrow's words.

"The bodies are gone."

"What?" said Collins. "What the hell are you talking about?"

"The corpses of the vagrants that you killed and buried here. One pool of wax for each body. They're all gone."

"More stupid lies!" snapped Bradford. "More lying shit to stop us doing what we've *got* to do!"

"I'm telling you the truth," said Lauren calmly. "The bodies are all gone."

"They can't be . . ." said Weldon.

"It's the easiest thing in the world to verify, isn't it?" *They're nearly here, Mother. And I don't know who they are!* And in her head, Lauren yelled. *It can't be any worse, Sparrow. We've got to get out of this so KEEP TALKING!*

"Give me that spade!" hissed Bolam, heading for the sarcophagus. On the ground, the unconscious figure of the innocent moaned. Terri moved quickly towards him and crouched on the steps close by, holding the stiletto in his direction.

"There!" said Sutton, moving back and pointing as Bolam returned with the spade. Like a man in the grip of fever, he stabbed the spade down hard into the nearest pool of wax and stamped down heavily on the edge of the blade.

"It's Ramsden," continued Lauren. "It's all part of his plan to return.

Just as Lorelei feared, he was making his own plans; keeping them secret from the Sabbarite. Eventually, he would have sacrificed you all in his main purpose."

Bolam attacked the ground furiously with the spade. The soil here was loose, and he knew that the body would not be buried deep, just like the others.

"But killing him didn't destroy him. He had already contacted those in the other place, those who had lived and died and now dwell in Hell. Quite apart from the pacts with the Sabbarite – the pacts that you all *knew* about – Ramsden had secret dealings too. Things of which the Sabbarite were never aware. And Ramsden had also made promises to some of them, promises which he was able to fulfil."

Bolam began to throw clouds of soil from the reopened grave onto the steps. Terri cursed and scrambled out of the way, still keeping her eyes on the young man on the floor. He was awake, but remained still when he saw the stiletto. He rubbed a hand over his face.

"You killed him – and his soul went to Hell. They were waiting for him there. The ones with whom he'd made pacts and promises. They wanted to return; the damned souls with whom he'd made contact. They knew that he had found a way to return, but his knowledge was incomplete. So they made a bargain. If he helped them, they would help him."

"There's nothing *here!*" yelled Bolam, frantically stabbing at the soil.

"It must be deeper than that!" exclaimed Sutton. He grabbed the spade from Bolam and forced him out of the hole. Bracing himself, he continued to dig.

"Illegal aliens," continued Lauren. "That's what all this is about." With each revelation from Sparrow, the feeling of sickness inside intensified. Lauren struggled to keep a calm face as she continued. "Smuggling them over the border."

"Don't talk in riddles!" snapped Weldon.

"The border between earth and Hell, between this side and the other side. Ramsden found a way to smuggle those damned souls out of Hell and back to our reality. In the discarded corpses of your own victims. Don't you see what a perfect revenge that is for him? He had already laid his own plans in the event of premature death, had made a failsafe plan in case any of the Sabbarite should try to wrest power from him. He has been able to resurrect the dead – the vagrants that you killed. And now they're walking the streets. Those damned souls with whom he made a pact are back and alive in those dead shells. Ramsden has brought them back from torment."

"I've seen them," said the innocent by the stairs.

"Shut up!" Terri lunged at him with the stiletto.

"Let him speak," said James.

Sutton cursed when the spade hit a buried stone and sent shivers of pain up his arm. He prised it out and continued, sweat now pouring down his face.

"They're out there on the streets, like she says," continued Randall. "Dead people. They attacked me and my friends. Mac, one of the street people, says that they're all over the place." Randall edged away from the stiletto point. In the few moments that he'd managed to pull himself around, he had weighed up the situation and knew that he was in worse trouble than before. "They want to kill me, because I know about them. Know that they're out there." He looked back to the American girl and her baby. Whether or not she was stalling for time, and despite the confused conversation, he had sussed out which side to take.

"There's nothing here!" snapped Sutton, wielding the spade. "We never bury them deep – and there's nothing fucking *here!*" On his last word, Sutton seemed to stagger in the newly uncovered grave. Now up to his thighs, he stopped quickly to look down at something he seemed to have found there. "Oh shit – oh *shit!*"

"What is it?" hissed Bolam.

"There's another . . . another hole here," said Sutton. "Like a bloody *worm-hole* or a tunnel or something." Trembling, Sutton clambered out of the grave. "Whatever was in there *clawed* its way out. Didn't come straight back up, just burrowed away, and out."

Still in panic, Bolam ran back to the sarcophagus and seized another spade. Feverishly looking around the chamber, he ran beyond Collins and Weldon to find another plot. With a moan that sounded like anguish, he began to dig.

"In return," continued Lauren, "the damned would help Ramsden. They would help him to wreak vengeance on those who had betrayed and killed him." *Oh God, Sparrow! The ones who are coming! The dead!*

No . . . no . . . it's not them. Not them. But it's someone . . . someone . . . who . . .

"I won't believe it," said Bradford. "He was never that powerful. Would never be able to do what you say."

"They're out there now," continued Lauren. "On the streets. Just waiting for the right time. Ramsden is on the point of returning, has been unable to return directly himself yet because he's been channelling all his energies in returning the damned and reactivating your victims. But that's all ended now. All of the damned with whom he has a pact have returned. Now he can concentrate on coming back himself."

317

"He can't come back!" yelled Terri. "He's at the bottom of a canal, slashed to pieces. Rotting."

"Oh, he's coming back all right," said Lauren. "And the damned owe him their part of the bargain now. They're coming back to honour their debt – and they're going to fulfil Ramsden's revenge by killing every single member of the Sabbarite."

Bradford whirled with the glass shard and lunged towards Lauren. Sutton could no longer protect her as he continued to flail dirt from the grave. James staggered awkwardly as Lauren tried to pull away, and it seemed as if there was no way that anyone could prevent Bradford from ramming the shard into her face.

Randall rolled fast and hard away from the stairs, and from under Terri's averted guard, slewing his body sideways and into Bradford's path. Their legs tangled, and Bradford fell headlong. Sutton cursed, leaping out of the grave – and swung the spade around hard. The flat of the blade hit Randall on the side of the head with an echoing *clang!* and he fell like an animal in the slaughterhouse.

"Shit, shit, shit!" exclaimed Collins. "Look . . . look . . . we've . . ."

"Get rid of him!" snapped Weldon, and Sutton grabbed Randall by the arms. Pulling him to the edge of what was now a four-foot hole, he dragged him over and then shoved him into it – face down. Randall made no sound, but his body lay crumpled in the grave, legs still sticking out of it.

"There's no one here, either!" shouted Bolam from deep in the chamber. "I know we planted this one in a shallow grave, but it's *gone!*"

Sutton began to shovel soil in on top of Randall, burying his head and shoulders.

"We've got to get back to the Council," continued Collins. "Tell them what's happening."

And then Bradford stood up, eyes filled with glittering hate. She turned, waving her arms – and tried to speak. A curious, fluting, gargling sound hissed from her mouth. She turned in a circle, glaring at them all, and Terri shrank back on the steps, away from this bizarre sight. Sutton dropped the spade. Then Bradford clawed at her chin, and when her hands came away, so did the thin lace-like ribbons of blood. Blood like treacle. Now, it was coming faster and this time when Bradford tried to speak, she opened her mouth wide. Inside her mouth, Lauren saw a faint glittering of light.

It was the tip of the stained-glass shard.

Bradford had fallen on it, and it had jammed up under her chin.

She fell croaking to her knees, scrabbling at her throat and chin.

The others watched in silent horror as she pitched forward and began to twitch and thrash feebly in the soil which had been unearthed from the grave.

"We've got to get out," said Fletcher faintly. "Let the others know . . ."

In the chamber, Bolam threw his own spade aside and rushed to join them as James bustled Lauren towards the stairs. Collins's face had changed to grey-white and Weldon looked as if she was on the verge of tears.

No! shouted Sparrow.

Lauren was dazed, both by what Sparrow had said and all of its horrible implications, and by the sickening violence here in the underground chamber. She could not react, despite that cry in her head as she allowed herself to be pushed towards the door.

No!

James reached for the door.

And then it burst open, swinging wide to hit the wall with an echoing crash.

James staggered away, dragging Lauren with him.

"Surprise!" yelled Harry Bennet, standing in the door frame.

And then he stepped aside to let two dozen of Gerry Tomelty's gang members through the door into the chamber. They burst in, whooping and shrieking. James let her go and Lauren fell to the soil floor. As Gerry's gang members leapt down the stairs and into the chamber, she clasped Sparrow tight to her breast and looked up at the young man standing in the doorway.

He smiled when their eyes met.

"I know someone who's going to be *very* pleased to meet you," he said.

Sparrow's psychic cry for help, his plea to the unknown empath, had also been heard by someone else.

It had been heard by his father, Pearce Ramsden – the Man Who Shines Black.

"All right, boys,' said Harry Bennet, his face set in the wide grin of Nektre. "Let's *party!*"

PART FOUR

HAVOC

61

They walk the streets.

They have waited impatiently and are hungry for the true freedom that will come only when they have fulfilled their bargain, and the Sabbarite have been wiped from these streets. They have bided their time, they have slept in shop doorways and under cardboard, oblivious to the bitter chill of the night air or the pangs of food-hunger. They have tried to remain hidden from prying eyes, have resisted any attempts at contact by do-gooders and social workers. They have even watched from the darkness as the black vans took away the prey, have welcomed those same victims into the fold when they returned.

And now that they have returned, each plans a different destiny; each has inherited different skills from their former abode, for in torment there is also knowledge – a knowledge attainable because, so far, very few have escaped from the place that the people here call Hell, but know so little about. In time, the decay and the death-wounds and the shattered limbs will heal. It will take months, perhaps years, but this healing process will eventually be complete. Any further injuries received will also heal miraculously: all part of the deal, all part of the pact with Ramsden. They will no longer require food or drink as sustenance; they will be able to survive and flourish without any need for it. They will only eat and drink for the physical enjoyment that it brings, nothing more. When the healing process is complete, and the diseased and shattered bodies which they have inherited have become whole, their bodies will be revitalised, youth restored – and that youth will be maintained. They will not age, they will not wither, they will not – cannot – die. Because they have already died once, and the Serendip decrees that just as in our world the guilty cannot be hanged twice for the same crime, neither can they be physically "killed" for a second time. All of Hell clamour for return to the place from which they came. Because that return would guarantee them immortality. But only those with whom Ramsden has made his pact – however he has been able to bend those rules – have been smuggled back. On this massive rock in space called earth, those among the forlorn and the damned with whom Ramsden has made his pact will live and experience all of its tactile joys for as long as the planet exists. Whether mankind will have the wisdom to plan its destiny, or whether it will simply collapse within its excesses, they will be there at the forefront, preying and feeding and taking all that is good and replacing it with everything that is bad. If the process of survival is not attained, then it will be the activities of the once-damned which will hasten the end.

They walk the streets – and have waited.

But now their time of waiting is at an end. The last of their conclave have come through, have re-emerged chrysalis-like from one of the Sabbarite killing places to join them. It has taken this last one four days to emerge, and they have been impatient to greet him. Impatient enough to try and take the three people from the street who had somehow sensed their purpose, sensed what they were. The one who had once been called Bernie had warned them. Whilst retaining no knowledge of the previous occupant of the raddled shell, the one in Bernie's skin knew that he had been recognised – and so the forlorn took steps to eradicate that threat.

But Ramsden had raged at them. Had accused them of breaking their pact, of reneging. With the power to return them, they had no other recourse than to back away. The three could easily have been taken, but were not.

The one who had been accosted by shopping mall security men had escaped.

And the ambulance which had taken away the dismembered parts of the one who had fallen beneath the bus had been hijacked. Those dismembered parts could meld and heal – in time. The ambulancemen would not.

The pact has not been damaged. All is as it was.

And with the final member of the conclave now present, Ramsden's attentions and energies can divert to the next stage of the agreement.

Leaving the forlorn to complete their part of the bargain.

Now, they walk the streets.

Hunting for the Sabbarite.

62

Howie Davidson's weakness was women.

Ramsden seemed to sense that straight away, without any evidence being necessary. He selected Howie from the Outer Circle, seeking him out with this uncanny ability – like radar. He had taken him under his wing, understood that his difficulties with under-age girls threatened to ruin his marriage, was on the verge of being made public. The gnawing inner fear had taken him, purely by accident, into the hands of the Sabbarite. On the verge of despair, thrown out on the streets by his wife, he had actually taken a leaflet from some hopeless idiot on the street, had actually followed the directions it gave to the nearest church. After all, he needed somewhere to stay. He had been completely unprepared for the enormouse sense of well-being that he would receive from the words of the man in the pulpit. Thinking of it afterwards, he couldn't remember a word of what was said. But the 'feeling' had been real enough. And after the service, it seemed that Howie had been singled out by the Church leader, Pearce Ramsden, a man younger than himself by a good ten years. Tall, dark, even saturnine-looking, Ramsden had seemed to see right into Howie, and all the dark secrets that lay there. He had been looking for someone, he said, just like Howie, to replace someone in what he called the Inner Circle. Someone who had died tragically. Normally, most people in the Outer Circle – the Latter Day Church – never aspired to the heart of the organisation. For those who did, it took years. But Howie was a special case – and Ramsden had initiated him quickly and willingly into the Inner membership.

After the first killing which he had attended, the prosecution case against him had mysteriously dissolved. On the second occasion, he had been driving a black van – and had attended. After that, his wife had come shrieking and weeping to him, begging forgiveness for ever having doubted him. There had been fear there, but fear of what Howie had no idea. However, he had also forgiven her – and everything at home had been fine since then. There was always a cooked meal on the table, never a cross word whenever he wanted to go out. And his wife mainly sat watching the television all night, eyes glistening in the light of the screen and constantly just wanting to make a sandwich, or fix a drink, or even go to bed if he wanted her to. On the third killing, he had been given the power. The power just to look at anyone he wanted, the power to go over and ask. And everyone he asked always came with him – and did it. He was a happy man, and very grateful for all that had been done.

But he had never been happy with the killing of Ramsden.

The others had been members longer than he had, but he still felt that they were overreacting to Ramsden's pursuit of his own pleasures. After all, were those pleasures really so far removed from his own? Nevertheless, he had not protested when they made their move. He was grateful to Ramsden, but he was after all only another disciple.

He had been present at the council when the conjuration of the Mechanics had taken place, after Lauren's escape with the child. He had voted with the others on the course of action when Lorelei and the chosen ones had gone out to get her at the canal. He may not have cared about Ramsden's demise, but he wanted to make sure that there was no chance of his return – and therefore any misunderstanding – taking place.

Which is why Howie felt so secure and whistled a tune as he worked in the pit beneath a customer's car. The business was thriving, had never been better. All of it due to the Sabbarite and the benefactions of the Anonymous One. He prided himself as a man with no extravagant ambition, but business was so good he had decided to work late at the garage, just for the hell of it. The options available to him now were endless, but he was happy to maintain this thriving business – until he changed his mind again.

When the outside garage door shuddered open, he at first presumed that it was Vince, calling in to say hello on his way back from late-night boozing. But when he called his name, there was no reply.

Howie returned to his work under the car. When something clattered in the garage, he twisted around to look up over the side of the pit.

"Vince?" Again no reply.

But now Howie could suddenly see a pair of sandalled feet up there, walking slowly around the car. Was it the young girl who had brought the car in? Maybe checking up. But at *this* time of night? He had every intention of screwing her before he handed the car back – and now was as good a time as any – but he couldn't remember her wearing sandals. No, the owner had been a pretty classy affair, and he was sure that she wouldn't be wearing sandals as scruffy as these.

"Mrs McNally?"

Again, no response. Cursing inwardly, Howie wiped his oily hands on a rag and made to climb out of the pit.

At that instant, the nozzle of the fire extinguisher was thrust into the pit, under the car. Howie was enveloped in a cloud of dry ice. That first blast hit him squarely in the face and open mouth. Gagging, Howie fell heavily back into the pit, jarring his head against the concrete side. The nozzle thrust further inwards, and the canister was emptied into the close confines of the pit. The heavier carbon dioxide displaced the oxygen greedily.

Within a minute and a half, Howie had suffocated.

The thing that had come into his garage threw the empty cylinder across the garage. By the time the clattering echoes had ceased, it had vanished into the night leaving the garage door to swing in the wind.

Pallister heard the commotion in his outer office, but felt sure that his secretary could handle it. They were working late, and he had no idea who could be barging in at this time of night.

He looked up from his desk, through the fluted glass door and tried to make sense of the jumbled movement out there.

"Excuse *me*!" That was Mrs Haining's voice. "Do you have an appointment? No, I'm sorry. You can't just . . ." Pallister saw the indistinct form of Mrs Haining jump up from her seat.

Pallister steeled himself. It must be Terry Campbell. The hulking shape that had burst into the outer office and was even now heading for the fluted door could only be him. He had already made stupid threats on the telephone about his divorce and the fact that Pallister was representing his estranged wife. So far, Pallister had handled matters in what he considered to be a professional manner. But if he persisted, as he was persisting now, then Pallister would be using his powers as an Inner Circle member to get rid of Mr Campbell permanently, and thereby doing the soon-to-be ex-Mrs Campbell a great favour.

Pallister forced himself to remain calm, picked up a propelling pencil from the blotter and watched as the shadow figure loomed large in the fluted glass door.

The door crashed open.

And Pallister recoiled in his chair.

This was not Campbell. This was some wild and demented tramp from the streets. The figure was tall, but had the same stooped shoulders as Campbell, the matted hair hanging in lank streaks across a horribly white face. The damp greatcoat had been torn in a dozen places and even as Pallister looked on in horror, a clod of soil tumbled oozing from a fold of that coat on to the office carpet. The man braced himself in the door. His gait had seemed unsteady and now he was swaying drunkenly in that door frame. Behind him, Pallister heard Mrs Haining telephoning for the police.

Pallister could not look away from the man's glittering eyes.

With great effort, clearing his throat, Pallister said, "Who the hell are you and what are you doing in my office?"

"*Pallister*," said the wild man. And the sound of that voice carved a great gash of fear in Pallister's soul. The voice barely sounded human, as if it had come from somewhere underground. Pallister rose from his seat.

"Get out of my way," he heard himself say and began to move around the desk.

The man staggered into the office, head lowered, glittering eyes still fixed on him.

And then Pallister attempted to hurry past and into the outer office.

The man moved swifly, catching Pallister by the collar in the door frame. In the outer office, Mrs Haining screamed. Pallister also cried out, a hoarse sound of terror. The smell of the man was overpowering: a gut-wrenching stench of decay. In defence as they twisted in the doorway, Pallister gripped the man's ragged shirt front and shoved. Incredibly, he tottered back – and Pallister stood frozen in horror with the rags of the man's shirt front still in his hands. Tearing the rotted shirt had revealed the man's torso.

Or what had once been a torso.

Instead, Pallister saw a bare ribcage, the grey-white bones held together in a spider-web tracing of rotted sinew and gristle. Inside that bony cage, living things glistened and writhed.

The wild man grinned; an insane, *hungry* rictus. And then he lunged forward again, taking Pallister by the throat and choking off his hoarse cries of terror.

Mrs Haining dropped the telephone in shock as both figures whirled in a mad dance away from the door frame and back into the inner office. She saw the wild man shoving Mr Pallister hard back towards the wall.

Towards the window.

Her scream matched the shattering of glass as both figures hurtled through that window, tangling momentarily in the window-blind before it was torn from its mountings. In an instant, both figures had vanished over the sill in a whirling spray of broken glass.

Later, when the police arrived, only one body was found on the pavement six storeys below.

328

* * *

When the store's front door juddered open, Bryan heard it immediately.

His living room was directly above the shop and at this time of the night sound carried. Despite his bulk, he was quick on his feet. Carefully placing his beer can next to its companions on the side table, he left the late-night horror movie and skipped over to the window. He nudged aside the curtain and looked down on to the darkened High Street. There was no sign of anyone directly below – so whoever was trying to burgle his place was already inside.

Right!

Bryan quickly pulled his boots on. Size twelve. Good for kicking heads in.

He kept his finger on the sneck of the living room door, not wanting to give himself away. Standing at the top of the stairs, he listened. But even though he had heard the door, the sounds of the television were covering any other furtive noise that the intruder might be making in his shop. Bryan started down the stairs, step by careful step, not wanting the smallest squeak in the boards to give him away. There was a bead curtain at the bottom of the stairs. Getting through that was going to be difficult.

A shadow moved across the beads.

Bryan froze on the step. His heart was hammering – and he was enjoying every minute of it. In his mind's eye, he had already worked out what he was going to do. He'd listened to those stupid bastards on the talk-shows, going on about how a person could only use reasonable force to confront or overpower a burglar. No way. Anyone caught in the act in his place was really going to *suffer*.

His attendance at the killings as a member of the Inner Circle had given him a taste for things he would have once considered inconceivable. Now, as a family butcher, the very act of dismembering meat gave him an erection. Something that had once shamed and dismayed him before joining the Sabbarite, now made the working day very pleasurable indeed. The prospect of his confrontation with a burglar was arousing him already.

At the bottom of the stairs, Bryan peered into the shop, looking for any sign of movement. There was none. Whoever had passed the beads had gone on, deeper into the store. Bryan carefully parted the beads, a hard job because of his bulk. Still holding them, he stepped through and pulled them back into position, carefully letting go and holding his breath while he did so. Behind him now, the meat counter. Moving quickly, he stooped below it, found the required tool, and re-emerged from the counter with a cleaver.

Weighing it in his hand, he moved around the corner and turned the L-shaped bend in his shop which led down into what he liked to call the Delicatessen Corner.

And there the bastard stood.

Bryan straightened up and breathed out. The cocky bastard was standing facing him. Not trying to hide or run away, but standing there with his hands at his side. It was impossible to make out any details here in the darkness, but by the size and the shape of the figure, this was an old man – maybe late sixties or seventies. He was wearing a woollen balaclava and bulky anorak. He was about Bryan's height – but God, how this bastard stank!

"What the hell are you doing in my shop?" asked Bryan confidently. There was only one way out of this place, and that was past him. And some dirty old sod who'd pushed his way in here off the streets wasn't going to steal any of his cash, or his food – or use the place as a bloody doss-house. Bryan was convinced now that this was a street beggar, the kind he often spat on when someone jangled a tin in front of his face. The figure did not answer his question. It stood still, and watched.

Bryan raised the cleaver in front of him, as if for the figure's inspection.

"Ever been to India. No?"

The figure remained unmoved.

"Me neither. But the professional shit-eating beggars there have gone one up on you and your kind. Did you know that?"

The figure inclined its head, as if genuinely interested in what he had to say.

"See, they sometimes chop parts of their own bodies off just to get sympathy. A hand or a foot. Do it to their kids sometimes. Then when they're sitting with their begging bowl, people go 'Ahhhhhh' and put a few extra coins down for them. So, look on the bright side – what I'm going to do to you is really a big favour. Going to put you streets ahead in the begging stakes compared to your pals."

Bryan stepped forward.

"So come on, make your play. And for what you are about to receive, may the Lord make you truly grateful."

The silhouette stepped forward, into the only faint glimmer of light from a streetlamp.

Bryan screamed then when he saw its face, raising the cleaver in defence.

Later, Bryan's begging potential in India was second to none.

63

Christ, Sparrow, thought Lauren. *I think they were killing them back there.*

Don't think about it.

I'm not sure how much more of this I can take. My head feels strange . . . I can't think straight . . . Oh God, Bradford . . . and that poor young guy . . .

I said don't think about it! And don't waste any pity on Bradford. You've got to think about us. We're away from that place now, that's the important thing.

Everything's so muddled.

Look . . . look . . . breathe deeply, take it easy and . . .

Where are they taking us and who ARE these people?

I said take it easy!

For a while there was silence. The car sped on through deserted streets and ragged back alleys. In a blur, she had been dragged out of that chamber and up the stairs into the ruined church. Lauren sat between two youths who had waited outside the church in this car. The young man who had ushered the gang into the underground chamber was driving the car. No one had spoken since she had been pushed with Sparrow into the back seat and the car had roared away into the night. She had no idea where they were. She could still see the bizarre smiles on the faces of the youths who had bounded down those stairs and into the chamber, could still hear their whooping cries of glee – like animals. And she could still hear the echoing shrieks and the crying and the pleas beneath that gleeful animalistic cacophony.

Did any of them . . . ?

No, they're all dead. They used the spades and the . . . sorry. Look, Lauren. Those people were Sabbarite. They were going to kill us, and you know how many they've killed themselves. They deserved to die. Now, come on. Pull yourself together, we're not out of this yet.

All right . . . all right . . . but speak to me, Sparrow. Tell me what you've been doing and what's happening now.

For a while there was silence as the car roared on into the night.

Sparrow!

Okay . . . I'm just getting my thoughts together. Everything I told you about Ramsden is true. He's coming back. He's made the pact, and the dead victims of the Sabbarite are out there now, hunting them down and carrying out Ramsden's revenge. That's good news for us since it's going to keep the Sabbarite off our backs. The bad news is – I don't know who THESE people are in the car. But they have something to do with Ramsden. I need time to search that one out. He's more powerful than ever, Lauren. And he's screened himself from me in a way that I can't break through.

These people are going to do what the Sabbarite were going to do, aren't they? But for different reasons.

I think so, yes. Ramsden wants me. He will embody in me, carry out what he's always intended before the Sabbarite killed him.

Who were you "calling" to? You said you thought you'd made contact with an empath.

The balance is wildly out of control, Lauren. The Serendip is easily tapped at the moment, since it wants some kind of order brought about. There's someone out there, a girl – she has psychic abilities. You remember how the Serendip suggested that Tony was bound up with our fate? It's telling me the same about this girl, wherever she is. I contacted her, I'm sure of it – but in that same moment, Ramsden caught the message, could see where we were – and I think sent these people to take us.

How can the girl help us?

I don't know. But we need her, and the one who's with her. Somehow, I don't know how, but he's actually more important.

More important?

I still don't understand it, but now I realise that I've been getting impressions about this man for a long time. But something about him doesn't scan. He's shadowy, but vitally important. I think maybe the girl is supposed to bring him to us.

Sparrow, are we going to get out of this alive?

I . . . I . . .

Come on, now.

The Serendip is working for us, but you know how it goes. There's no guarantee of a happy ending.

Well?

No, Mother. I think we're going to die. Whether we can stop Father or not – we still may die.

I thought so. Lauren swallowed hard and cradled her son tight to her breast. The youths on either side shuffled to give her room. Somewhere, a car horn blared as the driver cut across a central reservation.

Want some consolation?

Lauren laughed. A one-note sigh of resignation. *We're going to die, and you think you can cheer me up?*

Tony is still alive.

For a while, Lauren was silent. Then, swallowing; she thought: *What?*

While I was searching for the girl, I picked up his vibration. He wasn't killed back there at the canal. I don't know where he is or what he's doing. But he's alive.

Alive?

Yes . . .

Lauren could not hold it back any more. She buried her face into the shawl wrapped around her child and began to weep.

"Waterworks," sneered one of the youths next to her.

"Won't do no fucking good," said the other.

Lauren rocked her child between them, face buried and tears flowing. It was the first time she'd wept in over ten years. But these were not bitter tears; they were tears of relief, a breaking of the emotional dam inside her. And the confirmation of a crazy feeling inside that she had so far refused to acknowledge.

Sparrow had told her that they were going to die.

But her tears were cleansing.

64

Ranjana marched on ahead of Mac, down the railway track.

Since jumping from the train, they had not exchanged a word. Ranjana seemed to have landed awkwardly on the cinder track and appeared to be limping. But when Mac had caught up and tried to help her, she had roughly brushed aside his arm and marched on ahead.

Finally, when the silence began to irritate him, Mac said, "So where the hell are we going?"

Ranjana did not answer. Head down, she continued to march along the track.

"Ranjana!"

No answer.

Mac angrily caught up with her, walking alongside.

"What the hell's the matter with you?"

"We're pulling in different directions. You *know* that there are bloody strange things going on. You *know* that we're meant to do something about it." Suddenly, Ranjana stopped in her tracks and yelled directly into Mac's face. "We've just been chased all over the place by bloody *dead* people, for God's sake!"

"Take it easy, Ranjana."

"And you think we can just stay on some dirty old freight train and ride away from the trouble. Don't you see it? This is trouble that we can never escape from. This is something that is going to follow us!"

"I'm here, aren't I?"

Ranjana looked on the verge of launching herself at him again. Instead, she wiped the hair from her face, turned and kept walking. Mac followed.

"Things are bad enough," said Ranjana grimly as she walked. "But if you keep drifting in and out all the time, you may as well not be with me."

"All right, Ranjana. I'm going to tell you something now. Something that confirms what you're saying, and scares the hell out of me."

334

"I'm listening."

"Something happened back there when Bernie was killed. When he went into the water, when those people killed him and threw him in, I went into the water after him. Just like I told you. But something happened then."

Mac paused, struggling to find the words to express himself. Ranjana looked at him intently as they walked.

"A fire burning inside me was put out, was extinguished. Just as if the canal water did it. Before that, my life was . . . well, blurred to say the least. I still can't remember much about my life before I hit the street. You remember back there, on the slipway? When I was telling you what happened to me in the Falklands – things that you were able to *see* as I told you about them. The way you were able to see those things about me, the clarity of it all really shocked you, didn't it?"

Ranjana was silent for a while and then said, "Yes . . . I'd never seen things so clearly. And it's been like that ever since we talked."

"Same for me, Ranjana. That's my point. I hadn't remembered any of that stuff up until the moment that I started to tell you. It was like a revelation to me. There's still lots of things I can't remember, things about my life before I was in the army. But at that moment, I started to see things clearly again. It started with the canal, and then when you came along – the girl out of my dreams – it was as if something clicked into place. It's like something somewhere *meant* for us to meet up, just like you said. Like we were being guided together for some reason."

"It's to do with the dead people," said Ranjana.

"Yes, you're right. And that's what scares me, Ranjana. You said you felt that I was neither dead nor alive. And that's the way I feel about myself sometimes. Now that I've started to remember, is my mind going to clear completely, and will I get better? Or does this whole crazy business that we're getting drawn into mean that I'm going to end up just as dead as those other poor bastards out there? Look at me, Ranjana. Look at my face. This isn't *me*! Can you know what that's like? To walk around in a shell of a body, to wear a face that you don't recognise as your own. Since you came along, walked out of my dreams, the pain's stopped. The canal – and you – have both stopped it. But Christ, Ranjana, I couldn't bear to think about it coming back, of my mind slipping away again. It still does, I know. But it's getting less frequent."

"I'm sorry, Mac. I'm forgetting . . . it's just that this whole business . . . and Randall.'

She stopped then and looked at him.

"You don't have to stay," she said.

"That's not what I'm saying. What I'm telling you is that I'm going through with this thing, whatever it is. I'm going to see it through with you. But it's no use looking on me as a man of steel. I'm just as scared as you."

"You're a Superman, all right," said Ranjana. She moved to him quickly and embraced him. Mac stroked her hair and looked out along the track and into the night. Ranjana's eyes were gleaming when she stood back. "I don't know what's ahead of us, but I do know that Randall is alive. We're going to find him and save him."

"Where is he?"

"I'm getting really strong images. Like they're being sent to me by someone else. Strange. But it's a church, an abandoned church. Randall's been taken there. And it's not far."

"Okay," said Mac. "But look, we have to get off this railway line. If we follow it all the way back to that goods yard, we might just walk into those street people again."

"All right . . . we'll head for that embankment. Find the main road. The images are really strong. This place can't be far."

"Let's walk," said Mac.

Ranjana took his hand, and they headed for the embankment.

65

The car pulled up at the burned-out shell of a community centre standing in the middle of the council estate; windows boarded, covered in graffiti. There were already two cars parked in the deeper shadows of the building.

Lauren did not wait to be yanked out of that car when the two youths next to her climbed out. She stood watching as the driver moved quickly to the boarded door and knocked. The other two moved silently next to her, and took her arms.

"What the hell does he want *you* for then, love?" asked one of them.

"Shitting yourself, I bet," said the other.

"Watch your mouth, you little bastard," replied Lauren.

The second youth, crew-cut and acned, gripped her arm tight. She refused to cry out and returned his hard stare. His jaw muscles worked as he chewed gum. His eyes were dull and full of the stupid promise of mindless violence.

The driver knocked again on the boarded-up door, and this time it was pulled open. He turned and motioned to them, and then Lauren was pulled towards the building.

She smelled the burned-out and charred interior even before they stepped through that door. Inside, she could vaguely see the shapes of other young men, some of them with torches. A crazy zigzag of torchlight, like some directionless disco without music.

The driver picked his way through the charred litter towards what once seemed to have been a raised stage area. It had burned and collapsed, but there were four concrete steps there which had resisted the fire – and a figure was sitting on it, surrounded by others.

At their approach, the others at the stairs moved away from the seated figure. Lauren strained to see his face as they approached, but could make out no details. But something about the way that figure was sitting filled her with horror. Surely, it couldn't be . . . ?

Ramsden!

337

No, said Sparrow. *It's not him. It's someone that he's using.*

"Well, well," said Gerry Tomelty. "At last. The runaway mother and her baby boy."

The figure stood up from the steps and stepped slowly down as Lauren and Sparrow were brought forward.

I'm getting confused messages, said Sparrow. *The scent of Ramsden is really strong on this guy. But he hasn't embodied in him.*

"I can read your minds," said Gerry.

Lauren froze, and then realised with relief that the gangleader was holding his hands wide and addressing the others.

"Who the hell is the girl and the baby? Why the hell don't we get on with what we've planned? Well, as to the girl and the kid – that doesn't matter. Let's just say that someone very important is on his way soon to . . . collect them. But we don't have to wait for him before we burn this estate to the fucking ground."

Lauren looked around. In the bare light of the torches, she could just make out some of the faces. And it was clear that they were terrified of the figure who must be their leader.

"The other question you're asking," continued Gerry. "In fact, it's a question you've been asking yourselves for a while – why can't we use the Nektre, like the people we're giving it to?"

Nektre, Sparrow?

I'm not sure. Let me think . . .

"Well, you saw what it did to Quaid over there, didn't you? Now what would have happened if one of Andreas's people had just politely asked one of you who was supplying, and you'd been using the stuff? You'd have to say 'Gerry', wouldn't you? Power of suggestion, right? Do anything anyone tells you to, right? Well, that's the reason. And don't think I don't know what you've been up to, Jack."

Somewhere in the darkness, someone shuffled uncomfortably.

"Giving the girlies some of the stuff, and then asking them to go down on you. But that's all right . . . all right . . . because now the stuff's all over the estate."

It's a drug, Lauren. But not an ordinary drug. I think . . . think . . . they were given it by Ramsden.

"Mark was taking it. Despite the fact that he'd been told not to. Now, no one knows where Mark's gone. He was a *naughty* boy – so he got sent away. But all that's changed now. Because we're ready to begin. Mooney?"

In the darkness, someone said, "Yeah?"

"The kids you've been giving the stuff to – are they ready?"

"Yeah, got about fifty, maybe sixty ready to go. Down the shopping precinct. Petrol bombs, the lot."

"Good. Parks?"

"Yeah. The same, down by the wogs' community hall."

"Johnny?"

"Yeah, they're fuelled up on the stuff and ready to go."

"Good. When you get there, tell them to start. We've got the police and the Fire Brigade business all sorted. You're going to give them more Nektre when you get there – but make this lot *free*. Understand? When they take it, tell them to burn down the estate, smash everything. But listen, this is the most important thing of all. Tell them not to *listen* to what anyone else says to them once you've given them this next batch and got them sorted."

"What do you mean?"

"What I *mean*, stupid, is that the power of suggestion I've just reminded you about is still going to be strong. All it takes is for some copper to come along and say, 'Stop being naughty and go home' – and the chances are that they will. The trick is to give them an instruction that can't be countermanded. Now, does everyone understand what I'm saying?"

"What's countermand?"

"You fucking cretin! Just tell them to listen to everything you say, and to take no notice of anything anyone else says. Got it?" Gerry moved back to the stairs. "Good. Now, just because you've been good boys and done everything I've told you, I can relax the rules a little. Up until now, I've told you that it's hands off this stuff. Well now, everything changes. Because you've earned your right to have a little dabble."

The others in the community centre began to shuffle, the torch beams wavering.

"Yeah, that's right. I'm not joking. I'm serious."

Gerry reached down under the stairs and emerged with a cardboard box.

"Here's the stuff I want you to hand out to the kids who are waiting." Gerry moved forward again, placing the box on a charred beam. Taking two bags of white powder out of the box and holding one in each hand, he said, "And here's a little something to get you started."

The others shuffled again.

Gerry laughed. "Don't worry. No one gets their hands slapped. And you all know what to do, so I'm not going to give you it and ask you to cluck like a fucking chicken or something, like those TV hypnotism shows."

One of the shadows moved forward gingerly. Gerry laughed again and broke open a bag, pouring a small amount of powder into his hand. Now, the others were beginning to move forward eagerly in an excited hubbub.

"I gave some to the others before they went to church," continued Gerry. "To help them with the job. Good old smiling Harry helped me, right, Harry?"

Lauren looked at the driver, who was nodding; still with the horrible glacial smile she remembered being on the faces of the others who had swept into the underground chamber. The two youths holding her arms let go and moved forward to join the others, undisguised anticipation on their faces. Gerry put the bags back into the box and motioned for the others to get on with it, then moved away from the box, standing back and smiling.

"Help yourselves . . ." Then his eye caught Lauren once more. He moved back to the box and took out a pinch in one hand. Still smiling, he walked over to Lauren. She looked back at the boarded door and tried to calculate her chances at making a break for it.

Don't try it, said Sparrow. *You'll never make it.*

"How about you?" asked Gerry. "Want some?"

Don't touch it! snapped Sparrow in warning. *There's more going on here than meets the eye. The drug has the smell of Ramsden.*

Lauren shook her head.

"Just say no, eh?" said Gerry, still smiling.

"Why don't you try some?" asked Lauren.

"Someone has to keep a level head. Big things are going to happen soon."

"What has Ramsden promised you?" asked Lauren.

Gerry laughed, throwing back his head. Behind him, the others were swallowing and snorting their share of Nektre. When he'd finished, he reached out for Lauren's arm. She flinched from it, but Gerry laughed again, took it and guided her towards the burned-out stage, clearing a path through the others. When he pointed to the stone stairs, Lauren sat without question.

"See that?" He pointed to a small blue bag with a carrying handle. "That's a changing bag for the kid. Everything you need in there. Now how's that for fatherly kindness?"

Gerry turned back to the others.

"All right! Everyone sorted? Good. Now it's time for action."

The crowd were silent in the darkness.

"Ten of you know where to go and what to do. Helping out Mooney, Parks and Johnny. Three of you are going to stay here with me and watch over our lady friend and her little sprog. That's Chaz, Graeme and Danny. Right?"

Lauren looked at the horribly smiling, silent faces and felt sick inside. It was exactly the same look that she'd seen on the faces of the kids who had massacred the Sabbarite back at the church.

Riot, said Sparrow simply. *It's what Ramsden wants. Street riots –
and all the havoc it brings. Now I understand.*

"So go for it, you fuckers!"

Someone in the crowd whooped, a cry quickly followed by the
others. The torch beams swung wildly in the darkness and the sound
of Gerry's gang filled the community hall. The thunder and crash of
feet on the ruined flooring, pushing aside debris and yelling wildly in
anticipation.

*He's used this sick bastard to organise a riot for him. That's what
Ramsden needs, Lauren. All part of his plan. He needs an explosion of
violence to fuel his power and his ability to return. Once the riot starts,
fear and panic and death and horror will all fuel his emergence. He's
been working towards this for a long time. This, the murders of the
Sabbarite – they're all part of the pact.*

Oh God, said Lauren. *He'll be feeding on a vast amount of power once
the deaths begin.*

They've begun, said Sparrow.

The cardboard box and its contents had gone with Gerry's gang.

Outside, they listened to the sounds of cars revving up and roaring
off into the night. Soon, it had become very quiet again.

Gerry turned from the boarded-up door and began to pick his way
carefully through the charred debris, back to the stage where Lauren
sat with Sparrow. Behind him, the three young men he'd named idly
followed him with those sickly grins on their faces. Gerry picked up a
burned sliver of wood and began to tap it in the palm of his other hand.
He stopped, and looked back at the others.

"Now I wonder," he said, "how we can amuse ourselves until our
visitor arrives."

341

66

Mac and Ranjana had found a road over the brim of the railway embankment, running parallel with the line itself. Once on that road, Ranjana had stood for a while with her head down, as if deep in thought. Mac did not interrupt, knew that she was trying to pick up impressions again.

"Nothing . . . ?" he began to ask.

Without lifting her head, Ranjana held up a hand for him to be quiet.

Finally she looked up again; walked into the middle of the road and looked up and down. There was no traffic.

"This way," she said suddenly, and headed in the opposite direction from which they had just come.

"Are you sure?" asked Mac, following. "We're headed back the way we came."

"Only a little way. I think the place we want is over there to the left. And I'm pretty sure there must be another turn-off on the road back here which will cut through and save us some time."

"You should buy a crystal ball. We'd make a fortune at the carnival."

Ranjana managed a fragile smile. "There's still a lot of jumbled stuff coming through. I'm still getting something about – or even from – a child. That part of it makes no sense."

"We need to flag down a lift," said Mac, seeing headlights headed in their direction. They stepped quickly to the side of the road, and as the headlights drew nearer, Mac stepped out again waving his hand. The car went straight on by without slowing down.

"Oh God!" Ranjana suddenly halted in her tracks, holding her midriff as if she had suddenly been stabbed in the stomach. Then her hands flew to her head.

"What? What is it?" Mac was quickly at her side, taking her arm.

Ranjana drew in a deep breath, took another step forward – and this time doubled over, gagging in pain, clutching her temples.

"Ranjana!" Mac swept her up into his arms, felt how rigid she had become. He looked quickly around. The road seemed to stretch endlessly on either side into the night. God knew where they were. And there was no sign of any traffic. She groaned again, and Mac hurried to the roadside, laying her down there.

"What is it? What can I do . . . ?"

"It's Randall," hissed Ranjana through clenched teeth. "He's been hurt."

"Okay, take it easy." Mac felt helpless, not knowing what he could do. "Take it . . ." Ranjana convulsed again.

"Christ, Ranjana! What can I do for you?"

Ranjana gripped his arm tight as she contorted in pain. When the constriction lifted she gasped for air. "Something . . . something's happened to him . . . I don't know what. It's blurred. But he's been hurt, and we've got to get to him . . ."

Mac looked down the road again, then quickly stooped and scooped up Ranjana in his arms like a child. He strode down the centre of the road, feeling her trembling as if in the grip of fever.

"You said there was a turn-off somewhere, right?"

"Right . . . on the left."

"Okay, let's go for it."

Headlights flared in the night again, dead ahead. The car was perhaps four hundred yards away, but travelling fast.

Grim-faced, Mac marched on ahead to meet it.

The headlights flared larger as the car sped on towards them.

"He's hurt . . ." whimpered Ranjana. "God, Mac. Someone's hurt him . . ."

"It's okay. Ranjana. We're going to find him."

Mac gritted his teeth and kept on.

The light was blinding, and for the first time in a long, long time, Mac found himself praying.

A horn blared angrily – but Mac kept on walking.

Tyres screeched, and Mac wondered if this wasn't the best way for them both, after all. Wouldn't it be for the best if the driver slammed on his brakes too late and the car ploughed right into them? Scooping them up on the bonnet and hurling them into the air. It should be a clean and fast death. Not like the whole series of agonising deaths that might lie ahead of them.

The screeching tyres were like the screeching of a terrified, agonised human voice.

At the last, Mac stopped and waited, eyes screwed tight shut in the glare and holding Ranjana tight against him.

The screeching squealed to a stop, and he saw the car swerve and

343

skid to his right – no more than ten feet from where he stood in the middle of the road.

"What the bloody *hell* do you think you're doing?" shouted a voice in a thick Welsh accent. Mac could still barely see the car in the headlights' glare, but he heard the car door slam and saw the silhouette climb out.

"We need help," replied Mac, walking forward to meet him.

"What's wrong?" The man stepped in front of the headlights. Now Mac could see that he was a young man, in his mid-twenties, wearing a leather jacket and Levi jeans.

Ranjana struggled in his arms, and he put her down.

"I think I'm all right now," she whispered.

"No you're not."

"She looks okay to me." There was a note of trepidation in the man's voice now. Mac remembered how he must look to anyone belonging to the outside world. A trampish, vagrant figure.

"We need a lift," he said.

The man was backing away, reaching for the door handle again. "Like to oblige, but I'm already late. Like I say, she looks fine now . . ."

Mac moved faster than the man could appreciate, grabbing him by the arm and whirling him away from the car. The man squawked and tottered away into the middle of the road.

"Look," said Mac, "I'm really sorry about this, but we need your car. Get in, Ranjana." Without further prompting, Ranjana climbed into the passenger seat.

"You *bastard!*" shouted the man, clearly not wanting to engage physically with this big man, this wild vagrant.

"You're right, you're right. But I promise I won't damage the car."

"I'll . . . I'll . . . have the police. I'll . . ." The man could barely speak for the rage that had descended on him.

"Right. That's what I'd do in your position. Believe me, we don't blame you. We won't scratch it. When we're done we'll leave it somewhere safe."

"*Bastard!*" yelled the man when Mac climbed in and gunned the engine. He turned the car around in the opposite direction and then they roared on away from the man, leaving him shaking his fist behind him in the darkness.

"You're the most polite thief I've ever met," said Ranjana through gritted teeth. The pain was inside her head again.

"You won't believe this, but I don't think I've ever stolen anything in my life."

"You've got a flair, believe me." Ranjana sagged in her seat. Mac grabbed for her and pushed her back in the seat.

"Where's this turn-off?"

"Soon. You should see it soon." Now, for some reason, Ranjana was clutching at her throat. Mac was watching closely. Impulsively, he jammed his foot down on the accelerator.

"What? What now?"

"I can't . . . can't breathe. I'm choking. Mac. There's stuff in my mouth."

Mac quickly wound down his window. Chill night air swept inside the car.

"Open your window as well."

Ranjana wound it down and stuck her head outside, gasping at the night air.

Up ahead was a signpost, indicating left just as Ranjana had said. Mac quickly changed down, realising for the first time that he had no idea before they'd stolen the car whether he could actually drive or not. The car screeched into the turn. Ranjana's hair whipped in the night air and she bounced back into the car. Her face glistened with sweat.

And then the thought came to him: how deeply "linked" was Ranjana to Randall? How much did they mean to each other? Ranjana was suffering pain because Randall was suffering pain.

But what if Randall should die before they got to this ruined church, wherever in hell it was? What would happen to Ranjana then?

Mac changed quickly up into top gear and the car roared on into the night.

67

"We've heard nothing from Lorelei, nothing from the party that went to the church."

"Well, perhaps it's too early. This is too important to rush."

"But they should have let us know by now. That's why I've sent for you all."

"Send someone out there to Stanton. To the church. Just to make sure."

"I did. Two hours ago."

"And?"

"We haven't heard from them either."

"Well, telephone someone! Surely one of them has a portable phone?"

"No one answers. No one. And have you noticed something else?"

"We haven't time for guessing games."

"This is a Central Lodge meeting, called at urgent notice. You know the rules about attendance. There are never excuses for non-attendance. Eight Inner Circle members are missing."

"There's trouble on the estate. I haven't had a chance to consult properly with my junior officers yet, but it seems as if we have a riot brewing. I couldn't ascertain more, since the council meeting comes first. Perhaps the other members have been delayed by trouble on the streets. Hah, hear that! A police siren. Yes, I'm sure that's what's happened."

"But they should have let us KNOW where they are if they're in trouble, or delayed. There are no excuses, but they know the rules. Not one of them has been in touch. And there's something else. Tell the others, Jobling."

"We've been observing the Serendip since Lorelei and the others went out to get Lauren and Ramsden's child. The balance has been tilting wildly for over three hours and shows no signs of equalising."

"Ramsden!"

"We can't be sure. There are other unknown factors coming into play. It's as if the Serendip is sending in . . . 'antibodies' . . . to fight an infection in the order of reality."

"You mean we're *the infection? That's how it views us? Lorelei told us that our screens and balances would . . .*"

"*Not us. At least – not just us. So far, we've been able to keep the balance corrected by carefully spacing and timing our activities. But something else is happening out there, some huge build-up of power. And it's that which is tilting the Serendip.*"

"*Then it must be Ramsden. Like Lorelei told us. We know that he's dead, but somehow he's still up to something.*"

"*It can't be! How can it be him? He's dead, WE have the contact with the other side now, and we have his child. That child will be dead by now . . .*"

"*How do we know? How do we KNOW?*"

"*Oh, no . . . look . . . outside . . . down there.*"

"*Telephone your junior officers. Or do something.*"

"*What is it?*"

"*The riots you were talking about.*"

"*What IS it?*"

"*Outside on the streets, all around the Lodge.*"

"*Out of the way. Let me see.*"

"*Troublemakers. Tearaways. Look, they're all around the building. Coming down the street. Do something! That's your job, isn't it? There are dozens and dozens of them . . .*"

"*They're not youngsters, not . . . they look like . . . like tramps or vagrants or something.*"

"*God! Did you see that? They all looked up at once, towards this window. Now . . . they've stopped . . . they're coming on again . . .*"

"*Why are they smiling like that? For fuck's sake, somebody DO something!*"

"*It's all right . . . all right . . . everything will be . . .*"

68

Randall had no idea who this woman and her child were, but in the moment that the maniac in the power-dress clothes had made a lunge for her with that piece of glass, he had made his choice about whose side he was on. There was no time to think through his course of action, no element of bravery, just the knowledge that this bunch of maniacs were going to do him in anyway. He had slipped seamlessly from one nightmare into another, and was still in shock. His encounter with the Dead and narrow escape from death had unbalanced all sense of proportion; instead, only a lifetime experience of hard action on the streets and his response to the situations he encountered there remained. His head felt as if it was full of broken glass, and he knew that there was a split in the scalp behind his left ear. He had touched the dried blood there and felt the pain like an acid burn when he woke up. Even if he managed to stop the crazy woman, he had not thought through what would happen next. But after everything he had been through, he was not just going to lie there and take it.

But on the instant that his legs had tangled with the woman and brought her down, he had twisted to see the big bastard with the spade, swinging it down on him. He had tried to duck, but there was neither space nor time. The pain in his head was making him slow.

When the flat of the spade connected, it was almost on the same spot that he had been hit with the length of wood. He felt the flesh tear again; red-hot pain raged through his head. Vaguely he was aware that he was falling face first into a hole. But this hole must be hundreds of feet deep, because he was falling and falling and falling ... and there was no sign of the bottom. Something smashed into his face and the fire consumed his entire body.

Only blackness.

When the blackness spangled and shifted, Randall tried to suck in a deep breath of air – but his mouth filled with soil. He clawed at his face, discovering that only one hand was free. That hand was jammed

348

in front of his face, the other somehow compacted tight against his side. He shifted position, realising that he was lying face down and that his hand had instinctively flopped in front of his face before he had hit the bottom of the reopened grave. That hand had probably saved his face from being smashed, his nose from being broken. Randall clawed at his nostrils with his fingers, pushing out the dirt. His legs were still sticking out over the rim of the grave. His skull felt as if it had been smashed, his neck broken. And he could barely breathe. How long had he been lying like this in the suffocating darkness? He tried to turn his head again.

And then a spadeful of soil fell into the grave, covering his face. Randall tried to scream, scrabbling at his mouth with his fingers – and then a second spadeful entirely covered his head.

Randall twisted his head, ignoring the horrifying pain, fingers frantically twitching at his face like some burrowing, white five-legged spider. He squirmed frantically, fighting for breath and trying to pull free the arm that was trapped at his side. It was no good, he was jammed face first into the hole and could never get out.

Lights spangled in the darkness, behind his eyes.

He screamed, but no sound could be heard from above. And when he did scream, soil filled his mouth again.

Randall twisted his head face down and tried to twist the other way. The action seemed to compact his head even further.

Terror engulfed him and he gasped for air that was not there.

Gasped . . . and spasmed . . . and fought . . . and weakened . . . and clawed feebly and . . .

He was dying.

Impossibly, he was breathing again. His lungs were sucking in air. That air was stale and thin, but the oxygen it brought was clearing his head. He gasped at it greedily. His breathing came in great racking moans of relief. He prayed to God that he wasn't dreaming, or dead, or that wherever the air was coming from, it wouldn't suddenly cease. Randall tried to move, but was still stuck fast. When he wriggled the fingers in front of his face, he felt the soil loosening and crumbling. He froze, not wanting to cause a cave-in and make his problems worse. But that soil was still somehow crumbling away from his face. And then a great chunk of soil in front of his face seemed to shift and drop away. The air seemed to caress his face, and Randall knew that his face was somehow partially clear. It still smelled foul and rancid, but he sucked it in greedily.

Then he remembered something that the big man who had hit him with the spade had said just before Randall had made his move and earned himself the second smash across the head that night.

There's another ... another hole down here. Leading away. Like a bloody worm-hole or a tunnel or something.

That was it. The other hole burrowed out and away from the hole in which he had been thrown. It was still pitch black down here, but part of that second burrowed hole had collapsed, and literally given Randall breathing space. Tears of relief flooded his face, his breathing still came in sobs.

And then he heard the other distant sounds from above.

Sounds of screaming and yelling, and people whooping like wild animals.

What the hell was happening up there?

As he listened, he realised with sickening horror that people were being killed up there. The woman and the baby? Yes, probably, but there was more than one person screaming. And a child couldn't make a noise like that. Those sounds were the unmistakable and horrifying sounds of death. Had they brought others down here, others taken from the streets like him?

Randall tried to control his breathing as the screaming went on and on. The sounds were revolting and sickening, but now he realised that being in this hell-hole might be his only way of surviving. They'd thrown him down here and covered him over. He knew that his legs were still sticking out of the grave, but it was vital that he make no movement – and give away the fact that he was still alive. If they thought he was dead, then so be it.

And then someone fell across his legs.

The impact shoved him down deeper, pushing more soil into his mouth. The fire in his head and neck transferred to his calves. Randall scrabbled with his fingers again, gagging and spitting. Now, somehow, his hand was able to move a little more. And, thank God, the space that had been opened was still there. The weight was gone from his legs – as if someone who had been thrown down was now dragged from him and away. He fought to ignore the pain.

Please God ... please God ... please God ...

Someone shrieked, long and loud – and that sound suddenly dissolved into an utterly appalling *gargling* noise. Now, there were only the sounds of commotion, of a wild and elated whooping. But there were no more dying sounds.

Go, just go ... and leave me.

Someone seized his legs and began to drag him up.

Christ, no! Leave me here. I'd rather suffocate than die like that.

Two people had grabbed a foot each and were heaving Randall to the surface. Soil began to cascade around his face again. He tried to remain as limp as possible.

I'm dead, you bastards! Dead! Can't you see that?

They were hauling him up from the grave, and when they got him to the surface they would tear him to pieces just as they'd done to those other poor bastards. Randall tried to summon the strength to prepare himself. If he kept limp until they pulled him right out of this hell-hole, if he just flopped down when they finally got him clear – then maybe he could take them by surprise, maybe he could grab the nearest one . . .

Randall's hand flopped in front of his face. The arm that had been trapped at his side was clear at last. He could see both hands clearly now as he was heaved to the surface. But he could no more bunch those hands into fists than fly to the moon. There was no strength left in him. The last of his fight had been knocked out by the spade. He knew then that he was going to die. Not at the hands of the Dead, not beneath the wheels of a train, not in a reopened grave – but at the hands of the maniacs who were dragging him out. He could never fight back.

Randall wondered how long they would take.

And then someone from above said, "Leave him. Not worth the effort – he's a dead 'un."

The hands on his legs released him.

Randall dropped back into the hole for the second time.

The soil slammed into his face, filling his nostrils and mouth with packed dirt and blood.

And then the entire grave caved in around him, the soil completely enfolding him and destroying the worm-hole which had given him air.

69

They walk in the night.

In places on this estate, night has become as bright as day. Buildings are burning. Shops and stores have been looted and burned before being torched. And the light from these burning buildings remind those who walk of the place they have come from.

The night air is split with the sound of police sirens and loudspeakers, with the sound of fire klaxons as fire-engines race to the next burning store or house. There is the sound of One Great Voice on the streets; the same One Voice that speaks with such energy and passion and enthusiasm where any huge mass of people are gathered – at football stadiums, at religious meetings. But the sound of this Voice is different; this is a sound of rage and anger and hate. This is the sound of a million, million frustrations and bitter resentments being vented. This is the sound of vengeance. It is the voice of Gerry Tomelty – getting even in the crowd, acting on behalf of Pearce Ramsden. It is the sound of death and destruction – and it feeds Ramsden in the way that he had always intended.

In the tumult of the riot, they walk. As the crowds surge and the bricks and firebombs are thrown, they walk unnoticed.

As Gerry's gang and the Nektre-inspired members of their army hunt down and eliminate those whom they despise without reason, they walk and carry out Ramsden's vengeance.

Seven ragged figures emerge from the night, silhouetted against the burning beacon of a block of flats.

They walk to the edge of the canal. The fire behind them is reflected in the poisonous water, in the swirling pools of petrol and pollutants. Their ragged shadows weave and dance on the surface of the canal.

Something below the water is beckoning to them.

The first silhouette steps forward. It stands head down, searching the water.

And then it steps over the edge.

The dirty water enfolds the figure in a filthy plume of water. The figure bobs to the surface – and then dives, ragged legs kicking.

The others follow, plunging into the water after their companion. The night-black water is thrashed to a frenzy as they dive and search . . . dive and search . . . dive and search . . .

A long time later, the first figure claws at the side of the canal with its one free hand. It finds an iron ring there, jams what was once a foot into that ring and grips the rim of the canal, still holding on tight to what it has clasped in the other arm, tight to its chest. With water surging from its soaked body back into the canal, it heaves itself up over the side. Still cradling the thing under its armpit, it staggers to its knees. Then it rises, facing the burning buildings beyond and with water pooling around its feet.

It turns quickly, water flying from its body, and steps back to the canal. It waits there, watching the thrashing, foaming canal water.

A second figure crests from the canal, and strikes out back to the side – also with something in one hand. The figure on the canal side kneels down and proffers its free hand. The second figure takes it, and in moments there are two figures standing on the canal side, dripping wet, watching the search.

A third head erupts from the canal surface . . .

Soon, all seven figures have emerged from the canal and are standing on the canal side.

He has been retrieved.

The pact is almost complete.

They walk slowly back into the burning night with what they have retrieved, back on to the burning streets which look so much like home.

70

Randall remembered, with utter clarity, something that his grandmother had told him when he was seven years old.

She had died when he was eleven, and since then he had found difficulty bringing her face into focus when he tried to remember those days. The family photograph album had been taken by his departing mother, so he was unable to use a photograph to aid that memory. Now, however, he could see her face as if she was sitting opposite him. And she was telling him about how she had once nearly died. One night in bed and asleep, she had found herself rushing down a long dark tunnel towards a brilliant white light. She wanted more than anything else to arrive at that light, felt sure that there was great joy there. But something seemed to catch her and pull her back. A voice said, *It isn't time* – and the next thing she knew, she had awoken in bed feeling terribly ill. That illness had worn off and she had never gone to the doctor about it. But she had never forgotten the experience. Randall had asked what happened, and his grandmother told him that she supposed she had been dying in her sleep, maybe a heart attack. It was a story that she had heard was fairly common. And she had told him that story because . . . no matter how bad things got, he never had to worry about dying. Never had to fear death. Because the light was waiting.

Waiting . . . waiting . . .

And Randall saw the gleaming blackness on either side, like some black tunnel flashing past him at impossible speed. There was no wind accompanying that terrific rush, no air pressure on his face. But he could see a bright spangling light directly ahead of him: a sharp pinpoint of light that seemed welcoming and which he wanted to reach more than anything else. Now, he remembered what Mac had said back at the slipway – about "dying on the operating table" and seeing the tunnel of light.

But there was other light here, too. A light that his grandmother had never mentioned. Off to the left of that glorious, growing white light was another patch of light. This looked altogether less inviting than the white light. In fact, something about that dull, reddish-brown throbbing light horrified Randall, filled him with a hideous dread. He knew that he was heading for a crossroads up ahead, some departure point where he would either plunge right into the brilliant white, glorious light – or left, into that hideously throbbing red-brown light that seemed to pulse like some gigantic heart, criss-crossed with something that looked like veins and arteries.

Randall had never prayed, but he prayed now that he would go to the white light. The prospect of plunging left into that other place filled him with dread. He tried to push his flight in the right direction, but knew in that flashing voyage down the tunnel that he would have no choice in the matter. The crossroads was dead ahead, he could feel it, and prayed again as . . .

Something dragged at him from behind.

Something that slowed down his passage.

Randall fought back and resisted; more than anything else he wanted that white light.

But the force behind him was irresistible.

. . .Grandma . . . ?

The crossroads ahead was terrifying enough, but Randall did not want to go back. Not to that other place, wherever it might me. He could not recall where he had come from, not one aspect of it. He only knew that he was desperately unhappy there.

Please, don't take me back . . . please . . . please . . .

But Randall was now travelling back along the tunnel at incredible velocity, the brilliant white light and the horrific red light spinning away from him into the gleaming darkness.

No, no, no, no!

" . . .no, please God, don't let him be dead!"

Was that his voice?

The horrifying smothering blackness had descended on him again. Randall clawed weakly at his face, at the cloying suffocating clay and soil around his face. It was rushing past him as his backwards ascent continued.

Someone was holding his legs again and tugging hard.

The sudden light was faint, but somehow blinding to his eyes as Randall slithered out of that hell-hole and was dragged by the legs on to the underground chamber floor. A shadow fell on him, grabbing his head; delicate but strong fingers clawing compacted clay and soil from his nostrils, from his eyes and mouth, and all the time the new tear-filled voice was breathing into his face: "Oh God, Randall. Come back . . . don't die . . . please don't be dead . . . please come back . . ."

Randall turned over and retched on the floor of the chamber.

"He's *alive*, Mac!"

"God knows how," said another huge shadow looming over him.

When the retching had stopped, Randall began to tremble. That trembling soon became uncontrollable. The horror of suffocation, the tunnel that formed when that horror had become unspeakably bad, and everything else that had descended upon Randall in the last few nightmare days gripped him and shook him.

Ranjana seized him. She was kneeling beside him, but pulled his soil and clay-stained body across her lap as if cradling a child. She held him tight, rocking him and her soft tears washing his face. Randall could see Mac there, too – also kneeling and with a huge, scarred hand on his shoulder.

"It's okay, son. You're going to be all right."

Randall slept, his body still reacting to the horror of his experience.

71

They stayed like that for a long time, until Randall's trembling began to subside.

Eventually, Ranjana looked up at Mac.

"Those people . . ."

Mac looked up then, at the horrifying sight which had so sickened them when Ranjana had found this Godforsaken place.

Mac had followed her gasped instructions word for word in the stolen car, had taken the battered roadsign for Stanton despite his fears that she would suffocate before they got there. Ranjana kept her head out of the car window, fighting for breath, pulling it back in to shout an instruction. She had known exactly which road to take for the abandoned church. When the car had swung around a corner in that deserted ghost town and she had seen the derelict building with its toppled spire she had lunged back into the car and grabbed him by the arm. She was out of the car and staggering towards the church before Mac had a chance to stop the vehicle. He'd followed close behind, and it seemed to him as they staggered over the ruins that Ranjana was suffering some intense asthma attack. Were they really going to find Randall – or was she simply going to collapse on these fallen stones in her asthma delirium?

It was as if she had been here before. She seemed to know exactly where the studded iron door was hidden at the side of the collapsed altar. He had plunged on after her into the dimly lit gloom of that underground chamber.

And had nearly collided with her at the foot of the stairs. Ranjana had stopped there, hands braced on either wall, looking down onto that horrifying scene. Mac had carefully moved her aside and stepped down. He too was horrified and sickened.

There had been a massacre down here.

Dark, shredded forms were visible in the chamber. Recognisably human from the one or two white, blood-slashed faces that were

357

immediately visible. Two of them were naked – women, apparently. But the bodies were like tailor's dummies – with *parts* missing. Mac could see one of those tailor's dummy arms further away in the chamber, bent and clawing at the air. The other ragged bundles also seemed incomplete, and there were indeterminate ragged pieces scattered throughout the chamber. The dark soil on the floor was glistening.

Ranjana suddenly broke from the horror which froze her in the doorway, plunged past Mac and hurled herself at a jumble of those incomplete parts. Mac lunged after her as she dived down on to something. At first, Mac had thought that the calves and feet were dismembered, like the others. Now, he could see that they protruded from the soil. Someone was down there, buried alive.

Ranjana had feverishly clawed at the soil while Mac grabbed those legs and heaved.

Now, looking around the chamber at the indeterminate huddled forms of the dead, Mac turned to look back at Ranjana. Was it possible, or did Ranjana seem a hell of a lot paler than before?

"Those people," she continued. "They're all" – she swallowed hard, still cradling Randall in her arms – "all people from the vans."

"What, you mean the people who've been kidnapping and killing the street people?"

Ranjana nodded

"This is crazy. None of it makes sense."

Ranjana nodded again.

"The street people did it," continued Mac. "They got their revenge."

"I'm . . . I'm . . . getting jumbled messages again. I told you, I felt as if I was being sent messages about this place. But whoever sent them has gone, been taken away. I felt that they'd gone a while back on the road, but by then I was able to . . . to follow my own instincts to find the place."

"Well, we found him. He's alive, and that's all that matters."

"No, Mac. That's not all that matters. We're bound up in this nightmare, whatever in hell is happening. And we have to follow it through. It's . . . it's *drawn us in*. We can never get away from it, can never escape it by running."

"I know," said Mac. "I know . . ."

He whirled back to the doorway as something clattered and scuffled there. Ranjana jerked her head up.

A young girl suddenly staggered into the chamber. She was wearing some kind of old-fashioned smock. Her hair was braided but seemed encrusted with dirt, those braids lashing around her head as she was shoved into the chamber from someone following close behind. She clutched at the wall for balance, and now they could see that she was covered with dirt. Her smock, her face, her hands. Another shadow loomed behind her.

Mac clambered to his feet, bunching his fists. Had the killers returned?

And then a man stepped into the chamber behind the girl.

He was equally as filthy as the girl, as if both of them had been swimming through mud. He remained there, taking in the horrifying scene below. The man was carrying a rusted iron railing, wrenched from the church gates.

Holding the railing like a spear, the stranger's eyes locked with Mac's eyes.

And although Mac had never seen this man before, something seemed to register on the stranger's face; a look of recognition or astonishment or both. Mac saw that look falter and fade quickly as he stepped forward to join the girl. She suddenly whirled and flung herself to face the rough stone wall.

"They're dead, Dandridge! They're all *dead*!"

Dandridge?

The name seemed uncannily familiar to Mac. He grasped for a link or memory. There was nothing there.

"Sabbarite?" asked the man. He was standing ready, facing Mac now. Instead of recognition or astonishment, his face was grim – as if expecting to have to deal physically with Mac. Mac lunged to the soil floor, seized a blood-smeared spade and stood protectively in front of Ranjana and Randall. The man crouched instinctively with the railing, ready for an attack.

"Where's the girl and the baby?" snapped the stranger, eyes blazing.

They stood in the chamber, weighing each other up.

"Come *on*! Where are they?"

"What the hell are you talking about?" demanded Mac.

"They're gone," said the strange girl. "They've been taken away."

"What do you mean, taken away? You said they'd been brought here!"

"They *were* here, but they've been taken somewhere else by . . . someone."

Mac seemed to see an immense wave of relief sweep across the man's face.

"You're sure?"

"Of course I'm sure. Go look at those bodies if you like, you won't find them there."

"And who are these people?"

"I don't know who they are," said the girl. "They're not Sabbarite."

The girl turned away from the wall and faced them. Mac heard Ranjana's horrified intake of breath and looked at her.

The girl had no eyes.

Tossing back her filthy braids of hair, she stepped down the stairs. Somehow, *impossibly*, she was *looking* at them both. The eye sockets were hollow pits, but the girl's vision seemed completely unimpaired as she walked down the stairs and looked from Mac to Ranjana and back again.

"Fuck," she said at last. "That's all I need. Another empath."

"What?" asked the man with the spear.

"The girl," replied the blind one. "She's got psychic abilities."

The blind girl moved past Mac and Ranjana, moving silently and slowly to the corpses that littered the chamber floor. Mac adjusted his position so that he could keep one eye on the stranger and the other on the girl. Suddenly, the blind girl clutched at her stomach. It reminded Mac instantly of the way that Ranjana had clutched at herself just before their mad dash in search of Randall.

"*Ramsden!*" The word seemed to be torn out of the girl. It was a ragged, retching sound of a word.

"He's back?" said the stranger.

"No . . . no, not yet. But he's on his way. The bastard is on his way."

"Then who did this?" continued the stranger.

"I . . . I don't know. Father is . . . *cloaking*. But they were killed at his command."

"So Ramsden's got Lauren and Sparrow?" Again, that horrified look of concern on the stranger's face.

"What the hell are you two talking about?" demanded Mac.

"Who *are* these people?" demanded the stranger.

Lorelei stepped towards them again.

"The girl is a runaway. Her name is . . . Ranjana. She's running away from an arranged marriage."

Mac and Ranjana looked at her in astonishment.

"The boy on the floor is a runaway too. His name is Randall. And they've all had a run-in with us. I mean, with the Sabbarite. The big man is . . ."

Lorelei stood back again, her hands moving to her stomach. There was a look of fear on her face now. She began to shake her head.

"Who is he?" asked the stranger again.

Lorelei just stood and shook her head.

"Who *is* he?"

"I don't . . . don't know . . . don't *want* to know . . ."

"What the hell are you talking about, Lorelei?"

"There's something about him. Something 'cloaked'. But I don't know how or why. I've never come across anyone like this before . . . he's . . ."

"*What?*" snapped the stranger.

"Neither dead nor alive," said Ranjana.

"Another sister," said the blind girl, struggling to swallow her fear. "You there, Ranjana . . ."

Ranjana looked up at the stranger.

"She can read your mind. Don't let her. Find a way to keep her out if you can. She's dangerous."

Lorelei laughed. A hollow and bitter sound. "Dangerous? Little me? You should know by now that there are far more dangerous things out there in the night than me."

"You said Sabbarite," said Ranjana to the stranger. "Are they the people who've been killing the street people?"

Tony nodded.

"And that's who these people are?"

Tony nodded again.

"But there are more of us," said Lorelei.

"Not for long, you murdering bastards," said Mac, pointing with his spade at the mutilated bodies lying on the chamber floor. "Something out there wants you dead, that's for sure." Lorelei reacted to his words, shrinking back to the wall again, clutching at her stomach.

"Your father's doing, Lorelei," said the stranger, lowering his spear and coming down the stairs into the chamber. "If you want to get out of this alive, you'd do best to use your powers to help us, not hinder us."

"God," said Ranjana, a look of disgust on her face. "She *is* trying to see into my mind. And she's . . . she's . . . *evil*."

Lorelei laughed and tossed back her braids.

"Stop it, Lorelei!" snapped Tony. He jammed the railing into the soil and walked on past it towards Mac. Mac watched him come, still holding the spade defensively. He glanced quickly at Ranjana.

"I think . . ." She adjusted her position as Randall moaned and began to recover consciousness. "I think he's all right."

Tony stopped in front of Mac and held out his hand.

"My name's Tony Dandridge," he said.

Mac looked quickly back at Ranjana, and then lowered the spade. He took Dandridge's hand in his own.

"They call me Mac."

"Well, Mac," said Tony. "I think we're all in very deep shit."

"Never been deeper."

"I think we'd better talk. There isn't much time."

As the remaining candles guttered in the underground chamber, and their shadows reared and loomed, they shared their knowledge and experience.

Piece by jagged piece, they dragged together the horrifying jigsaw of their nightmare.

72

Somewhere in the night, something exploded.

The community centre seemed to shake, and a thin dust of ash drifted down from the burned-out timbers overhead.

"All . . . *right!*" exclaimed Graeme, hugging his leather jacket tight around himself at the sound.

"What was it?" asked Danny, with undisguised delight on his tattooed face.

"That's the first sound of the big changes," said Gerry, still smacking the burned sliver of wood into the palm of his hand.

"Fucking ace," said Chaz.

Since the others had departed, Gerry's companions had rigged up three portable car lights to provide illumination in the burned-out centre.

Still sitting on the steps and hugging Sparrow tight, Lauren wondered at the disparate nature of this gang. They looked as if they should all belong to different street gangs, different street cultures. The one called Graeme looked like a biker, Danny like a skinhead with the purple rose tattooed on his cheek and the crewcut revealing white scars on the scalp underneath. By contrast, the one called Chaz looked like the under-manager of a department store – in a suit with a tie.

What was it, Sparrow?

Not sure. I think it was a central heating boiler in a burning shop, or something.

So the riot's started?

It's been going for a while. Father's gathering great power.

"Gerry?"

He turned to Danny, whose attention had moved to Lauren.

"What about . . . you know, a little fun? With the girl, I mean."

"Yeah," said Graeme, stepping forward. "This Nektre stuff's giving me a hard-on."

"No," said Gerry simply. "She and the kid are special. We've got to wait."

"Ah, come on!" said Chaz. "What difference does it make? Whoever's coming to collect her won't mind." The Nektre had dissipated the growing fear of Gerry that all of his gang members had been experiencing recently.

Gerry seized Danny by the collar with one hand. "I said *no*!" He shoved him back and Danny staggered away, still with the Nektre grin on his face.

"Where is he, then?" asked Chaz. "This important fella you keep talking about?"

"Yeah," rejoined Graeme. "And *who* the hell is he?"

"All getting a bit uppity, eh?" Gerry slapped the wood in his hand again. "Not very grateful for what I've given you, are you?"

"Come on, Gerry." Danny's attention had returned to Lauren. "Let's party. You can go first, if you like." He stepped forward again.

Gerry stood forward to meet him, swinging the wood around sideways. It hit him across the side of the head with a hideous *crack!* Danny grunted and dropped to his knees, arms hanging limp at his sides. The others made no move; they simply watched – and grinned. When Danny looked up at Gerry, he still had that idiot smile on his face. There was a hairline tracing of red from his eyebrow, across the purple-rose tattoo on his cheek to the lobe of his ear. Suddenly, that thin tracing opened – and a wave of crimson flooded over his face, obliterating the tattoo. Danny never stopped smiling.

Not even when Gerry took a step back and brought the wooden spar down on his head in a two-handed blow.

Lauren recoiled, looking away. She heard Danny sliding to the floor.

When she looked back, Gerry's face was white – but he, too, was smiling.

Graeme and Chaz were leaning forward eagerly to look.

"Fucking hell," said Graeme. "Did you kill him?"

As if in answer, Danny groaned from the floor.

"Let us," said Chaz. "Go on, Gerry. Let me and Graeme finish it."

Gerry stood back, still white-faced and smiling, as Chaz and Graeme moved in on Danny.

But there was a new sound from the floor now. That groaning sound seemed to have changed. Each groan seemed to sound like some kind of effort, and at the end of that effort – a wet, cracking, splintering sound. Another groan – and more of that crackling and liquid splintering. Again and again.

Lauren saw the two would-be attackers stand back. But their faces were lit with inner joy; joy at some strange new development which was taking place on the floor.

Lauren! Sparrow's thought stabbed into Lauren's mind. *Something's happening. Something bad.* Lauren stood up on the steps, took a step back away from what was happening. Then she saw the expression on Gerry's face.

The smile had gone. Puzzlement was turning into something approaching horror, and as he stepped back he unconsciously dropped the spar on the ground. Chaz looked back at him, beckoned for him to come forward and see. Graeme laughed – a wild and uncontrolled sound. On the floor, Danny uttered a sound that was more animal than human: a ululating cry of pain, followed again by that horrendous, liquid cracking noise.

Then Danny sat up.

At last, Lauren could see what was happening to Danny.

Somehow, his hands and his face had bloated. Those hands were scrabbling at his face, and Lauren could see that the swollen skin had stretched and burst, shredding on his hands like strips of pink tagliatelle. Beneath that shredded patchwork of skin, Lauren could see the purple-red musculature of ganglions and tendons. Danny took his trembling patchwork hands away from his face – and Lauren almost screamed when she was what was happening there.

Danny's eyes had burst. Exploding in their sockets and running down the splitting and ragged flesh of his cheeks. The same thing that was happening to his hands was happening to his face. This time, when he made that horrid gargling, mewing sound a torrent of black-red blood spewed from his mouth and over his hands.

Danny's body was disintegrating, shredding and melting down.

It's the stuff they've been taking! said Sparrow anxiously. *That stuff he called Nektre.*

"The other side," said Lauren weakly, now stepping quickly down the steps and away from the sickening sight. "Ramsden got it from the other side."

I thought I was the psychic one.

Danny threw back his arms in a paroxysm of pain and rage, sending a spray of his own juices flying. Lauren recoiled, crying out in disgust.

Gerry began to shake his head.

"No, this shouldn't happen. You didn't tell me about this, Father. You didn't mention anything about this . . ."

Chaz and Graeme looked back at Gerry as he spoke. And in that one movement, Gerry saw the expression on their faces change. At first, they still held that idiot Nektre grin, that delight and amazement at what was happening to Danny. But now that expression changed, the grin began to vanish simultaneously from their faces, to be replaced by something like puzzlement, then an awareness that something was going on inside their own bodies.

Graeme's face began to move. That movement startled him. He probed the flesh of his face with his hands. It came again – a bubble of something under the skin of his cheek; swelling up and distorting his face; then suddenly vanishing. Another movement, another bubble of flesh – and now it was happening to Chaz, too. In horror and amazement, still shaking his head at this unexpected development – as if shaking his head could stop it from happening – Gerry saw that bubbling movement of flesh become a riot of seething movement under the skin on both their faces.

"You bastard, Gerry!" screamed Graeme. "What have you done to me?"

Chaz and Graeme clutched at their eyes and mouths, and Gerry could see that hideous bubbling movement happening on the flesh of their hands.

"*Help ME!*" screamed Chaz, staggering towards Gerry.

When Graeme's face suddenly ripped apart in a spray of blood, Gerry turned and began to scramble through the burned detritus towards the front door of the community centre.

Screaming, Chaz went after him.

Gerry had only covered a few yards when Chaz launched himself through the air and took him around the waist. They both went down flailing in the debris.

The thing that had once been Danny raised its ravaged and eyeless face, no longer screaming. Graeme was on his knees, disintegrating hands still clutching the ruin of his own face; crying and moaning as the cracking, splintering sounds engulfed his own body. Lauren could see hideous movement beneath his jacket and trousers – as if a thousand living things were under there, insects maybe, all swarming over his body and helping to disintegrate it. A horrendous image leaped into her mind. It was like one of those time-lapse shots from a nature documentary film – where an animal's corpse disintegrated in seconds.

The Danny-thing turned its glistening gaze to look at Lauren. There were no eyes in its sockets, but it was looking at her anyway – the way that blind Lorelei had been able to look. The sounds of change and disintegration seemed to have slowed. Lauren could only hear a low popping and bubbling sound coming from it.

It smiled at her. A hideous, ruined sight. Like something three months in the ground.

Somewhere near the entrance, Gerry screamed.

Graeme shrieked and howled over the sounds of his own disintegration.

"*Nice-looking girlie,*" said Danny – and began to crawl towards her.

73

"I still don't know what this Serendip thing is about," said Ranjana.

"Never mind the philosophy of it," said Tony. "We can discuss that later. The point is – Ramsden's coming back. To get revenge on Lorelei's people for what they did to their leader. That's what this is all about."

"And those dead people? The ones who chased us and tried to kill us?"

"You suggested as much yourself while we were discussing it. Victims of the Sabbarite. Somehow brought back to get that revenge. What do you say, Lorelei? You've been very quiet."

Lorelei had remained standing against one of the chamber walls throughout, arms folded across her chest. Face set.

"She's frightened," said Ranjana. "Frightened to open herself up to what you're saying – in case it's all true."

"Getting clever now, aren't you?" said Lorelei. "Well watch out, empath. Don't try to run before you can walk."

Tony turned from Lorelei. "I suppose we're all in this together now."

"In for a penny . . ." said Ranjana.

" . . . in for a pound," finished Mac.

"That makes four, if you're counting," said Randall. He had come around to listen in on the sharing of experiences, had told them all what had happened to him since they'd been separated at the goods yard. Lying in Ranjana's arms was the most comforting feeling that he had ever experienced in his life. He looked up at her smiling face as he spoke, and couldn't believe the way he was feeling. Ranjana smiled and kissed him, holding him tighter.

Tony could not explain the sudden wave of relief which flooded him. He had no idea why he should be so relieved when they were all so deeply into this nightmare. Yes, it had something to do with escaping from the Mechanic. That instinctive dread of his pursuer had vanished when he had managed, by the skin of his teeth, to send it back to Hell.

367

But the terror had never really gone, and now the fear of losing Lauren and her child was overwhelming. If they should fall prey to Ramsden in the way that they feared, then there could be terrible consequences for everyone. But there were deeply terrible *personal* consequences for Tony. The events that he had experienced and the horrors that he had endured had bound him to Lauren and Sparrow in a way that he could never believe possible. His fear for them was lodged deep in his gut, as deep as he might fear for his own life. But this other feeling of relief was strange – and awkward. It had to do with these strangers. At last, he was no longer in the nightmare alone. They too were part of it and something about them, the kind of people they were, drew him to them. They were as much a part of this horrifying jigsaw as he was – and he felt good about them.

And then two things happened simultaneously.

Ranjana suddenly drew in a hissing breath, as if in pain, lowering her head.

At the same time, Lorelei suddenly stepped quickly away from the wall, turning her blind face to the ceiling; twisting her head as if searching for the source of an unheard sound.

Randall reacted in alarm, shifting to a sitting position and taking Ranjana by the shoulders. "What is it? What's wrong?"

His nerves tuned to a fine pitch, Tony was ready to move.

And then Mac said, "It's okay. This has happened before."

"What's the matter with her?" Randall brought her face up gently with one hand. "Ranjana?" Her eyes were closed, but her face was screwed up intently.

"She's picking something up," said Mac. "A message." He moved to them both, kneeling on the rough soil floor and supporting Ranjana's back. Randall twisted to his knees, still holding her shoulders.

"A message?" sneered Lorelei. "More like a pitiful cry for help." Lorelei stood back against the wall, threw back her head and began to laugh.

"What the hell are you talking about, Lorelei?" snapped Tony.

"It's the child," said Lorelei indulgently, as if she was talking to a child herself. "He and Lauren are about to die. Ahhhh" – the sound she made was as if trying to placate that child into sleep, or stop it from crying – "he's been trying to contact the empath for a long time. Felt he'd found a soul-mate out there somewhere. Isn't that sweet? But she's only an amateur, I'm afraid. Got a lot to learn."

Tony moved angrily forward, yanking the spear-railing out of the ground as he moved and jabbing the point in Lorelei's direction. Lorelei flattened herself against the chamber wall.

"Don't let him touch me!"

"If half of what we've heard here is true," said Mac, "I'm not only going to stay here and watch him tear you apart, I'm going to hold his coat while he does it."

"Where are they, Lorelei?" demanded Tony, still moving towards her.

"You're too late! They'll be dead before you get there . . ."

"And you'll be dead if you don't tell me. So help me, Lorelei!"

"You need me . . ."

"We need you like we need rabies! *Where are they?*"

Ranjana moaned, and Tony looked back. "A community centre," she said, eyes still closed, head gently nodding from side to side. "Burned-out . . ."

Tony whirled when he heard a scuffling sound from Lorelei's direction. She was clutching her stomach, head down. In disgust, he walked away from her and back to the others, jamming the railing angrily back into the soil.

Lorelei remained where she was, trembling. But it was not with fear from Tony's threat. Something much more profound had affected her. Ever since her encounter with Tony at the canal she had put up her own psychic screens, believing that it might help her in the long run. If Sparrow believed her dead and was getting no psychic indication that she still existed, she might be able to use that to her advantage at some later stage. But her arrival at the church had damaged those screens. The murders of the remaining Sabbarite had been carried out by someone on behalf of Ramsden, and the *essence* of her father had been so very powerful down here. So powerful that she had tried desperately to put those damaged screens back up. She was aware then that things were happening, dangerous psychic emissions were in the ether. Sparrow's sudden call for help had been directed at the empath, but Lorelei had heard its power here in the underground chamber. Tentatively, she had explored that link between Sparrow and Ranjana, simply to taunt the others. But that had been a bad mistake.

That exploration had resulted in a lowering of her already damaged defences.

The immense power that was being generated in the ether flooded Lorelei's senses. In that one great flood of sensation came a complete knowledge of what was happening out there on the streets, and what was to come.

Lorelei saw in that one instant . . .

The Dead walking the burning streets.

The death and the horror – and the changes that were already taking place in those who had taken the drug called Nektre. A drug provided by her father. The death and the horror caused by those Nektre changes in the kids on the streets was feeding him, filling him with immense power. Just as he had always intended.

The killing of the Sabbarite.

The dreadful knowledge that all of the Sabbarite, all of the Inner Circle that provided the real focus for their activities, had been found – and vengeance enacted. The Outer Circle would dissipate and fall apart when the vibrations of well-being ceased.

All of the Inner Circle had been found – except one.

Her.

And the Dead knew that there was only one left, and they were out there looking for her now.

The shock of that sudden flood rendered Lorelei speechless and immobile. She sagged against the wall, head bowed, dirty plaited hair dangling.

Tony knelt down with the others beside Ranjana.

"Do you think you could take us there?" he asked.

"Yes," said Ranjana. "I think so." She wiped one hand across her face and struggled to rise. They all helped her.

"I've got a car," said Mac.

"Thank Christ for that," said Tony grimly.

"We've got to . . ." began Ranjana. "Oh God, we've got to *hurry*! They're in dreadful danger!"

"Then let's go!" Tony moved quickly back across the chamber and seized Lorelei by the arm. She did not resist when he dragged her back to the stairs. The others were already on their way up.

Looking back only once at the scene of hell below, Tony pushed Lorelei on ahead up the stairs and followed – towards the hell that awaited them above.

74

Lauren could not move.

As Danny struggled towards her through the burned debris on the floor, all she could hear was the conversation she'd had with Sparrow on their way here.

We're going to die. Whether we can stop Father or not – we're still going to die.

That knowledge immobilised her, and she clutched Sparrow tight as Danny staggered and fell to his knees again. His face was liquefying, and this time when he tried to speak, his mouth filled with viscous liquid.

Oops . . . Danny's shredded hand went to his mouth in a hideous parody of table manners.

Somewhere beside the entrance to this place, Gerry still thrashed and yelled hoarsely. Graeme uttered a feral, animal howl of pain as the cracking and splintering accompanying his transformation continued.

Danny reached for her.

Move, Mother! MOVE! Sparrow's "shout" stabbed across Lauren's mind. *You mustn't just give in!* The shock of his voice galvanised Lauren into action.

As the shredded claw-hand reached for her face, Lauren span away from Danny. She span again and almost toppled on the rubbish-strewn floor; saw the blackened and scarred bucket and its corroded handle; twisted and grabbed for that handle as Danny blundered after her on his disintegrating knees. In one swift and almost balletic movement, Lauren seized the bucket handle, whirled and swung the bucket at him as hard as she could.

It connected with his face at the same moment that she let go of the handle. Danny uttered a hideous *squawk!* as the bucket clattered to the floor.

And then Lauren was scrambling through the burned-out fallen timbers, making a wide circle and heading for the door as . . .

Gerry thrashed on the floor beside the entrance. Chaz had grabbed his left leg and was clinging on tight with shredded claw-hands as Gerry tried to pull himself away. Gerry seized handfuls of debris, throwing it back at Chaz and trying to kick himself free.

"Father, Father, Father! You never told me! Never told me!"

Chaz was uttering a hideous, chattering sound as his face fell apart. Gerry could see hideous movement under the jacket on his back as the flesh popped, split and stretched. Chaz dragged himself closer to Gerry, using Gerry's leg to haul himself along. *"Get off me, you bastard! Get OFF ME!"*

Gerry twisted on to his back, pulled his right leg back as far as it would go.

And then Chaz sank his teeth into Gerry's left calf, worrying his teeth-shards into the flesh. Gerry screamed, and kicked down hard with his right foot. The blow hit Chaz square in the head and dislodged him. Gerry saw the sudden eruption of blood from his leg before the pain came, saw that several of Chaz's broken teeth were still imbedded in his calf. Still screaming – but now in agony, Gerry kicked again; smashing his foot into Chaz's face. He felt the flesh skidding beneath the sole of his shoe under the impact, like cooked chicken's skin. Chaz's grip was gone, his head wagging from side to side like some horrifying, melting puppet. Gerry dragged himself away and despite the agony in his leg, pulled himself upright on a burned-out timber. He turned to stagger for the door – and then realised with horror that he was facing back into the community centre. Their struggle on the floor had twisted him right around. Now, Chaz lay between him and the door. He looked back at Chaz, still disorientated and clawing at his shredded face. Then back into the centre, at Graeme, who was still kneeling on the floor holding his face while his body convulsed and writhed under the transformation. Lauren was clambering towards him. Behind her, Danny blundered through the ashes and the jumbled detritus on hands and knees, clawing for her. Gerry clutched at his calf, and at the blood that oozed through his fingers. Graeme screamed again – somehow, it was taking longer for the change to be complete in him. Lauren stooped to grab part of a shattered chair, pausing long enough only to hurl it at Danny. He smacked it away with a shredded arm – and then Lauren was next to Gerry.

"Come on, you son of a bitch!" she yelled directly into his face. "There must be *some* other way out of here . . ."

Gerry did not answer. Instead, he staggered and hopped away from her towards a scarred and battered door. There was fresh graffiti on that door since the fire: *Nirvana OK*: an endorsement of the musicians,

372

or a promise of the after-life. Gerry hit that door hard with both hands. It banged open on impact, sending echoes chasing. Lauren was right behind him; saw an outer door beyond still with the faded words: *Fire escape.*

Thank God, a way out . . .

But it was not a way out.

Gerry slammed up hard against the outer doors, yanked at the door-lever, but the door would not budge. He slammed at the door with the flat of both hands, yelling, "Come on, come on, *come ON!*"

And then remembered that he had been responsible for the burning of the building, remembered giving instructions that the fire escape should be jammed so that anyone inside would go up with the centre; remembered how disappointed he'd been that no one had actually burned alive in this building.

"*Shit!*"

"Come on!" yelled Lauren. "They're coming!"

Gerry whirled and hobbled up the fire escape stairs. Those stairs were made of reinforced steel and had not burned with the building. The stairwell was filled with a strange, faint and undulating orange light. Lauren glanced back and saw horrifying, ragged movement there. Crying out, she slammed the inner door shut and clattered up the stairs after Gerry, clutching Sparrow tight. Now she could see where the light was coming from. There were three flights of steel stairs with small landings. Up above, at the top of those stairs, there had once been ceiling-height windows. They had been shattered in the fire, but that light was coming through the windows – because beyond those windows, parts of the council estate were burning. In the distance, fire-engine sirens caterwauled in the night.

Gerry clutched at a rail as he ascended, leaving a trail of blood on the stained metal. Lauren soon overtook him. The sounds of their flight echoed, rattled and boomed in the narrow stairwell. Lauren reached the top, rounded the corner – and then grabbed for the wall in alarm.

For a moment, she tottered on the edge of the girder, staring down into a ragged gap.

There was no floor here. The upper storey had burned through and the floor had all but collapsed into the community centre below. All that remained was a criss-cross section of burned timbers and battered girders. In horror, Lauren realised that if she had simply looked up from the stage stairs on which she had been sitting, she could have seen that there was no upper storey. She could see that stage area down below – and caught a horrifying glimpse of something that defied description glaring up at her. It was Graeme, now able to move despite the transforming disintegration. One baleful eye was fixed on Lauren, and he emitted a mewing snarl which made her recoil.

Lauren whirled back to Gerry as he reached the top of the stairs.

"You stupid bastard!" she yelled at him. "There's no bloody *floor* here! How the hell do we get out?"

Gerry staggered past her, face a white mask of shock and desperation. He hobbled out onto the only solid part – a twenty-foot square section that had not collapsed – and stared out across the ragged criss-cross of beams and girders. The community centre floor lay thirty feet below.

Something crashed at the foot of the stairwell.

Lauren whirled to look down just as the inner doors burst apart, and the thing that had been Danny fell through. His impetus slammed him to the floor and he lay there, thrashing feebly. He tried to rise, turning that dreadful disintegrating face up to look at her. Lauren stood back, hand to her mouth. One of Danny's arms remained on the floor as he came to his knees – it had rotted at the shoulder and fallen away.

A pair of shredded claw-hands braced themselves on the inner door frame. Another head thrust through the gap, turned and looked up at her. Chaz or Graeme? It was now impossible to tell.

Girlie . . . said Danny.

Gerrrrryyyyyy . . . said the thing in the doorway.

They were coming up.

75

It was like a drive through hell.

Stanton was a ghost town, and had remained untouched by the horror that was being visited on the streets tonight. But beyond Stanton, and into the council estates, it was a different matter. Mac was forced to take three different turns to avoid trouble. On one occasion a burning department store had collapsed into the street. Fire tenders blocked off the road but the avalanche of water from the hoses seemed unable to deal with the inferno. Ranjana had given new instructions and Mac had reversed the car and tried a different route. On both of the other occasions, the street had suddenly been filled with kids throwing stones or running from the police.

And in the night sky, the clouds roiled and reflected an unholy orange-yellow, a sure sign that there were fires all over the city.

Ranjana sat next to Mac in the front, giving directions.

Tony and Randall sat on either side of Lorelei in the back. Tony could barely contain his agitation. His window was open and he clutched at the upper roof as the car moved, drumming his hand on the metalwork. The window was open for another reason. The smell of Lorelei was making them all gag.

Now, they seemed to have found a clear stretch of road. Ranjana urged Mac ahead, and he put his foot down.

"How much further?" Tony's voice was harsh and clipped.

"Not far, I promise," replied Ranjana.

"Are they . . . ?"

"I don't know. I'm sorry, the messages have stopped and I'm getting . . . well, jumbled stuff."

"Christ!" Tony banged his hand on the car door. "What about it, Lorelei? Do you feel anything?"

Lorelei had not spoken since the underground chamber. Her head was still down, braids dangling. Tony forced himself to look at her. It was impossible to tell whether she was even conscious or not. He uttered a sound of disgust.

"Trouble ahead," said Mac

A crowd had suddenly appeared in the roadway, about four hundred yards ahead. Mac slowed down, and now they could see that the crowd's attention was focused on a building off to the right of the road. That building was also burning, but this didn't seem to be enough for the crowd. They were throwing missiles at it; anything they could get their hands on, bricks, lengths of wood and boarding, street signs. The fire tenders had not arrived yet, and this seemed to be another fire that was out of control. From the architecture and the aggressive attitude of the crowd, Tony guessed that it was probably a civic building.

Then the crowd saw the car coming.

"Watch it!" yelled Randall, as the first to see the car turned their attention away from the burning building and to them. A rain of bricks headed in their direction. Mac swerved hard as a brick thumped and skidded across the roof, making everyone in the car duck.

Then something cracked hard against the windscreen. Instantly, the glass cobwebbed, obscuring Mac's view.

He yanked hard at the wheel and the car screeched off to the left and away down a side street. Tony and Randall twisted in the back seat to look back as the car sped away. Half a dozen youths were chasing the car, throwing bricks. But even now, they were well out of range. The missiles bounced and exploded into fragments in the darkened roadway and then their pursuers turned back for richer pickings on the main road.

Tony and Randall turned to face front.

And then Lorelei lunged forward from her seat, shrieking like a wild animal.

She seized two handfuls of Mac's hair, dragging him back. Mac cried out in pain and alarm, one hand flying from the wheel to clutch at one of Lorelei's wrists. Shocked, Ranjana lunged from her seat, clawing at Lorelei's grip. But Lorelei clung on, even as Tony and Randall tried to drag her back into her seat.

Mac lost control of the car.

As Lorelei shrieked and shrieked and shrieked the car roared on. There was a roundabout ahead; a raised, cobbled island with a street sign. The car hit it hard, mounted the island with a juddering crash of suspension and swept straight on through the roadsign. Torn from its mounting, the sign smacked into the windscreen, imploding the already cobwebbed glass, then screeched on over the roof.

The car slammed to a halt.

And Lorelei was like a wild animal, clawing and scratching over Randall to get at the door. Winded and dazed, Tony tried to hold her back, but could not get a proper grip. Randall, still weakened from his horrific ordeal back at the church, tried to grab a handful of her hair. Lorelei shrieked in his face, fastened her teeth in his hand and tried to claw at his eyes. Randall's hands flew protectively to guard his eyes – and in the next moment Lorelei had found the door handle and twisted it open. She fell outside into the night, landed like a cat and in the next instant was running into the night: a ragged, wild blur.

"She's getting away!" shouted Ranjana, yanking open her door.

"Let her go," said Tony, shaking his head. "She's no use to us – and we're better off without her."

"He's right," said Mac simply. Already, he had shoved the car gears into reverse. The engine protested and for a moment something clattered and made a grinding noise beneath the wheels. Randall leaned out and pulled the door shut. Already, Lorelei had vanished into the night. Tony prayed that the car was still okay, that their crash hadn't damaged the chassis or the engine. And then the car slithered backwards away from the island, still with something clattering and banging beneath it. When Mac swerved and righted the car on the road, the roadsign suddenly clattered from underneath the wheels – the source of the noise. The gears made a horrific nerve-grinding clatter when Mac shoved them into first, but the engine roared into life and in moments they were headed around the island.

"Which way?"

"Right!" said Ranjana. "Next right . . ."

"Can you feel anything?" asked Tony again.

Ranjana did not answer. But he could see her tight face in the rearview mirror. Tony ran a hand over his sweating face, and the car roared on into the night.

76

Lorelei ran as well as any "sighted" person. The night was not darkness to her.

Since the psychic flood in her mind back at the church, she had fought mentally to keep her shattered defences together. But her instinct for self-preservation told her that allowing herself to be taken along with Dandridge and the others could only lead to one thing. Whatever happened, they were destined for a confrontation with Ramsden. And the last thing that she wanted now, knowing that she was the last of the Sabbarite – and the one who had wielded the killing-knife on her father – was a meeting with *him*.

Lorelei ran as never before. Her breath was tortured, her hair flying in the wind. Even now, she could sense the death vibrations in this city. Death and horror on a scale never experienced before. Although she had been bred by her father for the purpose of killing, and the reality of death was something which she not only understood but lived upon and embraced, she could feel those vibrations further eroding her mental defences. Her father was feeding well on it, and if her defences should crumble completely, she knew that her sensitivity would be her downfall. The accumulated vibrations of terror and violence in the ether must surely flood her mind and drive her insane.

Dandridge had called her insane already. How much further could she go beyond insanity, she wondered.

The sounds of screaming came from ahead. She could not "see" anyone there, but there was a crowd near – and something was happening in the crowd; something that was causing pain and terror amidst them. Somehow, she could sense that some of them were *changing* but she could not allow any exploratory psychic flash to find out more details, leaving herself open and vulnerable.

There was an alleyway at her left. Without pausing in her flight, Lorelei ran down it, feet clattering on cobblestones now. She skipped on to the sidewalk lest she give away her flight by that sound and continued on. She would have to stop soon and rest. Head down, she ran and ran. There was no meaning in time now; she had no idea how long she had been running. The alleyway seemed to go on and on for ever. Lorelei kept her head down, "looking" at her feet as she ran and ran and . . .

Lorelei staggered out from the alleyway into the open.

She collapsed to her knees, gasping for breath.

And when she looked up, she could see that she had run down to the canal. The water gleamed black in the night. Away to the the right, the factories which stood at its banks were silhouetted starkly against the night sky by the burning estates beyond.

Yes . . . yes . . .

The canal was a good place to be. Water. A protection, perhaps? She looked off to her left.

A group of figures were approaching along the canal side towards her. They were perhaps thirty yards away, only dark shapes in the night. But something about the deliberate and inexorable tread of those figures filled her with horror. Lorelei tried to rise, but her legs were too weak from the flight. She looked back along the canal to the right, where the warehouses stood.

More figures had emerged from the darkness, and were also approaching her with the same awful gait.

With each breath a sobbing gasp, Lorelei scrabbled on the ground, turning back towards the alley from which she had emerged.

More figures. Silhouettes darker than night, striding through the darkness. Eager to reach her.

There was only one way for her to go. Into the canal.

Lorelei dragged herself towards the edge. She paused, gasping for breath. Father was in there, wasn't he? His power was so strong, maybe this was the worst thing she could do. Or had he emerged? Realising with terror enfolding her that there was no other way, Lorelei continued to crawl.

And then a head suddenly thrust up over the canal side directly in front of her, spraying water.

Lorelei's heart spasmed in terror; she thrashed wildly away from it in horror. A claw-hand grabbed for her ankle and she kicked out at it as she thrashed away. The indeterminate figure fell back into the canal and water foamed over the canal side.

Lorelei twisted to look at the first figures she had seen approaching along the canal side. Suddenly, their very presence brought Lorelei's mental defence crashing. And in that crash, Lorelei realised with dawning horror that she had been manipulated. By the Serendip. In the tilting of the balance as the overwhelming forces of evil had grown and the weak forces for good had struggled to survive, that tilt had sent a pawn for evil running in a certain direction – not away from the horror, not away from her father as she had so desperately hoped – but straight into the hands of the very things she feared most.

Terrified, with each breath a racking sob, Lorelei was too exhausted to move as the ragged figures drew near. With each step, they became clearer. When she saw their terrible white and hungry faces, Lorelei tried to scream but did not have the breath. She slumped to one arm, shaking her head.

Each of the seven figures was holding something. Something that dripped with foul and poisonous canal water, just as did the figures themselves. Only twelve feet from where she crouched, they halted.

One held something that could be an arm from a tailor's dummy, still in a torn and ragged coat-sleeve and with the white fingers frozen in a clutching gesture. Another a leg, still in its torn trouser, still wearing a filth-encrusted shoe. Another a ragged bundle wrapped in clothing, the size of a man's torso. Another . . . and another . . .

But the dreadful and silent figure in the middle of that ragged group was holding something in both hands at waist level, like an offering. It was the size of a football, ragged and matted and indeterminate.

And then the eyes opened in that dark mass, eyes that could not possibly exist. Eyes that should have rotted a long time ago at the bottom of that canal.

When the mouth opened, Lorelei at last found the breath to scream.

"Et tu, Lorelei? How could you do it? To your own father." There was somehow an evil glinting of power and humour in those terrible eyes, but the horrific gargling voice which issued from that face sounded like a parent's admonition of a very small child.

"I'm sorry, Daddy," said Lorelei. In that instant, she had become that very small child.

"You're the last, my darling. The last before Lauren and her child. And you have to be punished for what you did. You know that, don't you?"

"Don't . . . don't hurt me, Daddy. I only wanted you to love me. Only wanted to be ordinary."

"You wielded the killing knife, my sweet. And you're the last. Why, this is almost poetic."

"Nobody loved me, Daddy," Lorelei began to weep. "Not even you."

"Of course I love you, my sweet."

Lorelei's tears were the tears of a lost and lonely child grieving for love and comfort. She held wide her arms to that rotting, severed head as the figures came on slowly towards her again.

"Come to Daddy," it said at the last.

77

Lauren shrank back from the top of the stairs, looking to Gerry as if he could find another way out. Gerry stood with his back to the scarred wall, looking out across the twisted criss-cross of steel girders and crumbled wooden beams. Lauren hurried back to the edge of the small platform on which they stood.

"So what do we do?" she snapped at him. Gerry just looked down and said nothing. His white face was still utterly bewildered. Lauren grabbed him by the collar with her free hand, banging his head back against that wall. "So what do we do *now*, Mr Big?"

Lauren tried to look sideways over the edge. Was it possible to climb down there to the ruined stage? If she could, then there might be a way to get to the exit again and away into the night before those things were able to catch up.

It was a thirty-foot drop. She could never make it with only one hand.

From the staircase, she heard the asthmatic wheezing and gibbering of the things that were coming; could hear the rustle and blundering fumble of their distintegrating limbs as they came on.

Sparrow? What the hell do we do?

Sparrow did not answer, and Lauren knew that wherever his energies were concentrated, it was better for them both.

Gerry blinked, as if coming out of a daze. Since Danny's sudden and hideous transformation, since reaching the top of these stairs, something like shock seemed to have robbed him of any mobility. These things should not be happening. Ramsden had told him everything, had planned everything so meticulously with him – but he had mentioned nothing about the Nektre having this kind of effect. And now, no matter how much he called out for his father in his mind the way he had taught him – no matter how much he pleaded – the Man Who Shines Black would not come to him. Since returning to his home and being attacked by Sharon, most of Gerry's mind and life had blurred. He only knew that the Man was acting through him, that everything was going according to plan. The day of getting even had come. But now, that blur was gone and Ramsden had gone. What had happened to Sharon? Had something happened to her . . . ?

Something growled from near the top of the stairs.

Gerry had been betrayed by the one person he trusted most. He had been betrayed by his father!

"*Noooo!*"

In an all-enveloping rage, Gerry lunged towards the stairhead, the pain in his leg forgotten. Lauren whirled in alarm at the sound and saw him reaching with both hands for something that was even now tottering inwards from the top step.

Danny's horribly decomposed and disintegrating skeletal face leered around the corner, one arm reaching out towards Gerry, skeletal fingers clutching at the air.

But Gerry seized that arm in both hands, screaming at the top of his voice, and dragged Danny on to the platform after him. Gerry twisted and – impossibly – flung Danny aside in one great heave. Lauren lunged backwards to the wall, holding Sparrow tight, face white in alarm. The distorted and deformed thing that had once been Gerry's henchman tottered on the edge of the platform. Screaming again, Gerry ran at Danny, raised a foot and planted it squarely in his back, shoving hard. Without a sound, Danny fell over the edge, ragged arm pinwheeling. A second later, they heard his body crash on to the ruined stage below.

Lauren hurried to the edge and looked over.

The Danny-thing lay on its back amidst the burned-out debris below, arm flailing and tattered legs thrashing amidst the wreckage. That movement was growing weaker as she looked. Lauren looked back. Gerry was still standing at the wall, breathing hard and with an insane grin on his face. The other two things were almost at the platform. There was only one way to go.

Without thinking about the height, or the possibility of falling, Lauren stepped out on to one of the ravaged girders that had once supported the floor. Swallowing hard, she stepped out along that girder and into space.

Keep walking, girl. Don't think about it. Keep walking.

The girder was ten inches wide, but Lauren refused to contemplate that width and slowly kept moving out. There was no other way. The girder connected with the far wall, but if only she could keep going and reach the far wall then maybe the things would be too clumsy to follow. Maybe they would fall apart even before they contemplated coming after her.

This place burned out and the girders held strong. So will this one . . .

(But what if the fire weakened the girder?) . . . *SO WILL THIS ONE!*

Below her, something sparked and ignited. Lauren found herself looking down against her will. Something was happening to Danny's body. His claw-arm had ceased to flail, his legs had ceased to thrash and kick. There was now no movement at all from him. But something seemed to be happening in his ribcage. There was movement deep within those shattered and decomposed innards. Movement . . . and light. Something was sparking and igniting. Suddenly, Danny's exposed ribcage erupted in flame. In a moment, that fire had spread to cover his entire body – his torso, arms and legs. Black, oily smoke began to gush from the corpse, drifting up to Lauren.

Don't look down! snapped Sparrow.

"Jesus!" Lauren tottered on the girder, one arm going out for balance.

Sorry, sorry. But don't look down.

"What is it? What's happening?"

It's the final stage of that hellish drug they've been taking. It'll burn them up. Keep going, Lauren. Keep going!

"Sparrow, what if . . . ?"

But he had gone again and Lauren continued on, step after careful step. That thick, oily black smoke was well behind her now as she continued but it was beginning to coil around the platform, obscuring it in black choking wreaths.

Behind her, Gerry suddenly realised that Lauren's route was the only way. Pushing himself away from the wall, he reached the edge of the platform, snatching at the coiling, choking smoke and trying to clear his vision. He stepped to the edge.

Something lunged from the doorway at the top of the stairs.

Gerry made to step on to a girder, saw that ragged movement and half turned. Just as Chaz's liquefying face thrust through the smoke into Gerry's own.

Gerry screamed and staggered back from the edge as those decomposing, erupting arms took him in a horrifying and ragged embrace. Gerry's hands went up defensively, cupping Chaz's chin and pushing up as Chaz tried to fasten that horrifying face on to his own in some hideous parody of a kiss. Gerry's hoarse cries of terror and revulsion intensified when his hands met nothing solid and his fingers sank into Chaz's lower face.

Chaz's face lunged forward unimpeded, engulfing Gerry's own face in that putrefying mass.

On the girder, Lauren heard the shrieking and quickened her unsteady step.

Her foot skidded.

383

Lauren's own scream echoed in the community centre as she fell.

She had almost reached a cross-section of girders at the midway stage. Lauren deliberately twisted as she fell, desperately pushing the momentum of that fall across the broader cross-section of girder and grabbing with her free hand. She landed heavily across it, keeping Sparrow tight to one side so that she would not fall on him and crush him. The impact knocked the breath from her body, and her legs were dangling over the side as she lay there. Lauren looked back the way she had come and saw . . .

Black, oily smoke drifting up from Danny's burning body and wreathing the platform at the top of the stairs. It was impossible to see what was happening there. But Lauren could hear what was happening, and wished she could not.

She could hear the scuffling, clattering sounds of feet performing a mad and shuffling dance. She could hear the grunting, animal sounds of something that was once human but was now something else. But above all, she could hear the hideous muffled screams of the gang leader who had brought her here. The desperation and pain and terror in those screams were the worst thing she had yet heard.

Deep in that smoke, on the platform, Lauren heard and saw something ignite. It was the same ignition she had seen taking place in Danny's ribcage below.

That small blossom of light suddenly erupted into a roaring ball of fire, cutting and flaring through the smoke. Lauren shrank back involuntarily as that burning, twisting mass of flame staggered, whirling, to the edge of the platform. Somewhere within that mass, she could hear a shrill and keening shriek.

Engulfed in flames from their mad and fiery embrace, Gerry and Chaz plunged over the edge of the platform. Like melting wax dummies, their joint blazing mass tumbled down on to the ruined stage in a twisting cloud of flame, directly on top of Danny's remains. The screaming stopped.

Lauren leaned over the edge of the girder. Involuntarily, she retched. But she hadn't eaten in a long time and nothing would come. Steadying herself, Lauren began to crawl along the girder, away from the flames. She didn't have the strength to stand and walk again; she would have to crawl, using only one arm and hanging on to Sparrow with the other. She dragged herself a few inches, then used her legs to push. The process was slow and painful. But at least she was moving away from the horrible conflagration on the ruined stage.

Below and behind, something popped and split in that crackling fire.

Lauren hauled herself another ten inches, pausing for breath.

Sparrow, am I hurting you, my darling?

Lauren looked back.

Just as a hideous and leering nightmare face emerged from the clouds of smoke around the platform.

"Oh, Christ . . ."

It was the thing that Gerry had called Graeme. And that face was very low on the platform, as if the thing was crawling . . . crawling through the smoke of its burning companions below, and out along the very same girder that Lauren was crawling on. There was no doubt that the thing was coming after her. For a moment, Lauren could not take her horrified eyes from that face. It was a contorted and horrifying mass; a leprous grin of disintegration. There was no nose, just the ragged bat-face gaps where the nose and nostrils had been. An eye had gone, exploded in its socket. But the other was still there, burning bright and luminous blue. It was the same glaring eye that had fixed on her from below when they first reached the top of the stairs. Changes were still taking place. The skin of Graeme's hairless scalp was blistering and bubbling, as if under heat. A rapidly decomposing arm flashed out from under that face and fastened on the girder. The leering, drooling mouth clamped shut with exertion – and Graeme began to haul himself along, after Lauren.

Lauren tore her gaze away and looked down. Could she drop Sparrow safely?

"No way."

Lauren pulled herself further along the girder, glancing back as the grinning monstrosity's arm flashed out again to grip the girder, and came on after her.

I'll swing around the girder on one arm until I'm hanging straight. Then I'll drop with Sparrow. I'll be hurt, maybe badly, but at least I have a chance to get to that exit.

Lauren looked back. The thing was falling apart – something fell from its torso even as she watched – but it didn't have a child to carry. It was bound to catch up with her.

But maybe this thing will self-destruct any second. Like the others. If I can just keep out of reach.

The thing behind her made a noise. It sounded like a snigger.

"Yeah?" snapped Lauren, turning. "Well, you can get fucked."

Keep moving, Mother!

"Sparrow!"

She's here, Lauren! She's here!

"Who, I mean what? I mean – shit! What are you talking about. This thing . . ."

Keep on the girder, Mother! Don't think about dropping. That thing's taking longer to burn out because its metabolism was different from the others. It took longer to change, it's taking longer to die.

"Thanks for the science lecture."

But it doesn't matter – because she's here! THEY'RE here!

"Who, the Seventh Fucking Cavalry?" spat Lauren, venting her fear and anger.

No, no, no! Her – and Tony!

"Tony?" Lauren snapped her head up to look out over the community centre. "Oh my God, is it him?"

He's here! Sparrow's sound of joy matched the feeling that erupted in Lauren.

"Tony, for God's sake, in here! TONY!"

The doors of the community centre juddered open and Lauren's cry of relief and joy was abruptly cut off. Sparrow had got it wrong. It wasn't Tony. It was more of Gerry's heavies, come to laugh and sneer while she dangled up there in mid-air. When they saw her hanging up there, they'd laugh and jeer and either wait until she fell, or until the thing behind her had caught up. The door had been pulled open by a big man who looked like a hobo or something. As he rushed in, he was followed by a black girl and a hard-looking young guy who certainly wouldn't be out of place in Gerry's gang.

"Come to laugh, uh?" spat Lauren. "Well, wait until you find out what happened to your leader, you . . ."

Then Tony shoved in past them and ran towards the stage.

Lauren opened her mouth to shout at him. But nothing would come. Her throat was constricted. Something that could be relief or joy, or even love, was preventing her from uttering a sound.

Tony rushed forward with the others. And then Lauren realised that their attention was fixed on the burning mass on the stage. She saw Tony's face when he saw it, saw him collapse to his hands and knees, saw him stare with horror into the flames. Then he held his head in his hands and bowed forward.

He was weeping.

"I'm not . . . not . . ." Lauren tried to speak, but the sound was barely audible. " . . . not . . ."

"Look!" The black girl was pointing up at the girders, pointing directly at her. The others looked up and saw what was happening above the stage.

"*Lauren!*" Tony leapt to his feet. "*Lauren!*"

And all Lauren could do was nod her head and weep – as the thing on the girder behind her slithered nearer.

"Oh my God, what is it?" said Ranjana in a horrified monotone when she saw the thing. It raised its claw-hand, reached out again along the girder and gripped. The next slithering motion brought it to within twelve feet of Lauren's legs.

"Lauren, keep moving!" Tony looked around desperately on the littered floor, found a chunk of masonry and stood back. When he threw it, the chunk of rock exploded against the girder on which the thing crawled. Instantly, the others had taken his lead. Mac grabbed another chunk of rock and threw it baseball-style. The rock smacked into the thing's midriff, its claw-hand wavered and gripped tight to the girder. Ranjana followed suit, hurling everything she could lay her hands on. Randall lunged into the debris, hunting for a spar of wood long enough to reach the girder.

Lauren forced herself to crawl onwards, inch by painful inch, as the others continued their bombardment. Randall found a length of wood – it was too short. Angrily, he discarded it and hunted for another. A chunk of masonry from Mac hit the thing in the face, sloughing away a chunk of skin. The smoke from the remains of Gerry and the others was billowing and choking them.

"Come on!" urged Tony. "You can do it!"

And then Graeme opened his liquefying mouth and began to howl at them.

For an instant, the sound of it froze them into inaction.

Smoke began to curl and wreath from around Graeme's torso.

As if sensing that the inner combustion was about to begin, Graeme lunged along the girder even faster than before in that horrifying slithering motion. His decaying, disintegrating face was a mask of hate. He would get to Lauren if it was the last thing he could do. Below, the others continued to hurl missiles at the thing in a frenzy. It clung tight, and continued on.

Lauren had reached the far wall. There was nowhere to go now but down, and the thing would be on her at any moment.

Tony rushed to the cornice, stood directly beneath her.

"Lauren, you have to drop him!"

"I know, I know!"

"I'll catch him. Come on!"

Mac pushed Tony aside. "No, let me."

Tony began to protest.

"Trust me," said the big man. Anxiety etched onto his face, Tony stood back. What *was* it about this man that affected him so much? "No time to think!" he shouted to Lauren. "Lower him and drop him!"

Lauren twisted around on the girder, bunched together Sparrow's shawl in her fist until she was gripping his front in a tight bundle – and began to lower herself over the edge.

Graeme hissed and howled, one lunging grab at the girder after the

387

other. Ranjana had found a beer bottle. It shattered across the thing's head. Graeme paused only momentarily to shake his head free of the glittering broken glass, and came on.

Lauren lowered herself until she was hanging by one arm from the girder, holding her Sparrow-bundle in the other.

I love you, Mother.

I . . . love you too . . . sweetheart . . .

The strain on her one arm was tremendous. She could hear as well as feel the muscles stretching in her shoulder. When that bundle was held as straight and as far down as she could manage, with the big man directly below her holding up his hands and shouting encouragement – she let him go.

The shawl opened and plumed instantly, like a streamer-parachute.

Lauren cried out when Sparrow twisted and spun out of the shawl, plummeting downwards to leave the shawl drifting in the air.

Mac readjusted by a step and caught the child in one fluid, swinging catch. He whirled with Sparrow, and held him close to this chest. The child made no noise. He looked quickly at his face. Sparrow was dazed, but fine.

And then everything happened very fast.

Graeme, his distorted body now wreathed in oily smoke, gave vent to a hideous scream of pain and rage, lunged across the girder in an impossibly fast, slithering motion – and seized Lauren's wrist.

"Quick!" Mac thrust Sparrow into Tony's arms. The child quickly wrapped his own arms around his neck and hugged tight as Tony instinctively whirled to the wall. Mac shoved them both out of the way and yelled, *"Now, Lauren! Drop now!"*

Lauren let go of the girder and dropped – her weight dragging the Graeme thing off the girder with her. Lauren twisted as she fell, and the thing's grip was torn away. In the next instant, Mac had lunged to position himself directly below her fall. She hit him hard, and both of them went down to the littered floor in a tangle of limbs. Graeme twisted away and crashed on to the stage area, claw-arms and legs flailing and gushing smoke.

Tony moved to help, but already Mac was on his feet, dragging Lauren with him. She was dazed, but they both appeared unhurt. Breath coming in sobs, Lauren fell against Tony. He took her and they embraced, Sparrow in the middle and with an arm around each of their necks. Despite the terror and the urgency of their situation, Tony could not believe how *good* that embrace felt. In the brief and flashing contact of their eyes before that embrace, he knew that Lauren felt the same way.

Not a good time for tears, said the child. *No time at all!*

But the tears were there for them both anyway as Mac shoved them aside.

The thing which had fallen on the stage was thrashing to rise. The fall had not stopped it; even now it was lunging through the burned-out timbers of the stage, lashing through the debris to get at them, scattering ash and with smoke gushing from its torso.

Lauren twisted to look back.

"Watch out!" she yelled. "It's going to burn!"

Graeme erupted from the stage, clambering on to the ruined stone stairs that Gerry had once used to "rally his troops". Throwing wide his smoking claw-arms he shook his head and uttered an inhuman shriek of rage. Viscous fluid spattered them. Somewhere deep inside his ragged torso, something ignited, lighting up his decaying ribcage and innards for an instant before the smoke billowed and enveloped him again. That hideous head swung around and fixed on its nearest target, knowing that death was near.

It was Mac.

Shrieking, the thing leapt from the stairs directly at him in a billowing cloud of black smoke.

Something hit Mac hard from behind before he could decide what to do. The impact threw him heavily to the debris-ridden floor. In the next moment, Randall had swung up the charred wooden spar that he had discarded earlier when they had tried to dislodge the thing from the girder.

The Graeme-thing landed straight on the stake, and was instantly impaled. The force and velocity of the thing's lunge carried it straight on over Randall as he ducked down to his haunches. The momentum of that death-lunge whipped the stake from his hands. The thing slammed face-down to the floor behind them, ramming the spar out through its back. Thrashing in the debris, it struggled to rise, the spar jutting from its back by a jagged four feet. Everyone remained frozen in shock. Lauren shouted again, "Keep away from it! It's going to burn!"

But already it was rising to what was once its knees and twisting its hideous head to screech back at them.

"Be nice," said Randall grimly as he strode towards it.

"No!" yelled Ranjana when she saw his intention. But she was too late.

Randall seized the stake protruding from the thing's back and shoved down hard, twisting to the side when the thing tried to grab for him. It screeched and thrashed there as smoke belched from its body, enveloping Randall. But Randall kept his weight on the stake, leaning down hard and pinning the monstrous thing to the floor. He turned his head away as the smoke engulfed him, choking for air. But his grip was unbreakable.

And then, with an oily *whump!* the thing was instantly enveloped in flame. A great surging blanket of fire erupted from its innards, surging like petrol-flame to its decayed arms and legs. It screeched and twisted, but Randall was with it every inch of the way, keeping his weight on that stake and the burning man-shape as its blazing arms and legs flapped weakly on the floor, scattering flying specks of soot and ash.

Ranjana grabbed his arm at last and dragged him away from the stake. The arms and legs continued to flap, but it was never going to rise again.

"You just can't reason with some people," he said simply as Ranjana pulled him away. She held him tight.

For a long time, they watched the burning shape on the floor, saying nothing.

78

Ranjana led Randall back to join the others beside the stage. Despite the billowing smoke from the far side of the stage and the Graeme-thing on the floor, no one seemed inclined to leave the building just yet. Mac rose to his feet as Randall drew level, placed a hand on his shoulder – and nodded. The expression on his face and the look in his eyes conveyed much more than words could do for saving his life.

"Reckon we've got something in common now, Mac."

"Apart from an ability to stay alive?"

Randall laughed. "Yeah, so far. But no – that's not what I mean. I've seen what you've seen, Mac. I've been there. Back there in the church, at the bottom of that bloody grave, I was dying. I saw the tunnel of light . . . and the darkness. I was on my way there, and you both brought me back."

"Welcome to the club, son," smiled Mac. "I've seen it so many times, I reckon I should have a season ticket."

"How about it, Ranjana?" asked Randall. "Does that make *me* dead and alive, as well?"

Ranjana tried to smile, but couldn't make it convincing. Her feeling about Mac remained the same. He radiated a strange aura. There was the sense of a great mystery about the man, something that she could not touch no matter how hard she tried. Even her heightening powers of perception as the nightmare unfolded could not bring her any nearer to the answer.

Outside in the night, the sounds of caterwauling police sirens and fire-engines still drifted to them; but now somehow an eerie calm descended on them all after the frantic and violent confrontations they had experienced. Were the sounds outside really a part of their nightmare? It was a shared feeling. After the chase to get to the community centre in time to save Lauren – someone they didn't know but whose existence they had taken on trust – Mac, Randall and

Ranjana were feeling a curious dislocation: a dislocation compounded by the thing that they had just confronted and killed, something that by rights should not exist but was yet another horrendous part of the nightmarish jigsaw puzzle in which they found themselves. Randall and Ranjana held each other tight. Their first meeting down by the river, and their encounter with the street gang, seemed a million miles away in time.

Mac sat watching them, and then looked at the others. Tony, Lauren and the child, looking like a ready-made family as they clung to each other. Mac turned away so that they could not see the expression on his face, and put a hand on his shoulder. He grimaced in pain. He had taken the full force of Lauren's fall, and had hurt his shoulder in the process. The pain was bad, but when he looked down at his hand he saw that he could still flex his fingers.

Tony looked over at Mac. Why did he feel that he knew this man, when he had clearly never met him before in his life? He stroked Lauren's hair and watched him flexing his fingers. Something about the big man was affecting him profoundly – but he could not rationalise it.

Is this a good time to talk? asked Sparrow.

No, replied Lauren. *We need this time together.*

It's important.

Not yet, Sparrow . . .

Mother, I have to be CHANGED!

Ranjana laughed and when Lauren looked over, she said, "I'm sorry. I didn't mean to eavesdrop – but I can hear what he's saying."

"You can?"

"It's thanks to him that we're here. He sent me messages, told me how to find you."

"So that's what you were doing," Lauren said to the bundle between Tony and herself.

Ranjana is the empath I was telling you I could sense. I've been feeling her presence for a long while. I think the Serendip helped us out there Lauren.

"Are you psychic?" Ranjana asked Lauren.

"No, I can hear Sparrow – but that's all. He tells me that we can communicate that way because of the mother/child bond."

"He has a nice voice," said Ranjana, moving away from Randall to join them. "How old is he?"

"Eight months going on eighteen years," replied Lauren with a laugh.

"Excuse me," said Tony. "But this conversation's going to be a little difficult for everyone else if we can only hear part of it."

"Sorry," said Lauren.

Ahem, any chance of a change of nappy? I'm a little wet.

"Please." Ranjana held out her hands. "Can I?"

Lauren smiled and handed over the child. The small changing bag was where Tomelty had left it by the stairs. She retrieved it and Ranjana got on with the job.

"I suppose we better fill Lauren in on everything that's happened," said Tony and recounted the nightmare. Lauren listened intently, and when he had finished she told them all everything that had happened to her including what had happened to the Sabbarite back at the church. She was visibly stunned when she found out that the figure who had stopped Bradford from killing her and who had ended up being buried alive was Randall. She had not recognised him.

When she had finished, Sparrow said: *We have to talk.*

Lauren and Ranjana exchanged looks.

'I'll speak for you, Sparrow," said Lauren.

Ranjana stood up, still holding him. The others looked at her.

"Sparrow's got something to say – as he speaks, I'll just repeat it for everyone, okay?" Randall and Mac moved forward until they were all sitting and standing in a tight ring. Outside, the police sirens still wailed and a noise like thunder seemed to break in the sky – signs of another burning building collapsing into the street. They all knew that they were relying on what the child had to say, and that whatever he did say would be taking them further in to the nightmare and not out of it.

"Okay, Sparrow," said Lauren, "Let's go . . ." Lauren paused to wipe her stained face, and then continued. "There's only one way to stop Ramsden. He's free now – free of the canal and ready to . . . what? . . . ready to *reconstitute*. That means he's ready to become whole again, take living shape. But that process involves Sparrow. His body and his life force. The street gang who brought us here killed the Sabbarite and brought us back here on Ramsden's orders. He's on his way now. So we had better make ourselves scarce pretty soon. But the only way to stop him . . . is to return to the place where Sparrow was conceived, the actual building. That's important. Since I was, as you might say, present on that occasion, I can tell you where it is. The place we've just come from. The deconsecrated church back in Stanton. So I'm sorry, folks, it means another journey back through those streets, back the way you came. And I have to warn you that things on the street are much, much worse – and getting worse all the time . . ."

Lauren paused and flashed a look at Ranjana. For a moment, Ranjana looked bewildered and horrified – then quickly covered her expression. The others hadn't seen the exchange taking place, and were waiting for Lauren to continue.

"We've got to go back there – and then Sparrow will call to Ramsden. Tell him to follow."

"Shouldn't we be getting the hell *away* from him?" said Randall. "Not letting him come to us."

"We have to try and finish him," continued Lauren. "Sparrow doesn't know how to do that yet, he's still searching for that information. Once we're back at the church, at the place he was conceived, he's sure that we can at least find a way of trying. Don't you see? We're all bound up in this together. Ramsden has put his mark on all of us for opposing him. Even if we turn and run away, he'll still find us, still find a way of finishing us – and it won't be pleasant."

Randall nodded grimly. His question had been a complaint, not a genuine suggestion. "Reckon he'd conjure up one of those Mechanic things."

"That's right," said Lauren. "He's made pacts with the other side. He'd have the ability."

"Then we'd better get moving," said Ranjana. "What other choice do we have?"

"None," said Lauren and Sparrow at the same time.

Outside in the night, another burning building exploded into rubble with a distant roar.

79

They walked through the burning night, unheeded and untouched by the violence and the terror and the death which surrounded them.

From the same shop doorways and darkened corners, the Dead waited and listened to those hideous sounds, knowing that the one with whom they had made the pact was drawing power with every scream, with every act of violence, with every death and with every horrifying "meltdown" engendered by the drug which they had supplied to him from the other side.

Only the seven bearers walked in this last night. The others waited in darkness, some watching them pass on their way to the last rendezvous. Debts would soon be honoured on both sides in this bargain. And once the reconstitution had taken place – the last act – then they would be free for ever. Free from the torment, and free to pursue whatever earthly pleasures they desired.

The doorway had been closed, and they knew with something approaching humour that they were despised and hated by those they had left behind. Despised because those others had not been given the chance to be smuggled across the border; hated because they were free.

On command, the seven bearers remained silent and still on the littered slope overlooking the community centre. The ragged figure in the centre of that group held up that which it clasped in both hands, like some kind of trophy. This was a moment to savour.

The moment of deliverance.

The figures descended the slope and crossed the flickering shadows of destruction towards the building. All around, the estate was burning. Power was emanating from every fire, crackling like static electricity in the ether.

The centre figure moved forward to the main entrance, stood back – and then kicked the front door aside.

They entered.

Moments later, the screams of rage began.

Screams of hatred and malice that resounded and echoed throughout the building, drifting into the night, and mingling with the sounds of death and destruction all around.

"Where are YOOOOUUUUU???"

80

It took a lot longer to get back to Stanton than the first journey from Stanton to the community centre. This time, Mac was forced to make six detours to avoid running crowds of people or looters and on two occasions the route was blocked by fallen masonry and burning rubble. The car had also been damaged by the crash on to the traffic island, and each change of the gears resulted in a grinding screech which seemed to draw attention to them as they sped through the night.

Ranjana had a ridiculous flash of guilt about the man from whom they'd stolen the car; ridiculous given the comparison between his loss and the whole series of nightmarish experiences they had endured. As Mac twisted the wheel and found new and hopefully quieter side streets to avoid trouble, she tried to catch Lauren's eye. They were both in the back seat now, with Randall. Tony sat next to Mac up front. But it seemed as if Lauren was deliberately trying to avoid contact, keeping her gaze fixed on the car window. Ranjana had heard everything that Sparrow had said to Lauren as she "translated" for the others. But she had left one very important and horrifying fact out, one very important statement that Sparrow had made.

I've been searching the Serendip, trying to make sense of the scales and balances. I can't find out what kind of chance we have against Father. I only know that it isn't good – but I have found something out. Something bad. One of us, if not all – but certainly one of us – will die. The Serendip suggests an innocent death in the battle we've got ahead. And it will *happen.*

So the chances are that none of them would come out of this thing alive. But certainly one was to die. Who would it be?

That's the point, said Sparrow in her head.

Ranjana looked at the child, and saw that it was staring intently at Lauren. When she looked at Lauren's face again, she could see that she had turned from the window to look directly into her eyes. Sparrow had overheard Ranjana's thoughts and conveyed them to Lauren – now

Lauren was speaking directly to her, this time using *Sparrow* as a translator.

It's going to happen. God knows what lies ahead of us back at that church, but I can tell you that it won't be pleasant. If I'd told them what Sparrow had said back there, everyone would be wondering: is it going to be me? We would paralyse ourselves with fear, may not be able to do what we have to do. Don't you see that?

Ranjana looked down, biting her lip. When she looked up again, she nodded. Sparrow turned to look at her for her answer.

You're right. I wasn't thinking.

Lauren leaned over and took her hand.

It might be me or you.

Well, let's just keep it to ourselves, thought Ranjana – and Lauren gripped her hand, turning again to look out into the night.

They were lucky. Although it was clear that things on the estate were very bad indeed, they didn't fall foul of any stone-throwing crowds. It seemed that the actual organisation of the riot had fallen apart. Occasionally, somewhere in the night, they could hear a howling or shrieking that was not a police or fire-engine siren – or anything human. They remembered what had happened to the Nektre-takers back at the community centre, and thought about all the others who had taken the drug on the streets.

Tony watched Mac's face as he drove. It seemed unnatural, as if the man was wearing some kind of mask. It was a curious sight, and something which just served to fuel the strange feeling which the big man engendered in him. On several occasions, he thought about talking to him as they travelled through the night. But their terrible situation and the prospect of even further horrifying ordeals ahead seemed to make that sort of discussion redundant. There was something about this man . . . something . . .

Stanton was still deathly quiet when they pulled off the main road and took the turning. Ranjana had half expected to see the owner of the car walking in the middle of the road in front of them, but he had long since gone. She supposed that his angry report about the theft had fallen on deaf ears at the nearest police station, given what was happening in the city tonight.

It didn't take Mac long to find the abandoned church again.

The silent shadows of the two cars which had brought the Sabbarite to their last rendezvous were still standing at the side entrance. The sight of the spire-less church and those cars made Lauren feel physically sick. Randall too seemed to be deeply affected. He leaned forward in the back seat and began to breathe heavily. Ranjana put an arm around both of them, herself feeling sick with fear but realising just what horror they had both endured already. Randall looked back at her.

"Never did like going to church," he said – and managed a smile.

Mac pulled the car up next to the others.

Without speaking, they climbed out into the night.

The night air should have been cold, just as it was when they had last been here. But somehow the edge had been taken off that chill. Could it be that the air was being warmed by the hundreds of fires in the city, the burning civic buildings and the police stations?

As they entered the side gates, Lauren forced herself not to think about the last time she had been forced here, tried to keep that horrifying memory at bay as they walked around the darkened side of the church – the memory that she was going with Sparrow to certain death. Because that memory, that relived horror would only feed the fear she was already feeling, and might well rob her of the strength to act.

At the ruined church portico and entrance, beside the great tumbled mass of masonry which had once been the church spire, they paused – and Lauren knew that the others were expecting her to lead them inside. Holding her breath for a moment, she tried to calm her nerves – and then stepped into that darkness within. The echoing sound of their footsteps was a familiar sound.

When they emerged from that greater darkness into the gloom of the ruined church itself, the stars were no longer visible through the shattered roof. Clouds of smoke had mingled with the night to make a grey-black barrier. It was as if the universe around them had ceased to exist. Lauren walked on ahead down the debris-strewn aisle. The others followed close behind, and no one spoke.

At the shattered altar, buried beneath the fallen masonry, Lauren turned.

The others gathered around her.

"Are you getting anything yet?" Lauren asked Sparrow aloud, for the benefit of the others. "Yes?" Lauren paused while she listened. "Okay, he's starting to sift – as he calls it. One thing's certain. Ramsden has discovered that we're not at the community centre."

"And he's pissed off," added Ranjana.

"You surprise me," said Tony.

"He doesn't know where we are yet, but he's working on it," continued Lauren. "Sparrow's trying to cloak – sorry, that means he's trying to keep where we are secret until he finds out more. Sooner or later, though, Ramsden will find out where we are."

Tony shuffled uneasily. "Where . . . where was Sparrow conceived?"

Lauren laughed. A bitter sound, without humour. "In less than romantic circumstances. Here in the aisle. On the floor. The pleasure was all Ramsden's."

Tony cursed himself inwardly for feeling the way he did about it, then asked, "Does it make a difference where we have to be, then? I mean, you said that we had to be back at the place of conception, but does it have to be right on the spot that it . . . happened?"

"Tony, don't lose track of what this is all about," said Lauren, "I was drugged high as a kite for the purpose, didn't know *what* the hell was going on. It was all part of Ramsden's plan. I told you that."

"Okay, okay."

Lauren turned back to Sparrow. "So, what about it, kid? Where do we go now?"

Another pause. Then Lauren nodded.

"Yeah, that makes sense." Turning to the others, she said, "As long as we're here in the building, that's the important thing. But we need a place we can defend. And I'm afraid that means it's back to that underground chamber, people. Thought we'd seen the last of it. But there you go."

Mac pushed on ahead towards the iron-studded door. The others followed, but when Mac pushed it open there was no light from below.

"Shit!" exclaimed Lauren. "Those candles have burned out."

"How about this?" said Randall, taking the flashlight from under his jacket and switching it on.

"Where did you get that?" asked Ranjana.

"The boot of the car, before we set off again. Reckoned we might need it."

"Would have made a great boy scout," said Tony.

"I lasted for three days, and was drummed out for conduct unbecoming." Randall's face as he switched on betrayed the tension behind his jocular remark. Mac made to take it from him so that he could go first. Randall waved that it was okay, and headed down the staircase. The others followed.

There was a new smell down here. Sweet, sickly and almost overpowering. The smell of the burned-out candles – or the smell of something else? No one raised the issue as they reached the chamber.

"We need more light," said Mac.

"That sarcophagus over there in the corner," said Lauren. "Sparrow says that there are more of those black candles in there."

While Randall shone the flashlight over the chamber to the sarcophagus, Mac hurried to it. They all tried to ignore the ragged shapes that the flashlight picked up in the darkness. The lid had been shoved to one side by Bradford – late of the Sabbarite – and Mac looked in to see a carefully arranged pattern of broken stained-glass window

400

shards. Lying around them were piles of black candles. Mac grabbed handfuls and hurried back to the steps. Silently, he handed them out. Tony had matches – and they began their silent round of the chamber while Randall shone the flashlight, still trying hard to ignore the bodies, and what had been done to them. It was difficult to do.

Soon, the chamber was lit by dozens of candles.

Randall looked at the ragged hole from which he had been dragged, and the feeling of suffocation threatened to overwhelm him again. Angrily, he turned from it and jammed the flash at the foot of the stairs so that the beam gave maximum illumination.

Lauren held Sparrow tight and tried to control her breathing. It was the same scene of Hell. As Randall passed, she took his arm.

"I never did get a chance to thank you properly for what you did."

"When it's over, we'll have a party," smiled Randall tightly. He squeezed her hand.

Is it him, Sparrow? Is he the one to die?

I don't know, Mother. I don't think I'll be allowed to know. Does it matter? We're all probably going to die, anyway.

You KNOW that?

No – and look, you're interrupting me.

Sorry . . .

"We've got to clear these . . . people out of the way," said Tony.

"You're right," said Mac, and something about the way he said it, the inflection in his voice, gave Tony that strange feeling again.

Randall gritted his teeth and joined them in dragging the Sabbarite to the side of the church. It was not a pleasant task, and when Randall came to drag Bradford away, he discovered at last what had happened to her. The fact that she had been trying to kill Lauren and her child at the time didn't make him feel any better.

When they had finished, Lauren cleared her nervous throat and spoke to them.

"Sparrow still isn't . . . isn't able to get anything specific. There's only one way, as he said before. We have to let Ramsden come here. We don't know how he'll come – or what he'll bring with him. But we have to let him come. Down here. With us. Sparrow says that the only chance he has – that *we* have – is for Ramsden to be in close proximity to him, bringing with him the power that he's soaking up. Sparrow might be able to tap into that. So – we have to make Ramsden think that we're going to give him what he wants. Sparrow. Make him think that we want to do some kind of deal."

"You mean like we're betraying the child or something?" said Ranjana. "Like we're using Sparrow to bargain with him?"

"Yes."

401

"But isn't it going to seem unlikely that Sparrow would tell him where he is, would call him here if he knows Ramsden wants him dead?" Tony was wiping his hand with disgust on his trouser leg.

"Sparrow can send the message in a particular way," continued Lauren. "Use his powers to cloak that message. Make him feel he's terrified. That we've vowed to kill him if he doesn't bargain with Ramsden on our behalf. Or I should say, *your* behalf – since he's also going to say that you've killed me to prove you mean business. Sparrow will make out that his only chance of survival, of living, is to let Ramsden come and absorb his life force. At least he'll still 'exist'."

"You said Ramsden's really powerful," said Ranjana. "Won't he sense he's lying? Won't he be able to see through it?"

Lauren shrugged. "We hope not."

"So we sit and wait for him to come?" said Mac.

"Christ, I'd give anything for a drink or a cigarette," said Randall. "Don't suppose you found any communion wine in that coffin-thing, did you? Or a box of twenty?"

Mac laughed and shook his head. "Don't you know? That stuff can kill you."

This time when they laughed, there seemed to be something about the sound. Despite the gut-wrenching tension and the horror ahead, it was a good sound.

"Ready?" asked Lauren, sitting on the rough stone stairs with the child.

The others nodded in unison.

"Sparrow?"

The child closed his eyes.

81

The candles gutter in the chamber, making it alive with the movement of shadows. But that is the only movement now. The night drags on, and now the fear has settled in their souls, like some dormant and dangerous beast. That fear will reawaken at any time, and all they can do now is try to rest their bodies. The time for talking is over. There is nothing more they can say.

Lauren sits with her back to the sarcophagus, trying not to think about how many Sabbarite murders have taken place down here, tries not to think about the graves and the things that burrowed their way to the outside and are now walking the streets. Even Sparrow is quiet. The call has been made and he has withdrawn quickly from the ether lest Ramsden be able to "home in" and discover the subterfuge. Lauren looks at him and wonders what the future holds. Is there any hope for them? The child looks directly into her eyes, and the expression is enough to steer her away from these bad thoughts. She hugs him, and wonders what a normal life would be like.

Tony stands at the sarcophagus looking down at Lauren and Sparrow. He feels drained and confused. So much has happened to him. The reality of the nightmare that he has been living has killed the other nightmares of Mount Longdon and the Falklands. He thinks back to the times before Lauren came into his life and can't believe that he felt life had dealt him bad cards. Nothing in his previous existence – no, not even the Falklands and that last horrifying encounter – can compare with the horrors he has seen in the last few days. But something else has entered his life, something that he could never have envisaged, something that he hasn't considered logically, simply hasn't had the time to weigh up. And that's the way he feels about Lauren now. He knows that she feels the same. But how long will that last? Will that all end for ever when Ramsden makes his appearance? Tony remembers the eve of battle when he was a soldier, remembers the fear in his guts just before they went into action. It feels like that now – but worse. Because then, he was facing flesh and blood realities; now, he is confronting things that defy logic and have their own rules. He looks down at Lauren and Sparrow again. Whatever comes, he's going to fight to keep what he's found and will not give it up readily . . .

Ranjana sits next to Randall, holding his hand – and thinks about this thing that Tony and Lauren have called the Serendip. Scales and balances between good and evil, they said. But if the scales can be tilted, and events sometimes manipulated and manoeuvred, what does that mean for Randall and herself? When did that manipulation begin? Was she meant to run away from home? Was the arranged marriage all part of that manipulation? How much of this has all been free will and how much part of this great tilting of balances? Ranjana tries to think through the logic as a means of keeping the fear at bay. She has closed down her psychic link, does not want to explore the way that she's now learned to do. She can sense the great powers abroad and fears that tuning into them will burn her mind into insanity. The Serendip, yes, the Serendip! Was she meant to find Randall? Was that all part of the complicated chain of events that led her to Mac and the Sabbarite and Sparrow?

Randall thinks about the tunnel of light, and what his grandmother told him about it. He's seen what lies at the moment of death, but he cannot forget that other hideous light at the end of the tunnel, cannot forget the crossroads leading to one or the other. Grandma never mentioned that there were two places at the end of that tunnel. Does that mean that because she had lived such a good life the light place was the only logical destination for her when she died? Or did she also see that place and just not tell him about it? No, it wasn't there for her – otherwise, why should she tell him the story to comfort him? Randall thinks about the dull, glowing thing covered in membranes, like some gigantic, closed eye. If the light place is Heaven, does that mean that the other place is Hell? Does such a place exist after all? Tony and Lauren have referred to it as another dimension, the place where Ramsden has come back from, the place where the dead street people have escaped from. If and when he dies, will he go there? Randall ponders this all, and wonders what he can do if and when he dies. He squeezes Ranjana's hand and she gives him a tight smile. He has never held a woman's hand like this before . . .

Mac struggles with the confusion in his mind. The new clarity that Ranjana's presence has brought seems to be clouding again. He ignores the throbbing pain in his shoulder, the pain caused by Lauren's fall, and concentrates instead on the confusing images which flash through his mind. The numbers are back again repeating over and over again. Three, seven, four, oh-two. Three, seven, four, oh-two. Three, seven four . . . and Mac has a renewed fear inside. A fear that his mind is drifting back again into the bad and forgotten place. He puts the palms of his hands to his eyes, and tries to squeeze the images away. The faceless soldiers are running through the night. The sounds of gunfire and of men wounded and dying. The silhouette of a man with his dripping hose of fire ... go away! Go away! Go away!

Incredibly, sleep ambushes them all. Even though a hideous threat is on its way, exhaustion takes its toll. Not one of them realises that it has happened. But it has come, and hours pass, and the night burns on, and ...

82

HE'S HERE! screamed Sparrow.

And somehow that psychic scream was heard by everyone in the chamber.

Instantly, they were awake. And so was the internal fear that they had all been struggling to contain until exhaustion had dragged them into sleep.

Lauren clambered to her feet from the base of the sarcophagus, Tony grabbing her arm as he also rose. The temptation to believe that everything was just a bad dream was very strong. Lauren turned away, and then Tony pulled her back. They embraced quickly – and then Lauren handed Sparrow to Tony as planned and hurried to the far wall, where the dead Sabbarite had been dragged. Mac, Ranjana and Randall moved to join Tony and Sparrow at the sarcophagus as she passed. Mac and Randall had two spades. Their attention remained fixed on the stairwell and the darkness beyond.

Lauren looked down and saw the hideously white, blood-streaked face of Collins. Her stomach revolted. Angry at herself and her lack of control, Lauren stooped and dragged the body aside. In the next moment, she had lain down next to it, amidst the other bodies. From her position, she could see the others and the doorway.

In her mind, Sparrow whimpered.

And as the others focused their dread on the doorway, and what might emerge from the darkness at any moment, Lauren realised just how much they had all come to rely on the child. She dared not throw a comforting thought at him, lest Ramsden somehow pick it up – and that knowledge fuelled not only a blossoming of mother-instinct but also a cold, hard rage. *All right, you bastard! So you're dead!* Lauren had resolved to try and keep her mind as blank as possible, but the anger consumed her. *You're dead – and you're probably not a pretty sight, all that time in a fucking canal. But we're ready for you. Right, Sparrow?*

Sparrow ceased to whimper.

And there was a noise from the doorway.

The sounds of someone descending. No – not one person. But the scuffling, shambling sounds of several people.

The others braced themselves. Mac and Randall raised their spades defensively.

The candles guttered as if a wind had entered the chamber. But there was no wind. Only the sounds of those who descended, and the wild dancing shadows in the chamber.

The seven bearers shambled across the threshold, heads down as if in obeisance. Each of them was carrying something, and they were leaving a trail of filth and dirty water behind them as they came. The others shrank back against the sarcophagus. Mac and Randall kept their spades raised.

And then, as if on command, the seven figures raised their heads to look at them.

They were the same hideously white, dead and hungry faces of the street people who had attacked Mac, Ranjana and Randall. Faces that had brought terror and fear. But somehow, impossibly, their grim and familiar presence was not as horrifying as the gnawing fear in their guts had led them to expect. Mac and Randall exchanged looks, then nodded as they stepped in front of Tony and Ranjana with their weapons.

But at last, they could now see what the seven bearers had brought with them.

"Oh my God . . ." said Ranjana with sick horror. And at her words, the dripping remains seemed to emit a revolting stench. On the other side of the chamber, Lauren jammed a hand into her mouth. The sight of those rotting and severed limbs was bad enough for the others, but it had a much more pronounced effect on her. Whatever had happened, Lauren could not rid her mind of past images. That man had cosseted her once, had hypnotised her. She remembered his eau de cologne, the drugged intimacies. Those hideous and rotting lips had once kissed her, those hands had caressed and stripped her. And of course, he had penetrated her.

The centre figure stepped forward to the steps leading down into the chamber. As if making an offering, the vagrant held up Ramsden's severed and rotting head.

Oh Christ, thought Ranjana. *Is that a* smile *on his face?*

The figure came down the stairs and the others followed.

Still holding his spade defensively, Randall moved forward. But Mac grabbed his arm and held him back.

One by one the street people moved slowly past them at the

sarcophagus, into the centre of the chamber. Carefully, reverentially, they began to lay the severed parts of Ramsden's anatomy on the soil floor. The others watched in fascinated horror. They had laid those pieces in rough approximation of order, like some hideous jigsaw puzzle of a corpse.

The figures stood back, looking down at their handiwork.

Again, at a given command, they turned and headed back for the stairs.

The others tensed again. But the figures did not come near them.

But as they passed, they turned their heads to grin hideously. Now there could be no mistaking what was taking place. This was the last part of the pact, the last part of their bargain. Ramsden had been returned for the reconstitution and their debt was almost honoured. Very soon, they would be free. But for the time being they were dismissed from this place.

They watched the street people file silently back through the archway and up the stairs. Darkness enfolded them once more. The others waited and listened. Soon, the scuffling sounds had ceased – and the street people had gone.

"Mac! Randall!" snapped Ranjana. "Sparrow says follow them up – but stay at the door at the top of the stairs."

Mac and Randall looked at each other, not believing that the street people hadn't attacked them, just as they'd attacked before.

"Go on!" snapped Ranjana again. "Do it!"

Still holding on to their spades, Mac and Randall darted up the stairs and vanished into the doorway.

"LAUREN!"

The voice seemed to fill the chamber, at once deeply powerful and sepulchral. Tony moved away from the sarcophagus trying to locate the source of the voice. Ranjana whirled, looking from floor to ceiling.

"Don't add insult to injury, my darling. Do you really think that playing dead is going to help you?"

Tony hurried towards Lauren as she climbed to her feet. Her face was a ghastly white.

"Christ, Tony. It's him. It's Ramsden."

"Playing dead is what I'VE been doing. And oh, what entertaining games I have in store for you."

"Where the hell is he?" said Tony.

"Why, I'm HERE. You invited me, remember?"

From the top of the stairs, Mac shouted, "Those bloody things are still there. Standing in the middle of the church and looking up at the sky. Like they're waiting or something."

"The head," said Ranjana, swallowing hard. "Look at the head."

"*Do you really think that after everything I've planned, you're going to be able to stop me?*"

Tony and Lauren followed Ranjana's gaze to the putrefying remains on the chamber floor. There was movement around the head – and when they looked again in horror, they could see without doubt that those lips were moving. And a liquid glinting in the candlelight revealed, impossibly, that Ramsden's eyes were open.

"*I commend you, Lauren. On being able to keep one step ahead of the Sabbarite. It should please you to know that our august society no longer exists. My colleagues assisted in . . . disbanding it. Your fellow survivors should also be congratulated – but I'm afraid that your efforts are to no avail.*"

They whirled at the sound of more clattering footsteps on the stone stairs. Mac and Randall burst back into the chamber again, and came to a staggering halt when they heard the voice.

"*Did you think that you could so easily be rid of me, Lauren? Didn't I tell you that I had other, greater plans?*"

"Modesty was never one of your strong points." Lauren could not disguise the trembling in her voice.

"*The child is quiet. Don't you want to welcome your father?*"

Sparrow remained silent.

"*Such ingratitude. You were conceived for a purpose, boy. I will live again in you. It's time to fulfil your destiny.*"

"You can't have him, Pearce," said Lauren.

The sound of Ramsden's laughter filled the chamber; an evil and indulgent sound.

"*And who's to stop me? A pathetic band of frightened little people – and a child.*"

Not quite so pathetic as you might think, Father! snapped Sparrow. *Lauren, get Mac and Randall to bar the door at the top of the stairs.*

Ramsden laughed again. "*Spirit, such spirit!*"

"Mac, Randall! Get back up there and bar the door any way you can. Quick!"

Mac and Randall vanished again.

You underestimate me, Father, continued Sparrow. *In a way, you even underestimate your own powers. I'm from your seed, you seem to forget that. And while you've been – gone – I've been growing. Keeping my psychic presence hidden from you, but growing nevertheless.*

"You have exhausted my patience, sweet ones," said Ramsden. "*It is time to begin.*"

From upstairs came the sounds of something heavy being dragged through the iron-studded door, Mac and Randall had retrieved a section of shattered wooden pew and were trying to jam it up against the inside of the door.

Back in the underground chamber, the others watched in horror as the dismembered pieces of Ramsden's corpse began to move. Those decayed and ragged arms were twitching and writhing, the spectrally white, semi-skeletal fingers groping and clutching at the soil. The tattered, filth-encrusted legs were juddering spasmodically; the disgusting mass of Ramsden's torso suddenly writhing with life, as if maggots seethed and fed beneath the rotted clothes. Only the head was still, the glittering eyes watching what was happening with insane glee, the lips spread wide in a hideous grin of decay.

Lauren! said Sparrow. *There is a way to stop him. So simple it's almost ridiculous. Tell the others!*

Lauren snapped out of the horrified trance engendered by the hideous squirming movement in the centre of the chamber. "Listen, Sparrow is telling me . . ." Tony and Ranjana remained frozen. "LISTEN!" She snatched the baby back from Tony, her face a mask of desperate conviction. They turned to her, and when she spoke again, it was with Sparrow's voice once more.

"There's a way! A ridiculously simple way to stop him. But we've got to be strong. Do you understand, it's not going to be pleasant – but we've got to be strong!"

"Okay, Lauren," said Tony.

Nodding grimly, Lauren looked back once at the squirming mass on the floor – and then hurried to the stone steps, shouting up the stairwell.

"Mac, you stay at the door. Keep it shut! Randall, back down here. We need you!"

Lauren turned back, walking towards the squirming mass.

Behind her, Randall emerged from the doorway, breathing heavily, holding his spade like an axe. "We've wedged a spar up against the door, I think it's going to . . ." He stopped halfway down the stairs, staring in disbelief at the horrifying spectacle.

"Remember what I said," continued Lauren. "We've got to be *strong*! Randall, bring your spade. Tony, Ranjana, find something – anything – to fight with."

Tony pulled the iron-railing out of the ground as Randall came down the stairs. Ranjana looked around, could only find a chunk of fallen masonry, the size of a housebrick.

"We've only got minutes," continued Lauren, voice tight and carefully controlled. "Ramsden's corpse is trying to . . . pull itself together again. He's going to reconstitute that rotting body back into one *whole* piece again. Once he's done that . . ."

410

"*LAUREN!*" Ramsden's voice filled the chamber again, filled with menace and threat. The voice trailed off once more, as if all of Ramsden's energies were being concentrated into the squirming effort on the floor.

" . . . once he's done that, once he's whole, he'll be able to steal my . . . Sparrow's . . . youthful essence, transfer it to his body. He'll use that essence to *invigorate*, make himself exactly as he was before the Sabbarite killed him. No longer decayed or rotting – but just as he was. Then he'll cast aside Sparrow's husk, just like some bloody spider. And he'll be free. Free from Hell. Fully returned."

"What have we got to do?" cried Tony in alarm. Already, he could see that the dismembered, rotting pieces were *crawling toward each other on the floor.*

"Simple," said Lauren grimly. "We've go to . . ."

"*LAURRRRRENNNNN!*"

" . . . got to make sure that his body doesn't reform. We've got to smash his body to pieces." Lauren whirled back to them. "Do you understand? Two or three months more in that canal, and he could never have been able to reform. His body would have deteriorated and rotted and dissolved to hardly anything at all. We have to smash his body. We have to smash that body into fragments so small he can never reconstitute!"

"*LAURRRRRRRENNNN!*"

From the stairwell came the sound of a crashing impact. They froze – and listened to the sounds of pounding on the iron-studded door. Mac suddenly reappeared in the doorway, spade in hand.

"Those things outside," he breathed heavily. "They're trying to get back in."

"Ramsden's called them back," said Lauren grimly.

"Stay at the door, Mac," said Randall. "Make sure they don't get in." He hefted his spade and looked at Ramsden's hideously living remains. "We'll take care of Ramsden."

"Give me your spade," said Ranjana. Mac hurried down the stairs and handed it to her, neither of them turning their gaze from the squirming mass. Ranjana took it without another word and joined the others. Mac paused for only a moment, then vanished back into the stairwell. The attack on the door had become frenzied.

Lauren lay Sparrow down on the soil floor well out of the way. Moving to Ranjana, she took the chunk of masonry out of her hand.

"Let's do it," she said simply.

They advanced on Ramsden's squirming, dismembered corpse.

Three, seven, four, oh-two. Three, seven, four, oh-two . . .

411

Mac shook his head as he reached the top of the stairs. The confusion and the fear of losing his mind again were bouncing around inside his skull. He clutched at his head, shaking it as the furious battering and clawing at the iron-studded door filled the small space at the top of the stairs. This couldn't happen to him again; he couldn't face losing his mind once more and drifting back to that dislocated and forlorn existence where fact and fantasy were seamlessly fused. Mac threw himself at the shattered pew, leaned on it with all his weight as the door juddered and rattled. Somehow, the things outside were directly connected with the mental battering at his defences, they represented everything bad that had happened to him. He hated them with a vengeance.

A centre panel in the door shivered and splintered.

Mac roared at the door, a great sound of rage and . . .

The sound of Mac's angry and defiant voice gave Tony the courage that he had been trying to summon. The others were standing in a circle around the squirming, crawling mass – all preparing themselves for a first blow. Tony used Mac's rage to give him that initiative.

Wielding the railing like an axe, he brought it down heavily on to the squirming torso. The impact spattered them with ooze. Ranjana cried out in disgust, but brought down her spade at the same time as Randall. She attacked a squirming arm, while Randall began to use the spade as it was intended, driving it down blade first onto a twitching leg, putting his foot on the rim and stamping down hard. Ramsden's foot crunched apart from his leg.

Lauren wielded the chunk of concrete, her arms feeling devoid of strength, crouching and battering at the severed head. The eyes glittered hate at her, the mouth worked soundlessly. Sobbing, she brought the rock down again and again.

The horror consumed them.

They were automatons, and a kind of manic resolution seemed to overcome them.

The candlelight flickered and guttered, mad shadows danced as they continued.

And far away above them, the sound of a storm. A storm of Undead hands battering on wood.

The masonry slipped from Lauren's hand, covered in the filth of decay. Only one remaining glittering eye was fixed on her as she scrabbled on hands and knees to retrieve it. She crawled back, sobbing, and raised the rock again.

Tony's iron pole pierced the ribcage. He dragged the railing out, tearing apart ribs and scattering them in disgust with his feet.

Randall had systematically chopped apart a leg, and felt as if he was going to throw up at any second.

Ranjana stabbed the spade down on Ramsden's hand. The fingers flew away, squirming like earthworms.

And then – as Lauren raised the chunk of masonry to strike again – the severed head screamed at her. It was a scream of malice and hate like nothing they had ever heard before. In shock, she recoiled. The others stood back. For a moment, the shattered head regarded them with its one hideous and glittering eye.

And then the sound began. It was a rumbling, shuddering sound. At first, it seemed to come from underground. But as that sound grew in intensity, it seemed to be coming from the very walls of the underground chamber. Like the approach of some train, travelling at nightmare speed and about to smash through one of the chamber walls, burying them beneath tons of masonry and smashing them to pieces.

Somehow, Ramsden was calling on unknown powers.

"No!" yelled Lauren over the now-deafening, rumbling sound. "Don't stop now!" Screaming, she smashed that rock into Ramsden's face. The others recovered, and recommenced their attack as . . .

The top of the stairwell seemed to be vibrating from that noise. The walls were shaking. And the attack on the door had taken on insane proportions. Mac bore down heavily on the spar of wood, felt it juddering violently – and watched in horror as the wooden panels of the door began to disintegrate under a flurrying, clawing attack that sent splinters of wood spinning and twisting into the stairwell. Something bad was happening. It seemed as if the very church itself, or what remained of it, was about to collapse.

Mac glanced back downstairs, not knowing what the hell they were doing down there but only hoping . . .

Three, seven, four, oh-two . . .

. . . only hoping that the kid knew what he was doing.

"Hurry and finish it!" he yelled over the crashing, rumbling noise of the invisible storm. "For God's sake *hurry!*"

In the next instant, the door exploded inwards, the wooden spar on which Mac lay splintering and shattering into pieces. He fell heavily as the door exploded around him. In a spinning, twisting blur, he saw the rough stone stairs swirling up to meet him. He was falling. The pain in his wounded shoulder became hideous agony as he landed on those stairs in a flurry of broken wood. He whirled again and hit the bottom of the stairs. Desperately trying to cling to his senses, aware that the street people must even now be clawing their way down those

413

stone stairs towards him, Mac struggled to rise, struggled to clear his head as . . .

An all-enveloping, shattering wind howled down the stairs. It hit him with the force of a hurricane. Mac was catapulted from his feet and flung through the open doorway into the chamber. His body tumbled and twisted, falling to the rough soil floor beside the sarcophagus, flipping its stone cover to the floor.

The wind exploded into the chamber.

Lauren was flung away from Ramsden's head, colliding with the stone wall.

The wind caught Tony as he raised the iron pole. It was snatched from his hands, and he followed it in a mad, whirling pirouette of arms and legs.

Ranjana was flung against Randall. They collapsed heavily to the ground and were whirled over and over in the nightmare hurricane.

And as the tornado raged in the chamber, Ramsden laughed: a mocking and hideous sound – as powerful as the wind.

83

Tony scrambled awake, hoping that it was a nightmare. But in the instant that his hands gripped the rough soil, and the sounds of a raging wind filled his ears – he knew that the real nightmare had not gone away, and that he was still in the middle of it. He struggled to his knees, and the sight which met his eyes froze him on the spot.

Lauren was lying unconscious not far from where he crouched, and he could just make out the figures of Randall and Ranjana, now beginning to stir like him. Mac was lying beside the sarcophagus where he had been flung, facing away. There was no way of telling whether he was alive or not. Tony presumed that they were all still in the chamber by the soil and the scattered, glittering pools of black candle wax beneath him, and by the sight of the sarcophagus. But it was impossible to see any other detail of the chamber.

They were in the eye of a hellish hurricane, a spinning vortex of wind and sound that obliterated the stone walls of the chamber around them. Those raging, whirling clouds of detritus and smoke obscured everything else. Above, only blackness. The force of that spinning whirlwind plucked at their clothes, ruffled their hair.

There was no sign of Ramsden's body.

Tony scrambled on all fours to Lauren and turned her over. She groaned, and began to recover consciousness. There was a dark bruise across her forehead where she had hit the wall and bounced back. Tony prayed that she had not been concussed – then wondered whether it would be better after all if she remained unconscious for whatever might lie ahead. Something flashed past in the spinning whirlwind, and Tony just had time to register that it was a severed human arm. Ramsden? He prayed to God that it was – but if that was the case, what was happening down here if it wasn't Ramsden's doing?

Lauren's eyes flickered open, registering alarm when she saw the spinning, howling vortex. Tony started to say, *"It's all right . . ."*

415

instinctively, and then realised what a bloody stupid thing that would be to say.

"Sparrow?" Lauren looked frantically around. Tony had assumed that the child was lying beside her, but was wrong. Lauren broke away from him, still on all fours, scrabbling around to see where Sparrow might be lying. But he was not in the chamber. Lauren seized two fistfuls of dirt and flung them down. "*Sparrow!*"

Ramsden had taken him.

Ranjana and Randall sat up together, at first dazed and then scrambling towards Lauren and Tony with their heads ducked protectively. Tony got to his feet, spun around and shouted, "Sparrow!"

"It's no use," said Lauren above the sound of the whirlwind, tears running down her face. "He's not here. Ramsden's reconstituted – and got him."

Something else flashed past in that spinning wind.

"Christ, that looks like . . ." began Randall.

"It's not Ramsden," said Ranjana tightly. She too had seen the ragged torso and the insane, waving arms. "It's the street people. They were caught in the blast of that wind. It tore them to pieces."

The others looked into the maelstrom and saw the dismembered, spinning pieces. It was a bizarre and surreal sight, but no more bizarre than the hideous experiences which they had already endured.

"Mac!" shouted Ranjana, and scrambled over the chamber towards the sarcophagus.

Before she could reach him, there was movement in the raging wind on Mac's left. Something was swirling and moving there. A shape was taking form. Ranjana halted in a skidding slide of soil.

And then Pearce Ramsden stepped through the raging wall of wind and into the eye of the hurricane. It was as easy for him as stepping through a curtain.

Ranjana scrambled back to the others.

They had all seen and endured horrors that threatened sanity in the last few days as the nightmare had gathered momentum. The instinctive dread generated by the Mechanic, horrifying attacks by the Sabbarite and by the street people, whose apparent imperviousness to pain and injury defied logic. The horribly transforming and decomposing things that had once been young men back at the community centre. All this and more, all of this and the sudden knowledge that there was such a place as Hell, that there were other truths and other aspects to what they had thought of as reality – should have prepared them for further horror.

But nothing had prepared them for their ultimate confrontation with Pearce Ramsden.

The sight of the thing that stood looking at them in the centre of the chamber was bad enough. Ramsden had reconstituted; his shattered, oozing and torn limbs had merged and melded, just as Sparrow/Lauren had said they would. He was still wearing the clotted shreds and rags of clothes that he had been wearing when he had been tied to the engine block and thrown into the canal. It seemed as if the very ooze from the bottom of that canal had been used now to bind his limbs together. The head was a hideous and terrifying sight. Lauren knew that she had smashed that skull in, but it was somehow whole. Nevertheless, only one eye glittered in that putrescent mass. But revolting and horrifying though this scarecrow figure was, there was something else about it which seemed to rob them of their strength, and rob them of any will to move.

Ramsden radiated an aura of utter *power*.

They could all feel it. An overwhelming vibration. Its all-enveloping touch was hideous in the extreme, touching something deep within their psyches; something which knew of death and desperation and loneliness and the utter abysmal distress of the soul. Instinctively, they knew that this man – this *thing* – could suck the very souls from their bodies if he so wished.

And Ramsden was holding Sparrow in his arms. The child was either asleep – or dead.

"Let him *GO!*" screamed Lauren through the wind, and thrust forward. Tony seized her and held her back.

The Ramsden-thing laughed. The sound seemed to resonate in the chamber, despite the howling, spinning rush of the maelstrom on all sides. Even the sound of that laughter contained the same dreadful, pervasive aura of power. Slowly, he bent to the ground, carefully placing the child next to Mac. Mac still did not move. And then, slowly again, the Ramsden-thing walked into the centre of the chamber, standing not twelve feet from them. The very presence of the thing was making each feel sick inside with fear.

Ramsden held up one horribly decomposed and dripping arm in front of him. The semi-skeletal grin widened as he flexed the rotting fingers in front of his one good eye.

"*You, black girl!*"

Ranjana tried to control the sudden lurch of fear inside.

"*It was a good blow. The fingers haven't quite melded. Let's see if I can pay you back in kind.*"

The glittering eye seemed to flash and spark like a turning diamond. Ranjana screamed in pain, hands flying to her head. It was as if she had received a glancing blow to the face, a blow which had knocked her backwards from her knees. Randall lunged to her side. She writhed

417

in his arms, enduring some kind of hideous, inner pain.

"All right, you bastard!" shouted Randall. "Stop it!"

Ramsden merely laughed again.

"*Stop it!*" Randall whirled from Ranjana, grabbing for the spade lying nearby. In one savage and fluid motion, he swung to his feet, wielding the spade in a sideways arc aimed directly at Ramsden's head. Lauren screamed a warning to him, but it was too late. In a blur of motion, Randall was slammed to the ground as if he had run into a brick wall. The spade whirled from his grasp, vanishing past the vortex and clanging against the invisible stone wall beyond. Randall squirmed there, twisting and shaking his head. Blood streamed from his nostrils as he grabbed for Ranjana. Ramsden had stopped whatever he had been doing to her mind. But her hands were still clasped to her head and she was moaning as Randall took her into his arms again.

On the soil floor behind Ramsden, Lauren saw Sparrow suddenly turn over on to his side and look at her. His eyes were wide and alert. Glancing around the chamber, he saw her – and their eyes locked. Tony too had seen the movement, looked from child to mother, mother to child and knew that something was happening. He glanced at Ramsden's grinning semi-skeletal face. He was still looking at Randall and Ranjana, enjoying what he had done – and apparently unaware that some kind of communication was going on beneath him.

"*And now,*" said Ramsden. "*To matters in hand.*" He began to turn back to Sparrow.

"You've broken your promise!" shouted Lauren desperately. And Tony knew that she was hunting for something, for *anything*, to keep Ramsden's attention.

Ramsden turned back. "*You may wonder why you're still alive, Lauren. You and your other pathetic little hopefuls. I could so easily tear your bodies and souls apart right now. But it seems to me I would be wasting so much pleasure. You've caused me such inconvenience. When I reconstitute, I'll punish you for that, Lauren – and oh, HOW I'll savour that punishment. You can't begin to imagine what I've got planned for you . . .*"

"You're not listening to me, you bastard! I said you've broken your promise. Your promise to the Dead you've smuggled back."

Sparrow turned on to his arms and knees, and began to crawl towards Mac. It was the first time Lauren had ever seen him do something like that. She tried not to look at the small bundle of movement, lest she draw Ramsden's attention to what was happening.

"You blew them to pieces in that whirlwind, or whatever it is. There are pieces of the poor bastards flying all over the place in there."

Ramsden began to laugh again.

418

"So you've broken your promise to them, haven't you? And if you've broken your promise, then the whole pact is blown. They won't allow you the power – whatever it is – to reconstitute fully. Because you haven't fully kept your part of the bargain."

Sparrow reached Mac, climbed slowly up to his unmoving shoulder and leaned over, apparently trying to look at his hidden face.

"They'll never be able to come back fully if you've blown them to bits."

"*You're ignorant, Lauren. And although knowledge is a wasted commodity on you bearing in mind your somewhat limited time remaining, let me tell you that this*" – Ramsden waved at the maelstrom, and for one horrifying moment, Lauren thought that he would see what was happening – "*this is nothing. Reconstitution, my darling. Did your compatriots tell you that in a confrontation with my friends, one of them fell under a vehicle and was dismembered? Yes? Well, she is dismembered no longer, is reconstituting and looking forward to her new existence. I do so like happy endings, don't you? Similarly with my friends . . .*"

"Even so!" snapped Lauren. "Not a nice way to treat your friends is it? Blowing them to pieces."

The "smile" seemed to vanish from that decaying face.

"*Tiresome, Lauren. Tiresome. And now . . .*"

Ramsden turned – and saw what was happening.

Energy seemed to flare and crackle as Ramsden made a liquid, hissing noise. He raised one rotting arm and pointed towards Mac and the child.

Sparrow turned his small head back quickly to look, and in that one moment it seemed that his eyes were filled with a blue luminescence. His face seemed to have an incredibly adult look of determination and concern.

In the next moment, Sparrow was suddenly snatched from Mac's side as if by an invisible hand. Arms and legs waving, he hurtled across the chamber towards Ramsden. Lauren cried out again, clutching at the air as if there was a chance that she might catch him.

But Sparrow flew into Ramsden's hands. Throwing back his head and laughing again, he dropped the child to the ground between his legs. Sparrow landed heavily.

"*Sparrow!*" screamed Lauren, scrabbling forward.

Ramsden lowered his head to look at her, and Lauren was frozen to the ground, unable to move. Then, looking down to where Sparrow lay still, eyes closed, Ramsden raised his arms from his side, raised them wide and held them up in the air. The feeling of a gathering energy was immense. The vortex around them seemed to spin faster, the howling of the wind growing strong. Ramsden looked down at the child, grinning and ready to suck the very essence from his small body. The reconstitution was to take place. There was nothing that they could do to stop it. Ramsden laughed again, long and loud and triumphant and . . .

Suddenly, that laughter had ceased.

Ramsden's "look" of triumph had vanished. For a long moment, he stood and looked down at Sparrow's unmoving body. Then, quickly, he stooped down and seized the child in one hand, shaking him. Sparrow still did not move.

Roaring, Ramsden stood erect again, grabbing the child up with him. He brought Sparrow's face close up to his own hideously decayed visage, staring at him with that one hideously glittering eye. Sparrow's head sagged.

Roaring again, Ramsden discarded Sparrow's body, throwing him back to the rough soil floor.

Sparrow's body was lifeless.

"*Sparrooooowww!*" Lauren could see what had happened. The grief which engulfed her was even greater than Ramsden's hold over her. She scrabbled forward, seized the child and rolled back to Tony, hugging him tight to her breast. She held back his cold white face and tried to will him alive. But there was no life in Sparrow's small body.

Ramsden threw back his head and raged at the darkness above.

Tony glanced at the iron railing, lying close to that vortex, but still within reach if he could move quickly enough. He tensed himself.

And then Mac turned and looked at them.

Tony was frozen on the spot before he could move, the first to see Mac's face.

"Oh my God," he said. "Look . . ."

The others followed his gaze.

Mac's eyes were shining with the same blue luminescence that they had just seen in Sparrow's eyes. They could not actually see his eyes, just two glowing orbs of that strange and fantastic light.

Ramsden looked down, still enraged – and then saw Mac.

"Lauren!" yelled Ranjana, still obviously in pain but now filled with something that was almost a fierce and angry joy. "Lauren! It's Sparrow! He's not dead! He's – he's *in Mac!*"

And Mac, a man whom Ranjana had described as neither living nor dead, slowly stood up from the side of the sarcophagus, those glowing orbs of light fixed on Ramsden. It was impossible to discern signs of emotion on Ramsden's hideously decayed face – but was there something approaching astonishment there? Mac drew to his full height, turning to face Ramsden directly. In those few words shouted

420

by Ranjana, they knew what had happened. Sparrow was Ramsden's seed, just as he had said. Again, as the child had said, his powers had been underestimated. Sparrow had been learning and growing strong all the time. Just as the spirits from Hell had been able to embody within the dead vagrant shells of the Sabbarite victims, Sparrow had been able to transfer his own essence into Mac.

"He's special!" shouted Ranjana. "I always knew that Mac was *special!*"

The Serendip had chosen him. A man who should be dead, a man who *had* died many times on the operating table. Now the very essence of his life spirit was a powerful channel for Sparrow – a vessel, a physical shell, filled with the essence of light which the Serendip had now allowed Sparrow to become and to embody. A vessel of light to stand against the vessel of darkness which Ramsden now presented.

Ramsden turned to face Mac.

Positive and negative.

Son against father.

The very fabric of the church beyond the maelstrom seemed to groan under the immense power which was, even now, building between the two figures. The whirlwind span even faster, the howling of the wind rising to a banshee shriek. There was a pulse in the ground, like the beating of a gigantic heart. That pulse began to increase in volume and frequency, like a huge underground drum. Tony turned away from the sight of that insane, spinning vortex, crouched down next to the others.

From above, a white light suddenly filled the chamber. It soon flared to a brilliant intensity as Mac and Ramsden stood, still facing each other, neither one of them yet moving. The others shaded their eyes. It was as if the core of a nuclear reactor was being exposed. There was no heat, but surely this terrifying light must fry them all to a crisp? Tony was blinded. He reached down to where Lauren still clutched Sparrow's body to herself. Something was going to happen. Something immense, when that white light reached whatever crescendo it was heading for. Behind them, Randall and Ranjana hid in each other's arms from the light.

"Look out!" shouted Tony, his voice completely lost in the raging of the wind. "I think it's going to . . ."

Something exploded with an all-enveloping roar.

Then, only blackness.

84

They are floating in limbo: Tony, Lauren, Ranjana and Randall.

They are "protected" by the power which Sparrow has finally managed to unleash within himself. Their physical and psychic presence during this titanic battle would surely burn out their minds and their souls – and so Sparrow/Mac has cocooned them instantly in a safe place while he engages with the evil that is Ramsden. Drawing on his father's own power, Sparrow has become an equal to Ramsden, a process hastened by the intervention of the Serendip – the scales of balance of order and reality. The intervention does not favour what humanity has called the forces of good, but has merely restored a balance between that and the forces of evil. Now, with an equal strength and an equal capability of winning out one over the other, Mac and Ramsden focus their energies upon each other in ways that defy human understanding.

Mac is a mountain of steel. Ramsden is a great sea of misery and torment. In the flash of an instant of our time, that sea has worn down the mountain in a billion, billion years until the sea engulfs the mountain top, and now ...

Ramsden is a snake, striking at Mac the eagle as he descends on the reptile, claws outstretched. Those claws seize and rend and tear. The snake strikes, but cannot fasten its fangs in that deadly fluttering of sharp beak and feathers as ...

Mac is a molten rock spinning in its thunderous atmospheres. In moments, that rock has cooled, oceans have formed, continents have sprung up and moulded. Life has coalesced in its seas, has crawled on to the land. The process of evolution has taken place in the time it takes to say so, and Mac is developing that process, eradicating all that is evil, eliminating all spiritual sickness, and destroying everything that Pearce Ramsden and his like stand for as ...

Ramsden is a comet, hurtling though space, impacting with that world and destroying it instantly, obliterating everything that has been achieved there and ...

MACABRE

Mac is a soldier ant, mandibles cutting through the strands of sticky silken web as the spider descends to take him. He is free, and the collective consciousness of the nest focuses on his plight. A stream of soldier ants swarm over the rock; the wave of forest detritus which they push before them collapses the web and the spider falls to the forest floor, writhing and slashing within its own trap. The soldier ants that are the collective consciousness of Mac descend upon Ramsden the spider, swarming over his upturned body as . . .

85

Instantly they were all awake again.

Each knew that something had happened to them; that they had been removed somehow from that chamber for protection, although physically their bodies had remained there. But now, something had happened. Something had changed.

The spinning vortex which had surrounded them was gone. The howling banshee shriek of that wind had vanished.

As they turned to look around the chamber, they could see that it was lit with a faint trace of the blue luminescence which had issued from Sparrow and Mac's eyes. The stone walls of the chamber were clearly visible in that light; the stairs and the arched doorway, the sarcophagus – just as they remembered. Around those walls, as if swept there by a great wind from the centre of the chamber, lay piled the dismembered and torn remains of the dead Sabbarite and the street people who had brought Ramsden to this place. There was no squirming movement there, no melding, no reconstitution taking place.

Mac was standing in the same position as before.

And Ramsden was on his knees, head down.

Mac's eyes still contained that blue phosphorescent glow as he stared at Ramsden's downturned head. Was he winning? Had he really brought Ramsden literally to his knees?

Somewhere beyond the chamber a wind whispered.

And then Ramsden began to laugh. A low, liquid chuckling which convulsed his frame – as if he had somehow thought of the greatest practical joke in the world. Mac shifted position, frowning.

"*Too late,*" said Ramsden. "*Much too late to stop it now.*"

"What . . .?" hissed Tony.

Ranjana clutched at Randall. "Oh God, he's done it. I know . . ."

"What has he done, Ranjana?" snapped Randall. "*What?*"

"He's called up a Mechanic. He's conjured it against Mac."

"That's never going to stop him," said Lauren. "It can't . . ."

424

"No!" said Ranjana, her face a mask of fear. "Not just any Mechanic. This is the biggest, most powerful Mechanic of all. It's a . . . collective of damned souls. Not just one. But a huge mass of the damned. Oh God, it's coming here now. Faster than I can think . . ."

Ramsden's chuckling became a monstrous and evil convulsion of laughter.

"It can't be turned back. And it has your name, my son."

The stone walls began to shudder at Ramsden's laughter. The ground beneath them seemed to groan. Outside, the whispering of the wind was building in strength, growing and changing into the sounds of a whirlwind or a hurricane as . . .

86

The Grand Mechanic comes.

Summoned in haste by Ramsden, it begins as a spiral of dirty wind in an alley. That alley is in the middle of the burning council estate. It begins near the site of the first building to have been torched by Gerry's late gang: a store owned by an Asian family. All the hate and the horror and the death has spiralled from this first act of violence – and the Grand Mechanic is drawn to it. It sucks up the hate and the fear, and the spiralling wind at last becomes visible as street debris is drawn fluttering and bouncing into it. In the alley, the garbage bins which have been left outside back doors suddenly explode into the air, disgorging their contents; that refuse and filth is quickly sucked into the spiralling wind as it grows more furious and stronger.

One of the alley walls splits and cracks. Masonry tumbles under the pressure of that wind. The burning store flares up. The flames have been fanned in one great and greedy suction blast from the wind. The firemen scatter for cover, pulling back their tenders. In moments, the very fabric of that store has collapsed upon itself in a furious ball of flame. The wind feeds on that destruction, spins roaring from the alley – and engulfs the first fire tender.

It settles there, tearing the tender apart while its personnel scatter and run.

And then the Grant Mechanic is on the move.

Growing larger and stronger by the second, its howling , shrieking progress is the screaming of a thousand damned souls. A looted department store lies directly in its path. It explodes through the ruined shopfront. The walls explode outwards into the street with a detonating roar, and the entire building caves in on the Grand Mechanic as it moves, scenting its prey. The roaring, shuddering collapse of that building does not affect it. It emerges in all of its roaring spinning vastness from the rubble and scythes a path through the council estate, growing bigger with each destroyed building. It sucks up the fragments of destruction as it

426

moves, adding to its whirling, howling bulk.

It is a great black tornado now, rushing through the estate, tearing the roofs from houses and scattering the contents into its mass. As the occupants of those houses are plucked into the air with the shattered remains of their furnishings, their screaming is joined by the terrible screaming of the damned.

And the Grand Mechanic comes on.

The concrete beneath it shatters and splits as it moves. It plucks automobiles from the roads it traverses, tossing them through the air like toys. A pedestrian bridge buckles and tangles under its passage, bursting apart and flying away like a child's construction, its bent and twisted girders raining down on the estate. The flames of the burning buildings in its path are instantly snuffed out as it passes over them; the flames are absorbed into the mass and the bulk of this hellish tornado.

The whirlwind explodes out of the housing estate. It twists and howls, its gigantic black bulk filled with the spinning, twisting mass of the destruction which it has caused. It pauses only momentarily on the main highway as cars skid and collide and screech into each other to avoid its sudden and hideous appearance. And then, as those bystanders lucky enough to survive will testify, it seems to ponder its next move; seems to decide its direction.

It twists from the highway, tearing up lamp standards and bringing down power lines in blue crackling traces of energy.

And then it heads towards the ghost town of Stanton.

87

Ramsden rose to one knee, still laughing.

"*Stalemate for now, my son. Until the Grand Mechanic arrives. And when it does, it cannot be stopped.*"

Tony had risen to his feet unaware that he had made the decision to rise. He was helpless in the face of these immense forces, but somehow a cold rage had enveloped him. Now, they were simply bystanders, and it seemed as if Mac/Sparrow had finally lost the battle. There was nothing that Tony could do, but in that cold rage, that inner instinct that they must now all surely die – or worse – he was not going to stand by and just let it happen. Uncaring of the consequences, he darted across the chamber and retrieved the iron railing. Lauren grabbed for him, but it was too late.

"*Noooo . . .*"

Her shouted plea made Ramsden turn.

The semi-skeletal face grinned as Tony charged at him, holding the railing like a lance. Ramsden laughed again, throwing back his head. Tony roared at him.

And then the railing seemed to hit an invisible wall inches in front of Ramsden. It buckled with a shivering *clang*! and Tony fell to his knees in a spray of soil as his weapon buckled and twisted in the air. Bent into a shrieking iron loop, it whirled away and hit the stone wall before clattering to the ground. Tony hugged his arms to his midriff, the shock of the impact convulsing his body. Ramsden laughed again, and stood up.

Tony was only a couple of feet away from both Mac and Ramsden now.

And he could only watch as Lauren screamed from behind, and Ramsden stepped towards him. A decayed, skeletal hand came slowly down to fasten on his face – and suck away his soul.

Mac strode forward. Two simple and purposeful steps. As he moved, he reached inside his tattered jacket pocket and pulled something out.

428

"Father!"

Ramsden looked back at him, corpse-face still grinning, and that terrible hand descending.

Mac leaned quickly forward, and slapped something on to Ramsden's decayed chest. It lodged there, stuck in the glutinous mass between his neck and chest, one fold of it now glued behind part of Ramsden's rotting jacket.

Incredulously, Ramsden looked slowly down at what Mac had planted there.

From his kneeling position, Tony could see it clearly in every detail.

It was an army identification card. It contained the name and rank and photograph of a face that Tony knew only too well, in a plastic-wallet cover.

Serial number: three, seven, four, oh-two.

Tony looked up at Mac in utter amazement. He looked at the ravaged white face, the face of a stranger. For the first time, in a burst of understanding, he saw the thin white trace-lines of surgery around Mac's eyes and ears and face. Those eyes were still burning with that blue light, but he remembered what they looked like beneath that light. And that, he realised, had been the source of his fascination and puzzlement about this big man. The face was different, utterly different, but the eyes were still the same – and he had been unable to reconcile that instinctive recognition.

They were the eyes of Cameron MacKay Stevens.

5th Battalion Parachute Regiment.

Missing in Action – Presumed Dead.

Alive, if one could call it that, wandering the forlorn streets and searching for his lost self.

"Cameron!" Tony's yell was a yell of pure joy, the immediate horror of his predicament forgotten. *"For Christ's sake, Cameron!"*

Ramsden recoiled from Tony, clutching at the photograph. The decayed fingers tore the identification card free, hurling it to the floor.

"Too late, Father," said Mac. *"The die is cast. The deed is done."*

"No!" shouted Ramsden. *"The Mechanic is conjured in your name, Sparrow."*

"What name, Father? You never allowed me a name. The one called Mac and I are one."

"But you can only do this in the presence of the Mechanic! The Mechanic MUST be here!"

"It IS here, Father!"

The underground chamber was filled with the sound of a great rending and crashing. The wall of the chamber shuddered and cracked. Tony hurled himself back to the others as great shivering

429

cracks appeared in those walls and clouds of dust gushed inwards. Ramsden threw his head back, his one eye glittering with panic.

And then the entire roof of the underground chamber split apart with the sound of a hundred storms. The mildewed and dripping masonry erupted upwards and away, flooding the chamber with a bitterly cold wind. The ground beneath their feet shuddered and cracked.

Something had torn that roof off – the ground floor of the church above – like some huge and hideous beast searching for food beneath a rock. The Grand Mechanic was all around the chamber; looking down on them – and once more they were at the centre of a hellish hurricane.

As Tony and Lauren, Randall and Ranjana struggled to their feet, the ground bulged and moved beneath them. Gaping cracks and fissures suddenly appeared in the soil. There was a hideous, glowing orange light in those cracks as the ground bulged upwards, as if they were suddenly standing on the floor of a once-extinct but now suddenly erupting volcano. Clouds of steam gushed from those cracks, under pressure from below.

Instinctively, Tony pulled Lauren towards the arched doorway leading out of the chamber. She still clutched the lifeless body of Sparrow. Ranjana and Randall followed close behind.

Overhead, in the night sky, the air was filled with a great roaring and hissing. They glanced up as they ran to the stairs, seeing a huge nebula-shaped spiral of blackness in the sky, swirling and descending. The sounds of destruction were all around them. At the entranceway, Tony pulled Lauren to a halt. The Grand Mechanic had arrived, was descending on the church, and in that descent, it was tearing the ruins of the building apart above them. The archway shook, the ground beneath their feet rumbled and shuddered. They crouched there, waiting. To go up there now was to risk being buried beneath falling rubble, but to stay down here also must surely mean death at the hands of the Grand Mechanic.

And in the sky, the swirling black mass suddenly seemed to be a gigantic cloud of bees, hissing and buzzing as they descended in the centre of the storm.

Ramsden began to scream, head thrown back, arms wide apart.

Mac walked around him, heading towards the stairs.

The swarming blackness funnelled and chanelled downwards into a thin black tentacle of hissing, buzzing life. Crouching on the stairs, the others were suddenly filled with the instinctive fear and revulsion generated by anything human in the presence of a Mechanic. But this was much worse than anything Tony had experienced in his flight from

430

the first one. Prolonged exposure to this hissing, writhing cloud must surely drive them all insane within seconds. Now, Tony could see that the swarm was not a swarm of bees, it was a hideous swarm of the same mantis-like creatures which he recognised of old. Not mantises, not priests-in-cowls, not machines, not animals. But some hideous combination of them all.

Ramsden was still screaming when that descending spiralling mass swarmed into his mouth.

The scream abruptly ceased, and Ramsden stood in the same pose, shuddering and convulsing as the swarm continued to enter him, exploding from his ribcage, surrounding and engulfing him in a hideous, twisting black mass.

The walls of the chamber were cracking and falling apart, the ground splitting and disintergrating.

Mac turned and lunged for the stairs.

And then the entire floor of the underground chamber caved in. With a thunderous roar, the zigzag patchwork of fissures suddenly widened, split and fell away in a collapsing mass of masonry, soil and gushing steam.

Ramsden was suddenly able to scream again as his body fell twisting with the collapsing floor into a bottomless pit.

As the others shrank back into the stairwell, the ground fell away beneath Mac's feet. His right hand fastened on the bottom step – and he swung in empty space as Ramsden's scream and the collapsing roar faded away beneath him.

The chamber had suddenly become the top of a vast and bottomless pit. The sides of that stone pit glowed orange as if there was indeed a volcano lava-pool far below.

Mac twisted and brought up his other hand, grasping the bottom stair.

Randall was suddenly there, face white in shock, grabbing Mac's left wrist as he groped upwards and looking down past Mac into an unimaginable, bottomless, hellish pit. Tony's face joined Randall's and he too was grabbing for Mac's other hand. Ranjana scrambled behind them, ready to grab Mac's collar or shirt – or anything she could get her hands on without impeding the others. Far away beneath Mac, they could see only a red-orange glow, seemingly hundreds of miles below.

It was a pit into Hell.

And Ramsden had been consigned there.

Suddenly, as Mac swung there on the bottom stair, the horrifying, destructive wind and its hideous swarming of mantises had gone. Above, there were no more sounds of destruction. Ramsden's scream had vanished with the tumbling masonry into that bottomless shaft – and now there was only the sound of exertion as Tony and Randall braced themselves on the edge of that pit, struggling to drag Mac back over the rim. Agony flared in Mac's left shoulder and the arm that had taken the brunt of Lauren's fall back at the community centre. His hand lost its grip and tore away from Randall.

The sudden weight dragged Tony over the edge. Randall flung himself on to Tony's legs, stopping him from falling as he clung to Mac's hand. Moaning, Ranjana dived back and grabbed Tony's legs, hauling back and bracing herself.

Tony looked down to Mac, spinning in mid-air, and could see that the blue light in his eyes had gone out.

Tony could see those eyes so clearly now.

"We've got you, Cameron! You're okay. We've got you."

"Cameron . . .?" grunted Randall.

The step beneath them cracked and shuddered.

"Oh *Christ*!" shouted Tony.

They heaved, Mac braced his legs against the stone side of the pit beneath those overhanging stone stairs and brought a knee up on to the stair.

And then the stair dislodged from the side.

Mac deliberately let go his grip. Randall grabbed Tony's jacket and hauled back on to the next step, dragging Tony with him.

"*Nooooooo!*" yelled Tony, lunging back to the ragged edge.

For a long moment, it seemed that his eyes were locked with Mac's eyes. There was a curious expression there. Not horror or fear or remorse. Just a profound sense of sadness. Suddenly, they sparkled blue – that same luminescent light as before. But as quickly as it came, that spark had vanished.

And Mac dropped away soundlessly from them into the pit.

His body soon became a ragged silhouette, whirling and turning silently.

Tony gripped the side of the pit, watched him fall in horror.

Beneath Mac, the billowing orange clouds of flame.

The silhouette of a soldier, advancing through the night with his dripping hose of fire. Mac suddenly there, bringing the soldier down in a rugby tackle.

Mac whirling and falling.

The flaring mass of flame from that thrower. Engulfing Mac. The lost best friend who had saved his life, and now haunted his dreams.

And Tony yelled his name over and over into that pit. Suddenly, Mac's distant shape was engulfed by the rumbling orange flame below, vanishing from sight into that inferno.

"No, no, no, no, no! Not AGAIN!"

That orange light was rumbling and climbing the sides of the pit, just like an eruption of lava. A huge and hideous force was climbing the ragged stone shaft, heading up towards them. Tony watched it come.

"There's nothing we can do for him!" yelled Randall. "Come on!"

Tony could not resist as Randall dragged him back from those cracked stone stairs and into the archway. Lauren seized his other arm and Ranjana was weeping as they bundled into that archway. Mac had gone, and it was tearing her heart apart. They scrambled up the stone stairs, hearing that great rumbling behind and beneath them. It was the sound of an avalanche of fire on its way. The staircase was filled with the scattered and broken remnants of the door. They tore their way through it and out into the night air above. The air here was pure and clean, the ice chill of it invading their lungs.

All around them, the ruined walls of the church had been shattered and thrown to the ground.

The aisle ahead was still clear, and they headed towards it, looking back to see that the same hideous glowing light was pulsing from where the underground chamber had once been, throwing out the remaining ruins in jagged relief. They staggered down that aisle towards the main entrance, seeing at once that it had collapsed. Off to the left, the church wall had crumbled and fallen, showing a clear way through to the side gate.

The ground beneath their feet was still rumbling and shuddering as they picked their way over the rubble and out of the church.

"Thank Christ!" said Randall. "The car's still there – not buried under tons of fucking rubble."

They had reached the gates when the first eruption split the night air.

They ducked instinctively, looking back through the gap in the church wall as the shaft exploded into the night with a thunderous roar, like a dynamited oil-well. The church wall crumbled further, the eruption blasting the surrounding ragged ruins to the ground in a cloud of toppling black masonry. An orange-red fireball belched into the sky from the shaft, lighting up the ghost town of Stanton, making their own shadows leap and rear.

Randall shoved the others towards the car as the rumbling continued and the gigantic cloud of fire was swallowed by the night. Their danger was far from over. Yanking open the doors, he shoved the others in as a rain of debris began to hit the ground around them. Soil and dirt rattled on the roof of the car like a hailstorm shower as Randall twisted the ignition keys, gunned the engine and twisted the wheel hard. The car lurched away from the church, wheels roaring in a spray of gravel.

From behind them came another shattering and explosive roar. In the rearview mirror, he saw another massive cloud of flame leap into the sky from that shaft into Hell. The car swerved as the ground beneath them wavered. Randall righted the car, and put his foot down. The next blast blew apart the wall through which they had escaped, ripped the iron gates from their brackets and shattered the two remaining cars of the Sabbarite.

But by then, their own car was roaring away from the church – and from the flames of Hell.

88

A half-hour later, on a hill overlooking the town of Stanton and its destroyed church, they stood and watched as those clouds of flames belched from the Hell-shaft.

Behind them, the council estate burned with myriad flames, the sounds of police sirens wailing in the night. But there was no longer the sound of that one hideous voice on its streets, hungering for death and destruction. The riot, the havoc – and those who had perpetrated it – was at an end.

The pact was uncompleted – sundered by Ramsden's defeat and return to Hell.

Those who had occupied the bodies of Sabbarite victims had also been returned. The damned could no longer use his powers as a doorway to smuggle themselves out. That doorway had been closed. Perhaps for ever – or maybe only until the next time. The damned were damned again, returned to the place from whence they had come. The decayed and rotting shells of street people littered the burning streets, no doubt to create myriad problems for the ensuing coroners' investigations.

Gerry Tomelty's gang, and the unfortunate takers of Nektre, were no more. Guilty and innocent consumed alike in the balancing of the scales. No side – good or evil – favoured.

The Inner Circle of the Sabbarite, now all destroyed, and the Outer Circle destined soon to wane and disappear from the streets for ever.

There was another detonation down in Stanton. This time resulting in a gigantic, roaring mushroom of flame. And this time, the detonation was quickly snuffed out, the flame instantly dissolving – it was the final explosion to snuff out that oil-well from Hell.

As they watched, it seemed that some great ocean liner was

sinking to the bottom of an unfathomable sea. The remaining ruins of the church crumbled and collapsed, masonry tumbling and rolling into that pit. The surviving buildings around the church began to crack and fall apart, clouds of bricks and mortar and shattered wood and glass flying through the night towards that shaft – all of it being *sucked* into that gaping and ragged hole like the undertow caused by the sinking of a great vessel, finally shuddering down into the depths and dragging its debris with it.

The ground beneath their feet shuddered and trembled.

And then was still.

Smoke engulfed the entire devastated area once occupied by the church.

There was no more sound from the ruins of Stanton.

Only the gushing, spiralling smoke – a pale spectre of that which had descended upon it from the night.

"It's not fair," said Ranjana, at last. "It's just not bloody *fair*!" She hated herself for the tears, hated more than that what had happened to Mac. "Why did Mac and Sparrow have to die like that? I don't understand. Why did the Serendip say that an innocent had to die?"

"What?" Tony moved to Lauren. She was still holding Sparrow's lifeless body to her breast.

"It's true," said Lauren simply, eyes red, face stark white with grief at the loss of her child. "Sparrow found out that one of us – if not all – were destined to die. I suppose we should count ourselves lucky . . ."

"Lucky?" cried Ranjana. "*Lucky?* You didn't feel Mac's pain the way I felt it. Years and years on those bloody streets, struggling to remember, find himself – all that pain. And now . . . now . . ." Ranjana was consumed with her own grief. "And . . . I'm sorry . . . Sparrow."

"Christ, I don't believe it," said Randall – and they looked back down to Stanton.

The spiralling, gushing clouds of smoke had cleared, dissipating into the night sky. And what remained down there defied their senses.

It was as if the church had never been.

There was no debris, no rubble, no smoking pit. Instead, the entire area which the church had occupied seemed to have been *levelled* flat. A great unbroken expanse of land in the centre of town. The buildings which surrounded the vanished church were still there, still smoking and ruined. But in the centre was no devastation, no pit, no shaft into Hell. It was almost as if something had bulldozed and landscaped the area flat.

"But it *was* there," said Randall in disbelief. "The church and the pit and everything . . ."

"It was there," said Tony. "Now it's not."

Ranjana nodded, trying to recover from her grief about Mac and the child with whom she'd developed such an intimate psychic link. "The Serendip."

Randall looked at her.

"Hell is a place – but it's not down there. Below ground."

"I don't understand."

"Everything that's happened – it's like reality has been thrown through a loop. Hell exists. But not the way some people think. Anyway, Ramsden's gone back there. That's all that matters. And Mac . . ."

"I knew him," said Tony. "Mac. God help me, I knew him. But that wasn't his name then. We were both soldiers together in the Falklands. He saved my life . . ."

"What?" Ranjana pulled herself together, wiping her face and moving forward to them.

"His name was Cameron MacKay Stevens. He was my best friend. But his face was different . . ."

"Plastic surgery," said Ranjana. "He was 'Missing in Action – Presumed Dead'."

"Lost his memory," said Randall in wonderment. "Probably didn't know you from Adam – or else he would have said."

"I don't understand this," said Tony. "I've got this feeling. Almost like we were supposed . . ."

"To meet up again?" completed Ranjana.

"Something like that. I don't know."

"The Serendip!" said Ranjana excitedly, eyes glittering.

"But what the hell for?" snapped Tony, suddenly angry. "You mean we're all manipulated by this fucking thing, haven't got any bloody free will of our own?"

"That's what I thought at first," said Ranjana. "But it's not like that at all. We're free to do what we want, I'm sure of it. But the scales and the balances mean that . . ."

Lauren suddenly gasped, her eyes wide.

Tony held her shoulders, trying to help with what seemed to be a delayed shock reaction. "Look, it's all over. It's finished . . ."

But Lauren was looking down, eyes filled with amazement.

As Sparrow squirmed and moved in her arms.

"Oh, God. *Sparrow?*"

The child moaned and turned his head, as if in sleep.

"Oh dear God, he's alive, Tony! Sparrow's *alive!*"

Tony pushed close, turned the child's head to look at his beautiful face. He could not speak, could find no adequate words to explain what he felt inside. Grief turned to joy, inside out – and his throat was constricted. Tears flooded Lauren's face; she crushed her face down to Sparrow's own. Tony looked back to Ranjana and Randall in amazement.

"The Serendip," said Ranjana simply, and the words choked in her own throat with joy. "But look again. I can feel something. Look at the child again . . ."

Lauren lowered Sparrow to look at his face once more. Tony and Randall craned forward to see.

Sparrow opened his eyes.

"But they're not – " Lauren could not understand – "they're not *his* eyes. Sparrow's eyes are green."

"Jesus Christ," said Tony in awe, looking at the child's startling blue eyes. "They're *Mac's* eyes."

"It's Sparrow . . . and Mac," said Ranjana. "Sparrow transferred his essence to Mac – and then back again at the last."

Tony remembered that last spark of blue luminescence in Mac's eyes before he fell into the pit. This time, *both* of their essences had been transferred into the lifeless body of the child which Lauren clutched to herself as they made their escape. Just before Mac's body – his shell – had fallen into the inferno below.

"But I don't understand how . . ." continued Lauren.

"The Serendip has balanced the scale, Lauren," said Ranjana. "Sparrow no longer has powers, no longer has the same essence." Ranjana sobbed into her hand, controlled herself again and continued. "He's just a normal child, with no remembrance of what has happened, no knowledge, no psychic ability. And his essence has combined with Mac. The two are one. His spirit lives as well, Lauren. Don't you see? Now, they're truly one."

"Two minds in one," said Lauren, eyes glittering. "Surely that's not possible. That's like . . . schizophrenic, or something."

"Believe me," said Ranjana. "I can feel it. They're truly one."

"A second chance for Mac," said Tony. "And for Sparrow. A chance to live their lives normally. A chance to start again."

"Maybe a chance for all of us to start again," said Randall, putting his arm around Ranjana's shoulder.

Lauren wept again. Tears of pure joy. She pulled Tony close and embraced him.

When they moved apart again and Lauren kissed Sparrow's upturned face, the child was smiling.

Tony found his voice again.

"I'll be the second-best bloody father Mac ever had," he said.

"Maybe I should put in for adoption," said Randall, grinning.

Sparrow, Mac, thought Lauren. *Maybe now we'll find you a proper name.*

All together, they headed back to the car.

AUTHOR'S POSTSCRIPT

Something to think about . . .

There are 250,000 people missing in Britain at any one time. That's equivalent to the entire population of Derby. In real terms, this means that 700 people walk out of their homes every day. Over half of that number go missing to avoid financial obligations and bad debts. For others, it can be depression, Alzheimer's disease, sexual abuse – a whole range of reasons, although statistics are few. In about two-thirds of cases, people are found, return or make contact in forty-eight hours. Several thousand disappear for more than a few days, but a large number are never found again. Many head for London – and in 1992 alone, fifty-one bodies were recovered from the Thames by the River Police.

In recognition of the problem (and in the year that *Macabre* is published), police forces in Britain are now obliged to file all missing reports centrally with the Missing Persons Bureau in London. Currently, there are 2,000 names on file for the capital city alone.

The Cult Information Centre in London estimates that there are 500 cults operating in Britain alone, many of them with connections to other countries.

Something else to think about: with so many people taking to the streets and vanishing from their homes for ever – who will miss them if they disappear a *second* time?

Research shows that organisations, on limited funds and against great odds, are struggling to provide shelter, food and support for those who end up on the streets. In recognition of this fact, I've therefore deliberately set *Macabre* in an unidentifiable city to avoid any negative inferences for those who are providing such a vital service.

And finally – on 25 February 1994 a former Scots Guard Corporal was awarded £100,000 by the Ministry of Defence in an out-of-court settlement. The ex-Falklands veteran, who fought in the battle for Mount Tumbledown and who performed a life-saving tracheotomy on an injured colleague by forcing a hole through his windpipe with a bayonet, sued the Ministry for failing to diagnose or treat his post-traumatic stress disorder and subsequent nervous breakdown.

The Ministry settled the claim without accepting liability. It was the first such claim of its kind.

S. L.   March 1994.

440